# THE C...
# —OF HUNTER COUNTY

**LEWIS CODY:** He speaks his mind, takes no nonsense, and answers to his conscience. An ex-soldier and ex–big-city cop, he's now smashing the myth of the Southern sheriff in a small town facing very big troubles. . . .

**IVY JOE CULPEPPER:** He was Hunter County's school custodian for as long as anyone can remember—and friend to generations of townsfolk. But a secret life may have earned him a lethal enemy. . . .

**LUCIA DODD:** Filled with anger and her own private guilt, she's determined to wreak righteous vengeance on Hunter County—and the murderer of her grandfather, Ivy Joe. . . .

**COLEBY BUTLER:** Cody's Vietnam comrade-in-arms, confidant, and dearest friend. A dedicated doctor to the people of Hunter County, he cannot heal the pain of his own tormented life. . . .

**LOIS ROSS:** Venomous queen bee of prostitution in Hunter County, she has friends in high places, as well as under rocks—and a score to settle with Lewis Cody. . . .

**CASSIE SHELOR:** She was a girl-woman with insatiable erotic appetites, a craving for older men, and a rage to live—dangerously. . . .

**THE SLOANS:** Brutal, lawless brothers Lanny and Danny are the moonshining, drug-pushing, thieving scourge of the county—and the prime suspects in Cody's murder investigation. . . .

# SHEPHERD OF THE WOLVES

## William S. Slusher

**POCKET BOOKS**

New York   London   Toronto   Sydney   Tokyo   Singapore

This book is a work of fiction. Names, characters, places and incidents are products of the author's imagination or are used fictitiously. Any resemblance to actual events or locales or persons, living or dead, is entirely coincidental.

An *Original* Publication of POCKET BOOKS

 POCKET BOOKS, a division of Simon & Schuster Inc. 1230 Avenue of the Americas, New York, NY 10020

Copyright © 1995 by William S. Slusher

ISBN: 0-671-89546-X

First Pocket Books printing September 1995

10  9  8  7  6  5  4  3  2  1

POCKET and colophon are registered trademarks of Simon & Schuster Inc.

Printed in the U.S.A.

# Acknowledgments

It is trite but true that an author cannot acknowledge everyone who was kind enough to aid him in the writing of his novel. In a sense, everyone an author has ever seen, heard of or read about contributes something to his work. Still, with thanks to all who have helped, and with apologies to those I cannot cite here, there are five I will recognize.

*Shepherd of the Wolves* is dedicated with gratitude to Jamie Loomis, then my editor and so much more; to Nancy Wagner, my tireless literary cheerleader; to Nelle Chilton, without whose unsolicited courtesy I would still be in search of a publisher; to Bill Grose, who consented to read still another manuscript for still another friend who had a friend who had written a book; and last but hardly least, to Dr. Linda Shields, my Linda, the link, the lady and the love.

—William Slusher
January 1995

# SHEPHERD OF THE WOLVES

# Prologue

My name is Lewis Cody.

I am a six-foot, two-inch, 190-pound, Caucasian male born the year of the atomic bomb. My gods all died in Vietnam and my politics lean gently to the right on most issues.

I love women, well-raised children, cold Norwegian beer and The Mother Blue Ridge—not necessarily in that order. I hate arrogance, cruelty, bleeding-heart liberals and smokers—not necessarily in *that* order. I believe capital punishment is woefully underutilized in America, yet I was "sensitive" decades before it became trendy in heterosexual American men. I speak my mind, and I don't much give a damn if it comes out "politically correct" or not.

I am Sheriff of Hunter County, Virginia. I will try to tell you what happened to Ivy Joe Culpepper and, thus, what happened to me.

# Ivy Joe Culpepper

**I** was staring a twelve-foot-long buffalo in the face that cold, cloudy Monday in November when the call came in. This beast lacked fearsomeness, even dignity, its brown color faded and speckled with adolescent graffiti. It was fiberglass and stood behind a sign: "HUNTER COUNTY HIGH SCHOOL, HOME OF THE FIGHTING BUFFALOES." School was out for some teacher function in Richmond, so the place was abandoned to the autumn wind and me.

I had been lulled by years of exquisite peace and quiet in these mountains, the ancient home of the Powatan. The population of Hunter County is less than twelve thousand and the county seat town of Hunter boasts only 481 registered residents, a tad shy of a metropolis. Hunter County is as remote as the South Pole, and Hunter Countians like it that way. Teenagers who grow up here temporarily hate it for its isolation from the mainstream America they see on television. They vow to leave it as soon as they can and never come back, but most of them return a few years later to raise families and grow old, having found out the televised pasture wasn't so green after all.

Perhaps I can be forgiven for not seeing it coming, for not smelling the wolf on the wind and not sensing the evil in the cold air.

Years ago, when I was a cop in Washington, D.C., you

found drug traffic in schools only in those dismal, graffiti-smeared ghetto "educational" institutions patrolled by armed guards. Now, here in Hunter County at this small mountain high school, I had found signs of drug movement.

Under the stairs leading down from the biology lab to the cafeteria, I found little wadded balls of aluminum foil in the dust. I was carefully opening one with my knife when I heard the call on the radio.

You spend four years as an army helicopter pilot, six as a D.C. city cop and almost twelve as a rural county sheriff and your brain delegates a portion of itself to monitor the radio and not disturb the rest of you unless it's important.

"County . . . Sheriff Six!" I could hear my deputy, Haskel Beale, heaving for breath between words. I lifted my head and tilted it to better hear against the wind.

Now I have this neat old black broad for a combination desk sergeant, dispatcher and jailer—Milly Stanford. Milly had been the janitor and cook at the county jail for eleven years when I was hired as a deputy after I left the D.C. police. I had learned by the time the county elected me sheriff that Milly knew a lot more about running the jail and the sheriff's administrative office than the lazy, pilfering slug who was then desk sergeant. So I promptly fired the slug and installed Milly at sergeant's rank and pay. Reaction to this innovative personnel change varied from shock to raging apoplexy, but in a few weeks even the worst skeptics admitted the whole jail and office operation flowed much more smoothly and efficiently than ever before. Milly had a sumo wrestler shape, a heart the size of a basketball and a flair for quelling small jail riots with a broken walnut table leg. She steadily graduated in the minds of prisoner and deputy alike from "that ol' nigger jailhouse maid" to "Sergeant Stanford" or "Ma'am."

Calm as always, Milly answered, "Six this is County, what chu need, baby?" Milly's radio persona could stand some work.

Haskel was still struggling for breath. "Sarge, I got a 10-45-I, possible fatal, off County Twelve about four miles up from the Roanoke Highway. Send me the rescue squad and a wrecker on the hurry-up; victim's trapped in the wreck. An' git the Sheriff up here, quick!"

As Milly answered, "Ten-fo', Sheriff Six," I could hear her snapping her fingers, and I pictured the office staff snatching up phones for the appropriate calls.

I hit the lights and siren and got under way, and I radioed Milly to find Pierce and get him up on the scene also.

My predecessor, former Sheriff Oscar Wheeler, had the ethics of a leisure-suited lounge lizard, a trait he shared with his brother-in-law Homer Poff, the only Dodge dealer in the county. It struck a few folks as curious that, in all those Wheeler years, Poff Chrysler/Plymouth/Dodge always somehow managed to win the bidding process for Sheriff's Department patrol cars. Not the least curious were the Chevy dealer and the Ford man, whose bids were always marginally high, no matter how competitive they attempted to be.

When I ran for Sheriff, opposing Wheeler's fourth term, no one in the Wheeler political machine took me seriously until rumors began to trickle in that more than a few Hunter Countians were sick and tired of Wheeler's business as usual. Alarmed, Wheeler and his cronies, including Homer Poff, scrambled for damage control but found to their dismay they'd made too many enemies for too long. Suck on that, Oscar.

When I was soundly elected, Homer Poff took the high road and sent me a two-thousand-dollar Huntley-Rogers shotgun as a "token of congratulations." He also invited me to be his guest on his annual hunting trip to Mexico where, he assured me, the ladies were "real friendly" if I knew what he meant.

None of this, I'm sure, had anything to do with the fact that the Hunter County Sheriff's Department was about to let its annual bid for patrol cruisers. Nonetheless, I borrowed a demonstrator Chevrolet and drove out to Poff Dodge to return the shotgun. Vietnam had sort of ruined me on killing things for fun, I explained to Homer, and while I was as fond of "friendly" ladies as the next guy, I would pass on Mexico, too, thank you very much. "By the way," I said, leaving him simmering in his office, "I've decided to let the car bids in two-year contracts from now on." Homer's eyes widened at that as he realized it more than doubled the size of the upcoming purchase. "You may wish to examine the braking performance requirements very closely," I said, closing Homer's office door behind me.

When Homer figured out that, in that year, independent lab testing had placed Dodge panic-stopping distances at more than twenty-two feet longer than my specification in the bidding standards, but that both Ford and Chevrolet qualified, he screamed loud enough to register on seismic charts. He roared even louder when his attorneys reluctantly allowed there was no way to beat the process in court because I had the authority to set departmental safety standards wherever I wished and, in fact, Homer's cars didn't qualify that year. It would be four years before they did and six before Homer won another contract, legitimately. Shame on you, Homer.

Chevy won the bid that first year and, for many of my deputies who had plied their trade for years in the big-block Dodges, this was a heresy second only to making a nigger jailhouse maid a desk sergeant. They pissed and moaned until they began to swear by the Fords and Chevys as well, seeing once again the omniscient wisdom of Sheriff Lewis Cody. Oh, they of little faith.

We were in Chevys at the time I'm telling you about; mine was dark green and unmarked, sort of accenting my khaki uniform with dark brown Western boots and narrow brimmed Stetson, creating a fashion statement that will go worldwide any day now.

One of the joys of being a lawman is you not only get to shoot your gun and blow your siren but you get to drive like a wildman, too. In eleven minutes, I was on the accident scene high up on that section of County Twelve cut in the side of Saddle Mountain.

Haskel was soaked in sweat in spite of the fall air, and as I parked in the road because the goddamned gawkers' cars had the shoulders blocked, he threw a spent fire extinguisher on the ground and met me, frowning.

"Sheriff, it's ol' Ivy Joe Culpepper. He's done drove that

ol' truck a' his right through the guardrail halfway to the goddamn valley. Musta turned over about fifty times. The truck hung in some pines about a hunnert yards down the slope or it'd be in the river on its way to Roane County by now. They was a small gasoline fire but I done put it out."

"Is he alive?" I asked.

"He was when I left the wreck but, Sheriff, it ain't good. He's got the doorpost stove plumb in his chest. It's gonna take tools and time to git him out. We ain't got the tools and he ain't got the time. And, Sheriff?"

"Yeah?"

"He's been askin' fer you."

"All right, Pierce is on the way. Ya'll get these gawkers out of here; hang paper on anybody who moves slow."

As I stepped through the splintered gap in the old wooden guardrail and began to descend the steep slope, I heard Haskel bellow. "Awright, people, this ain't the goddamned circus! Anybody that's still here a minute from now gets wrote and towed! I might even bust me some headlights! Let's move it, people, now!" It sounded like a NASCAR race lighting up on that highway. Haskel's never going to win a Nobel Prize for diplomacy, but he gets the job done.

The slope was steep and there was a trough through the pines where Ivy Joe Culpepper's old '53 Studebaker pickup truck cut a trail down the mountainside. When I got down to the wreck, there was a cluster of six citizens standing around with their hands in their pockets, sucking on burning stinkweeds and staring at the inverted, mangled old red pickup. The tail end was charred, one wheel was missing entirely and the hood hung open. Steam and smoke rose from the upturned greasy black bottom of the wrecked truck.

I told the gawkers, "Ya'll get on up to your cars and get out of here and I don't mean later." One or two moved upslope a few feet, then stopped and resumed staring. I really hate gawkers.

I threw myself on the pine needles and crawled under the downslope side beneath the hood to the broken windshield. There, impaled upside down by the windshield cornerpost in his chest, was Ivy Joe Culpepper.

Nobody, probably including Ivy Joe, knew how old Ivy Joe Culpepper was, but everyone who had attended high school in Hunter County in the last sixty-odd years knew Ivy Joe as the kindly old gray-haired black gentleman who was the school custodian. He was a timeless fixture in these hills. No one could remember when he wasn't sweeping the school and smiling, and now it was impossible to envision a time when he would not.

Every school kid in Hunter County for over half a century had their own private, affectionate memory of Ivy Joe Culpepper. Mine was the day in my junior year when that old battle-ax, Mrs. McKenzie, saw Patsy Nolan looking out of her third-period English classroom door into the hall at me, though Mrs. "McFrenzy" didn't see me. I saw Patsy blanch and heard McFrenzy's polio boots clopping the floor in my direction. I split in a cold panic as I was supposed to be in Algebra class, not roaming the halls lusting after Patsy Nolan. As I rounded the corner from the hall into the auditorium on a dead run, I crashed into Ivy Joe Culpepper, spilling him ass over mop bucket. I put a foot in his chest and kept right on truckin' because, buddy, Mrs. McFrenzy meant *business* and corporal punishment was quite the vogue in those days. I hid in the seats as McFrenzy arrived to find poor old Ivy Joe picking himself up, soaked in mop water. She demanded to know who I was, and I held my breath because I knew Ivy Joe had gotten a good look at me and, count on it, Ivy Joe Culpepper knew *everybody* by name.

Mr. Joe said, "Don't reckon I know, Mrs. McKenzie. Went by so fast I don't even know if it were boy or girl!"

When McFrenzy stomped back to her classroom, I surfaced to apologize and help Mr. Joe clean up the mess. "Lewis," Mr. Joe said to me, "why in the name of the Lord ain't you on the football team?"

For over half a century, a highlight of each school year was near Christmastime when Ivy Joe Culpepper would take the stage before the entire school and play the piano and sing Christmas carols. He always closed his exquisite annual program with an achingly slow rendition of "Silent Night" that made you cry. That raspy whisper of a voice held God knows how many years of the knowledge of man, of suffering and love on a scale most people never fathom, let alone experience. "... *Hoooooly Infant ... so tender ... and mild ... sleeeeeep in heavenly peeeeeee-eeace ...*" When the last note faded all you could hear was sniffling until Ivy Joe Culpepper rose from the grand and bowed with regal dignity. The standing ovations always lasted forever. Then a representative from each class would come on to present that class's Christmas gift for Mr. Joe.

He was a gentle old soul who never had an angry or unloving thought in his life.

And now, hanging inverted here before me was the bloodied, carriage-leather face of Ivy Joe Culpepper, who was clearly dying.

His eyes were squinted with the pain, but he opened them as I crawled near. The corners of his mouth twitched in an effort to smile. I smelled gasoline and pine resin.

"Lewis," he said. Blood dripped from his mouth along the sides of his broad nose.

"Easy, Mr. Joe," I said. "You've been in an accident, sir, but don't you worry. We're going to get you out, you're going to be okay—"

"Nooo ..." Mr. Joe groaned and then he coughed in agony, spitting blood in my face.

"Hang tough, Mr. Joe, help's on the way, sir."

"Lewis! It wa'n't no accident, Lewis!" he rasped, bubbling blood. His speech was slurred—the word *accident* sounded like "azz-dunt." I struggled to understand him.

Then he said something that sounded like "loz loz!" or "loz roz!"

I pulled myself closer. He coughed again. "What was that, Mr. Joe?"

"Loz loz ... loz rahz. Lewis ... it wa'n't no azz-dun ..."

"What happened, Mr. Joe?"

"Roz loz ... shot ..."

"Lois Ross, Mr. Joe? What do you mean 'shot'?"

"Loz rahz! Roz lahz!"

"What about Lois Ross, Mr. Joe? Tell me!"

He must have seen the distress in my face, for then he reached out a withered, trembling hand and touched my cheek. I seized his hand; we both knew he was going soon.

"Don' you fret, boy," Joe squeaked out in sudden agony, "Ah know . . . ah know . . . you done . . . all you could."

His eyes were still open, but I've seen a lot of dead eyes in my time. I knew he was gone. Ivy Joe Culpepper had died a slow, violent, painful death. Silent night, Mr. Joe. Sleep in heavenly peace, Mr. Joe. I felt his neck for a pulse I knew wasn't there. Goodbye, Mr. Joe. If there's a heaven, you own it, sir.

I pushed back from beneath the wreck and stood, shaken. I felt tears welling up.

The gawkers stood near, smoking and staring. One of them, about forty years old, a fat, dirty man with belly showing between his shirt and pants and tobacco-juice dribbles in his beard, stepped past me. He bent over to peer beneath the hood. He spat. "Well," he said, "that ol' nigger's dead, ain't he, Sheriff?" He turned his head to smirk at his chums. "Tha's one less nigger, I guess!" He laughed through his nose and the chums tittered.

That did it. I lost my temper. I planted my feet and kicked that fat ass as hard as I could. He grunted with the impact and sprawled forward to his belly under the hood of the truck. I straddled him, grabbed him by his pants and collar and heaved him over the slippery pine needles until his face was six inches from Mr. Joe's dead white eyes. The fat man recoiled in horror.

"You tell *me,* you fat fuck!" I roared. "This is what you came to see, isn't it? *Hanh?* What about it, *doctor?* In your professional opinion, doctor! Is he dead or not? *Hanh?"*

"Aaaaaah! God, let me go, please!" he shrieked in horror, eyeball to eyeball with the very late Ivy Joe Culpepper.

"Answer me, goddamn it!"

"He's dead! He's dead! Lemme up! Lemme up!"

I scrambled backward and dragged him out by his belt, pulling his pants below his pale white ass in the process.

"On your feet!" I grunted, heaving him up. He struggled to pull up his pants. The three women and two men with him looked on in gape-mouthed shock.

Lardass had a pouty look on his face. "Sheriff—" He whined.

*"Shut up!* You aren't from around here, are you, fatboy?"

"No, sir! I'm from—"

"You know why I know you're not from around here?" I seethed, my nose to his.

"No, sir," he whispered, his eyes twitching.

"Because!" I shouted in his face. "Around here *we didn't call him nigger!"*

"Yes, sir!"

"Now take your esteemed colleagues and get the *fuck* out of here and if I ever see any of you at a wreck in Hunter County again you better goddamn well be *in* it!"

The message soaked in this time. Up the slope they went like a herd of mountain goats. Not a very professional display on my part, but it sure as hell felt good.

Watching them go, I saw my huge chief deputy, Percy "Pierce" Arroe, scuffling down the slope with a pair of chain come-alongs and a first-aid kit. When he saw my face, he stopped scrambling and walked.

We call him Pierce or occasionally Broken Arroe, since we don't wish to die for calling him Percy. At six-eight and 270, he's much bigger than me, but he's a much nicer guy, too. Pierce is married to one of those salt-of-the-earth women who is happy to raise kids and cook all day and fuck your brains out all night. They have five splendid kids anyone would be proud of, and God knows Pierce and Brenda were. Pierce and I went through army basic together back in the Stone Age, and we flew in Vietnam together for a while, he as a crew chief and me as a pilot. We're friends—real with-you-right-or-wrong, kill-for-you friends.

"Aw shit," Pierce said. He has a voice like a grizzly in a cave, and now I could hear it cracking. "Old Ivy Joe's dead?"

We were halfway back up to the road when Pierce grumbled, "Hunter County'll never be the same again." He was dead right about that.

On the road, Haskel had run off all the gawkers. The local undertaker, Lawrence Weeks, and his son, both conveniently volunteer fire department medics, were unloading a gurney from an ambulance. A wrecker from Stout's Texaco was arriving. The wrecker's yellow flashing lights mixed with our blues and Lawrence's reds, giving the whole scene a surreal, unworldly look.

Lawrence and his boy were hustling to the gap in the guardrail with something called a Miller Board, used to carry patients.

"You can take your time, Lawrence," I said. He stopped, comprehending.

"Understand it's old Ivy Joe Culpepper," Lawrence said.

"Yeah," I replied. "Was."

"That's a shame. We'll take him over to East Hunter to the colored funeral parlor."

"Not yet," I said. "Take him to Coleby Butler's clinic and tell Coleby I need a complete autopsy ASAP."

Both Pierce and Lawrence took on quizzical looks. "An autopsy, Sheriff?" Lawrence said. "On an old ni—ah, on an accident victim?"

"Goddamn it, Lawrence, did I stutter?"

"Well, no, Sheriff. I just wondered, that's all."

"Wait till Stout gets the wreck up. Pierce, before this scene is further disturbed, I want you and Haskel to do an investigation of the accident, photos and all. You know what to do. Have it on my desk in the morning."

"Sure, Lewis, color it done." Pierce looked to see that Lawrence, his son and the wrecker driver were out of earshot. "What's up?"

"Probably nothing. It's just something Mr. Joe was rambling on about before he died. He said it wasn't an accident."

"Ivy Joe said that? Lewis, who the hell would want to hurt Ivy Joe Culpepper? He didn't have an enemy in the world and God knows he didn't have any fortune for anyone to inherit! Christ, I don't think he even *had* any heirs."

"I can't imagine anyone wanting to harm old Joe either, but that's what he said, so we'll play it out as far as it goes."

"Sure. That all he said?"

"No. He kept saying something like 'lohz rahz.'"

"Lois Ross?"

"Could be. He was pretty fucked up and difficult to understand."

# Shepherd of the Wolves

Pierce thought for a moment. "You know, Lewis, even though we ain't been able to prove Lois Ross is dealing shit through the school, I *know* she's behind that coke and them pills we recovered off them kids. You don't reckon old Joe had something real on her, do you?"

I looked at the stars appearing in the twilight. "Who knows? It sure don't seem likely. Joe was the kind to mind his own business."

"Yeah. Well. Still, I wouldn't put even murder past Lois Ross. That's one bitter bitch."

"I think it's thin, Pierce. Old Joe was drifting into senility recently. Hell, he was a million years old. He was pretty shaken up down there. He may not have known what he was saying and I might have misunderstood him."

"Ummmm. Still, if anybody, especially Lois Ross, killed Ivy Joe Culpepper, I'd sure like to get a piece of 'em, you know?"

"Bet your ass."

# 2

## Lois Ross

I went home. I just radioed Milly and told her I'd be at the house if I was needed.

Ivy Joe Culpepper's was hardly the only death I'd worked in eighteen years of police work, but somehow his passing saddened me. I guess it was that if anyone as harmless and gentle and loving as old Mr. Joe could get murdered, if that's what happened, not in some grimy inner-city alley, but up here in the clean mountain air, then something was very, very wrong.

My grandfather left me a solid old frame farmhouse and a barn on forty-six acres of Bram's Ridge. When my daughter . . . died . . . and Elaine left me, I resigned from the D.C. police, moved up here and took old Granddad's place out of mothballs.

A Hunter County deputy sheriff didn't make much eleven years ago, still doesn't actually, but I didn't need much. Granddaddy's home was isolated, full of antiques and old chinaware and it smelled of wood smoke. It was a place where a badly injured man could crawl to heal. Or try to, anyway.

It wasn't a fancy place, but a tired and vaguely depressed country cop could come home to it, turn on his old Joan Baez tapes and sip a cold Norwegian beer while watching the sun's glow fade beyond the distant Appalachians. You big-city rich guys can eat your hearts out. Ya'll who never heard of Joan Baez can fuck off, too.

Over the years I took on two boarders: an incredibly ugly English bulldog puppy I found on the Cain River Bridge after some sorry bastard bungled an attempt to throw him into the river from a moving car, and a Belgian draft mare about the size of an elephant. I bought the mare as a filly from Lon Sutley the year he broke his back and could no longer plow behind the filly's dam and had to auction his farm. The bulldog's name is Gruesome and if you could see him you'd know why. The horse is called Moose for similar reasons. Moose was no plow horse for me because I was no farmer. I kept her to ride and to pull my cruiser out of the mud in the spring rainy season.

When I arrived home, I turned my unmarked Chevy cruiser through the gate over the cattle guardrails (which hadn't guarded any cattle in twenty years) and parked by my old faded silver four-wheel-drive pickup truck, a classic hillbilly chariot complete with rifle rack. Gruesome came snarling out from under the porch like a self-propelled chainsaw until he got close enough for his goofy eyes to register, whereupon he wagged his entire ass in apology. I pushed him on his wrinkled butt and he sprang up and grabbed me by the arm as if he'd really hurt me. It was an old ritual. Gruesome and I are also with-you-right-or-wrong, kill-for-you friends.

Inside I popped a Norwegian brew, poured a small amount in Gruesome's water bowl and sat down out back on the porch with the rest. In the dying twilight, I could barely make out Moose walking up from the creek to the barn.

I thought about the untimely demise of Ivy Joe Culpepper.

Pierce was right about Lois Ross. She was one bitter bitch, but I didn't see murder in her. Still, one thing you learn fast in this business is you never put anything past anybody.

What Pierce was fond of calling the "whore war" began right after I took office seven years ago. Lois Ross owned and operated a tavern and motel called Saddle Mountain

Lodge way out on the Roanoke Highway just this side of the
Hunter/Roanoke County line. While you could buy a meal
in the restaurant, a drink at the bar and rent a little cottage
in the pines for a night, no one was confused about Lois's
place being a front for prostitution.

Lois had operated in Roanoke County for years until vice
ran her out. Then she bought the old Saddle Mountain
Lodge at a tax auction and set up house about a quarter of a
mile on my side of the county line. Her old clientele still
drove up from Roanoke, and now business from Hunter
County was hers as well.

No argument so far. For all I cared, prostitution per se
could be legalized. The problem is, of course, there is no
pure prostitution. Anywhere you have prostitution you have
assholes who traffic in underage girls and drugs; it never
fails and Lois Ross was no exception. If grown pussy had
been all Lois sold I'd never have darkened her door, but it
doesn't work that way in the naked county. Lois was
thought to deal marijuana, coke, crack and PCP on a
limited scale, but she was good at it and evidence was tough
to come by. She also blatantly handled moonshine, more as
a distributor than as a distiller, and she dealt in guns of
mysterious origin.

I don't run hysterical over a grown woman electing to sell
herself. Likewise, I don't see pot or moonshine being all that
tragic as long as you don't drive under the influence of
either. I wasn't even too concerned about Lois dealing in
guns because the good ol' boys are going to have their guns
and, at least in Hunter County, they used them primarily
for shooting deer and bear and not for robberies and
homicides. But Lois wasn't satisfied with dealing to adults,
or even *with* adults. She sold to anybody with the money,
and some of the girls she sold in the Wheeler years were
rumored to be as young as fourteen.

My daughter, Tess, would have been seventeen this year.

The infamous Sheriff Wheeler was known to be on the
take from Lois, and her operation flourished in those years.
When I was elected, the situation took a turn.

The week of my swearing-in, I drove out to Saddle
Mountain Lodge and calmly read Lois the riot act. I told her
to keep a low profile so the Christians would stay off my ass,

deal no drugs, keep the girls age twenty-one or over, and I'd not muddy her water. Otherwise, I'd cut her off at the knees. Seemed reasonable to me; I wasn't asking for a payoff and she could still earn a good living.

When Lois calmed down from her laughing fit, she said Oscar Wheeler had warned her I was a smartass but she knew how to handle smartasses. "I been doin' business my way in Hunter County for sixteen years, you little shit!" she told me charmingly, "and I ain't changing it for you or no damn body else! Now git outa here and take that silly badge with you!"

"Ooooooo K," I said.

She wasn't laughing when I came through her front door with a warrant and eight of my deputies the following payday Friday night at prime time. We impounded the homemade booze, some pot and the guns, and we photographed her customers before running them off. We found enough to book Lois for possession with the intent to distribute and she did sixty days in the state workhouse.

· The next time I drove out to parlay with her, she was inclined to be a little more reasonable. She said she'd cooperate, but I had no illusions. I knew she hated my soul and would move on me sooner or later.

It was about a month later. She had four of her thug minions, including this pretty-boy she was in love with, jump me one night when I answered a false call at a roadhouse in town. Fortunately, these morons had been bragging about what they had in mind, and someone I'll never know, but will always be grateful to, dropped a dime on them. About two minutes after they threw a tablecloth over my head, Pierce Arroe and a few of the boys came through the door with blood in their eyes. It was teeth, hair and eyeballs all over the place. (You don't want to be around when cops catch up with cop fighters because a "get-'em-before-they-get-one-of-us" mentality sets in and things get evil. Right or wrong, that's how it is.)

That night there was a crashing-in of Lois's bedroom window at the lodge. A body barely alive landed next to Lois in a shower of glass. Lois turned on the light and began to scream. Pretty Boy wasn't pretty anymore.

Pretty Boy left Lois when she nursed him back to health.

He was a posturing excuse for a man anyway, and he'd only hung in with Lois because she kept him fed and fucked. When he could walk again, he did—right out of Lois's life. The episode crushed Lois, and you might say it served to direct her attention to subtle changes in the prevailing power structure in Hunter County. It took the fight out of her.

For almost eight years, Lois kept a low profile as ordered. I got occasional reports of an occasional young girl, but I could never get enough evidence to hit Lois again.

Recently, though, a little coke and a lot of pills had been turning up at the high school. I'd been working with the principal, Gene Sweet, on it, but hard information was scarce. Some of the boys, however, were known to frequent Lois's Saddle Mountain Lodge, for a delicious dinner, no doubt. Pierce and I had been working on the possibility that Lois was distributing again. Could it be possible that one of the kids either said something to Ivy Joe Culpepper implicating Lois or maybe he overheard same? Even so, Mr. Joe wouldn't have been stupid enough to confront Lois about it. He would have called me. If he'd had time. But would Lois murder a harmless old Negro school janitor over a drug implication? Why? How? Maybe Joe knew more about Lois than I could guess right now. But what? And how did I even know Joe was implicating Lois with his dying words? They were, after all, unclear. He sure didn't appear to be shot, like he said, although Dr. Coleby Butler would tell me for sure about that in the morning.

Then, too, wasn't it possible that Joe or I or both of us were just confused in the stress of the moment? Wasn't it even likely that the great unbreakable law, the law of averages, caught up with ancient Ivy Joe Culpepper and he just lost control of that old truck and killed himself? But then why would he have sent for me and said what he did?

The sadness still hung heavy in the cold evening air. Gruesome shouldered the screen door open, waddled onto the weathered porch planks and belched. I scratched his ears and, as though he knew something was eating at me, he launched himself into my lap and cuddled.

Maybe you're wondering what a forty-plus lawman was doing living alone in the hills with an ugly dog and a giant horse. Specifically, you may ask, where were the women in his life?

I wondered that too actually. I knew my little girl was dead. And I knew Elaine was remarried to some jive-ass attorney up in Baltimore. Hadn't seen her in years and I guess you could say I'd gotten over her. I guess.

Since the divorce, there'd been some dates and a couple of close women friends. I made friends with women more often than I made lovers of them. I was hoping to someday do both with the same girl. Soon. I'd thought I was reconciled to living alone, but recently it was getting harder and harder to justify a life void of . . . meaning, of anything or anyone to look forward to at the end of the day.

When I was a rookie in D.C., after Vietnam, I used to hear all those tales about lonely, disillusioned older cops sucking on their revolvers. I even knew one who did. I used to think it was just a few mentally disturbed guys who took the coward's way out. I used to think that all the psychological explanations for cop suicides put forth by the psycho/socio experts was just a lot of esoteric balderdash dreamed up to justify their jobs. Lately I was beginning to wonder.

But at the moment, I had to figure out what happened to Ivy Joe Culpepper.

# 3

## The Gentry

Gruesome knew I'd blender his dick if he woke me up early, but part of our deal was that, once the alarm went off, he could go as hysterical as he wanted. When I heard the clock beeping, the morning after Ivy Joe Culpepper's death, I instantly covered my face and lamentably underutilized privates with my hands because I knew Gruesome would be on short final with his clawed, knobby feet. I felt like a pro quarterback fading back to pass who suddenly hears snorting and heavy footfalls behind him and notices a huge shadow beginning to form around him.

It was November cold and predawn dark when Gruesome and I trotted out for the morning run. The eastern sky was beginning to glow when we staggered back, each forswearing beer forever for the thousandth time. I dived in the shower and Gruesome went tits up and tongue out by the gas heater in the kitchen. Normally Gruesome minds the house, but occasionally I take him to work with me. This morning he eagerly leaped in the cruiser's right seat, ripe with enthusiasm for finding someone to lock up and/or bite.

We country folk place much stock in our rituals. So it was that every weekday morning, barring emergencies, I joined The Gentry for breakfast at Lady Maude's Cafe on the square in Hunter. "Lady Maude" always sounded a little pretentious to me to befit the grand old, perennially smiling operator of the cafe, who was easily the best cook in recorded history. I parked in the no-parking zone by the fire hydrant, and Gruesome promptly anointed it.

The smell alone of ham, bacon and biscuits in Lady Maude's prehistoric cafe was reason enough to go there. The Gentry were assembled at the long table in the rear as always, and a chorus of greetings went up for Gruesome and me. Gruesome went quickly to each of The Gentry with his precious pet-me-or-I'll-kill-you look. Pete Floyd, editor of the *Hunter Press,* gave Gruesome an obligatory pat, then wiped his hand on his napkin. Burt Willis, the barber, greeted him with enthusiasm, which was returned. Amos Cotter, the postmaster; Merlin Sowers, with the bank (also chairman of the County Board); Fire Chief Arnold Webb; and Dr. Coleby Butler rounded out the table.

Dr. Coleby Butler was my third and last unconditional, with-you-right-or-wrong, kill-for-you friend. I met Coleby when the North Vietnamese shot me down north of Pleiku late in the war. They flew me and what was left of my crew to the medevac hospital in Pleiku, and one of those masked and gowned in green, standing with his sterile hands up in the air like a praying mantis as I was wheeled into receiving, was Captain Coleby Butler, a U.S. Air Force physician.

My Huey had been hit in the tail with an antitank rocket as we hovered over heavy mountain jungle, dropping ammunition to an American platoon in contact with a company-size NVA force. In the crash I broke my jaw in three places, broke some ribs and got cut up, but more critical, I felt, were the splintered ends of my right tibia and fibula that extended out the back of my calf.

In the shock, pain and nausea of the first few days in the hospital, my dominating concern as a young pilot was whether I would ever walk again, especially well enough to pass a stringent military flight physical and return to flying status. I became obsessed with this concern as doctor after doctor making the rounds dodged giving me a straight answer. "Well," they'd equivocate, "we'll just have to see . . ." This, to me, was doctor talk for "You're going to be a cripple the rest of your life, Ace." More than painful, those first days of recovery were terrifying in their uncertainty.

At some point, I opened my eyes to a blond-haired young

doctor whose premature widow's peak and patrician face made him a dead ringer for Ashley Wilkes, the doomed Confederate Cavalry officer from the movie *Gone with the Wind,* the Southern aristocrat Miss Scarlet never quite got over loving.

"Hello," he said pleasantly, "I'm Coleby Butler; I'm an orthopedic specialist. I thought—"

"Dahg!" I mumbled with swollen lips, through mandibles sutured shut, "Dahg! Am Ah gong ta wahg again? Am Ah gong ta wahg again?"

His brow creased with concern and he held my hand. "Are you going to walk again?"

"Yez!"

Coleby's smile at that moment outshone the smile of my own mother. "Of course you will, my friend! I set your leg myself and I've studied your X-rays carefully. In my opinion those bone fragments will meld together quite nicely. It will be a few months, of course, but in less than a year you'll be back in the cockpit." He bent closer to me and touched my forehead. "Trust me," he said, smiling. I did.

In later rounds we were delighted to discover we were both Virginians. The name hadn't rung a bell, but Coleby's father had been the late senator from Virginia, Carson Butler, and Coleby had grown up in Richmond. We also discovered we enjoyed chess and had no one to play it with. Coleby started coming by on his off time with a chess set, and we'd play the ancient game and talk for hours. When I fell asleep or succumbed to the pain drugs they had me on, he would slide the board under the bed and come back when I was alert.

Coleby possessed the sort of sensitive, gentle refinement that is frequently mistaken in men for homosexuality. I wondered about it at first, but it was wasted concern. I learned in the hours over the chessboard that Coleby Butler was simply a genuinely nice guy. So rare are they these days, we are reluctant to believe them when we see them. I came to know Coleby could be believed.

Coleby wrote me when they moved me to Japan—he seemed to hurt for someone he could be himself with, someone he could talk to without having to guard what he said. A year later, we ran into each other at the officer's club

## Shepherd of the Wolves

at Andrews Air Force Base. It took over an hour of cruising the few stores open at nine P.M. before we finally found a cheap plastic chess set. We kept in touch and occasionally got together in D.C. when I was a cop or at his family estate in Richmond to play chess and solve the world's problems over some cold beer. Coleby had been a child when his father died; I attended the funeral of Coleby's mother after the war.

Coleby was the scion of one of the wealthiest families in Virginia, drove a silver Rolls-Royce Corniche convertible and occasionally played polo ("horse-hockey," I used to kid him) with Washington quiche-eaters. Yet he had not the slightest trace of arrogance, the trait I despise above all others. Dr. Coleby Butler could have practiced anywhere he wanted to after the name he made for himself in U.S. Air Force medicine, but he'd inherited a self-sustaining fortune and he was quite content to settle in Hunter County, at my urging, and take over the little clinic there and the post of County Coroner. It was Hunter County's blessing. Dr. Coleby Butler was one of a vanishing breed of physicians who actually gave a fat damn more for his patients' health than their income or insurance. Yeah, he could afford to, that was true, but it wasn't his wealth that made him sing happily to babies he delivered or weep quietly in his closed office after an especially tough patient succumbed to forces beyond his control. He put in more hours than any doctor I ever knew. He was the shepherd of Hunter County; he cared and Hunter County loved him for it. So did I.

Unfortunately, it was commonly known that his wife didn't love him. The arrogant bitch certainly made no effort to conceal the fact. Coleby met Sarah Elizabeth McCormick when her father was a power at Johns Hopkins in Baltimore. Sarah was a cellist for the Baltimore Symphony Orchestra, a "middle-fiddle stroker for the Baltimore beat-blow-and-stroke folks," Coleby and I used to quip. We thought it rather rich, but Sarah never laughed. She married the Butler fortune while Coleby was still a U.S. Air Force doctor, fully anticipating he would take up his rightful place in Baltimore medical society upon his discharge. To her profound shock she later learned he intended to move up into the hills to practice at some outback family clinic in

Hunter, Virginia, forty miles from the nearest country club! Poor guileless Coleby loved Sarah deeply and assumed she loved him the same way, and, thus, what did it matter where they lived? Coleby was convinced Sarah would come to love the Blue Ridge and would share his enthusiasm for realizing an opportunity to be of service to people who needed him. For her part, Sarah was convinced Coleby would in time see the folly of it all and move her back to Baltimore. She never did and he never did. Their marriage was not made in heaven. Coleby loved Sarah, but he knew he was not of a nature to be happy in Baltimore and he further came to know that what was wrong with him and Sarah would not be cured by a change in address. Sarah, he then knew to his grief, loved only Sarah.

Coleby was blessed with two beautiful daughters. Anne was seventeen the month Ivy Joe Culpepper was killed— she was a senior at the exclusive Madeira School near Washington, and Elizabeth was ten. They, unlike their mother, loved him without reserve, and Coleby was blindly, wildly devoted to them both.

In recent years the strain between Coleby and Sarah had grown. I was worried about its effect on them all, especially on Coleby. I could see the misery growing in his gentle eyes.

But enough of this cheery shit.

Lady Maude doesn't employ a waitress younger than sixty, so although the service is good it's slower than a crippled turtle. No matter; we came to talk, not just eat. Gruesome agreed to stay under my chair if I passed him every second sausage.

"Lewis!" Coleby Butler said as I sat down. "I'm starved for a good game of chess. I insist you join us for dinner this evening. I'll have Polly prepare her splendid corned beef and we'll chill some of my best Norwegian pilsner. No objections will be considered."

"Who could say no to that?" I replied. "I'll be there. Thanks." I wondered if Sarah would find a way to spoil it.

"What the hell is *pilzer?*" Burt, the barber, asked.

"A pilsner!" Coleby laughed. "It's an excellent imported beer, Burt."

"Humph," Burt grunted, wondering no doubt why any-

24

one would pay to ship in weird-tasting foreigner beer when all the Bud you could ask for was in the Piggly Wiggly by the case.

The food arrived. Everyone settled down to eating it until Pete Floyd, the newspaper editor, opened the can of worms.

"Lewis," he began, feigning casual interest, "what's the latest in the murder of Ivy Joe Culpepper?"

Jesus, there are no secrets in Hunter County. I knew Pierce Arroe would never have said anything, so Pete could only be fishing in a pond of rumors derived from the wrecker driver or Lawrence Weeks, the undertaker, and they didn't know shit.

Nonetheless, all conversation and chewing at the table came to a screeching halt.

"What gives you the notion Ivy Joe Culpepper was murdered, Pete?" I responded, equally casual. "You know something I don't?" I kept eating.

"Come, come, Sheriff," Pete said with exaggerated pleasantness. "You don't order the county medical examiner here," he said, nodding at Coleby, "to perform an autopsy in a routine single-vehicle traffic accident without a reason."

"That 'routine single-vehicle traffic accident' killed a man, Pete. That's reason enough."

"Now, Lewis," Pete said, a little testiness now in his tone, "there's more to this than you're telling. I can smell it, and the people have a right to know."

"Bullshit. The people have a right to know the truth where it affects them, Pete. Don't try to pull that freedom of the press crap on me; I'm not impressed. I've seen you press people fuck up too many innocent people's lives. Ivy Joe Culpepper died in a car wreck. That's all the facts there are right now. When I know something real, you'll know it. I've always cooperated with you."

"Well! Who appointed you to the Supreme Court?"

Amos Cotter, the postmaster, interrupted. "You think ol' Ivy Joe was done in by foul play, Pete? How come?"

I interrupted. "See what I mean, Pete? Ivy Joe was widely revered, and now you're going to unnecessarily stir a lot of people up with the as yet unsubstantiated and ill-chosen drop of the word *murder*. Now that's—"

Burt Willis couldn't hold back the gossip he'd apparently been hoarding for the right moment. With style and relish, he butted in to announce, "Well! They was a guy in my shop last night whose sister was at the wreck and she said they overheard Joe tell Lewis he was shot by Lois Ross!"

"You don't say!" cried Merlin Sowers.

"Shot?" Pete asked, perking up. "Lois Ross?"

"Ah, Jesus," I said, exasperated. "I was there and it was very difficult to tell what he said. The poor old man had a truck sticking out of his chest! He wasn't very lucid."

"Ah, shit," Burt whispered to Amos, "what's *lucid?*"

"Lewis, what exactly did you understand him to say?" Pete demanded, clicking a ballpoint over a napkin. "After all, I understand he specifically asked for you!"

"No kidding?" Merlin Sowers crowed like he'd just been told Martians had landed in the town square.

"Goddamn it, Pete!" I said. Haskel knew better than to talk shop on the outside. Some gawker must have overheard him talking to me at the scene.

"Gentlemen!" Coleby, the statesman, interrupted. "I believe I can and should lay the matter to rest before hostilities escalate between our good guardian of the truth here and our sheriff. Ordinarily, the results of an official autopsy are not for public consumption, at least not before running the appropriate channels, but in this instance I think Lewis will agree no harm is done. The late Ivy Joe Culpepper succumbed to severe traumatic invasion of the cardiopulmonary cavity, resulting in the subsequent failure of both associated major organ functions."

*"What?!"* Burt sputtered.

"The crash fucked up his heart and lungs and he croaked, Burt," I said.

"Oh."

"No gunshot wounds?" Pete insisted, obviously disappointed.

"None," Coleby replied amiably.

"Maybe that old truck broke a tie-rod," Merlin volunteered.

"Well, I tell you what *I* think!" growled Fire Chief Arnold Webb, standing and tossing some bills on the table, clearly miffed that no one had asked him what he thought. "I think

**26**

that old nigger just fucked up and drove off the goddamn mountain, that's what I think! I never knew a nigger that could drive no ways." Arnold stalked out.

"Well, I guess that settles that," I said.

"Not quite," Pete retorted.

I just looked at him.

"Lawrence Weeks said you also ordered an in-depth investigation of the accident. Said Pierce Arroe measured and photographed the whole scene and examined that old truck with a fine-toothed comb. Now, Lewis, you know I'm gonna want the results of that investigation."

I stood up and dropped my own bills. "When I know the truth, Pete, you'll know it. Off your ass, Gruesome, we're leaving. Coleby, we'll see you tonight. Thanks for the invitation."

"Certainly, Lewis. I'm looking forward to it."

At the mention of his name, Gruesome sprang up and headed for the door.

Gruesome, Pierce Arroe and Coleby Butler. Best friends a man could ask for. Without friends, life is shit.

# 4

## Captain Jedidiah Hunter

The Hunter County Sheriff's Department offices and jail were together in one large building constructed of the ageless gray stone which has been a curse on area farmers for over two centuries. The building sat among towering hemlocks and had a six-foot wrought-iron fence around the grounds. The fence looked like hundreds of ugly black vertical spears linked together. In short, the sheriff's department and jail looked like a medieval dungeon of the most odious order. I loved it.

My office had been the judge's chambers when the building was the county courthouse before the "new" courthouse was built about forty years ago. It was full of rugged antiques, not by virtue of any decorator's finesse, but because, for a hundred years, the county had been too cheap to purchase new furniture for the dungeon. No matter. I liked the massive old walnut desk, the cracked leather chair, the wooden file cabinets, the built-in bookcases and the soot-blackened stone fireplace. Straight out of a John Wayne western.

Over the fireplace was a large old brownish tintype photograph of a rank-looking dude with a preposterous walrus mustache, wearing a long black coat and a bowler hat. He sat astride a killer mule, and a well-oiled .44-caliber hand cannon hung casually from the hand he draped over the saddle horn. The dude wore a silver star like mine. The dude was my great-grandfather and he was the sheriff of Hunter County for twenty-six years.

The interior door to my office opened onto what was now the booking room and office cubicles for Milly and the secretaries and clerks. It was the courtroom in the days the place was a courthouse. In the frames of the main front doors and windows, there were carefully preserved bullet holes. They were reminders of the day my great-granddaddy and his deputies shot it out with the Berle family, when they tried to take Thomas Berle out of the court trying him for knifing his lover's husband to death. A deputy was killed before a slug from Great Granddad's .44 sent Old Man Berle to hell. The deputies killed two of the Berle brothers and captured the wounded third. He and Thomas were hanged together in due course. Tough shit, boys.

In the front yard stood a statue of the noble Captain Jedidiah Hunter, who rode with Jackson in the Valley Campaign. Captain Hunter seemed to be studying faraway vistas, one arm draped atop his saber. I thought he looked suspiciously like a young Custer, but such a thought was blasphemy in these parts.

The statue of Captain Jedidiah Hunter was erected by the Daughters of the Confederacy, who annually held a ball in the good captain's memory, he having been the only of Hunter County's sons decorated both for bravery by Jackson and service by Lee. When I was first elected, I was expected to speak at the ball. I tried to beg off but was told by the board it was an annual ordeal the sheriff was required to endure. I went to the library and dragged out some dusty old volumes on the period but was unable to find anything on ol' Jed that wasn't already engraved on his monument.

I figured that if I had to do this speech I should do it right. There are always Civil War buffs in every Southern community, and some of them are extremely knowledgeable, especially with regard to their own pet locale. I asked Coleby, the most educated man I knew in Hunter County, if he knew of anyone who could give me something fresh on Captain Jedidiah Hunter.

"Lewis," Coleby answered, "I've got the proverbial good news and bad news."

"Um-hmm," I said.

"Unquestionably one of the finest Civil War historians in the state is Mrs. Beulah Vaughn."

"Has a farm out in Mossy Hollow?"

"That's her. She's almost old enough to speak from direct experience. She's provided artifacts for the Smithsonian and she has been named as a source by the likes of Douglas Southall Freeman and Bruce Catton."

"So I'm waiting for the other shoe," I said.

"Unfortunately, Mrs. Vaughn suffers a distinct shortfall of cordiality, emphasized by her regrettable tendency to shoot at anyone who comes calling uninvited, and that's just about everybody. UPS leaves her packages down by the highway, and you may rest assured she was omitted from the last census."

I drove out to Mossy Hollow and up the rocky dirt trail to Old Lady Vaughn's log home one night shortly after dark. The porch light was on, which I took to be a good sign. I parked what I thought was a safe distance from the porch, chirped my siren and hailed her over the car's loudspeaker. I was confident that, as long as the old gal knew who had come to see her, she wouldn't dare shoot at the ranking law-enforcement officer in Hunter County. I squinted in the darkness and could barely see her, dimly silhouetted by the parlor window, just to the left of the porch light. She was leaning on some sort of heavy crutch.

"Good evening, Mrs. Vaughn!" My amplified voice echoed up the hollow. "This is Sheriff Lewis Cody, Mrs. Vaughn. I'd be grateful for the opportunity to have a short talk with you."

The "crutch" suddenly came up horizontal and a thunderous kaBOOM was the next sound that echoed up the hollow. I could hear the shot slicing through the tree leaves behind me.

"You git the hell off my land, asshole!" Old Lady Vaughn's witch's screech required no loudspeaker. She punctuated her charm with another charge from what sounded like a ten-gauge goose blaster that could drop a satellite from orbit. I flinched at the sound of the shot cutting the treetops.

Fortunately, Mrs. Vaughn's hospitality was rivaled only

by her marksmanship. She couldn't have hit a dairy barn with a machine gun if she had been standing inside it with the doors shut.

I popped my trunk, got my oiled and pampered M-14 rifle from its sheepskin case and benchrested it across the roof of the car.

Mrs. Vaughn completed a reload of the old double-barrel goose gun and had just clacked the breech shut when I let go with one very carefully aimed round from the extremely accurate M-14. She had just gotten out "I *said,* you git the—" when the porch light fixture exploded in a shower of glass and porcelain.

While she tap danced about her porch, avoiding flying shards, I called to her, "I can see you are a sporting lady, Mrs. Vaughn! Tell you what. I'll trade you shot for shot till one of us hits. How about it?"

Old Lady Vaughn was a cranky old witch, not a stupid old witch. "How about *a drink,* Sheriff?" she screeched, breaking open the old shotgun.

In her living room, Mrs. Vaughn poured me an excellent whiskey, no doubt of dubious origin, and she commenced telling me about Captain Jedidiah Hunter.

Two weeks later, the night of the Daughters of the Confederacy Ball, I got up before all the fat cats, debutantes and dandies and told about how much I admired the spirit of Captain Jedidiah Hunter, which was true. A classic Southern gentleman, a brave warrior for the cause he was, I said, which was true. But most of all, I continued, I admired Captain Hunter for the way he died: bashed in the head while charging his horse under a low tree limb in the dark, stone drunk and buck naked with a distraught and equally naked Richmond harlot belly down across his saddle! Which was *true,* verified by an original Confederate Army incident report in Old Lady Vaughn's collection! Now there, I admitted, was a man I could truly admire.

That took care of that. They haven't invited me back since.

Incidentally, the night I dropped the bomb on the D.O.C., everybody went into a tight-ass freeze except Dr. Coleby Butler and Mrs. Beulah Vaughn, who cackled until they cried. They got invited back, though.

I parked in the spot marked SHERIFF OF HUNTER COUNTY and strolled through the front door with Gruesome to a chorus of "Morning, Sheriff Cody!" from the office staff and a warm smile from Milly, my big momma desk sergeant. The office staff cooed appropriately about how cute Gruesome was, the old love-the-boss's-hideous-dog routine. The little bastard fawned shamelessly. I suppose that if a half dozen sweet-smelling honeys were petting me I'd fawn some myself. I hoped he'd go to humping their legs again. Drives 'em wild.

Gruesome finally left the girls and trotted toward Milly, who fixed him from the corners of her eyes. "Git away from me you ugly little tub a' shit, 'fo' I kick yo' wormy ass." Milly has such a way with words.

To this, Gruesome did his little stiff-legged pissed-off dance and barked a few snappy comebacks.

Milly replied, "Think I'll stomp you' little butt and hang you out in my garden to scare off the starlin's!"

Gruesome danced furiously and barked back the canine equivalent of "Not before I saw your toes off at the hip, meaty woman!"

Milly howled loud enough to be heard in the street. "Come here, Gruesome, honey, come to Momma!" Gruesome squealed in delight and fired himself into her huge bosom for a cuddle session. I went into my office.

As usual, Milly had the computer printouts from the NCIC and state nets laid out on my desk, along with any incident reports from the night watch she deemed pertinent. I sat down in my antique chair and scanned the activity sheets. Ivy Joe Culpepper's death was the most significant incident of the twelve-hour period. There were a couple of notes from the state police about some car thieves suspected of bringing stolen cars from Roanoke into the hills off County Nine to strip. Pierce would have assigned a deputy to check that already.

There was also a note that Cassie Shelor's mother had called to report Cassie "missing" again. Cassie Shelor went missing every time she met some good-looking guy who wanted to run off to Virginia Beach for a few days or take her to a frat party at UVA overnight. Each time, Helen Shelor would report Cassie missing, and every time Cassie came in on her own when the party was over or the boy ran out of money. I saw Milly had made a few calls without result. We'd give her a few hours; she always turned up. Cassie Shelor. I had to yank my mind back to the matters at hand.

Milly's secretary, Cindy Barron, came in with my regular morning hot chocolate. I hate coffee. Sometimes I suspected that, even though Cindy was a hell of a fine secretary, Milly hired her with half a notion of marrying her off to me. Matchmaking would hardly have been beyond Milly, who was devoted to me. Nor would Milly have discounted the fact that Cindy was divorced with a little girl and could use a match herself. Cindy would never be crass enough to spell it out, but she had let it be known in subtle ways that advances by me wouldn't be unwelcome. I had to admit she gave me a twanger just walking a hundred yards upwind and I came close to moving in on her in my weaker moments, of which there have been several, but fucking the help is one of your little management no-no's. Besides, sweet though she was, Cindy just wasn't the right girl for me then, even if I did faint when she bent over.

Cindy put the tray down, smiled and walked out with just a touch of style. I sucked her perfume deep into my lungs.

Milly waddled in with my smug dog under her arm. "How's it hangin', Lewis?"

"Right now, Milly, it's standing straight up. In fact, I'm giving some fine thought to nailing your black ass to the rug right here and now."

Milly cackled that glass-breaking laugh. "You should live so long, white boy. This black ass been nailed by some *pros,* and you ain't even a good beginner! You want nail somethin', nail somethin' mo' on you' amateur level like that sweet li'l Cindy."

"I could suffer through that."

Milly snickered. "Look here, Sheriff. Ol' Broken Arroe in his office wif dat accident report when you ready. Ivy Joe's funeral tomorrow at ten—you goin'?"

"Yeah, I'm going. Let anybody off who wants to attend. Tell the deputies on traffic to look sharp. And send Pierce in, please."

Pierce Arroe coming into my office reminded me of that

scene where Frankenstein's monster looms in the door of the old blind man's cottage. If I hadn't known what a nice guy he was, I'd have wet my pants.

He spread several photographs and diagrams on my desk. "Now, Lewis," he began without preliminary, "to pack it in a nutshell, the evidence here is inconclusive, but I got a sour taste in my mouth about it, you know? If you look here, you see these skid marks beginning here and extending to here, see? Now I done the weight, contact patch and friction coefficient calculations on the computer, and old Ivy Joe woulda had to be doing a little over fifty to lay streaks like that. Did you ever see Ivy Joe Culpepper do more than thirty-five or so your whole life? And look how they wobble; a skidding unloaded pickup truck just don't slide like that, Lewis—none I ever seen did. And the rubber pattern for the rear wheels is inconsistent, like the weight that bore on the tires varied during the slide, almost like the back end was lifted off the road at times. And this ol' guardrail, Lewis"— Pierce tossed a black-and-white photograph before me— "granted, it's wood and was erected in the fifties, but it was ten inches of creosoted oak and, I checked, they wadn't no rot anywhere in that rail. Also, look at the angle of contact. Ol' Joe woulda had to steer deliberately into the rail to hit hard enough to penetrate it with a twenty-eight-hundred-pound pickup truck."

"Spell it out."

"Well, I got this hunch that somebody with a pretty powerful vehicle rammed him from behind, is what I think, and forced him through that rail but, goddamn, Lewis, I cain't prove it 'cause the whole ass end of that truck was burned. Wadn't no paint on it and no way to tell what damage might have been done by his pusher and what was done bouncing down Saddle Mountain."

I sipped the steaming chocolate. "Did Haskel see the accident happen?"

"No, sir, he was coming back from a call when he seen the smoke and the busted guardrail. If he hadn't got down there when he did, ol' Joe woulda been a crispy critter."

"So we don't know how long before Haskel arrived that the, uh, crash, occurred?"

"Well, there's no good way to calculate it, but I'd guess

the truck hadn't been burning more than about five minutes when Haskel showed up. 'Course, ain't no way of knowing if the fire ignited at the time of the accident or some unknown period of time afterward. But I doubt Joe woulda been alive when you got there if he'd been injured like that more than a few minutes, don't you?"

I nodded. "For the record, Pierce, did you look at Haskel's cruiser?"

"Yeah, Lewis, I thought of that. Ain't a mark on Haskel's cruiser and I cain't imagine what motive he woulda had to shove Joe off Saddle Mountain anyway. Besides, it was him kept Joe from burning up."

I sighed. "I agree, of course. But who would have had any reason to kill Ivy Joe Culpepper? If it was Lois Ross that Joe was trying to tell me about, why would she kill him? And why did he say he was shot? Coleby verified there were no bullet holes in the body—did you find any in the truck?"

Pierce drew a deep breath and let it out slowly. "No. No bullet holes, Lewis, but I did find this. In the glove box." He tossed a clear plastic evidence bag full of encapsulated pills on my desk. "Nothing to write home to Momma about, just an assortment of strong prescription uppers, but what would Ivy Joe need with over three hundred of 'em in one plastic bag?"

"Oh Christ, Pierce. You're surely not suggesting he was dealing this shit. I'm just not ready to believe Ivy Joe Culpepper was dealing even mild drugs to the kids."

Pierce looked pained. "Damn, Lewis, the idea don't thrill me either, but there they was in his glove box. How'd they get there? Much as I hate to think it, they ain't much other way. Maybe he was movin' a little shit to the kids for Lois. It's possible. It stinks, but it's possible."

"No, it's not possible, Pierce. Not Mr. Joe. If a man of uncompromised moral integrity ever walked this planet, he was Ivy Joe Culpepper."

"Lewis," Pierce said, putting his gargantuan hand on my shoulder, "I know how you loved that old man, hell everybody did. But I ain't tol' you all of it yet, I'm afraid. You know that little punk kid that drives the wrecker for Stout, Ronny Woods?"

"Yeah. What about him?"

"Well, I got to talkin' to him last night at the scene. He admits to being one of Lois's regulars and he swears he seen Ivy Joe's truck parked out at Saddle Mountain Lodge twice in the past two months. Also says he seen Joe coming out of Lois's place this week."

"What? Are you serious?"

"Yeah, that was my reaction, but Ronny swears he got a good look all three times, and he's too stupid to lie. Besides, why would he make that up?"

"This isn't making any sense, Pierce. Lois and Joe were on opposite poles of the human quality scale. Christ, I've known that old man all my life. I can't imagine him ever going anywhere near the lodge!"

"Lewis, I know this is hard to swallow. Ol' Joe was a local saint. But, hell, he was human! Maybe he just got tired of living off a janitor's pay. Maybe he was knocking off a piece of ass. Lois keeps a couple of nigger girls. You know that."

"Are you nuts? He had to be at least seventy years old, maybe as much as twenty-five years more than that!"

Pierce just shrugged.

I sighed. "You say you think he might have been rammed off Saddle Mountain. What about damage to the rear of his truck? Had to be some, right?"

Now Pierce sighed. "Lewis, Ivy Joe's pickup truck was built in 1953. It wadn't made of plastic and tin foil like they do today, it was built like a small tank. Besides, Ivy Joe had Bealor's Garage weld a back bumper on that truck a few years ago when the old one rusted out. Bealor made it out of four-inch steel pipe. Now it had some scratches on it but none any other bumper wouldn't have. You coulda hit that bumper with a train and not marked it. As for paint, the fire burned it clean. I'll tell you one thing, though."

"What's that?"

"The bumper was higher than standard height. I bet whatever hit him took some damage."

"What about fingerprints?"

"There were a few that couldn't be identified as Joe's, but God knows who's rode in that truck in the last few weeks. Also, this ain't the bag I found the pills in. I sent it to the state lab for ultraviolet and all, but I don't expect they'll find anything or, if they do, it'll just be Joe's prints."

# Shepherd of the Wolves

We stewed for a while in silence until the buzzer on my phone sounded. I pressed the intercom switch and put it on the speaker. "Yes, Milly."

Milly's voice had a palpable taste of contempt, which got my attention. It was unlike her. "Sheriff, they's a . . . *lady* out here been waitin' to see you about ten minutes. Now she be gettin' all hostile, say she *demand* to see you, now."

I could tell from Milly's tone that she personally didn't give a happy damn what the "lady" demanded but she thought I should be aware of the situation. Wonderful, I thought, just what I needed this morning, a riled-up woman with some complaint. Probably one of my deputies wrote her precious kid a speeding ticket.

"Okay, Milly. Pierce and I are about done. You can send her in when he comes out."

To Pierce I said, "Okay. So what do we have? A borderline senile man with no enemies makes a dying statement suggesting murder that possibly implicates Lois Ross. Some mention of being shot but no bullet holes in the body or the vehicle. A quantity of mixed controlled uppers, far beyond any that might have been prescribed, found in the victim's vehicle. Suspicions that the victim met with foul play but no real evidence of same. Evidence from a questionable source that the victim had recent repeated contact with the suspect he named. Am I right?"

"In other words," Pierce said, "we got plenty of questions but we ain't got shit for answers."

"And every time we turn over a new rock in search of an answer, more peculiar questions crawl out. All right. Let's start making tracks in the snow. Have the men watch out for vehicles with fresh front-end damage. Advise the state boys and the local body shops. And let's keep our ears open. This is a closed community in which secrets are hard to keep. Have Otis Clark circulate the pool halls over in East Hunter and try to find out if anybody was known to have it in for Mr. Joe. It's a long shot, but it's got to be tried. We still don't know for sure that anything outside of a common car wreck happened to Joe, but we'll play this out by the numbers, just in case. We owe that to Ivy Joe Culpepper."

"What about Lois?"

"You and I will pay Lois Ross a visit after lunch. I've got

some busywork to get done here and I better find out what's got Milly in a stew about this woman who's waiting to see me."

"Yes, sir." Pierce gathered his papers and photos and stuffed them in the file which he left on my desk. He collected the evidence bag with the pills to secure it. The old walnut floorboards creaked under his 270 pounds of beef as he walked out, dipping his head at the door. Good ol' Pierce.

Milly marched in with that exaggerated swagger she affected just before she switched out some rowdy prisoner's lights with her table leg. From the way she puckered those big lips I knew she was struggling to control her temper.

"Sheriff, they's a *Ms.* Dodd to see you. Won't say what she want."

Milly stood aside, folded her arms and allowed passage through my door to one of the most beautiful women I had ever seen in my life. She was dressed way too fashionably for Hunter County and she carried herself with authority. She was as black as Ivy Joe Culpepper, and she was real angry.

# 5

## Lucia Dodd

Now beauty, especially beauty in women, is different things to different men, and it never quite makes it from the seeing eye to the written word. Most black women didn't appeal to me physically, which was not intended to put them down—I suspect most of them would consider me as handsome as a syphilitic wart hog—that's human nature; it just works that way.

But this woman stunned me to distraction.

She was short and somewhere in her thirties. She wore a smart but conservative grayish suit over a crimson silk blouse that matched her shoes, which were those thin-strap-around-the-ankle pumps that tripped my fetish alarm every time. Her shiny black hair was tied back in a bun that only served to highlight the extraordinarily feminine impact of her face. Oddly, the strictly-business suit did the same for her nice body. Her lips were symmetrical and full but not huge, and she had large, compelling, warm brown eyes framed in long lashes beneath neatly sculpted, arching brows. She wore red lipstick, but if she wore any other makeup it was so expertly applied that I couldn't tell. What I could see of her legs beneath her conservative hem was sweet and the rest of her matched. And her skin! It was hypnotically smooth and soft and splendidly brown. You can tell how she affected me by all this dumbstruck rhetoric

I'm running off at the mouth with. Not to put too fine a point on it, she was a walking wet dream.

For those of you whose foreheads crease because she's black, tough shit. When they look like this girl, I don't care if they're green.

The woman and Milly scalded each other with their eyes as she walked in with the gait of a model and a carriage of authority. I stood, still struck by her beauty, but she appeared not to notice me. She exuded education, sophistication and class. What in the world was she doing in the Hunter County dungeon?

She wore a look of bored disdain and she gazed about my office like it was decorated in roadkill skunks. Milly rolled her eyes and left, closing the door.

The woman finally looked me in the eyes and I controlled an impulse to jump over my desk and kiss that shiny red lipstick right off of those plump wet lips. She extended her hand, I thought to shake mine, but when I put out my own hand she ignored it and set a business card on my desk. Then she inspected one of my chairs—for herpes or something—and sat down and stared me in the eye.

It was clear she was underwhelmed by me.

I picked up the card and sat down. The card was traditional white and read in raised embossment: H. LUCIA DODD; PELHAM, WELLS, PAINE AND DODD; ATTORNEYS AT LAW; 1 LAFAYETTE PLACE, WASHINGTON D.C. Oh goody. This was turning into one of those days that make you want to burn your calendar.

Her perfume reached me then and I damn near died. Somewhere in that sweet fragrance was the distinct smell of woman that nature must've put there long ago to insure the cave men would stay busy making little cave babies. It still works.

By now I'd figured out that a drama was under way; this entrance was too stylish not to have been calculated. I looked up to find those big brown eyes still on me, displaying cool subtle contempt and just a trace of arrogance.

A girl I once knew told me I have wolf eyes. I'm not sure what she meant, but over the years I have found I can stare a lot of people into submission, thus averting my having to beat them into same, a useful talent for a cop. Some people might spit in my wolf eyes, once anyway, but more than a few are intimidated. Okay, I thought, I'll play her game; nobody takes charge of me in my own dungeon. I gave her my best Clint Eastwood make-my-day look and held. We probably looked like a couple of idiots.

After a moment, she sighed without taking her eyes from mine and said, "My name is Lucia Dodd. I am an attorney and I am here to find out exactly what you are doing about the murder of Ivy Joe Culpepper."

Jesus Christ, Ivy Joe, couldn't you have just died in your sleep or something? Silent night, Mr. Joe.

I leaned back in my creaking chair and continued to meet her stare until she finally broke it off, ostensibly to look at her Rolex no-less watch. Score one for Clint. Good thing. I was getting a headache.

"Before we go any further, Ms. Dodd, suppose you tell me what your interest in the matter is."

There was a pause during which she studied me carefully. Then she spoke. "Ivy Joe Culpepper was my grandfather."

Things were sure getting complicated in my peaceful little mountain county.

"My condolences. I didn't think Ivy Joe Culpepper had any living relatives."

Lucia Dodd pursed her lips with obvious irritation. "He had a daughter. She had one, too. Now I want to know what you are doing about his murder."

"What makes you think he was murdered?" I asked.

She sighed again. "Look, Mr. Cody, I really didn't hope to find law-enforcement genius at work up here, but you're becoming more of a disappointment than I expected. I must warn you that my time is limited. I've come for answers, not questions, and I do not intend to leave without them."

I paused, studying her now. "Ms. Dodd, there is no evidence that your grandfather was murdered. He was in a truck accident and—"

"Mr. Cody! I spent last night in East Hunter—'Niggertown,' as I'm sure you and your ilk refer to it—and I listened and I asked questions. Perhaps you should do the same. I know my grandfather told you he was shot by a Lois Ross or someone in her employ, possibly the so-called Sloan brothers."

The Sloan brothers! Lanny and Danny Sloan, the two-man Ku Klux Klan? What did they have to do with this? My deputy, Otis Clark, would know by afternoon.

"Ms. Dodd, I was the only one who heard exactly what your grandfather said, and while he was very difficult to understand, he never mentioned the Sloans—"

"Then he was shot by this Lois Ross."

"I didn't say that. I'm not sure he said Lois's name. He didn't—"

"Then who shot him?"

"Nobody shot him. He—"

"You are a liar, Mr. Cody. Witnesses overheard him tell you he was shot!"

I was on my feet. "Just a damn *minute,* miz lady lawyer, I made no reference to what he *said,* I just told you he wasn't shot. Now, if my word won't cut it for you, I'll waltz you up to the county clinic and you can eyeball his cold corpse for yourself, but you're *not* going to find any bullet holes!"

Her eyes widened, then narrowed. "You are a crude bastard," she said softly.

"Now there's the black calling the kettle a pot! My people checked the county records, lady, and Ivy Joe Culpepper was never married. Sounds to me like the real bastard was your mother and the only liar in the room is you!" I was on a roll now. I am not a model of restraint.

"Let me tell *you* something, Mr. Cody. My grandfather's marriage to my grandmother was common-law but, by God, my mother was as 'legitimate' as yours! Furthermore, I loved that old gentleman and if you think for one minute I'm going to let some dimwitted country constable allow his murder to go uninvestigated for lack of interest, you are mistaken!"

I snatched up Pierce Arroe's file containing the investigation of the crash and flipped it at her. It struck her in her rather noticeable breasts and its contents spilled out in her lap.

"That, *Ms.* Dodd, is only part of an investigation that has been going on since yesterday and will continue to its logical conclusion."

She glared at me, then she examined some of Pierce's photographs and diagrams while I stood, fuming, hands on my hips. Then she drew a sharp breath, closed her eyes and put a hand to her lips. Her other hand dropped to her lap and I saw the photograph it held. The dead white eyes of Ivy Joe Culpepper stared vacantly through the windshield cavity of his shattered old Studebaker pickup.

I said sincerely, "I just got that report when you came in. I haven't studied it yet. I didn't know that picture was in there. I'm sorry."

She rose and tossed the file on my desk. She looked at me with open contempt. "I'm sure you are."

"Have it your way. You can lead a horse to water but you can't shove her stubborn face in it."

"You, Mr. Cody, have no idea how stubborn I can be, but you will most certainly find out if you try to sweep my grandfather's murder under your lumpy rug, or if you fail to pursue it with all your resources, however limited they may be. I am an attorney with a respected firm not without influence with the State Attorney General's office. If you think this is just the inconsequential death of some old 'field nigger' that you can put in your circular file, you're wrong. I intend to see that justice is done, even in this backward bastion of white ignorance!"

I was seething inside, but I maintained my cool. You can't shoot folks for arrogance, unfortunately.

"Ms. Dodd," I said pleasantly, "are you or your firm licensed by the Virginia Bar?"

Lucia Dodd took pause as the lawyer in her figured that one out.

"Well, no, but—"

"But, my ass!" I said. Her eyes widened slightly. My cool was fading. Lovely eyes. "Item one: in the state of Virginia, you are not an attorney, you're an arrogant, presumptuous, hot-headed outsider. Item two: if you're half the attorney you brag to be, you know damn well the State's Attorney isn't likely to meddle in an intracounty affair. Item three: there is no evidence—remember *evidence?* You must have heard the word somewhere in law school—there is no *evidence* that your grandfather was murdered. Item four: I *am* investigating the matter with all my backward, ignorant white resources as well as all my backward, ignorant black resources! And item *five:* by God *I* loved that old man, too!"

"Mr. Cody—"

"It's *Sheriff* Cody to you, young lady, and item six: if you loved Ivy Joe Culpepper so goddamned much, how come I've never seen you in this county in all the years I've lived here?"

"You have!"

"The hell you say!"

"Yes, you have! Of course, you wouldn't have noticed, let alone remembered, a little 'nigger' girl in East Hunter on the few occasions you went there with your daddy in his big fancy car!"

"My daddy ran a country hardware store and drove a Buick. He was hardly a plantation slavemaster. And when he went to East Hunter, it was usually to collect from someone who'd abused the credit he always allowed them. And, no, I don't remember seeing you."

"Well, I was there!"

"Yeah? And how many times since you escaped from the backward bastion of white ignorance have you been back to see your beloved grandfather?"

"That's none of your business!"

"Because I got a few friends in East Hunter, it might surprise you to know, and if a black woman of your style and offensive arrogance had set foot in this county in the last eleven years, I'd have heard about it. That's really what's eating at you, isn't it, Ms. Big-time Lady Lawyer? You loved Ivy Joe, all right, but not enough to soil yourself by returning to the ol' bastion to pay him a lousy visit, right? Now he's deader than four o'clock on Sunday morning and you're all eaten up with guilt, and all this saber rattling is your way of trying to make up for neglecting him. I got your *number,* lady!"

Lucia Dodd continued to meet my stare, but I didn't miss the almost imperceptible tremble of her lower lip or the watering in her eyes. In a moment, she spoke, but with less heat in her tone.

"I am here, Sheriff Cody, for one reason only. To see that my grandfather's killer is pursued and prosecuted to the fullest extent of the law. My reasons are none of your affair."

"Well, let me assure you, Mr. Joe's death will be thoroughly investigated, and if it develops that he met with foul play, every effort will be made to bring his killer before the court."

Lucia Dodd sneered. "Either you're a fool or you think I am. I grew up in this county, Sheriff Cody. I know how . . . conscientious . . . the Hunter County justice system, including you, is likely to be about the death of a poor black man. Civil rights are forty years behind the times up here in these mountains. You go ahead and run whatever passes for an investigation in the Hunter County Sheriff's Department. In the meantime, I will be conducting an independent investigation of my own, just in case yours should leave anything to be desired. I am quite serious, Sheriff Cody. The law is my field. I know how to ask questions and get answers."

"Knock yourself out. Just remember two things. This isn't Washington; it's the bastion of white ignorance, and you'll go farther on a little less arrogance and a lot more courtesy."

"And the second thing?" she asked, her sculpted eyebrows rising.

"And the second thing is you'd do well not to break any laws or violate anybody's civil rights in the course of your investigation or you're going to get a real good look at one of the oldest cell blocks in the United States."

"Sheriff, if you or one of your flunkies lay a hand on me, you'd better have all your legal *i*'s dotted and *t*'s crossed or I'll have the courts all over you."

"Then we understand each other," I said, walking to my office door, "and now you can get out of here because I have work to do." I jerked open the door to find Milly stooped with her hand at her ear. Instantly, she pretended to be dusting the door frame for Christ's sake. She flashed me an innocent, wide-eyed look and dusted her way back to her desk. The whole outer office was busting a gut trying to look busy and unconcerned.

Lucia Dodd walked out, exchanging drop-dead looks with Milly. Through my office window, I watched Lucia Dodd get into a bronze-colored Lincoln Towncar. I jotted down the tag number. I knew I hadn't seen the last of her.

I walked quickly to the door and caught Milly watching from her desk. "Sergeant Stanford!"

"Yes, sir, Sheriff!"

Good. When she called me Sheriff instead of Lewis, she knew she was in trouble. "How long have you been working here?" I said loudly. "Not counting tomorrow!" I slammed the door behind me.

"Yes, sir, Sheriff!" she called through the door.

No secrets in Hunter County.

Except, what the hell happened to Ivy Joe Culpepper?

# 6

## Cassie Shelor

Before lunch I got a call.

"Sheriff Cody, have you found my Cassie yet?" Poor Helen Shelor. Being a nervous, high-strung widow didn't make her the best candidate for mother of an independent, oversexed seventeen-year-old Lolita like Cassie Shelor.

"Mrs. Shelor, I'm going to tell you like it is. We've made some calls, but we haven't otherwise looked for her and we won't for a day or so. You know and I know Cassie comes and goes as she pleases. She's stayed away for days before and she always comes home when she's ready."

"Oh, yes, I know, Sheriff, but this time it's different. I just know it is. Cassie's been troubled lately. She took the car. Something's wrong, I know!"

"Troubled how, Mrs. Shelor?"

"I don't know! Just troubled! You ever try to talk to a seventeen-year-old? She's been different lately, Sheriff. A mother knows these things!"

"Nothing you can be a little more specific about, Mrs. Shelor?"

"I, no, I don't know, Sheriff Cody! She's just been different lately and I have a bad feeling. A mother knows these things!" she said with frustration.

Then how come a mother doesn't know where her kid is? I wanted to ask, but I knew that in Helen Shelor's case that would be unfair. Cassie had been a free spirit before her daddy died two years ago. Without him, she just went where the wind blew her.

"Mrs. Shelor, with nothing specific to indicate that this occasion is any different from Cassie's dozens of other absences, don't you agree we could wait a day or so before getting too worried?"

"Well . . . yes, Sheriff Cody, I know you're right. I just got a bad feeling. A mother—"

"Knows these things, yes, I understand. Tell you what. If we haven't heard from her by tomorrow, I'll send a deputy to get a report from you and get the wheels turning. In the meantime, if you learn anything specific we can go on, please let us know. How's that?"

"Oh. Okay. Thank you, Sheriff Cody."

I creaked back in my old cracked and faded black leather judge's chair and stared at the ceiling. Involuntarily, blood flooded my cock as my own encounters with Cassie Shelor spilled out of memory. Sound peculiar? You don't know the half of it.

I'd known the Shelor family, and peripherally Cassie, for years. Jonathan Shelor had been a respected insurance agent and community figure before his heart attack. I'd never noticed Cassie in any particular way until one day I was driving down Main and noticed the sweet sway of a gorgeous fanny and lush thighs in a snug skirt walking away from me on the sidewalk. I remember I was slightly chagrined when I passed her and realized she was only Jon Shelor's little girl, what was her name? Cassie, that was right. Jeez, was she growing up. I was further surprised to see her looking directly at me with a quizzical smile, as though she'd read my every thought. Great, I thought at the time, she'll probably run home to her squirrely mother and tell her the sheriff was leering at her baby girl.

Then, about six months before the death of Ivy Joe Culpepper, I rode in behind one of my deputies on a traffic accident where one of Cassie's college beaus trashed a Porsche, drunk, with Cassie in the car. Neither of them were seriously hurt and my deputy charged the kid with DWI. When the ambulance attendant passed on Cassie, I told her I'd radio to town to have her mother come out and pick her up. I tried not to be too obvious about it, but the unavoidable stark truth was that Cassie Shelor was a physically blessed young lady, a lithe blond beauty with the most compelling look in her jewel-blue eyes. That night she wore a long and loose designer skirt and one of those strapless elastic blouses that require healthy, pointed tits to keep it up. Cassie's blouse stayed up just fine. Her eyes had a disturbingly piercing quality.

"No," she said. "Mom's not home; she's in Roanoke at her sister's. She thinks I'm spending the night at a girlfriend's. Please, Sheriff Cody, let's not upset her. Couldn't you just drive me home, please?"

Well, it was true that Helen Shelor didn't need to be upset any more than she usually was, so I drove Cassie home. It was on the way back to town anyway. When I pulled into the driveway of the dark Shelor place, Cassie said she was feeling weak.

"Please, Sheriff," she said, staggering a little, leaning on my unmarked cruiser, "would you mind helping me inside? I feel like I'm going to fall."

On the front walk, she did fall. I caught her and picked her up, telling her I was going to take her to the clinic.

"No," she said, "please, just take me inside. I'll be all right in a moment." She put her arms about my neck. Disgusted with myself for getting into this embarrassing predicament, and hoping none of the neighbors were watching, I carried Cassie into the living room of the comfortable Shelor home.

When I flipped on the light with my elbow, I found her eyes open and her lips wet. Before I could react, she had locked onto me with an industrial-grade kiss.

I know, I know. She was sixteen at the time and I was over forty and I ought to be ashamed and all that. I don't know what to tell you except that Cassie Shelor was a stunning example of a female body in its sexual prime and I was no eunuch. This was a time when I'd been physically celibate for months and emotionally celibate for a lot longer than that. It was a time when I was spending many hours of solitude wondering if a life of such loneliness and absence of promise was worth all the effort it took to live it. You may think *you'd* have cast her off in righteous piety like a good boy, but I was there. Her lips were so plump and ripe, her tongue so . . . desperate. She had such a fever about her that was contagious. Sure my conscience roared at me to break it off and flee, but the rest of me replied, *"Fuck* your morality! She tastes too *fine!"*

I set Cassie on her feet and she went for me again. I pushed her back a few steps—I had to think. She stood there with a wide-eyed look of sympathy, as though she read my mind and knew what the struggle was doing to me. She unzipped her skirt, letting it fall down her slender legs. A scent of her heat and perfume washed over me. She slowly drew that stretch blouse over her head and dropped it, her rigid nipples bobbing with the effort. She stood in heels and thin-ribboned peach-colored panties darkly wet at the crotch. She was devastating and I was galvanized, suddenly hard as a carbon drill bit. I never wanted, yearned for, needed, *desired* anything in my whole life like I did Cassie Shelor at that moment.

She whispered in a throaty voice, clearly under a sexual strain of her own, "Please . . . Lewis . . . I neeeeed you! Pleeeease . . ."

You have to know the primal seduction in that voice, in that beautiful face. My heart pounded like a steam locomotive on a long grade. She walked to me and I swear to you I could not move. She kissed me in that starving way again and the skin at the small of her back was so incredibly smooth and firm and warm.

Part of me screamed, Are you *crazy!?* Another part of me said, If you don't take her, you will certainly die right here and now.

She clung to me, pressed her belly against my hardness and gouged at me with her tongue. She whimpered plaintively with a tremor in her tone. My God, it wasn't enough that every nerve in me clamored for her. Her own urgent desire so vividly compounded my lust.

I've kicked myself a hundred times for what happened next. I don't know why it happened, it just did. I seized her by the shoulders and wrenched her back from me at arm's length. Her eyes, they knew! She knew how much I wanted her, yet she knew what held me back and she knew what the conflict was doing to me.

# Shepherd of the Wolves

"Pleeease . . . Lewis," she whispered in my ear, breathing hard, "do it with me. Please, love me now."

I uttered a cry of equal parts rage and pain and I released her, the most impossible task I ever accomplished. I backed away, sucking air through constricted nostrils, unable to take my eyes from her naked and overpowering body. She sank to her knees, looking at me with those commanding wet eyes. Her expression told me plainly my rejection left her not only physically starved but emotionally wounded as well. I felt like a bastard *and* a fool. I strode for the door without looking back, as I could feel the second thoughts leaking in fast around all my seams.

Just before the door closed behind me, I heard her whisper: "Anytime, Lewis. Anytime!"

I didn't sleep well for days. Masturbation didn't help. Even thinking about what would happen to my career if I'd made love to her and anybody found out about it didn't help. Minutes later her perfect white breasts, the smell of her, the taste of her lipstick, that pleading expression, they would invade me again. "Anytime, Lewis . . ."

I tried to write it all off as the loony reaction of a spacy teen queen with a uniform fetish under the influence of alcohol. I wasn't likely to encounter Cassie again, and if I did, she'd either not remember it or be too profoundly embarrassed to acknowledge it, let alone repeat it.

I didn't know Cassie at all then. But I was about to.

Because of her youth, I suppose, I grossly underestimated two traits of Cassie Shelor's. One was her phenomenal, instinctual understanding of the sexuality of men. In a mature woman of average physical charm, such an insight into what turns men on would have been a little intimidating to a man, but it would have been intoxicatingly sexy as well. In a frighteningly young, exquisite beauty like Cassie, this uncanny intuition was both terrifying and devastatingly erotic.

This sets the stage for the second gross underestimation of Cassie Shelor—that, where lust is concerned, nothing can compare to a sixteen-year-old girl, hard of nipple, wet of vulva and utterly determined of mind.

A week after I fled Cassie's living room to escape her desire and my own, I was sitting in my office at the dungeon when Cindy Barron tapped at the door and entered, carrying a small box wrapped in brown paper, about the size of a box of tissues.

"Sheriff," Cindy said, a little puzzled, "somebody left this for you."

"Who?" I asked.

"Well, nobody seems to know, Sheriff. There've been a lot of folks in today for various reasons. We just found it on the main booking desk."

"Oh, great, Cindy," I said. "Did it occur to anybody out there that it might be a bomb?"

"Oh!" Cindy gasped and promptly dropped the box on my desk, where it bounced and settled right in front of me.

"Well," I said dryly, "at least we can rule out motion and shock detonators."

"Sorry, Lewis—uh, Sheriff, I never thought of a bomb."

I picked the package up. It was very light and was addressed "Personal to Sheriff Lewis Cody" in a pretty handscript, but it bore no postage or return address. It didn't rattle and it didn't tick, but by today's bomb standards that was meaningless.

Cindy still stood before my desk nervously. "It's okay, darlin'," I said, "I can't imagine anyone wanting to bomb us either, but in this crazy business nothing is impossible. Next time this happens, if it does, don't touch it, just come and get me."

She rewarded me with a sweet smile. "Yes, sir, Sheriff!" she said, and she spun on her heel, causing her loose skirt to spin out from her thighs. "Thank you," she said, closing the door.

Thank me. Hoo. Whatever it is that Nature imbued us bulls with, it's still in there kicking.

I studied the little package. It was not uncommon for people to bring cakes, cookies and the like to the dungeon. People either love cops or hate them, depending on their need for them at the time, and occasionally those who loved us brought little gifts for us. I recovered Emmett Cutter's old tractor once, for instance, and Emmett brought me one of his home-cured country hams. We generally discourage this sort of thing, but sometimes it's simpler to accept a modest token of appreciation than it is to hurt the giver's feelings with some bullshit about not accepting gratuities. There is a difference between Emmett Cutter's ham and Homer Poff's shotgun. It's a judgment call.

Still, I mulled, citizens almost never wrapped what they brought us, which were usually homemade food items of some kind. I cautiously slit the outer wrapping with my knife and removed it only to find the box nicely gift-wrapped in a pink metallic paper and a yellow ribbon. Now I was really puzzled. It had been better than two years since I had any involvement with a woman that might have evoked a gift.

The Hunter County Sheriff's Department budget didn't allow for such exotica as bomb squads, so I considered taking the package to Coleby's clinic and having it X-rayed, but then I began to feel silly. This wasn't D.C., L.A. or Chicago—this was Hunter County, Virginia, where if someone had it in for you, they usually shot you point-blank. They certainly didn't mess with gift-wrapping bombs.

Nonetheless, I unwrapped it gingerly and removed the department-store-style gift-box lid. Whatever was in it was properly sub-wrapped in folded tissue; someone had very carefully prepared this mystery.

I folded back the tissue to find demurely folded therein a pair of peach-colored, lace-trimmed nylon panties and a small folded white card.

A stunning flooding sensation ran over me as I lifted the underwear from the box and realized where I'd seen it before—the sole garment on Cassie Shelor a week prior, its cotton-lined crotch damp with her arousal. Pam Undies, size six, one-hundred-percent nylon, exclusive of decoration.

My mind still spinning from surprise, I unfolded the card and read the feminine script: "I am not a child, Lewis. Soon you will come to know this."

The Comanche say, "In all men dwells the wolf." I take this to mean there is an element of animal deep within the core of us all. The undeniably aroused wolf now stirred within one Lewis Cody.

The Sheriff in Lewis Cody now said, This is silly; some oversexed teeny-bopper has a cop fantasy and here you get all weak-kneed. You bet your ass, the wolf replied, your knees aren't the only reason you can't get up from that chair right now, and you know it. You want her so bad you'll risk your career, even jail, to have her. The hell I will! said the Sheriff. Yes, the hot-eyed wolf answered, stone confident, you will. I won't! the Sheriff protested.

The Sheriff found himself unable to stop his hand from lifting the silky garment and pressing the crotch to his face and inhaling long and slow. The pungent fragrance combined of perfume, sweat, urine and the passion of Cassie Shelor seared all the way to the center of his soul, and he was now afraid. He was terrified because he knew. The wolf was right.

Two weeks later, still about six months before the call I just got from Helen Shelor, I was taking advantage of an unusually warm Saturday in May to give Moose, my enormous Belgian mare, a bath in Bram's Creek, down the draw from my home on the ridge.

As she stood patiently in the creek with me, I threw bucketful after bucketful of water on her and lathered her down. It took enough water to power a hydroelectric dam. The exertion of heaving the buckets in the sun sweated me to the extent that I peeled off my shirt and tossed it on the bank near my boots and socks. The sound of my labored breathing was covered by the white hiss of the water running over the smooth stones of the creek.

I had finished rinsing Moose and was laboriously wire-brushing her, tossing huge glots of her winter coat to float downstream, when she snorted and threw up her head. I pushed back to keep one of her massive shifting hooves from crushing my bare feet on the wet stones.

I turned to see what startled her and was no less startled myself to see Cassie Shelor watching me from astride a handsome barebacked appaloosa stallion.

The horse stood on the wet clay bank, heaving and lathered in sweat. She'd apparently ridden at some pace from the Shelor place in town ten miles away.

Cassie's blond hair hung over one eye. She was barefoot and she wore a man's oversize flannel shirt, the sleeves rolled up above her elbows, unbuttoned nearly to her navel and tucked into a long brown suede riding dress.

# Shepherd of the Wolves

It was disconcerting how this girl kept catching me off guard, leaving me dumbstruck.

"Hi . . . Lewis," she said, staring at me intently with those mesmerizing crystal blue eyes. "You weren't at your house or barn, but I followed the tracks of your incredible horse. She's such a magnificent beauty!" She spoke slowly, watching me carefully. She smiled with wet pink lips around straight white teeth.

I finally found my tongue. No self-declared sexpot was going to best me in my own creek. I smiled slightly, deciding to find out what this nutty kid had in mind. "Thank you," I told her. "You better water your own gorgeous animal or you'll be walking back to town." I continued to brush Moose.

Cassie smiled again and her eyes narrowed with a pronounced sporting sparkle shining out. "I may not go back to town," she said with that amazingly sexy, throaty voice.

I met her teasing gaze again. "Well, water him anyway," I said. "Walk him upstream aways, though. He's making this mare nervous and she's hard to hold."

"Mmmm," Cassie said, "I know that feeling."

Slowly she walked the appaloosa up the creek. I splashed cold creek water on my sweaty face and chest and watched her. I was getting hard in spite of my nerves, but I made no effort to conceal it. Cassie dropped the reins and the barebacked stallion sucked at the creek. She threw her right leg over the horse's neck and slid down from him. In the doing, her skirt rode high up her taut white thighs.

She splashed to her feet and walked toward me in the water, still drilling my eyes with her own. She stopped about five feet away. She was upwind and I could smell the horse and Cassie's perfume and heat on the breeze.

She fluffed the loose shirt over her naked breasts to cool herself. I saw her look down at my lumpy jeans. Her calm gaze held, then drifted slowly up the length of me to lock again on my eyes.

"I need a bath, too," she said, her eyes widening in mock innocence. "See?" She then lifted her skirt to her face and chewed on the hem like a little girl. This move exposed her long, muscular dancer's legs, spread and slippery to the thighs with the sweat of the horse. She wore no panties now and her soft brown pubic hair glistened in the sunlight.

My face tightened and I sucked in a hard breath. Deep inside, the hot-eyed wolf howled in triumph.

I made a decision. I threw the brush to the mud-slick bank of the creek and splashed toward her. I could see her breasts rise higher as her breathing quickened. She dropped the hem of the skirt and spread the fingers of both her hands. I extended an arm, seized her by the front of her shirt and yanked her to me. She cried out from the violent pull, but when she hit my chest she rubbed her face in the sweaty hair and licked at my left nipple. My heart hammered. I took her by the hair and turned her face up to me. Those penetrating ice-blue eyes met mine, her nostrils flared with the strain of her breathing and her expression screamed: "You don't dare!" I kissed her fiercely, and she moaned and clawed to get a grip on me. I grabbed the folds of the shirt and spread them hard. The lower buttons flew into the creek and her breasts swayed, the tiny blond down on them glinting in the sun, her nipples stiff. I pinned her arms behind her, stripped the shirt from her and threw it to the bank. She heaved for breath but her eyes never left mine. I lifted the dress above her head and she held up her arms to let it pass. It landed on her shirt on the wet clay edge of the creek.

Now totally nude, she smiled as though in her own triumph and she suddenly pushed me hard. I stepped back on the slick mossy rocks and caught my balance. She splashed to her knees and tore at my belt and jeans, pulling them down to my ankles in the water. My cock bobbed straight out before her and she reached for it, but I seized her wrists and pulled her to her feet. I could see the veins in her neck pulsing. I kicked the soaked blue jeans onto the bank. Holding her wrists, I straightened my arms above my head, lifting her out of the water against me. She wrapped her thighs about my waist and locked her ankles. I released her arms, which fell around my neck, and I gripped her ass in my hands. She kissed me savagely and I fought back as I carried her to the bank. There I laid her on her back in the wet clay, held her down and sucked at her twanging nipples. She grunted and squirmed, still holding me with her legs.

# Shepherd of the Wolves

We rolled over and over in the wet brown mud, coating ourselves like two pigs. We slipped toward the creek. She hung about my neck and I put my hand between her legs and pulled her upslope with me. She began to pant audibly. I coated my hand in the slippery clay and stroked and squeezed her pussy, the clay squirting between my fingers. I slipped a middle finger into her and she gasped and clung to me and humped frantically at my hand. My penis poked about her mud-slick hip and she groped to find it, but I turned so she could not reach me. She took a fistful of my hair and yanked, and I slipped from my knees and fell upon her. She squirmed and wriggled in a panic to spread her legs.

"Please!" she cried out. "Please, now! Put it in me now!" She reached to guide me into her, but I blocked her. In the struggle, we slid again to the water's edge. I gripped the first stones in the cool water with my toes, took her by the thighs and spread her. *"Yes!"* she almost screamed. "Yes, now, Lewis. Fuck me now!"

"Now?" I panted.

"Please! Do it to me now!" she pleaded, the challenge in her face now replaced with desperate need. She reached for my bobbing cock again, but instead I kissed her ferociously one last time and then threw her back on the slick wet clay.

I stood, staggered weakly into the creek and rolled in the water, cleansing myself of the sweat and mud. I stood before her still hard but drooping a little, heaving to get my breath.

Cassie lay in astonishment, propped on her elbows, a stricken expression on her face, her sweet thighs still spread, her pink cleft still gleaming in the curly wet hair.

"Not now!" I gasped between breaths. "Not now!" I splashed more water on my face and stumbled to my things on the bank near her.

Cassie was struck with disbelief. She stared at me with wide questioning eyes, her breasts rapidly rising and sinking.

"Not now!" I said, still struggling to get my breath. I heaped my boots and jeans into a sack made from my shirt, knotted it and stood over her glorious, naked, muddy body. "Not now, not tomorrow, Cassie. Not until I'm damn good and ready, and that won't be for about ten years!" I splashed across the creek, reached toward Moose's mane and threw the sack up as I leaped and pulled myself onto her back.

"Lewis!" Cassie cried plaintively, closing her thighs. "You can't leave me like this!"

"Cassie," I said from astride Moose. "You are a stunning beauty. I'd give one of everything I've got two of to fuck you till you squeal, but the time is not right for you and me and nothing can change that." I stabbed a finger at her. "Don't tease me again, girl!"

Moose shifted about in the creek nervously. "Yah!" I yelled. I leaned forward and gigged the huge horse with my heels. In a cascade of flying water, she charged out of the creek and up the ridge toward the home of my grandfather.

A half hour later, I sat on my back porch, dressed in sweat pants, holding a cold beer against my aching temple.

I watched Cassie ride the appaloosa slowly up the mountainside from the creek. She now wore the muddy suede skirt and she had knotted the shirt securely about her breasts. Her wet hair swung over one eye. She stopped the horse by the porch and gifted me with a wry but genuine smile.

"Sheriff Lewis Cody," she said, "you are something else."

"Cassie," I replied, "if I live to be a thousand years old, I will never forget you and this day."

Cassie smiled tightly, as though she were holding back tears. She laughed richly and heeled the pony. She looked back once as she rode away. She was still smiling.

Even as I sat at my desk now, the thought of Cassie Shelor made me uncomfortably hard. Lord, Milly, don't send Cindy in here right now. Better yet, do.

Gruesome eyed me suspiciously.

# 7

## Lois Ross

**T**he time had come to have words with Lois Ross. I had Milly radio Pierce to meet me at a rendezvous about five miles from Lois's Saddle Mountain Lodge down near the county line. Gruesome could sense something in the works and he was on his knobby feet psyching himself up.

In the parking area outside the dungeon, I encountered my deputy, Otis Clark, in from the recon in East Hunter I'd had Pierce send him on. Otis was so mellow you wondered sometimes if he was awake, but I'd learned he was actually as quick of mind as a pro quarterback. He was dressed in those jive threads he liked so much, but other than being loud as a chartreuse 747, he looked pretty sharp.

"Hey, Lew!" he said without moving his lips. Otis's lips never moved except minutely for the occasional necessity of pronouncing *P* and *B* phonetics. Somehow Otis could say "Momma's mad this morning" without moving his big lips. Knocked me out. "Say, Lew, I been shootin' a little pool over on the east side, man."

"Figured you might have."

"Lew, you ain't gonna believe this, but ol' Ivy Joe was hangin' out at Lois Ross's lately! Some of the dudes says they seen his truck out there! My man Cletus Johnson, drives a bread truck, you know? Well, Cletus say he done seen Joe at Saddle Mountain Lodge three of the last six deliveries he done made out there! Cletus ask Joe one time,

59

he say, 'Man, what chu *doin'* out here?' and Joe, he just say, 'Takin' care of business.' Takin' care of business?! What chu reckon that mean, Lew?"

"I don't know," I answered, but I had a terrible feeling I did know what kind of business Ivy Joe Culpepper had been taking care of with Lois Ross. I hated to believe Lois could have been moving pills or other controlled substances to the kids at the high school through Mr. Joe.

"Well, that ain't all I found out, Lew. Come to find out the Sloan brothers was after his black ass! Blowed my mind, too. The two most race-crazy motherfuckers ever drew breath; make Hitler look like a Kennedy! Anyway, word is Joe had somethin' to do with Lanny Sloan's little girl, Peggy; she in the eleventh grade at the school."

"What!?"

"I'm tellin' you, Lew! Say he talk to her about somethin', don't nobody know what, and she go home and tell ol' Lanny, and now Lanny and Danny is lookin' to kill Joe's ass. Or was."

"Great. Just fucking wonderful. Is that all you learned?"

"That's it, Lew."

"You do good work for a dumb nigger."

"Sheeit. Somebody got to do the po-leese work in this county, goddamn! The sorry-assed, limp-dick, hunky faggot we got for a sheriff sho' ain't worth a fart in a hurricane!"

"I resent that. I am *not* 'hunky.'"

Otis laughed and raised his hand for the obligatory high slap, which I threw him.

"You a skit, Sheriff!"

"Hey, Gruesome," I said, "how about some dark meat for lunch?"

"Git dat little dragon-ass motherfucker away from me 'fo' I blast his ugly ass with my nine mil!"

"See you at Joe's funeral tomorrow, Otis. Nice work."

"You got it, Lew."

I joined up with Pierce about twenty minutes later. We drove our cruisers into the woods about a quarter mile from Saddle Mountain Lodge and walked in through the trees, turning down the volume on our belt radios. Lois Ross kept a sentry in a gatehouse where the drive to the lodge turned off the highway, and we didn't wish to arrive announced.

# Shepherd of the Wolves

Gruesome was pissed at being left in the car.

At the edge of the woods, we surveyed the big log lodge with its expansive shake roof. It was a rustic old three-story structure, not without a certain character in spite of the 'business,' that got 'taken care of' inside. Even at slightly before noon, there were several pickup trucks parked around and a few expensive cars from out of county. Pierce and I recognized some of the vehicles. Most belonged to plowboys who minded their own business, but there were a few local toughs and shady types inside, we judged from the other cars we saw.

Inside, we were aware, was a long brass-railed bar off a cavernous dining and dance hall. There was a kitchen in the rear and Lois's private quarters were in the back on the far side. The dance hall great room extended from floor to beamed roof, and there were rooms off a circular interior balcony on the second level. To one side of the lodge, for a hundred yards into the woods, ran a row of little pine cabins. From thirty meters away, we could hear loud country music punctuated periodically by raucous laughter or the squeal of a woman.

Shotgun in hand, Pierce slipped through the trees until he was even with the rear of the lodge, then he trotted swiftly across the drive and stood behind a Dumpster. He eyed Lois's blue Cadillac carefully, but I could see from where I was there was no damage to the car. I wasn't surprised. It wasn't likely Lois herself had shoved Joe off Saddle Mountain; she'd have paid someone to do it for her. Pierce looked at me and nodded. I walked across the drive, up the broad split-log steps and across the porch to the heavy double front doors. I took off my sunglasses and strolled inside.

As we had evaded Lois's lookout, my entrance was greeted by those inside with varying degrees of shock, alarm and/or contempt. While the loud music boomed on, all conversation died instantly in the bar and shortly thereafter in the dance hall. In spite of the poor light and the smoke, I saw the black bartender's hand go beneath the cash register—an alarm signal to Lois's rooms, no doubt. Several questionable cigarettes were being unobtrusively dropped on the floor and a few caps were tugged down over the eyes. As best I could see, no one's hand went to their belt or beneath a coat. The place reminded me of that scuzzy outlaw bar Han Solo had to phaser his way out of in *Star Wars*.

There was a startled squeal from behind the swinging kitchen doors. Some cook had discovered Pierce coming in the back.

Guarded conversations resumed and people watched me from the corners of their eyes. One tubby fortyish guy in a three-piece suit withdrew his arm from around a girl who faded quickly toward the kitchen. He quickly got up and looked around nervously, finding to his dismay there were no other exits from the room. He walked casually toward the front doors, giving me as wide a berth as possible. I felt I knew him but I couldn't pull up his file. I stepped in front of him. He gave me a worried look and I remembered.

"Well!" I hailed him loudly against the music. "Councilman Arnie Dreyfuss of the great city of Roanoke. Fancy meeting you here."

He coughed. "Ah, I was just looking for someone, Sheriff, but, ah, I see they're not here so I'll be on my way. Good day." He moved to pass me.

I threw my arm around his shoulders. "Oh, well, I sure don't want to hold up the important business of the Roanoke County Council being conducted in a Hunter County cathouse, Dreyfuss. I'm sure the Roanoke County voters would be downright miffed at me for interfering with all the good work on their behalf you do here."

Dreyfuss tried to shrug off my arm, but I held him. "Goddamn it, Cody! You're a little too cute sometimes. Turn me loose!"

He was turning red. I released him.

"You don't scare me!" he announced, boldly pointing a fat finger at me. "You can be handled, you know, and I'm the man who can do it. You keep your goddamn hands off me, Cody, or you're going to be standing in the unemployment line with the other trash." He tugged his coat about him, glared at me fiercely and moved to push past me. I stopped him with a stout palm in his chest, which backed him up a step.

"You know, Dreyfuss, that little honey you were conducting all that council business with just ran out back. What she doesn't know is I have two hundred and seventy pounds of deputy back there *whom* I suspect has impeded her escape. Suppose we go ask her how old she is?"

Dreyfuss continued to stare belligerently, but he swallowed and his lips quivered. I reached and drew his expensive silk necktie from beneath his vest, and I cinched it tight around his chubby neck. (This is why, incidentally, all on-duty street cops wear only the clip-on variety of necktie.) I jerked his bloated, reddening face to within an inch of mine. "Councilman," I said just loudly enough to be sure he could hear me over the music, "you ever threaten me again and I promise you you'll headline the *Roanoke Times* for a solid week. Do we understand each other?"

He couldn't speak for choking, but he nodded vigorously. I drew my knife, cut the tie off at the knot and tucked the trails in his coat pocket. He was quaking, but he elected to leave without further ado.

Pierce came in from the kitchen with the girl from the councilman's booth in tow. She looked about sixteen in spite of too much cheap makeup. Her nipples bobbed around beneath her low-buttoned blouse and her shorts were so brief and tight that pubic hair puffed out at the crotch. She was as pissed as Gruesome.

Pierce handed me a driver's license that showed her to be nineteen. Gina Turnrow. A Roane County rural address. Gina jerked the arm Pierce held, but she may as well have tried to break chain. "Turn me loose, you fucking gorilla!" she said, snarling, thrashing wildly. Pierce just kept his eyes moving slowly about the room behind me. "Goddamn you, motherfucker, I said get your hands off me!" Pierce never looked at her or changed his expression, but I noticed the skin on his hairy hand grow tight as he torqued his grip about five hundred foot pounds. Gina's eyes and mouth opened wide. "Aaaaaah! Okay! Okay!" Gina calmed down, her eyes watering, and Pierce loosened his grip.

I was jotting down the information from Gina's driver's license when Lois Ross arrived.

There was probably a time when Lois Ross had been a pretty woman, but years of nightlife take more of a toll than other years. Her cheeks were hollow and her face had more lines than a New York City road map. She looked more awful than usual now, because she'd apparently been awakened from a sound sleep, though it was beyond me how anybody could sleep within a thousand meters of this din. Her brittle bottle-blond hair was a mess and she had pulled on a flowery pink housecoat. The look in her eyes told me she'd cheerfully piss on my grave.

"Top of the morning, Lois, my love!"

"Fuck you, Cody. What do you want?"

"Conversation. Here?"

Lois stared raw hate. She pursed her thin lips and walked off. We followed her across the dance hall and down a long carpeted hallway to a closed door. Beyond it was an office and beyond that was Lois's apartment. I could see an old upright piano to my surprise.

Lois flounced into a worn chair behind a cluttered desk. Pierce unclamped Gina and went out to take a position where he could watch the approaches. Gina sulked and rubbed her arm. I tossed my Stetson on the sofa and sat down by it. As I did, Lois suddenly snatched open a desk drawer and jammed her hand into it. I went cross-draw for my SigSauer nine-millimeter automatic. Staring at the heavy black snout of the pistol, Lois froze. Gina gasped and jumped back.

"Bring that hand out slow and empty, Lois," I said, standing, holding the sights on the bridge of her nose.

Lois had paled but lost none of her fire. "You goddamn storm trooper! I was gittin' out a bottle! I want a drink! Okay? You gonna shoot me for takin' a goddamn drink?"

I walked around her desk and shoved her roller chair back with my foot. I looked in the open left desk drawer, where there were only office supplies, a couple of shot glasses, some makeup articles and a bottle of Chivas Regal. I opened the center drawer and found a nickel-plated .38 revolver, which I removed. The other drawers held some interesting medicines, among other things, but no weapons.

Lois was reaching a boil. "Satisfied now, you trigger-happy asshole?" She grabbed the bottle and shakily poured herself a shot. "That gun is legally mine, by God! You ain't got no right to take it!"

I holstered the Sig, opened the cylinder of Lois's gun and shook out six live rounds onto the floor. I held my thumb at the breech to reflect light up the barrel and found it rusty. It hadn't been fired in a long time. I dropped it on her desk, empty, cylinder out.

As I sat back down, Lois snapped her head toward Gina. "I never saw this little cunt before in my life. She musta just wandered in here this morning."

"What!?" Gina shrieked. "Why you lyin' mother—"

"Shut *up*, girl!" Lois warned.

"Both of you shut up," I said. "Gina. You wanted for anything, anywhere else?"

"I ain't done nothin'." She glared at Lois.

"If you're woofin' me, girl, I can fix it so you wish you hadn't."

"I been busted in Roane County for holdin' some grass. That's all. I swear. I ain't wanted nowhere . . . in more ways than one." She sniffed.

"You got a car, Gina?" I asked her.

"Yeah, I got a car."

"Well, here's your license. Get in that car and drive it out of Hunter County and don't drive it back in again." She took the license with a surprised look on her face and went to the door. "Hey," I said. She turned to face me. "Underneath all that shit on your face right now, you're a pretty girl. You stay in this business very long and you're going to wind up looking like her. Promise."

"You bastard!" Lois hissed.

Gina looked at me, then she looked carefully at Lois for a moment, and she left.

"Let the kid go!" I called to Pierce down the hall.

"What are you?" Lois said, snarling. "A fuckin' social worker now?"

"Right now I'm a poet, Lois, and I want to recite some classic verse to you. You have the right to remain silent. Anything you say may be used against you in a court of law. You have a right to consult—"

"I know all that shit! What is this? What the fuck do you *want*, Cody?"

"I want to know why Ivy Joe Culpepper said your name to me before he died yesterday, Lois."

Clearly, Lois was stunned. Nobody acts that good.

"Wh—what?" She sat forward.

"You heard me."

"Now wait just a damn minute. I heard Ivy Joe was killed, but that ain't got nothin' to do with me!"

"It does if you killed him."

"You're fuckin' crazy! It was a car wreck! Why would I kill some old nigger?"

"You tell me. He was out here several times recently."

"The hell you say!"

"Witnesses!"

"Uh, well, maybe he was. Hell, I don't see all the customers all the time."

"Bullshit. Nobody comes or goes on this place that you don't know about. Now, Lois, watch my lips. I've got witnesses who will place Joe out here often and recently, he had three hundred controlled uppers on him and *he said your name when he died!*"

"I don't know what you're talkin' about!" Lois wiped her mouth and sucked on her shot glass.

"I'm talking about murder, Lois. Did you know seventy-one percent of Americans favor the death penalty and Virginia just cooked one two months ago?"

"I didn't kill him!" Lois was beginning to sweat.

"Where were you around three P.M. yesterday?"

Lois paused, watching me. "Drivin' back from Roanoke."

"Alone?"

"So what?"

"Who'd you see in Roanoke?"

"Nobody. I went to, ah, I went to see somebody but they wadn't home."

"Somebody? What's this 'somebody' shit, Lois? You need an alibi pretty bad. You better make with some names, pronto!"

"I had nothin' to do with Ivy Joe gettin' killed!"

"And pigs fly and the good don't die and the Pope does a disco mass. Why was Ivy Joe out here recently, Lois? Come on! What about it?"

Lois's eyes narrowed as she stared at me. She leaned back in her chair. "You know, Cody, somethin' just dawned on me. If you had anything solid to connect me with Ivy Joe's death, we'd be havin' this chitchat in your jail, not out here. You're fishing, Sheriff, and I ain't biting! Now if you got all this evidence, you arrest me. Otherwise, get the fuck out of here."

Lois hadn't spent twenty-five years outside the law without learning a thing or two.

"Hah-haaaah! That's it, ain't it? You ain't got shit for real on me!"

I stood and put on my hat.

"I knew it!" Lois crowed, running around her desk. "You're bluffin'! Get off my property, you asshole, go on! Git!" She was on a roll. Her breath stank of whiskey-soaked tobacco and would have gagged a goat. Lois laughed with glee. "You hear me, you prick? I said get your ass off my— ach!"

I had seized her by the throat with my left hand. "You want to talk underage girls again, Lois? Huh? You want me to hit this cesspool every weekend until you fold?"

Her eyes glowed but she shook her head.

"Then shut your pornographic face. I'm going to keep digging until I find out what happened to Ivy Joe Culpepper. And if you killed him, I'm going to see you twitching and smoking in the electric chair, so help me *God!*"

I pushed her back and opened the door. Lois rubbed her throat.

"I hope . . ." Lois coughed, her eyes wet. "I hope somebody kills you an early, slow and painful death."

"Sheriff!" Pierce's voice boomed from outside. The floor shook as he ran down the hall. I met him halfway.

"I just took a phone call from Milly, Sheriff. Cassie Shelor finally turned up."

"I figured she would," I said, vaguely puzzled by Pierce's urgency.

Pierce gripped my arm. "Lewis," he said in a low voice, "Cassie's dead!"

# 8

## Questions, Questions, Questions

A rabbit scrambled as we ran through the woods to our cars. On the way, Pierce relayed what was known.

Pursuant to the state police bulletin on stolen cars, Pierce had sent Haskel Beale into the hills off County Route Nine to see what he could find. He found something.

Where Nine crested the ridge leading to the peak of Saddle Mountain, there were several worn places in the trees overlooking the stunning Shenandoah Valley. These places have been collectively known as Lover's Overlook since before my great-granddaddy drove his own true love up there in a buggy for a Sunday picnic. It's safe to speculate that a legion of virginity bit the dust in those pine groves and the Shenandoah was not the only splendid view beheld on Lover's Overlook.

The big Chevy V-8 sucked wind loud enough for the howl to be heard over the siren as I turned off the Roanoke Highway and charged up County Twelve along the side of Saddle Mountain.

A second unexpected death in my hills in two days had me a little wired. The fact that it was the, shall we say, unique, Cassie Shelor, who had "been different lately," did nothing to relieve my shock and anxiety. Intensely erotic images of her kept flooding my brain.

Tires squealed in protest as my cruiser slid through the

mountain turns. We zoomed past the splintered gap in the old wooden guardrail where Ivy Joe Culpepper had crashed only eighteen hours earlier.

A thought struck me. Where was Lucia Dodd? I swept her and her dead granddaddy from my mind. One dead folk at a time, please.

When I reached the point where Nine dead-ends into Twelve, my pace slowed. At the crest of the ridge, I pulled up behind Haskel's cruiser and Pierce slid in behind me. Haskel had a distinctly unpleasant look on his face. He tossed away his cigarette, exhaled a blue cloud and inclined his head toward the tree-shrouded crest, about fifty yards away.

"Was lookin' for them stole' cars the state was bitchin' about, Sheriff. Thought I'd found one but it's just ol' Helen Shelor's Buick Riviera. I ain't opened it up yet"—he looked at me with drawn eyes—"but I ain't got to be no coroner to know that girl is dead. I done like you always said, I ain't messed with nothin'. Drove down to Emmett Cutter's place to phone in the call, keep it off the radio. So far as I know, the scene ain't been disturbed 'cept for me walkin' up to the car and back."

"You did good, Haskel. What time was it when you found her?"

"Well, I didn't think to look at my watch till I got down to Emmett's at twelve-ten, so it musta been about noon I found her."

"Good. Let's check it out."

"All the same to you, Sheriff, I'd just as soon stay here."

"Been a long twenty-four hours or so for you, huh, Haskel?"

"I've had better."

Pierce had gathered equipment from his trunk, and together we walked carefully, single file, up the edge of the rocky trail through the woods to the crest, where the rear of a copper-colored Buick Riviera could barely be seen. Both of us studied the ground as we walked, being careful not to miss or step on anything which might provide a clue.

I was all right until we got close enough to see the back of

Cassie's blond head through the rear window of the car, canted to the left against the driver's window, then I felt strangely anxious. This wasn't going to be just another body for me, I knew. She sure as hell wasn't "just another body" when she was alive and I dreaded seeing that vibrant, passionate girl dead. But I had to see.

We stopped alongside the car—me on the left, Pierce on the right—studying everything in view. I realized I was scrupulously avoiding looking at where Cassie sat behind the wheel. I felt the hood and the exhaust; both were cold.

With effort, I looked at her. Her head lay against the driver's glass, tilted slightly back, her face pointed up directly at me. Her lips were parted and her eyes were half open in a vacant, sleepy way. Her flesh was a blue-tinged white and she had begun to swell. Cassie Shelor was quite dead. I tore my eyes from her.

I sat on a rock ledge while Pierce moved around the car and surrounding area, taking dozens of photographs and dusting the door handles and outer-door surfaces for fingerprints. I felt sick. Such a fabulously vital, sensual girl, dead at seventeen. Why? How? My mind kept snap-flashing from Cassie's dead, bored face to the incredible color and wetness and *life* it radiated that day in Bram's Creek. "Anytime, Lewis . . ."

"Lewis!" Pierce called, for what must have been the third time. He pitched me a paper packet containing rubber surgical gloves. He handed me a tape recorder which I hung on my belt, clipping the microphone to my collar. I took a deep breath, let it out, and began to speak.

"Twelve-fifty-eight P.M., October nineteenth. I am Hunter County Sheriff Lewis Cody. With me is Chief Deputy Pierce Arroe as we examine the deceased body of a Caucasian female known to both investigating officers as Cassie Shelor, seventeen years old, discovered approximately noon this date by Deputy Haskel Beale. The body is seated normally in the driver's seat of a Buick Riviera, Virginia tag AJJ978, located at a point where County Route Nine crests Saddle Mountain, known locally as Lover's Overlook.

"Before opening the vehicle, it appears that the condition of the vehicle is not unusual in any way, both doors are unlocked, hood and exhaust are cold to the touch, the key is in the ignition and is switched to the off position."

I tugged on the powdered rubber gloves that, oddly, made my own hands look as dead as Cassie's. When I opened the door, her body slumped slightly against the seat-belt shoulder strap, her left arm hung bent in the position in which it had been propped on the armrest. Pierce opened the other door and we stepped back to let the autumn breeze ventilate the car. My guess was that she'd been here at least overnight but not more than forty-eight hours. The cold weather had retarded decay slightly, but the inevitable odor seeping from the car was already nauseating. While Pierce photographed the interior and took more prints, I waited, speaking into the recorder.

"The body is seated normally in the driver's seat; the seat belt and shoulder harness are in place normally. The body is clad in a light blue sweater, a dark blue pleated skirt, and brown leather shoes. Visible on the left wrist is a yellow metal watch and upon the ring finger of the right hand is a yellow metal ring set with clear stones. I observe nothing unusual within the vehicle. A maroon leather purse lies on the right front seat."

I pushed Cassie's now stiff body upright in the seat, flinching at its uncharacteristic coldness and hardness. I pulled out the neckline of her sweater and looked down it, then I lifted her skirt and dropped it back on her knees.

"The body is underclad in white bra, white slip, panty hose and blue underpants, all apparently in place normally and undisturbed. The body displays no apparent sign of injury or violence. The hair is neatly combed and the makeup, including lipstick, is normal and undisturbed. The posture of the body and all clothing are apparently normal and undisturbed.

"Contents of the purse are apparently normal and undisturbed. A maroon leather billfold is within and contains two credit cards, Texaco and Visa, and . . . sixty-six dollars in cash and . . . ninety-one cents in change. There are articles of makeup, a plastic tampon case which is . . . empty, sunglasses, a plastic case of numerically sequenced pills—probably a birth control prescription—and a checkbook. Additionally, there is a package of chewing gum, two ballpoint pens, several scraps of paper on which are written some phone numbers, and . . . a recipe for . . . apple cobbler.

"The parking brake is not set. The climate control is set to seventy degrees and is on automatic. The glove box is closed; inside it is the car owner's manual, a box of facial tissues and . . . some makeup items. The radio is set to FM one-zero-seven. When the key is switched on, the vehicle displays all appropriate lights, the radio is set at a low volume and the power antenna rises as per normal. The engine starts as per normal. The fuel gauge indicates approximately one-third capacity."

And so it went. There was nothing peculiar under the seats, in the trunk, under the car or anywhere near it. There was nothing at all unusual anywhere except Cassie Shelor was dead.

I stood by the rear of the car and shouted to Haskel to call for an ambulance to transport the body to Coleby Butler's clinic for an autopsy. Pierce collected his gear and joined me.

Fittingly, the sky had clouded overcast, gray and cold. There was a smell of snow in the air.

"Pierce," I said, sighing, "what the hell happened here? I mean, an autopsy should tell us a lot, but what's your gut feeling?"

"I don't have one, Lewis. It's a sterile investigation so far. On the surface, it appears we can rule out robbery, rape and/or murder. As for suicide, we can pretty much rule out weapons and carbon-monoxide poisoning. Maybe she OD'd on something. Reckon?"

"I don't think so," I said, studying the rocky dirt trail behind the car as it led down to County Nine.

Pierce saw me eyeballing the trail. He looked also but saw nothing. Neither did I.

"Why would Cassie Shelor kill herself?" I asked.

"Who knows, Lewis? Kids are waxing themselves all over the country these days. Maybe she couldn't handle her dad's death anymore. You told me yourself on the way from Lois's to our cars that Helen told you Cassie was troubled lately."

"I still don't buy suicide, Pierce. Not over her dad's death two years ago. Besides, there's nothing physical to indicate an accidental OD or a suicide; no container, no wrapper and no note." I continued to examine the trail.

"Inconclusive," Pierce replied. "What the hell are you looking at?"

"I'm looking at the main reason I don't think Cassie did herself. See it?"

Pierce eyed the trail intently. He shrugged. "I'm sorry, Lewis, I don't see shit."

"That's exactly it."

"What?!"

I looked at him. "No tracks, Pierce! Look. No tire tracks. What'd she do, *hover* this car in here?"

Pierce stooped and sighted down toward the road, frowning. "I don't know, Lewis. This ground is pretty rocky, dry and hard."

"But look, Pierce," I said, walking toward the road, "there's nothing all the way down to the roadway. There'd at least be an impression in the dirt spots, wouldn't there? Did you look at the tires? That car is almost new—the tires are, too, and they've got dirt in the treads. Why no tracks? Maybe somebody swept the trail or something. Look. There's Haskel's footprints and yours and mine. But no tire tracks except about three feet behind the rear tires. Why would Cassie think, let alone go to the effort, to eradicate her tire tracks all the way up from the road and then get in the car and OD with no container and no note?"

Pierce walked the trail, peering at the surface. He looked at me, hands on hips. "Okay, what if somebody scrubbed the tracks. Why? The car is visible from the road and some kids would've come up here and found this long before anybody thought to follow any tracks."

"Suppose somebody else had a vehicle of their own they wanted to erase trace of?"

Pierce shook his head. "I don't know, Lewis. I ain't so sure this trail has been scrubbed. For one thing, the texture of the surface just makes it too hard to tell. For another thing, why would anybody want to kill Cassie Shelor? And more confusing, how? There ain't a mark on her. No blood. No bruises. No cuts or punctures. No sign of assault or struggle. It don't look like she was either raped or robbed. If not, why would anybody want to cover their tracks? It don't make no sense."

"Just like the death of Ivy Joe Culpepper," I said.

Pierce squinted at me. "You sayin' they're connected some way?"

"I don't know, Pierce, but think about it. They occurred about three or four miles apart in geography and probably within hours in time. In both cases, we have bodies and a vague suggestion of funny business but no motives and no methods."

"Inconclusive for a connection."

"Granted. But we can't rule it out."

"Granted."

We joined Haskel at the cars.

"Lawrence Weeks is on the way out, Sheriff," Haskel told us.

"Thanks. Pierce, you and Haskel complete the scene investigation when they get the body out. Tell Lawrence to take Cass—to take the body to the clinic and have Coleby do the whole nine yards on her. That ought to tell us something useful."

"I sure hope it tells us a damn sight more than Ivy Joe Culpepper's autopsy told us," Pierce said, grumbling, staring at the graying cold sky.

"I'm going to town and give Helen Shelor the news," I said.

Haskel grunted. "Better you than me, Sheriff."

Helen Shelor took it hard.

There's no easy way to do this kind of thing. When Helen opened her front door, smiling, to find the Reverend Harper and Charlene Watson and me, it took her about a full second to get the message. She threw up both hands and an awful wail built quickly to a blood-chilling scream.

Who said only the good die young?

Helen collapsed on Charlene and Rev Harper, and they struggled into the living room with her screaming all the way—the very same living room, I could not help thinking, where the late and lovely Cassie Shelor stepped free of her clothes and invited me to make love to her barely six or seven months ago.

I went to the kitchen phone to call Pete Floyd at the paper to do him the courtesy of hearing about Cassie's death firsthand. I told him there was no evidence of the cause of her death yet but it appeared that there was no violence and that neither robbery, rape, suicide or murder appeared to be factors at this time. He asked for a few details and I obliged but omitted any mention of my suspicions. Just the facts, ma'am, as Jack Webb would have said.

"Damn!" Pete said by way of gratitude. "Lewis, I wish you'd have let me know sooner so I could have come out and gotten some photographs!"

"Sure, Pete," I said, a little chapped, "that's just the thing to do. Listen. Hear that noise, Pete? That's poor Helen Shelor screaming her lungs out. She really needs several thousand pictures of her daughter's bloated dead body spread all over the county. Maybe you could send her one suitable for framing."

"That's not a judgment for you to make, Lewis! It's not for you to decide what's fit to print and what isn't! That's—"

"You're welcome, Pete," I said and clapped the phone on its hook. Immediately, it rang and I picked it up. "Shelor residence."

"Sheriff?"

"Yeah, hi, Milly."

"Listen, Lewis, we just took a phone call from Peggy Sloan, Lanny Sloan's little girl, you know?"

"Yes."

"Well, she all outa breath and all and whisperin' and cryin' in the phone. She pretty upset."

"About what?"

"Lewis, she say that little lawyer girl what was in here this mornin', she out there at the Sloan place now askin' a lot of questions and all—"

"Holy shit! Lucia Dodd is at the Sloan farm?"

"Yeah! And Lewis, little Peggy say we better send somebody quick 'cause they gon' kill her!"

"I'll handle it. 'Bye."

As I ran to my cruiser, two cars were pulling up out front

with friends of Helen Shelor's in them, neighbors gathering to see Helen through her time of need, her second time of need in two years. No secrets in Hunter County.

Except why were all these strangely dead people turning up in my peaceful little mountain county? And what the hell was Lucia Dodd doing going up solo against Lanny and Danny, the two-bigot klanny?

Questions, questions, questions.

# 9

## The Sloans

The first snow of the new fall began as I slipped through the town of Hunter on the blues and siren and shot out Route 619 toward the cutoff to the Sloan farm. The flakes were sparse and the cold swift wind dried them on contact with the road. Fall was my favorite season, but right now I wasn't enjoying much of it.

Lanny Sloan was in his late fifties and his brother Danny was about ten years younger. Danny was an all-purpose do-it man for Lanny, who now dominated their clan since a tractor accident addled old Clancy Sloan. Lanny, his wife, two sons and daughter lived in the original huge farmhouse on Trace Mountain with what was left of Old Man Sloan. Danny and wife and two children lived in a mobile home dragged up by the main house.

There were many stories about the Sloans in these hills, all partially embellished but rooted in truth. They dated back to prohibition days when Clancy Sloan and *his* father and brothers warred with competing moonshiners for equitable shares of the illicit whiskey trade. More than one rival clansman and an occasional federal lawman had simply disappeared in the smoky Blue Ridge Mountains in those days, never to be heard from again.

One story held that Lanny Sloan was dishonorably discharged from the U.S. Marines over a statutory-rape incident. Shortly after he returned home to the hills of Hunter County, he decided ripe young Brenda Sowers would be his bride. That revelation didn't set well with Brenda, let alone her fiancée, John Billy Henderson. Another player not so thrilled with the whole idea was Brenda's father, Gabe, the patriarch of another fight-now-and-think-later mountain family. As it happened, old Gabe Sowers didn't think that John Billy was worthy of his daughter either, and the ill feeling between the two of them was well known. Ultimately, Gabe Sowers was stretching on his front porch one morning when a high-powered rifle bullet went through him like a photon torpedo and he was beamed up. Permanently. Just as John Billy was about to report the mysterious theft of his favorite rifle from his pickup truck, the badges descended on him and said, never mind, *we* found your rifle and shame on you for perforating Old Man Sowers. John Billy screamed all the way to prison that he didn't kill Gabe Sowers. Pragmatic to the end, Brenda said what the hell and married Lanny Sloan about two months later. The story ain't over.

Nine years later, John Billy Henderson hit the bricks on parole and went forthwith in search of Lanny. They came together late one Saturday night in a Roane County honky-tonk where neon beer signs flashed, the air was blue with smoke and Hank Williams sang loudly of cheating hearts. Never one to become enmeshed in preamble, John Billy announced he had come to cut the fucking black heart out of Lanny Sloan, and suddenly Hank's famous voice was drowned out by the snarling howl of a chainsaw. The saloon patrons gave John Billy *lots* of room. Understandably motivated, Lanny Sloan stepped lively about that honky-tonk while John Billy made sawdust out of three tables and carved out a section of the bar before the saw stalled. As John Billy ripped smartly on the starter rope, Lanny nailed him in the cerebellum with the blunt end of a pool stick, sending him to live out the remainder of his days staring at the floor of the Virginia Psychiatric Observation Center in Radford. Better luck in the next life, J.B.

My own story about the Sloan clan evolved from a time in my freshman year at Hunter County High School when I found Danny Sloan groping Patsy Nolan in the band room, much to her distress and protest. I asked him to stop. He told me to go to hell, but I switched him off from behind with a steel folding chair, instead. A week later, Clancy Sloan, with Lanny and a still-bandaged and dazed Danny, ran my father's Buick and me off the road and hauled me out to dim my future. I fought, but I was never much good at fighting three hillbilly goons at once, and I was taking the short end of things when Clancy Sloan noted that in his righteous glory he had neglected to set the parking brake on his truck and it was rolling swiftly backward down the mountain road. In the resulting hysteria, I jumped into Daddy's car and left them watching their truck hit a bridge abutment. Safety first, boys.

A few years ago, I got some strange information about the Sloans attempting to form some sort of paramilitary 'Aryan Protection Group' based at their farm. There were some stories about a few training sessions with similar gun nuts from out of county, but it never went anywhere. I decided at the time the Sloans were far too independent and self-centered to be capable of organizing any coordinated effort, however odious.

The Sloans were farmers by guise, moonshiners, minor drug dealers and broad-based thieves by trade and cop fighters by hobby. They were a cunning, treacherous bunch, and they were racist in a way that would make the Nazis look benevolent. They generally minded what they saw as their own business, but on the other hand, they repelled trespassers with a vengeance. Assuming they weren't too tripped on whiskey and/or PCP, I doubted they'd actually kill Ivy Joe Culpepper's granddaughter, but they might well give her cause to wish she was dead.

It was dark enough for the headlights by the time I turned off the highway onto the dirt road running along Trace Creek to the Sloan farm three miles away.

I was concentrating on missing the biggest holes in the road and, of course, it was the last thing I expected to see, so I initially thought my imagination was playing games with me. Then I jammed on my brakes with shock. Standing in my headlight beams was Lucia Dodd. She was totally naked.

She appeared to be in a state of shock, but then she stood straight, casually covering her breasts and pubic fluff with her arm and hand. She breathed rapid puffs of vapor and she stood tall, proud and defiant, except that her hair was mussed, her feet were bleeding and tears streamed down her cheeks. She was trembling violently.

I popped my trunk lid release and bounded out. I pulled my winter coat from the trunk and walked quickly to her. She took the coat, turned her back to me and put it on. I was still dumbstruck when, without a word, she walked painfully, shivering, past me to the driver's side of my car and got in. I thumped my own door shut and turned the heater fan on high.

Lucia Dodd said nothing; she only stared straight ahead, gasping and shivering. Two minutes passed. Slowly, she brought her breathing and trembling under control. Still, she neither spoke nor looked at me.

Finally, I spoke. "Miss Dodd, have you been raped?"

A few seconds ticked by and she tried to speak but her voice caught. She tried again and failed. She drew a long quivering breath.

"Na—na—no." She breathed again deeply, her arms wrapped tightly about her. "The—they said," she said very precisely, "they said, 'Any white man who ... who ... would fuck a nigger should have his dick cut off.'" Lucia Dodd fought for control. "They, they took me to the edge of their farm. They drove my car into the creek. They ... then they ... stripped ... me. Stripped me. They held me down ... and tore off my clothes ... all my clothes. They threw my clothes in the stream. They laughed at me. They put my panties and bra on their radio antenna and they drove away and left me. They laughed at me. They laughed at me." She began to tremble and gasp again. She was close to folding.

Saying her first name felt strange on my tongue but seemed more appropriate than "Miss Dodd" under the circumstances.

"Lucia, I'm sorry." I placed my hand on her shoulder in an unconscious gesture of comfort.

Her scream was deafening in the closed car. Her arm slashed out at me. "Don't *touch* me! Don't touch me! You *bastard!* You goddamned white bastard! Don't you *touch* me!" She cringed against the door and wept in heaving sobs.

I had jerked my hand back as though burned, but she was so vulnerable, so hurt, so scared and humiliated. My heart went out to her and I reached to comfort again without thinking.

"Get *away!*" She screamed. "Get way from me! You white savage bastards, I *hate* you! Get *awaaaaaay!*" The sobbing overcame her.

I kicked open my door, got out and slammed it. I didn't blame her, of course. The treatment she'd received was more traumatic and degrading than a rape might have been.

I walked a few laps around the car in the dark, a certain familiar rage building in me. The last time I remembered feeling that rage was when I found Gruesome on the Cain River Bridge the day some maggot had attempted to throw him into the river from a moving car. The puppy had struck the superstructure and bounced into the road, and the maggot had just kept going. Gruesome was broken and bleeding and whimpering when I came along, and I cried. I cried like a baby. I vividly remember how bad and how long I ached to find the heartless trash that did it and kill him. The sheer rage kept me awake, off and on, for two weeks. That was how I felt, pacing around my car, waiting for Lucia Dodd to regain her control.

Gruesome! Jesus, I forgot he was in the back seat. He'd prudently kept a low profile, and he couldn't bite her through the prisoner screen even if he was inclined to, but I knew if he popped up by surprise, she'd lose her mind. I got back in the car, my head feeling tight from the rage rising in me.

She had calmed down somewhat. She continued to stare ahead.

"I don't want you to be further upset," I said, by way of warning her about the dog, "but—"

"I know!" She finally looked at me with scalding contempt. "I know! There is 'nothing you can do.' No witnesses other than the perpetrators and no Hunter County jury is going to convict white men of assault on their own land on the word of an 'uppity out-of-town nigger girl'! So just save your breath!". Bitter sarcasm dripped from her words.

"That wasn't what I—"

"It's true!" she snapped. "I know it. I'm an attorney. There is nothing I can do. *Nothing!* God *damn* you white heathens!"

"Now wait a minute—"

*"Fuck* you!" she shouted. Somehow, the expression seemed so alien to her sophisticated demeanor I felt slapped. "Just take me back to East Hunter—'niggertown,' to you."

Gruesome had had enough of this, too. He put his front feet on the screen near her ear and went "snork."

"Oh!" Lucia shrieked, jumping forward on the seat. In so doing, she released the heavy coat which parted in front, exposing her smooth brown thigh and left breast. She jerked the coat together over her. "Enjoying yourself?" she asked with acid.

I sighed. "I tried to tell you about the dog but you wouldn't shut up."

"And I thought that odor was you," she replied.

I just chunked the car in gear and drove up the rough rocky road toward the Sloan place, the gate to which was still half a mile away.

"Where are you taking me?" Lucia demanded with alarm.

"To your car."

"I told you, they drove it into the stream."

"Got any other clothes in it?"

"Oh. Yes."

The bronze-colored Lincoln Towncar was nosed into the shallow creek bed, its headlights just above the gurgling cold water still reflecting into the trees. I got hip boots from my trunk and waded out to it. The keys were in the ignition but it wouldn't start. I shut the headlights off, popped the trunk and removed Lucia's suitcases.

While I waited behind the car, boiling inside, thinking about redneck bullies stripping a dignified girl and leaving her to freeze, Lucia Dodd dressed herself in designer jeans, a heavy drape-necked sweater and boots. She combed her shining black hair and tied it back. She cracked the window down and said, "I'm dressed, Sheriff. Now will you please take me back to East Hunter?"

"Not just yet," I said, and I walked past her to the metal cattle gate of the fence surrounding the Sloan farm. I unchained the gate and it swung open of its own accord.

"What are you doing?" Lucia asked, warily.

I passed her window on the way to the rear of the car. "Pop the trunk," I said.

"What for?" She was beginning to get nervous about my mood.

"Pop the goddamned *trunk!*" I shouted.

The trunk lid swung up and I removed the old M-14 rifle I had used to adjust Old Lady Vaughn's attitude. I inserted one twenty-round magazine, racked the bolt, and put two more magazines in the pockets of my bomber jacket.

The time had come to do a little business with the Sloans.

I slid the big rifle across the floor as I got back into the car. Lucia Dodd gaped at it.

"What are you doing?" she asked. "I won't waste time with a warrant, you've got no prosecutable case. There's nothing you can do!"

"The hell you say," I replied. Gravel churned from the rear wheels. Lucia was silent but she watched me carefully.

A single mercury vapor flood lamp on a pole illuminated the big gabled Sloan house, a mobile home on blocks, two tractors, several cars and a heavy pickup truck with white panties and bra dangling from the radio antenna. Junk car parts lay about. Beer cans were strewn all over. Falling snowflakes looked huge and bluish in the cold light.

Lucia Dodd had begun to sense what was happening in me and her apprehension showed. Gruesome had picked up on it and was pacing the back seat.

I drew up in the wide yard before the big house. I left the engine running and got out, pulling the rifle with me. Snarling dogs charged up. Gruesome slobbered insults at them.

"Lock the doors," I said. "If there's any trouble I can't handle, drive yourself out of here."

"Sheriff Cody, I—"

I slammed the door and waded through the barking mongrels. I leveled the weapon and fired several fast shots into the dirt beneath the elevated front porch. The noise, the buck of the rifle, the muzzle flash and the brass casings showering onto the car roof were just goddamn gorgeous. Greyhounds had nothing on the Sloan mongrels; they set the world land speed record for parts unknown. Gruesome ricocheted about the inside of the car like a golf ball teed off on a racquetball court.

"Get the *fuck* out here, Sloan!" I roared.

Inside, I could hear cursing voices, thumping footsteps and objects falling. The front door flew open and out strode Lanny Sloan, followed quickly by his brother, Danny, and his two sons, one big raw-boned kid about twenty-five, the other about eighteen. All were armed and all were visibly enraged at this disrespectful invasion of their turf.

Lanny Sloan was as big as Pierce Arroe but possessed of a ponderous gut Pierce would never tolerate. He wore a Lucifer's mustache and goatee and his hair and eyebrows were shaggy. He looked like something born nine months after Pancho Villa's mother did an all-nighter with a Cossack mess sergeant.

They spread out on the wide covered porch with menacing expressions. Lanny and Danny carried big Colt magnum revolvers, the oldest boy had a rifle and the younger a shotgun. Lanny clumped down the steps. I leveled the M-14 at his face. "Tell these clowns to drop the shit, Lanny, or you'll be the first to go."

"Cody, you crazy son of a bitch! This is my property! You got no——"

His eyes got real big as I let go a shot past his knees into the dirt under the porch. The flash lit his ugly face.

"Jesus, mother*fuck!*" he said eloquently, jamming to a halt.

"Tell 'em, Lanny!" I demanded.

Danny Sloan squinted through the smoke rising from a cigarette clenched between yellow teeth. He came up with his revolver. I snapped the rifle at him and aimed. "Listen, goddamn it! I didn't come here to negotiate. Put the weapons down or this place is going to be wall-to-wall widows and orphans!"

Danny grudgingly let the gun slide from his hand. It clattered off the porch into the snowflaked grass. Cautiously, the boys put down the rifle and the shotgun. They jumped from the porch and formed up around Lanny, who was livid.

I leveled the muzzle at Lanny's nose; he stared at it and let his pistol drop. He wiped his beard with the back of a huge hand. He was quaking with fury.

"Cody, you crazy motherfucker! You got no right—"

"Don't you talk to me about rights, asshole!"

Danny piped in with his nasal whine, pointing his cigarette at me. "If this is about that smart-mouth nigger bitch, Cody, you got nothin'. *Nothin'!* It's our word against hers and you'll never get a conviction, and you know it!"

"Shut up, shit-for-brains, I didn't come here for an arrest or you'd all be wearing handcuffs by now. I want a little information."

"Fuck you, Cody!" Lanny bellowed. "We ain't answered no questions for that nigger cunt and we ain't got shit to say to you!"

I swung the rifle on Lanny's kid's Camaro and blew out the windshield.

"Hey! Goddamn!"

"Holy shit!"

"Goddamn you, Cody! What the fuck do you—"

"Where were you assholes about three P.M. yesterday?"

"What?" This took Lanny by surprise.

"You heard me, monkey breath." I loved insults.

"None a' your goddamn busi—"

I blew out the expensive high-performance tires on the Camaro, which sank hissing to its hubs. The ejected casing hit Lanny in the face.

"Gaaaahd*damn!*"

"Daddy, he's wreckin' my car!"

Lanny stepped toward me and I stabbed him in the gut with the muzzle, knocking him back. He grunted, but I imagine he was thinking how easily the rifle could have gone off.

"*Damn* you, Cody!" Lanny howled, his voice cracking. I wondered if Lanny had a family history of, oh, say, stroke or heart attack.

"Where were you?"

"*Fuck* you!"

I turned on Danny's nice new Ford pickup truck and shot out the glass and tires on my side. The Sloans' incredulous expressions were illuminated in blinding white-yellow muzzle flashes.

"Aaaaaaach!"

"Oh no!"

"Shit!"

I fired into the grill of Lanny Sloan's expensive four-wheel-drive pickup. Antifreeze flowed onto the ground. The bolt locked open on the empty magazine; I slapped in another and dropped the bolt.

"I asked you inbred cretins a question."

"You son of a bitch!" Lanny seethed, purple faced. "So help me God, I'll—"

*Bam, bam, bam.* The nearest tractor squatted to its hubs.

"All right! All right! Goddamn you! We was cuttin' wood up on Saddle Mountain! So what?"

"I hear you killed Ivy Joe Culpepper!" I shouted.

"What?" Danny squeaked, obviously alarmed. "What'd you say?"

"Shut up!" Lanny commanded. "You listen to me, Cody. I'll tell you right in front of this nigger bitch that I'm tickled to death that ol' nigger is dead but I'm sorry to say I didn't kill him. None of us!"

I collected the Sloan guns and locked them in my trunk. Then I strolled around, examining the fronts of the Sloan vehicles. Lanny's antifreeze-dripping truck had fresh damage to the grill and plastic underpan, and the bumper was scratched.

"How'd you get this damage, Lanny?"

"I've done told you all I'm—"

I snapped up the rifle.

"Ah! That bumper got fucked up when I was pushin' some ol' boy's truck off that wouldn't start."

"What 'ol' boy'?"

"Hell, I don't remember! Didn't know his name!"

"Right. What was your beef with Ivy Joe Culpepper?"

"He was a fuckin' nigger, for one thing. For another, he tried to play Daddy to my girl, Peggy. And I don't want no stinkin' nigger playin' up to my daughter, tryin' to get in her pants!"

# Shepherd of the Wolves

I discovered Lucia Dodd had rolled her window down in the cruiser. She began, "My grandfather would never have—"

"Keep quiet!" I said. "I'm doing this. Sloan! Your kids wouldn't dream of talking to a black person unless they had some real good reason. What do you suppose it was?"

A clear flash of worry registered on Lanny's face. He paused to think.

"Brenda!" he yelled.

"Yeah?" came a nervous voice from the house.

"Git Peggy out here!"

In a moment, Peggy Sloan came hesitantly down the steps, staring at her toes. She was a thin girl of about fifteen years, cursed with her father's beaky nose but otherwise mildly attractive. When she drew close, I saw her lips were swollen and there were abrasions on her cheeks.

Lanny glowered at her. "Tell this asshole about that nigger janitor!"

The wretched girl looked up at me with pleading eyes. I got the message; please don't tell them I called.

"Ah . . ." Peggy stammered. She flinched as Lanny yelled again.

"Tell him, damn it!"

Tears ran down her face, collecting in the crevice of her puffed lips.

"Daddy, I—"

"Tell him, Peg! Tell him how that old dirty nigger was always playin' up to you, talkin' sweet to you!"

"Yeah," Peggy mumbled, looking at the ground. "That's what he done."

"See?" Lanny barked.

I said, "Peggy. Look at me, honey." She looked up, agony in her face. "I want you to know something."

"Now listen here, Cody! You ain't got no—*Unnh!*"

"Shut up, Lanny!" I said, sticking him hard with the rifle again. "I'm not talking to you." He stepped back, eyeballs bulging, probably weighing in his mind whether I'd really shoot him if he went for me.

"Now, Peggy," I continued, "you listen to me. There ain't a law in this state that allows him to beat you up. You don't have to put up with it. You can come with me now if you want and I promise you he'll never touch you, or you can go anytime to the county social services office in town or come to the jail and see me. There are means for taking care of you."

"She ain't goin' *no*-goddamn-where! Are you Peg?" Lanny breathed at her ear.

Peggy hung her head. "No."

"Git in the goddamn house, girl!"

Peggy fled.

*"Now,* by God!" Lanny snarled, shifting from foot to foot. "We gonna talk about the county payin' for all these shot-up cars, you son of a bitch! You ain't got no right to——"

I cut loose a short burst at the remaining tractor, and antifreeze streamed from its radiator.

"You mother*fucker!*" Lanny reached critical mass. "I ought to kick your——"

In the army, they teach you a thing called the "butt stroke," which I decided at that moment was invented for chickenshit child beaters like Lanny Sloan. I planted my feet, took a death grip on the big rifle and pivoted the stock end up hard. It caught Lanny in the jaw with a concussive *chunk,* and he went down like a polled hog. Lanny's stringy-haired oldest kid went for me and I almost didn't see it in time. The kid's big fist whistled past my cheek like a Klingon warship. The inertia of his missed swing threw him off balance; I popped him in the back of the head as he went by and he moled in next to Lanny. I turned on Danny, who threw up both hands in surrender, but I clubbed him anyway so he wouldn't feel left out. Lanny's younger boy had backed away to the porch steps, looking as though he had wet his pants.

Lanny Sloan staggered to his feet wiping blood from his beard. "You fucking pussy!" He croaked, shaking with rage. "You wouldn't be so goddamn brave without your goddamn gun!"

I stepped at him, and he threw up his heavy arms, expecting to eat the M-14 again, so I kicked him hard in the stomach and kneed him over onto his back. I tell you, it felt great.

"You're absolutely right, Lanny," I said, "but *with* my gun I'm your worst nightmare. That's why you will never find me without my gun. Momma didn't raise any fist fighters, you fat freak, but I pull triggers with the best. I look forward to the day you give me a legal reason to pull one on you, and don't you forget it."

Lanny's older kid sat up, massaging his head. "You're a fuckin' coward, Cody! In a fair fight, I'd kick your ass!"

I laughed. "What would a punk like you know about fair fights, you little maggot? Is stripping a woman four to one and leaving her to freeze your idea of a fair fight? Or maybe beating up little girls, like your old man, is more your style."

"What about my goddamn car?" the kid whined. "The county's gonna pay for all this damage, Cody. You gonna git fired!"

"No shit, Junior. You know what I think? I think it's your word against mine, and you'll never get a conviction, that's what I think! You Neanderthals aren't exactly universally loved in this county, you know. Hell, there's almost nobody left in Hunter County you haven't stolen from at one time or another. Tell you what, though, Junior. You send the department a bill. As soon as we check that all the titles on all these vehicles are kosher, and there are no outstanding traffic warrants in three states, and the serial numbers are all present and legit and aren't in the computer, and you got receipts and bills of sale for all those fancy wheels and stereos and engine parts, and if *all* that checks out *I'll* pay the damage out of my own pocket! *But* . . . if I find anything dirty in all that, *you* are going to do a little paying of your own!"

Junior mulled on that while I backed away to my cruiser.

"Hey, goddamn it!" Lanny choked, getting to his feet. "Them fuckin' guns in your trunk is mine!"

"I won't be taking them far, Lanny. You'll find them at the bottom of Trace Creek about where ya'll put her car, give or take a mile."

I walked to Lanny's pickup truck and broke the antenna off of it. I removed Lucia's lacy underwear from the stub and tossed it through the window to her. She looked at me strangely.

"What's this all about, Cody?" Danny sneered, suddenly brave. "How come you to take up for some nigger girl? You knockin' off a little chocolate pussy, Sheriff?"

Lucia Dodd's eyebrows shot up.

"Yeah," Lanny growled. "He's just the kind a' son of a bitch who'd fuck niggers."

I walked toward Lanny casually. "You boys could do with a few days at charm school, you know it?" Lanny correctly figured he was on his way to the cold ground again, and he backed away quickly. He stopped and leaned forward so his blood dripped onto the ground.

"All right, Cody, you motherfucker, you holdin' all the cards right now. But your time is coming! We'll git your ass, and soon!"

I faked with the rifle and kicked him again. Some folks are just slow learners. He sank to his knees. I set my feet, and kicked him onto his back. Again. I fired a three-round squeeze-off in the snowflakes by his ear.

"You crazy bastard!" Lanny fairly screamed, clutching his ringing ears. "I'll kill you! I swear I'll kill you!"

"Listen carefully, Sloan. You guys are taking up star billing on my shit list. By morning, all my deputies and the local VSP troopers are going to know it, and it's going to rain hot piss everywhere you go. And if I find out you had anything to do with the death of Ivy Joe Culpepper, life is going to get a little slender for you. You can take that to the bank."

Lanny Sloan's eyes bulged with rage and the veins on his forehead stood out, but he elected to decline comment.

"Just one more thing, you assholes!" I said, getting back into my car. "I'm running for re-election late this month; 'course I'm running unopposed but I know I can count on your vote and enthusiastic support anyway, right?"

I watched them in the mirror as we drove away, lest they come up with another weapon for a parting shot. They didn't.

By the gate, I wedged the Sloan guns in the cattle guardrails and ran over them with my car. Now the Sloans could shoot around corners.

We were all the way down to the highway before Lucia Dodd spoke.

"That was the most incredible display of constitutional travesty and police brutality I have ever witnessed." A few miles later, she said, as though speaking to herself, "That was amazing. In any civilized jurisdiction in this nation, you'd be arrested for what you did back there."

"Yeah," I replied, "well, we do things a little differently up here in the ol' bastion."

I dropped her in front of Ivy Joe's little home on Eldridge Street in East Hunter and set her bags on the walk. I could feel the neighbors' eyes on us. I looked at Lucia Dodd. Her expression said nothing.

"I'm not through, Sheriff Cody. I'm not scared off easily. I'm not leaving until I know what happened to my grandfather."

"I sort of figured that. Good night."

"Sheriff?"

"Yes?"

"I may have misjudged you. I apologize, sincerely." She picked up her suitcases and marched for the house.

I made a decision. "I'll pick you up at noon tomorrow after the funeral," I said to her.

That gave her cause for pause. "I beg your pardon?"

"I'll have your car towed in tomorrow, but it'll be a day or so before it's fixed. You can't do much investigating on foot. You can learn what I learn and I can try to keep you from getting yourself lynched in the meantime. Such a deal I have for you."

Plainly, she didn't know quite what to make of this proposition. After some deliberation, she said, "Very well." And she went inside and closed the door.

Snow filled the air. I checked my watch. I'd have time to get a couple of things done at the dungeon before driving out to the Butler estate for dinner and chess.

Maybe by then Coleby would know what killed Cassie Shelor.

Maybe he could help me figure out what happened to Ivy Joe Culpepper.

# 10

~

## Coleby and Sarah

The Butler estate was called Mountain Harbor and was built in 1878 by a sea captain named Hiram Braithwaite who had made his fortune running guns to the Confederates, then investing wisely. Mountain Harbor was Captain Braithwaite's retirement home. It was said that when he sold his ships he vowed never to look upon the sea again. He didn't. His weathered marble sarcophagus was surrounded by a wrought-iron enclosure at a point on the edge of the plateau that offered a tranquil view of the Mother Blue Ridge to the east and her daughter, the Shenandoah, to the west.

Captain Braithwaite planted the thick spruces that now towered over both sides of the long driveway winding up from the highway to the mansion. Over the years, succeeding generations added on until the stately, weathered-brick home had about fifteen thousand feet of living space on two floors, a six-car detached garage over which there was a duplex apartment for the staff and a serious stable across the creek that flowed behind the home. It was what people of Coleby's breeding called "comfortable."

As luck had it, the Braithwaite descendants, then in California, were not interested in keeping Mountain Harbor when their grandmother died, so they put the estate up for sale about the time Dr. Coleby Butler was to be discharged from the U.S. Air Force. I lost no time advising him and he fell in love with the place on sight. We tried desperately to help Sarah Butler appreciate the grand old home, but she had cancer of the attitude from the very beginning. She never forgave Coleby for taking up country medicine, which she blamed and despised me for.

In this automated age, the Butler staff consisted of a rotund Irish housekeeper named Polly, who who was born to cook, and an elderly but alert stable hand named Arthur.

I drove around back and parked by the six-car garage. I noted Sarah's Mercedes sedan, the oldest daughter Anne's Mercedes coupe and the family Jeep, but not Coleby's Rolls-Royce Corniche convertible. Grimly, I wondered if Coleby was still at the clinic field dressing Cassie Shelor. Jeez, I thought, the world would be a less colorful place without her.

Coleby wasn't still at the clinic. He met me at the French doors opening from the broad brick veranda into his spacious sunken den, handing me an iced bottle of my favorite Norwegian brew. I kicked the snow off my feet.

"Come in the house, Lewis!" Coleby crowed, as though I were his long-lost brother. He affected the Portsmouth accent that made 'house' sound like 'ha-ooose.' "Good evening, Gruesome," Coleby said to my mutt, "your beer is in your bowl in the kitchen." Gruesome jumped up on Coleby's leg to accept a little ear scratching and then split promptly for the kitchen.

"Where's that jalopy of yours, Coleby?" I asked. "I thought you weren't back from the clinic yet."

He laughed. "I had it taken to the dealer in Washington, Lewis. The top folding actuator failed on it, and that's not the sort of thing Stout's Texaco keeps parts for."

"Uncle Lewis!" Coleby's oldest daughter, seventeen-year-old Anne, rose from the sofa and trotted across the expansive sunken den, her breasts bouncing beneath her sweater.

"Holy shi—uh, sugar, Anne. Want to get married?" I said.

Anne beamed, embraced me and kissed my cheek. "You darling lecher! Good to see you again. Better be careful how you make that offer. I might just make an honest man out of you."

"Ooh. Easy there, girl, my old batteries can't stand the strain." I squeezed her tight.

She laughed. "You're my favorite pervert, Uncle Lewis."

"It's good to see you, too, sweetheart. What are you doing home from school?"

"Teachers' conference," she replied, taking my bomber jacket. I slid my holstered Sig and handcuffs from my belt and handed them to her. She walked toward the towering foyer, calling, "Haven't been home since school started, so I thought I'd run down for a couple of days. I miss everybody!"

I took a seat in a leather chair near the twelve-foot stone hearth. The crackling fire felt good. The beer felt even better.

"Sorry to show up in uniform, Coleby, but I've been up to my ass in problems today and didn't have time to get by the house and change."

"Yes. A tragic thing, the death of the Shelor girl. You know you don't have to apologize in this house, Lewis. Kick off your boots."

Anxious though I was to know, I was sure Coleby would get around to telling me the results of the autopsy in his own good time.

Coleby's ten-year-old Elizabeth ran breathless into the room, bounded down to the sunken floor and threw herself on me. "Hi Uncle Lewis I got a new horse oh he's beautiful you've got to see him where's Gruesome in the kitchen Gruesome!" The lovely child was out the door to the long brick-floored kitchen.

Polly waddled in from the kitchen with a silver tray of sausage pinwheels, hot and crisp. "Anne!" I called out. "Our engagement's off. I'm marrying Polly instead." Polly chuckled. It took both my long arms to hug all of her.

"Eat these here pinwheels while they hot, boy!" She shuffled toward the kitchen, cackling.

Gruesome zipped in, beer foam all over his ugly mug, and took up station by my chair to mooch pinwheels. Elizabeth followed and threw herself on the rug beside him.

"Oh dear," Coleby said, "it appears Gruesome has contracted hydrophobia!" Gruesome fawned at the mention of his name and Elizabeth giggled and wiped his jowls.

## Shepherd of the Wolves

Anne rejoined us. We talked about how well she was doing at Madeira, a private school near Washington, where she was a senior, and her recently confirmed acceptance at the University of Virginia. We were discussing her quandary as to what to choose for a major when her mother arrived from upstairs.

Behold the Brahmin beauty. Sarah Bernhardt Butler— "of the Baltimore Bernhardts," she was found of saying— was a tall, striking woman with rich black hair and the carriage of an aristocrat. She was a little thin for my taste, but she was undeniably a classic Roman beauty whose only physical flaw was that she'd forgotten how to smile years ago.

"Good evening, Lewis," Sarah said offhandedly, meeting social necessity. Sarah had never seen much socially redeeming value in me. She eyed Gruesome as though he were a rectal tumor. He ignored her. Gruesome had never seen any socially redeeming value in Sarah, I imagined.

It was minutely apparent to a cop's eye that Sarah had been drinking.

Dinner was splendid—steaming corned beef and cabbage. Conversation was topical in an extra-county way but Sarah declined to contribute. At one point, Anne said, "Uncle Lewis, I was so sorry to hear about dear old Mr. Culpepper and I was shocked about Cassie Shelor! I knew her in elementary school."

Sarah cut in, her sarcastic tone just noticeably fuzzy at the edges. "Anne . . . dear. I'm certain that if you make the effort you can think of more appropriate dinner conversation than the . . . deaths, of two . . . locals."

Anne eyed her mother briefly. There were bits of ice in her reply. "Yes, Mother."

After dessert—smoldering apple dumplings—Sarah excused herself. "I . . . have letters to write. Polly. I'll have a brandy in my study at nine."

"Yes, ma'am."

"Elizabeth," Sarah said, "dinner was late." She glanced at me making this remark. "It's your bedtime."

"Oh, Mother, there's no school tomorrow. Can't I stay up and talk to Uncle Lewis?"

"No," Sarah said, as blunt as the flat side of an ax. She left without another word.

We retired to Coleby's library, a warm leather-and-walnut enclave where a man could think and learn. The chess table sat on short legs between two leather armchairs before a small elevated hearth. We built a fire, and Gruesome flopped down near my chair. Anne came in with two bottles of stout and sat on the rug, her arm over Coleby's knee. I drew white and opened with a conventional pawn center attack. The game was on.

At nine, Elizabeth came in wearing her nightgown to kiss us all, including Gruesome, good night.

By ten o'clock, there were two more empty green bottles on the hearth, Coleby and I were engrossed in the game, Anne was sleepy and Gruesome was snoring. The game had become one of slashing queen and rook moves, the bishops and knights having met early fates. Anne rose, kissed us both and excused herself to bathe and sleep. We watched her go, full of grace and sensuality.

"There goes a rare young woman," I remarked.

"Thank you, Lewis. She is beautiful, if I say so myself." Coleby paused in thought, staring into the fire. "You know, Lewis, there is nothing on this earth more lovely than a beautiful girl in her late teens. Nature is at her kindest to women then, I believe."

"Few women Anne's age have her poise and grace. Most think the latest rock group or the right designer jeans are the pressing issues in life."

"Indeed. It distresses me so to see what they eat, the drugs they take, to see them smoking and drinking on a devastating scale, even when pregnant. I tell them what they're doing to themselves and their babies. They just nod vacantly and light up another cigarette as soon as they're outside the clinic. It's sad and frustrating. Would that women's minds and bodies matured in concert."

While I contemplated my next move, Coleby changed the stereo disc. "You'll like this one, Lewis, with your penchant for the Oriental. An incredibly gentle Japanese flute piece."

He was right. It was so gentle it slowed the cardiac and respiratory rates. You could hear the breath of the musician flowing down the bamboo, passing in perfect pitch and fading like wind in the pines. Jeez, I thought, I am some kind of poetic when I'm drunk.

I told Coleby about the intriguing Miss Lucia Dodd, her abuse at the hands of the Sloans that afternoon and the, er, abuse of the Sloans at the hands of Sheriff Lewis Cody.

Coleby listened intently, especially as I related the malicious statements the Sloans made about Ivy Joe Culpepper.

"My word, what bigoted animals the Sloans are. They certainly are malcontents and thieves. You should be careful with your frontier style of personal justice, Lewis. In this case, it was richly deserved, but someday someone is going to sue you blind."

"Point taken. It's always a risk in this business whether you're playing by the rules or not. I just beat them at their own game for once. Where the system fails, men must prevail."

At one point, Coleby said, "Hmmm. Dodd. Seems I've heard that name before, but I don't remember in what context."

Coleby drew two more green bottles from the oak ice chest on wheels that Polly had brought us before retiring. The beer was just a hair away from freezing; it was ice-fire in the mouth. I savored the flawlessly balanced flavor—not as heavy as the Dutch brews but so much richer than the American beers. I looked up from the chessboard to find Dr. Coleby Butler staring at me.

"Heart failure," he said simply.

"You're kidding! Cassie Shelor?" I was stunned.

Coleby nodded.

I sat up and shook my head. "Seventeen-year-old Cassie Shelor had a *fucking heart attack?!*" I was astounded. A body that perfect had a bad heart? I was, for the umpteenth time since it happened six months before, inclined to tell Coleby about my incredible encounters with Cassie Shelor, but a middle-age lawman is instinctively reluctant to relate his sexual encounters with a minor to anybody, even best friends. Besides, this hardly seemed the time.

"It's rare, of course, Lewis, but not unheard of. She's been my patient since she was a child. She's always had a heart murmur; it's been in her records for years. She just sustained a load on her heart the ventricular wall could not bear."

"Sitting stock still in a car on Lover's Overlook?!"

Coleby took a swallow of beer. "Lewis, one doesn't have to be running the Boston Marathon to overstress the heart. Emotional stresses are frequently the greatest. Loss of a loved one, rejection by a lover. Even sex can put a strain on weak hearts."

Between the beer and the bizarre revelations going down here, I was considering having a heart attack of my own. I struggled to think. "Cassie was fully clothed. Did you find any evidence of a recent sexual encounter?"

"As you know, Lewis, I'm not able to determine that categorically, but I can tell you this. All the detached pubic hairs I found on her were those of a Caucasian female, probably her own, as they exhibited no differences from the attached hairs. There were no traces of semen in her vagina, rectum, mouth or stomach, nor on her exterior. Nor was there any tissue distress of the vulva or other membranes which chafe first upon dry or extended copulation. In fact, there was no tissue damage upon her anywhere. I don't have the lab results, including those on the secretions in her underwear, back yet, but I do not anticipate anything out of the ordinary. It was the heart, Lewis. The ventricular wall had a congenital thin spot. Something caused it to open into the adjoining ventricle and the heart simply could not develop sufficient blood pressure. It probably was not even particularly painful. Just a growing lethargy that became death."

I let this soak in. It was unsettling, yet at the same time it was a relief. It meant one less suspicious death to muddy up my water.

Erotic mind shots of a nude and pleading Cassie conflicted like water in a fuse box with the thought of her split open and decapped, her organs lying in puddles on stainless-steel scales.

I shook my head hard and drew on my brew. "Coleby, was she using a tampon at the time?"

"No."

"Was she pregnant?"

Coleby's eyes narrowed. "No, Lewis. Why do you ask?"

"I've got a dead kid on my hands, Coleby. Her mother said yesterday that something was troubling Cassie lately. And there's another reason. There were birth-control pills in her purse bought in a Christiansburg pharmacy. Hell, you prescribed them, in fact."

Coleby nodded. "Ovulon Eighty. So?"

"So it looked to me as though they hadn't been taken recently. They were out of sequence for the date. I had Milly check with the pharmacist in Christiansburg and he agrees. The prescription was four months old and had not been completed."

"Perhaps she misplaced it, bought another prescription which she kept at home, and later happened to find the original prescription and just failed to dispose of it. It happens."

"It's conceivable. But there's something else."

"Yes?"

"A tampon case. Empty. Wouldn't she have been likely to be carrying spare sanitary protection if she was ovulating regularly?"

"Possibly, yes, but, as Pierce Arroe is so fond of saying, that's inconclusive."

"Granted. There are just too many loose ends."

"I'll tell you something conclusive, my friend." Coleby smiled. "Cassie Shelor was definitely not pregnant—that's in my report, which is already at your office. I know this is unusual, Lewis. Your professionally skeptical policeman's mind is suspicious, but you can relax. It was the girl's heart. Her health records document the murmur all the way back to the time of her birth. Copies are also in the report."

We sacrificed our queens and the battle became one of elaborate strategies for reaching the opponent's back row with a pawn so it could be made an all-powerful queen to turn the tide decisively in favor of whoever accomplished the deed first. Coleby was winning in that he could get there one move ahead of me. Unless he slipped up.

"I thought she was murdered," I said.

Coleby's eyes snapped at mine. "Are you serious? Why?"

"Nothing real, Coleby. Nothing substantive. Just nagging little loose ends that don't add up. Like Ivy Joe Culpepper.

"Really, Lewis? Like what?"

I realized at that moment how silly I sounded. "Oh, Jesus. I guess I sound like a dime-novel Charlie Chan, don't I? To call a spade a spade, Coleby, I don't have shit. I can't prove either Joe or Cassie even died of foul play, let alone how or by whom. Plainly, what I've got here is an old gentleman who died in a car wreck, whose final words were unintelligible or senseless, and a young girl whose long-standing heart murmur finally caught up with her. I'm seeing wolves where there are only rabbits. That's one of the prices your mind pays for a career in law enforcement."

"You're just tired, Lewis, and your diet is awful. You eat fast food by day and canned chili at home."

"I hate cooking."

"Nonetheless, your body needs fresh food. You should prepare yourself nutritious salads and vegetable dishes. You could even grow your own——"

"I'm a cop, not a farmer. I couldn't grow grass."

"Nonsense. I've known you for years. You've abused your body by eating poorly ever since . . . ever since you divorced Elaine. You've got to——"

"I didn't divorce Elaine, and you know it. She divorced me. When Tess . . . was killed, there was nothing left between us, and she left me for that asshole lawyer in Baltimore.

"Lewis," Coleby said softly. "It's over, my friend. Don't allow it to keep hurting you so——"

"No. No, it's not over, Coleby. It'll never be over for me. If I hadn't had that last row with Elaine, we wouldn't have put Tess on that goddamned plane to spend a week with her grandmother while Elaine and I sorted things out. Then when the fucking thing crashed, she wouldn't have been on it——"

"Lewis, Lewis——"

"And she wouldn't have been burned alive!"

"Lewis, no."

I was weeping like a baby. Again. "I always told her I'd take care of her, Coleby. I used to tell her I'd never let anything hurt her!"

"Let it out, Lewis, let it out."

"She was all alone," I sobbed. "I can hear her screaming,

'Daddy!' in my sleep even now, afraid, alone, terrified. Oh God, oh God, there was nothing left of her to bury but her teeth . . ."

I just wept. It was the beer, I guess. And Coleby was right. I was tired, physically tired and emotionally tired of a life with nothing and no one in it but work. I stared into the fire, its heat warming my eyes.

Coleby leaned forward across the chessboard and put his hand on my shoulder. "Lewis, your grief distorts the truth. They struck a mountain in fog at three hundred miles an hour. You're a pilot. You know no one aboard lives a nanosecond after a crash like that one. Tess died instantly, painlessly, knowing no fear, Lewis. You must believe it, my friend. She was happy at the prospect of seeing her grandmother. She knew no terror, no pain. Don't torture yourself. Please."

In a moment, I straightened up. I wiped my face and drained my beer. When I set the empty on the hearth, I noticed Gruesome was on his feet by my chair, looking at me with what I interpret as concern. I scratched his ears and he lay back down.

"Oh shit," I said, sighing. "You can tell a man has had too much to drink when he starts blubbering. Fuck it. Give me another beer."

Coleby smiled, fished out two more and opened them. I pulled on mine and stared at the flickering fire, letting my tears dry. Tears of Tess.

"I'm sorry Coleby, I haven't been very cheery company. I just loved that child so much." I looked at him and smiled. "But you know how that is, don't you, my friend?"

Coleby wasn't smiling now. He was staring at me but he was looking way beyond me. "Yes, Lewis. I do know how that is. I love my daughters with all my heart and soul, but I'm not as strong as you, Lewis. If I lost them, I'd perish. Their love and adoration is all that gives substance to my life."

I knew what he wasn't saying—that Sarah lent his life no substance. What a grand and gentle man was Coleby Butler. How sad that he should be wasted on so self-centered a shrew as Sarah "of the Baltimore Bernhardts."

I studied the battleground of the fine mahogany chessboard. I deliberately moved my best pawn within range of his king-side rook.

Coleby held his hand to his lips, and his eyes flicked over the board. Still, his mind seemed to be elsewhere.

"Sarah wants a divorce," he said.

Poor Coleby. He was willing to live without the love of a good woman just for the privilege of loving a bad one. And she wasn't going to let him do even that.

"I said no, Lewis. She wants a settlement that would ruin me, many times over what is required for her to live as she is accustomed. And worse, she wants exclusive custody of Elizabeth. She says I've turned Anne against her and she'll not permit me to do that with Elizabeth. I never did that, Lewis. I never disparaged Sarah to anyone, except perhaps to you when the frustration was so great, but I never wanted to bias anyone against Sarah. In fact, I've had to defend Sarah recently both to Anne and Elizabeth."

"Anne is no baby, Coleby; she sees Sarah for what she is. That's Sarah's fault, not yours."

"Still, Sarah insists on nothing but the rarest weekend visitation rights to Elizabeth. I couldn't live with that, Lewis, you know that."

"Yes. So fight her. Have you talked to an attorney?"

"I had a preliminary discussion with Bob Whitney about three weeks ago. He says Sarah has no grounds, that I've been a good provider, husband and father, which is demonstrable in court and, in the absence of an adultery charge, even mental cruelty won't stand up."

I could see Coleby aging before my eyes. How ironic. The only mental cruelty in the marriage was being inflicted upon Coleby by Sarah.

"I would let her go, Lewis, if she would simply be reasonable and not try to be vindictive through Elizabeth and the estate. I love Sarah, but I know she isn't happy with me. I know she has seen a couple of other men in recent years. I hoped perhaps that would relieve some of her dissatisfaction and give us a better chance together, but it only intensified her disdain for me. I do love Sarah, Lewis. But life with no love, only her eternal cold contempt, has been hard on me. I—I'm not a man who can live without love. We . . . haven't shared sex together for years. More devastating, Lewis, she hasn't had a kind or even pleasant word for me in all that time. It hurts, Lewis, it hurts. I love her. You know?"

It was my turn to sympathize. Yes, I knew. Coleby was a man who knew how to love and who needed love in ample measure. In this, Sarah was barren. Hence the love and adoration of his daughters was all the more dear to him. A man like Coleby, for that matter any man, could not survive starved of affection, warmth, praise, encouragement . . . love.

Coleby went for the pawn with his rook. He was now up a pawn, but the move was nevertheless a mistake. He wasn't thinking of chess.

"Depriving Elizabeth of your influence, condemning her to life alone with Sarah, wouldn't do her any good either. I think you're doing the right thing, Coleby. Where does that leave you with Sarah?"

"A stalemate of sorts. I imagine her own attorneys have told her she can leave anytime, but before she can take Elizabeth and most of my family holdings, she'll have to demonstrate stronger grounds. So she is here under protest. She says she is waiting for me to make the first legal mistake she can use against me and take what she wants from our marriage. For my own part, I like to believe that in time her hate will die and I can salvage us." He managed a sad, unhappy smile.

I wanted to strangle Sarah's bitchy neck. The spoiled, narcissistic brat. She commanded, wholly undeserved, the love and devotion of one of the most sterling men flowering on this weed patch of a planet, and it wasn't good enough for her. She wasn't woman enough to appreciate and nurture it; she had to be a hateful, destructive ballcutter to boot.

Coleby was eyeing the board. He leaned forward, his brow wrinkled. In a moment, he looked up at me and smiled. "You treacherous dog!" he said with admiration. "No offense, Gruesome. Lewis, you *gave* that pawn away—I should have seen that. The capture puts me one move too late to stop you from queening your king's-knight pawn.

The game is yours." He tipped over his king and extended his hand. "Well played, Lewis." I hoped to someday have a tenth of his graciousness.

"Well, my strategy to make you feel sorry for me and get lost in your own woes worked, huh? Took your mind off the game."

Coleby laughed. "You won fair and square, Lewis. It was a good game."

We wobbled out onto Coleby's big veranda, now covered in snow. Enormous snow crystals filled the air, which tasted cold and sweet. There was the quiet that is unique to a snow-muffled night. Gruesome beat it for the bushes to take care of business. In the snow, he looked like a football with ears.

"Coleby, I would arrest me for driving in the shape I'm in. How about I take one of your guest rooms for the night?"

"You know you needn't ask, Lewis. *Mi casa es su casa.*"

I looked at Coleby. His noble face reflected the misery he felt so acutely. He would've cried like me except he was a better man than me, a man too proud, too well bred to wear his agonies on his sleeve.

"Go to bed, Coleby. It won't seem so bad in the light of day."

A moment passed while he stared out into the night. One of Coleby's horses neighed from the stable. When he spoke, the strain rendered his voice brittle.

"I couldn't live if I lost my girls, Lewis. I can endure it all, but not that. Every man has his breaking point, and if anything happened to alienate or take my daughters from me, I couldn't handle it, Lewis. I'm not the man you are."

"Easy, Coleby. I was just thinking the same thing, that I'm not the man you are. Besides, your daughters adore you—you could never alienate them. We're both tired and drunk, my friend. Let us rest. Tomorrow is another day."

He looked at me with watering eyes. "Whatever I do, I do for them, Lewis."

"Good night, Coleby. It's time for rest."

He looked again at the night and turned and walked for the open French doors to the den.

"Whatever I do, I do for them."

I stayed outside awhile, washing away intoxication with

icy breaths and wet snowflakes bathing my face. Soon I was shivering. I whistled to Gruesome and we went inside. I called the nightwatch and told them they could reach me at Coleby's the rest of the night. Gruesome followed me up the carpeted, curving stairway to the room I used on occasion. I saw Anne had anticipated I'd be staying the night as she had put my jacket, gun and cuffs on the bed.

The room was huge by my standards, dominated by an antique four-poster bed. I dropped everything on the floor, went into the sort of shower/hot tub arrangement in the bathroom and marinated in the steaming water. Under cover of the running water, I underwent another attack of the weeps for Tess, for poor, gentle Coleby Butler and, yes, for myself. Felt almost as good as kicking the shit out of Lanny Sloan.

There was a teak-handled razor in a brass tray on the sink next to an electric shaving cream dispenser, for God's sake. I felt elegant as hell, shaving.

I looked at my watch as I hit the sheets. Midnight.

I don't know how long I'd been asleep when I snapped awake to Gruesome's low-throated growl. Then I heard what had set him off. The door knob was turning. I reached to the floor to silence Gruesome and felt about under the sheet for my gun, feeling half silly for doing so. There was no light on in the hall, but I could still tell that the door had opened and closed behind someone. Then there was the peculiar smell of perfume weighted with brandy. Sarah.

I flipped on the bedstand light and squinted.

She was a beautiful woman, if I must say so. She wore an expensive dressing gown over God knew what. She was composed but she swayed slightly.

"Well, well," I said, rubbing my eyes. "This year's Nobel Prize for happy homemaker goes to . . ."

"My. He is sober enough to speak, at least."

"Mrs. Butler, would you tell our viewers what life as an alcoholic shrew is like?"

"How's your wife, Lewis?" she asked sweetly, sitting demurely at the foot of the bed. "The one who left you for a man of substance, I mean."

I sighed. She had won. "If Coleby finds out you're here,

it'll crush him, Sarah, and I swear I'll choke your loveless eyes out."

A Mona Lisa smile formed on her face. "I'm afraid your plebeian posturing is in vain, Lewis; Coleby is not the saloon dweller you are. Alcohol puts him very soundly to sleep."

"Mmm. A problem you clearly don't suffer. Why don't you tell me what's on your mind? It shouldn't take long; then you can bug out and let me sleep."

Sarah studied me as though trying to find a key to me. "Did Coleby tell you I'm divorcing him?"

"Get serious, Sarah. You know I'd never discuss Coleby with you."

A slight crease appeared on her high forehead. "Why do you hate me so colorfully, Lewis?"

"I don't hate you, Sarah, I'm just disgusted with you because you wreck the happiness of the best friend I'll ever have."

"My God. You sound like a cub scout."

"So be it. What the *fuck* do you want?"

"You are the most tactless dullard I have ever met."

I leaned forward. "Listen carefully, Sarah. One of the advantages to being a tactless dullard is I don't feel obligated to sit here listening to your chickenshit repartee. Furthermore, I'm just tactless enough to rise out of this bed buck naked and throw my hostess out of one of her own guest rooms if she doesn't get to the goddamn point. Forthwith. Pronto."

Sarah stood, striking a pose like one of those New York clothes horses in the fashion shows. "Very well, Lewis. If you truly are as maudlinly devoted to Coleby as you profess, you can do him a very great favor by persuading him to grant me a divorce on my own terms."

Jeez, I had to give her credit for brass. "I happen to feel, of course, that Coleby would be infinitely better off shed of you, Sarah, so he might enjoy the many good women in this world who are capable of appreciating him. But your 'terms' amount to cheap cruelty and you know it. The only persuasion I'm going to offer Coleby is to cut you off at the knees." I gave her both wolf eyes, right in the face.

Not a muscle in Sarah's face moved a millimeter, yet her

expression turned the color of rage. "Very well. As you wish, Lewis. I'll do it the hard way, without your help. But I promise you Coleby will suffer the more. Sooner or later, I will come up with the legal cause to take what I want from this regrettable marriage. In the meantime, I shall see if I can, in my own special little way, motivate Coleby to become, as you so quaintly put it, 'shed' of me. On my terms!"

"Fair warning, Sarah. Don't ever put yourself in a position where I can move against you."

If my eyes were those of the wolf, hers were those of the leopard. "Lewis, you are merely a lower-echelon civil functionary, a rather barbaric one at that."

"You're dismissed now, Sarah. Nothing about you is needed or desired."

She gazed calmly at me for a time, and then she left.

It was women like Sarah who gave divorce a good name.

# 11

## Goodbye, Mr. Joe

The next morning was cloudy, cold and white everywhere.

Short of a plane crash, it was a blessed day for the funeral business in Hunter. The drive in from Mountain Harbor took me past Weeks's Funeral Home, where, I presumed, Lawrence had spent the night making what was left of poor Cassie Shelor presentable. Cars were gathering.

Rolling quietly on the packed snow past the offices of the *Hunter Press,* I saw Pete Floyd shoveling his sidewalks. I called to him to relay my regrets to the breakfast club this morning and kept moving. I was in no mood for questions. What I needed were answers.

I pulled up at the East Hunter Salvation Memorial Chapel and talked with my deputy handling the traffic already arriving en masse for the funeral of Ivy Joe Culpepper.

"It's colder than an empty mailbox, Sheriff. Funeral procession's gonna be a real thrill in this snow."

"You can handle it, Bobby. I'll have Milly call Stout's Texaco and have his boys stand by with a couple of wreckers for those who get stuck. I've already asked State Roads to plow the approach to the colored cemetery this morning. I'll get you some help up here before they move to the cemetery. How you fixed for coffee?"

"Thermos is empty. Been freezin' my balls off."

"Well, run down to Lady Maude's and get it filled. I'll stand by here till you get back."

While I waited, I flipped on my commercial radio and listened to the news. I wondered if some Russian country policeman was sitting in his car listening to whatever passes for news there and wondering why he bothered to bust his ass protecting the citizens when humanity was so universally screwed up.

Wow, I reflected. The events of the last couple of days, culminating in last night's depressing episode at Coleby's, had sure left me in a glum mood.

I watched a church van full of singers in choir robes walk into the chapel.

Hunter County black folks really knew how to lay on a good funeral. There would be a first-class gospel spectacle here today—I'd seen it before. The Reverend Mr. Scopes would start out slowly eulogizing Brother Joe, working scattered amens from the mourners in the packed chapel. As he progressed, he would get louder and more emphatic and so would the amens. The choir would pick up the pace. At the right moment, Rev Scopes would chant, holding the last syllable, ". . . and Brother Joe, he dwell on High now wid de *Loooooord!*"

"Aaaaa*men!*" the mourners would reply, swaying in the pews, clapping.

". . . where he look upon the blessed face of *Jeeeeeesus!*" Rev Scopes would cry.

"Aaaaa*men!*"

"An' all his trials and trib-a-*la*shuns, they now be *ooooover!*"

"Aaaaa*men! Glo*ry Halle-*lu*-yah!"

". . . 'cause Brother Joe, he be*lieeeeved* in the Holy Spirit *all* his many years!"

"Aaaamen! *Yes,* Lord! Halle*lu*yah! Aaaamen!"

They'd all be rocking and rolling, high on the Spirit, smiling, standing, swaying, clapping, shouting.

"Aaaamen! Aaaamen!"

It would go on for an hour. Everyone from the rug rats to the fossils would participate, and by the time the service ended, they'd all be happier than kids at Christmas. Now that's the way to lay a man down. Fuck death.

**109**

Making a party of a funeral wasn't the way of the whites. For this reason, because they felt neither comfortable nor welcome at this private part of the service, whites would not attend, I knew. Yet I also knew that at the cemetery they would come in legions, for old Ivy Joe Culpepper was loved by generations of white Hunter County school kids as well. This notion was borne out by all the flower arrangements, some of them costing hundreds of dollars, which had filled the chapel by yesterday and now crowded the snow-covered lawn all the way out to the street. And they were still coming.

Silent night, Mr. Joe.

I don't know why I looked up at that moment but I did, and on the porch of the chapel I saw Lucia Dodd being led in by Rev Scopes and others.

Lucia Dodd, I imagined, seeing her beauty endure through the somber black suit and veil she wore, was caught in between. Black she was and proudly so, yet I knew she'd absorbed too much of the white world outside Hunter County to be able to join in the chanting and singing, to cast herself into the joy like the rest of East Hunter. Part of me respected that, because it narrowed the gap between her world and mine, but part of me felt sorry for her, too.

Then she spotted me, or more likely the unmarked police cruiser. I lifted my hand. She was close enough to see me but she made no gesture in return. She looked very noble, I thought, as she watched me for a moment. Someone spoke to her. She nodded and accompanied the man to the entrance of the chapel. At the doors, she stopped, looked once again at me, then went inside.

I had a sudden, intensely erotic mind shot of her nude body in the snowy road to the Sloan farm, of her lacy underclothes.

Bobby's voice sounded on my radio: "'Preciate it, Sheriff." I looked over my shoulder and saw Bobby's cruiser pull up in the street before the chapel. I waved and drove away.

At the dungeon, a bleary-eyed Gruesome followed me stiffly inside. From Hap Morgan, the local vet, I knew Gruesome endured nearly continuous pain from his long-ago injuries. He never let it interfere with his love and enthusiasm, but it clearly affected him. It was why I let him drink as much as he did. The girls said hi to him, too, but he just gave them his kiss-my-ass growl. "He's hungover," I explained.

"Look like he ain't de only one," Milly mumbled as I walked by her.

A fire crackled in my office fireplace, which made me grateful the place had been a judge's chambers in the days the building was a courthouse. The room smelled of wood smoke. It was good.

Gruesome collapsed with a tired sigh on the hook rug by the fire. I felt like doing the same.

My head felt like an overpumped tire about to blow. I was massaging my shoulder and neck muscles when Cindy Barron breezed in. She carried a tray with hot chocolate and a glass pitcher of water, and, Lord, did she look good this morning. She wore suede boots and a plaid wool skirt and matching sweater. Her hair was done up, exposing the sweet back of her neck, which is one of—*one of*—my favorite parts of a woman. Oh Lordy, Lordy.

Cindy set the tray on my desk and gifted me with a lovely smile of straight white teeth. I reached for the chocolate, but she lightly slapped my hand. "First things first, Sheriff." She poured me a glass of water and plunked two Alka-Seltzers in it to fizz. God, her perfume was sweet.

Then she did the damndest thing. She stooped on her heels, facing me beside the hearth, to pour water in Gruesome's bowl. In so doing, her loose skirt draped to the floor beneath her. Her knees were demurely together, but nonetheless I had a marvelous view of her thighs, her bottom and the tender panty-covered part where her cunt, her thighs and her ass came together. It was by all appearances an accidental, unconscious display, except most grown women know exactly what they are displaying and when. When Cindy saw me looking, she made no effort to alter what I could see. Looking at her, and knowing she knew I was looking, was sexier than an outright strip. She poured the water slowly, talking lightly about the snow, then stood. She smiled again and left, unhurried.

I was a nervous wreck.

When I got enough blood out of my dick and back in my brain to think, I read the activity sheets. The results were back from the state lab on the pill bag from Ivy Joe's truck and the secretions in Cassie Shelor's underwear. They divulged nothing. Great. That fit right in with all the other nothings I had.

The autopsy report on Cassie contained photocopies of health records dating back to her birth, confirming that Cassie had indeed had a heart murmur. No tissue trauma, no pregnancy, no drugs. Her stomach, blood, hormone levels and bowel contents were all normal. Everything was normal, normal, normal. I was beginning to hate that word.

The plastic bag with all those boosters, which Pierce had found in the glove box of Ivy Joe's truck, had no fingerprints on it, according to the lab report. None? Not even Mr. Joe's?

Pierce came in for the morning briefing. He told me the computer had come back on Gina Turnrow, the little girl I ran off from Lois's tavern, confirming she had no record of arrests, besides possession of marijuana, for which she had drawn a suspended sentence. She was an NCIC-listed missing person but had gone home to her family and was looking for a legit job, according to a note from the Roane County Sheriff's office, which was pleased to be able to close its file on her. Sometimes, you win some.

I told Pierce about Lucia Dodd and the Sloans and asked him to send two men with the wrecker driver when they recovered her car. I told him to tell the deputies and the state police regulars that some leaning on the Sloans was in order, that they were beginning to get out of hand again and needed to be tightened up before somebody got hurt.

"There was some damage on the front of Lanny Sloan's pickup truck," I told Pierce.

"You think they killed Ivy Joe, Lewis?"

"I think they know something they're not telling. I can read it in them. Danny nearly pissed himself when I tried to connect them with Joe's death, but Lanny shut him up fast. They say they were on Saddle Mountain cutting wood at the time of death and never saw Joe. With no more to go on than we've got, it'll be hell to prove otherwise. Christ, we don't even know for certain he didn't just die by accident."

Pierce was as astounded as I had been by the news of Cassie Shelor's heart attack. He looked at the report.

"Well," he mumbled. "Heart murmur. At least we can eliminate murder there. That's a relief."

A little before eleven, I put on a white uniform shirt and tie and my dress uniform coat. I drove over to the Weeks's Funeral Home.

There were several parlors at Weeks's. It didn't take a detective to figure out which one Cassie Shelor was laid out in. At least a dozen weepy schoolgirls were consoling each other or were being manfully comforted by several boys. There were a number of out-of-towners in the crowded parlor as well as many locals. A white casket stood on a stand among floral pieces at one end of the room. In it rested the memorable body of Cassie Shelor. I removed my hat and paid a brief respect. Lawrence had plied his trade well and she looked as nice as a dead girl can look. I turned away quickly. I'd seen too many lifeless bodies already and I preferred my memories of Cassie to be those from her living room and Bram's Creek—a young, sensuous and vitally alive young beauty.

Helen Shelor was sitting among a group of relatives and friends, including Lawrence Weeks, at the opposite end of the parlor. She was appropriately dressed but her face looked like forty miles of bad road.

"Sheriff Cody," she said, taking my hand. "Thank you so much for coming."

"Certainly, Helen."

"Cassie thought so much of you, Sheriff Cody. She used to say how handsome you were and how you reminded her of her daddy."

Oh Jesus.

"I, ah, I was very fond of Cassie, too, Helen. She was a lovely girl and I'll miss her."

"She wasn't a bad girl, Sheriff. She always came home. Each time she left, she always came home. She wasn't a bad girl."

"I know, Helen, I know. All kids are troubled these days. It's the times we live in."

"Thank you, Sheriff, you're so kind."

I knelt down. "Helen, do you feel up to answering a couple of questions?"

"Whu . . . why? Cassie's poor heart failed her. She had a murmur, you know."

"Yes. There are a few things I'd like to ask you just to get them out of the way. Do you mind?"

"Oh. Well. Yes, I mean no, I don't mind."

I turned to Lawrence, who was listening intently. "Lawrence, I wonder if we could have the loan of your office?"

"Of course, Lewis! Right this way."

Charlene Watson helped Helen to Lawrence's plush office. Lawrence was clearly disappointed to be asked to wait outside. "Call me if you need me," Charlene said, and she turned to leave.

"Why don't you stay, Charlene?" I said. "Do you mind, Helen?"

"No, of course not." They sat on a couch, hand in hand.

"Helen," I said, watching her carefully, "why was Cassie at Lover's Overlook? What was she doing there?"

"I . . . I don't know, Sheriff Cody. Kids have been going there since before I was a young girl."

"But not alone. Who was Cassie . . . romantically involved with?"

Distress registered in Helen's face. "What are you saying, Sheriff Cody? Cassie was a good girl! She died of heart failure! Why are you asking me this?"

"Please, Helen, I'm only trying to tie up a few loose ends. Who was Cassie dating, in love with, seeing regularly?"

"Oh. Oh. I don't know. She didn't talk to me very much. I can't think of anybody she was . . . ah, involved with."

Charlene Watson spoke. "May I, Sheriff Cody?"

"Of course."

"Helen, honey, didn't you tell me that up until about, what, six months ago, Cassie dated many boys but that about . . . uh, May or so she just stopped dating altogether?"

"Yes! Well, I mean she didn't stop going out. In fact, she went out even more but never with anybody. No one ever came to pick her up like before; she just left in the car. When I asked her where she went, she always said to a girlfriend's or a movie in Christiansburg or just to be alone. Sometimes she was gone overnight. Said she was tired of dating boys. Didn't want to anymore."

# Shepherd of the Wolves

I leaned closer to Helen. "You told me yesterday morning Cassie had seemed troubled lately. 'Different' was the word you used. How?"

Helen frowned. "She never would say, Sheriff Cody. At first, she was very happy for months—happiest I've seen her since her daddy passed on. She even seemed to grow up so much in the way she acted. She used to say she felt like a woman at last. Then, about a week ago, she got real quiet, depressed like. Cried a lot. Wouldn't say why. Young girls are like that, Sheriff. Moody. Sometimes quiet. You know?"

I knew. Cassie Shelor was real quiet now.

The colored cemetery was on a bleak hillside in East Hunter. It was studded with several emaciated pines, that leaned painfully away from the wind that always blew up from the valley. Today, the wind blew cold and was peppered with new snowflakes.

Pierce had laid on additional deputies to help with the traffic that had greatly overrun the cemetery grounds and was lining both sides of the two streets approaching. Cars were backed up for a quarter of a mile and they were still coming. I heard a short chirp of siren and saw Billy escorting a panel truck stuffed with floral tributes through the throng making its way to graveside. Haskel Beale was shuttling old folks in from the parking areas. Old Ben Lomas, the black funeral director, looked worried. Between the massive crowd and the snow, he was in over his head and he knew it.

"Sheriff One? County." Milly's voice came over the county net.

"Sheriff One," I replied.

"Lewis, Otis say they ready to move Joe from the chapel to the cemetery."

"Ten-four."

I drove over to the chapel. Otis Clark was in uniform, of course. He and another of my black deputies, Thomas Bonner, were bearing the casket along with James Chilton, the county school-board supervisor, and three other men. They gently slid the casket into Ben Lomas's ancient but gleaming black hearse. Following, among a group of black women, was Lucia Dodd, composed, her head held high.

On the last long ride of Ivy Joe Culpepper's, Otis and Tom went in the lead marked cruiser and I brought up the rear. Passing motorists pulled to the side of the road and held their hats. Other people walked from their places of business to put single flowers on the slowly passing old black hearse. Some were obviously offering prayers. Some waved. Some cried.

The wind whistled and bit on the exposed hillside of the cemetery. The funeral was to be a record setter for attendance. There were at least a thousand whites standing quietly in the snow, in addition to about two hundred blacks, and more mourners were still pouring in. Mostly, they came in old but clean yeoman cars and pickup trucks, and they wore faded dresses or blue bib overalls with a necktie beneath the collar of a workshirt. One elderly white farmer even arrived on a tractor towing a wagon of hayrolls, in spite of the forbidding weather. Yet there were some elegantly dressed out-of-towners as well, black and white, in their Cadillacs and Mercedeses and Porsches bearing tags from as far away as Texas.

Hunter County was here to do Ivy Joe Culpepper proud.

How could Mr. Joe have been dealing drugs to children for the likes of Lois Ross? I wouldn't believe it. Not until irrefutable proof slapped me in the face would I believe it.

I parked and joined the throng. I could see Pete Floyd of the *Hunter Press* scurrying about with his cameras and tape recorder.

As the casket was borne from the hearse to the grave, waves of men's hats were removed. There was no sound under the clouds, save the mournful song of the autumn wind and the muffled sobs of some of the women.

Rev Scopes commended unto Jesus the remains of Ivy Joe Culpepper.

Somehow, I expected "Amazing Grace" or "Swing Low, Sweet Chariot," but the legend of Ivy Joe Culpepper had followed him to the grave. As Rev Scopes stepped back, a black woman about three feet wide, with a voice that could carry a note to Pluto and back, began to sing the only appropriate piece for this occasion.

*"Siiiiiiiiilent niiiiight . . . hooooooooly niiiiiight . . . Allll*

*is calm, allll is bright. Round yon virgin . . . mother and child . . . Hooooly Infant, so tender and mild . . ."*

She sang the exquisite hymn achingly slow, bearing each note forever with power and laser clarity. Women wept, men had pursed lips, tight faces and they dabbed at their eyes. I didn't dab mine. I just let the tears flow. Another original was gone and the world was a lesser place. Goodbye, Mr. Joe. I'll miss you, sir.

*"Sleeeep in heaaaaavenly peeee-eeace . . . Sleee-eep in heaaaavenly . . . peeeeeeeeeeace . . ."*

Snow fell heavy from the cold gray sky.

# 12

## Black and White

I didn't like the looks of the weather. We already had four inches of snow on the ground, and now as the funeral traffic dispersed, drivers were turning on headlights for the renewed heavy snowfall. I decided to get my truck in case the unusual snow got as bad as I suspected.

I drove from the cemetery to the dungeon and exchanged my dress coat for the bomber jacket. I collected Gruesome and drove up on Bram's Ridge to the house. Even with snow tires, I barely made it up the narrow, steep one-lane road.

I parked next to the big silver four-wheel-drive pickup truck and cranked it to let it warm. I took Gruesome in the house and fixed him a bowl of hamburger and oatmeal with raisins, one of his favorite dishes. He dived into it, sounding like elephants tap dancing in a swamp.

Moose, my mammoth horse, had retired to the barn, I noticed. She was such a magnificent animal. Even in her shaggy winter coat, her fine strong musculature was evident. I fed her, ran some water in her trough and shoveled out her stall. She nosed me in appreciation, nearly sending me sprawling. I didn't want her out with a winter storm building; it could turn very cold if a front passed in the night, so I closed the barn doors and slid bars into the braces to secure them.

I transferred my shotgun, rifle and ammunition to the

truck. It was already wired with a radio console and equipped with blue lights in the grill and on the dash.

The big Ford truck was a dinosaur. It was six years old and had an engine that bit gasoline pumps off at ground level, but it was powerful and very capable in this kind of weather. On the way to East Hunter to pick up Lucia Dodd, I radioed to Milly that I was back in service. "Sheriff One is ten-eight, Milly."

"Ten-fo', Sheriff One. Signal twenty-one."

That was odd. Signal twenty-one meant call the office by phone. I wondered what Milly had to tell me that she didn't want to put out over the radio, which, of course, was monitored by anyone with the interest and a commercially available receiver, such as any number of radio hobby freaks and Pete Floyd of the newspaper, among others.

I also wondered, as I drew up in front of the late Ivy Joe Culpepper's neat little house, if Lucia Dodd still intended to join me in the quest for what, if anything, really happened to her grandfather.

I left the truck rumbling and crunched through the falling snow for the small covered porch of Mr. Joe's home, which sat on a pampered quarter-acre lot surrounded by a white picket fence. As I reached out to knock on the door, it opened, and there stood Lucia Dodd.

I'd expected her to look haggard after the events of the previous day and this morning's funeral, but she was lovely, dressed in a loose Irish sweater, a long split riding skirt and, sensibly, calf-high leather snow boots. I was somewhat struck by her professionally business-like yet distinctly feminine impact, as I'd been the morning she entered my office. She reminded me of an English noblewoman out for a casual ride in the country, except there aren't many black English noblewomen I would suppose. Actually, a fine smooth brown, rather than black. Her hair was coal black, though, and was tied back in a bun secured by a thin yellow scarf. Her lips were a wet carmine. She carried a heavy hooded ski coat.

She looked at me with the expression the guards at The Tomb of the Unknown Soldier use, totally devoid of emotion.

It dawned on me I must have been staring at her for several seconds. Her unusual beauty was, for me, staggering.

"Ah. Ready to go?" I said, always one for clever repartee.

"Yes. Where?"

"To eat, first. I haven't had breakfast and I'm hungry. It'll give us a chance to compare notes."

"I wasn't aware you had any 'notes.'" She paused, eyeing the scratched, dented old truck grumbling in the road. "Are we going in that?" she asked coolly. She was clearly as underwhelmed by our transportation as she was with me.

"Oh, hell no, the limousine will be here any minute. Of course, we're *going in that*. We may be bumper deep in snow by nightfall and I don't fancy being stuck in a snowbank with—being stuck in a snowbank."

"'With me,' you were about to say." Her head was tilted forward so that she looked at me out of the tops of her eyes. Still no emotion. Considering the emotions she was capable of, maybe that was a good thing. She got into the truck and clunked the door shut.

Wonderful. Things were off to a ducky start.

"Put the seat belt on," I growled, buckling my own. She studied me for a moment as we drove off, then she snapped her belt.

We were a big hit at Lady Maude's Cafe. Back in the late fifties, Lady Maude fancied herself a one-woman civil rights advocate and went out of her way to invite blacks to eat at her place, and a few still did, regularly, but most of Hunter's black community ate in East Hunter at the Bean and Rib. Everybody just seemed to prefer it that way. Additionally, Lady Maude's Cafe was the undisputed Cheyenne Mountain command center for North American gossip. Consequently, when the sheriff strolled in during the lunch rush with that rich nigger gal from D.C. who was rumored to be the illegitimate granddaughter of the late Ivy Joe Culpepper, the entire joint went into a tight-assed freeze. Having eagerly anticipated the same all morning long, I put my hand affectionately on Lucia Dodd's waist—which astonished her beyond reaction—and gave everybody a smug grin that plainly said suck on *this* a while, you motor-mouthed busybodies. I hoped there would not be any fires or other local emergencies in the next half hour because the antiquated Hunter County telephone system was going into massive overload in about five minutes.

Old Adelle Sowers waited on us with all the hustle of a slug on Valium. "Afternoon, Sheriff," she grunted at me, eyeing Lucia Dodd suspiciously. Adelle really was forty years out of sync with the civil rights movement and would doubtless die that way.

"Hello, Adelle!" I crowed, still richly enjoying the spectacle. "I'd like you to meet my sister, Lucia; Sis, this is Adelle Sowers, fastest waitress east of the Pecos."

Lucia nodded at Adelle and looked icily at me. Adelle was obviously confused as to whether she should sing or dance at this point. Oh, it was rich. "Uh. Heh, heh, uh-hum" was Adelle's snappy comeback. She stumbled through taking our orders and hobbled away.

"That little witticism was in poor taste," Lucia observed. "Further, it probably cost you a vote in the next election."

"I thought it was funny as hell. I didn't get elected the first two times by running on the kiss-ass ticket, and if that ever becomes necessary, I'll just lose. Meanwhile, I'll do the job and behave the way I want to. Besides, so far I'm running unopposed, and, furthermore, ol' Adelle probably won't live long enough to get back with my lunch, let alone vote in the next election."

"Speaking of doing your job, what have you done about my grandfather?"

"So far, all I've done is help Hunter County give him a slam-bang send-off, but, then, modern law-enforcement miracles take time. Listen, there's something you may as well know right now. We found over three-hundred controlled amphetamines in a plastic bag in Mr. Joe's old truck."

Lucia stared at me over her coffee cup. "So?"

"So it appears there's a possibility he might have been selling drugs for Lois Ross, a local flophouse operator we've long suspected of a number of nefarious activities in the county."

"That's absurd and insulting to my grandfather's memory!"

"Then you tell me what a bag full of uppers was doing in his glove box when he went off Saddle Mountain."

She paused, thinking. When she spoke, her reply was hard. "I don't believe there was, Sheriff Cody. I strongly suspect that, when I made it obvious to you I would not permit you to sweep my grandfather's murder under your lumpy rug, you invented that alleged drug possession to discredit him and dissuade me from pressing the matter."

Boy, what a lightning romance we were having. "It's in the report which, you may remember, was already on my desk before you ever showed up," I said tersely, chapped at her accusation.

"So you say."

"Come on, Miss Dodd! Why would I—"

"Sheriff Cody! My grandfather was no drug pusher! And I resent your assertion to the contrary!"

"Jesus Christ, *Ms.* Dodd! How'd you ever get into a respected law firm? By being the token woman and/or black? I'm talking *evidence* here! You're talking sheer emotion. You gonna do this as an attorney or as a doting granddaughter?"

"How dare you question my credentials! If you were such a legal eagle yourself, you'd hardly be a common paper hanger up here in, in, Hunter County!"

"In the 'bastion of white ignorance'?"

"If the shoe fits, wear it!"

Our conversation was flowing like the frozen discharge from an airliner lavatory.

"Listen, lady!"

"No, *you* listen!"

"Coffeeeee?" Adelle sang pleasantly.

Lucia Dodd and I sulked while Adelle poured coffee for her and hot chocolate for me. A long silence passed after Adelle fairly flew to the kitchen to alert the world that the sheriff and the fancy-dressed nigger woman were having a fight!

"We ain't gonna accomplish much like this," I said finally.

More silence.

She sighed. "Your observation as to my objectivity with regard to my grandfather's death is well taken," she admitted.

"Hot damn. That's better. When you start using fifteen words to say what ordinary folks say in three I know the lawyer in you is coming out at last."

I smiled. She didn't.

In a moment, she said, "I am simply not prepared to believe my grandfather could have been involved with anything illegal or anyone 'nefarious.' It just wasn't his style."

"At last we arrive at a point upon which we can heartily agree. Please try to keep in mind I loved the old man, too, and I had only the highest respect for him. But . . . my deputy *did* find those pills in his truck. Furthermore, I must tell you we have witnesses who place him at Lois Ross's establishment often and recently." I expected another tirade but instead she only studied me through the steam rising from her coffee.

Adelle brought our food. I watched, fascinated, as Adelle's quivering hands set each item on the table without spilling anything; it took her a solid minute.

We ate in silence for a while, Lucia sitting bolt upright, one hand in her lap, with grace and poise. I wondered how she got from East Hunter to her present level of sophistication.

I told Lucia about the revelations gleaned from Stout's wrecker driver and from Otis Clark's friend, Cletus, about Joe being at Saddle Mountain Lodge. I also told her what Cletus told Otis about the threats made against Joe by the Sloans, but I didn't elaborate on their motive, which was supposed to be a result of some mysterious involvement Joe had with the Sloan daughter, Peggy. I deemed it prudent to let Lucia absorb the pill bag story a while before raising any allegation that the poor old guy had been a drooling pedophile *and* a drug lord.

"I've got to call my office," I said, suddenly remembering Milly's signal-twenty-one call. I went to the pay phone on the wall by Lady Maude's antique brass cash register, which sounded like a train wreck every time it rang up a bill. *CHING! CHANG!*

"Lewis!" Milly said. "Dat Ross woman, she called here about a hour ago. Say she got somethin' to show you."

"Show me? What would Lois Ross have to show me that ain't already been seen by half the men east of the Mississippi?"

Milly chuckled. "Don't know, Lewis, she wouldn't say. But she say it done got somethin' to do with Ivy Joe's death."

Hmmm, I thought. "Great, Milly. We're up to our asses in snow and related problems, and now Lois wants to do show and tell. Well, hell. Where's Pierce?"

"Busy."

"Haskel?"

"Busy."

"Bobby?"

"Busy, Lewis—"

"Billy? Otis? Tom Bonner? What the hell, Milly, did my whole damn department resign? Who's available to back me up?"

"They all on traffic calls, Lewis! Everybody be out celebratin' the first snow by wreckin' they cars! The deputies be workin' all over this eight-hundred-square-mile mountain county. They ain't out dining no outa-town smartass city girl at Lady Maude's."

"Well, fuck it. I'll go out there anyway and see what she wants to show me."

"You watch yo' ass, white boy. Dat bitch traffic with some evil folk."

"Yeah she *is* an evil folk. I'll be careful, don't worry. Besides, I got a partner with me."

"Who? Dat wormy little dog? He ain't gonna help you hol' off a saloon full a' drunk rednecks."

"No. Gruesome's at home sobering up. I'm talking about Lucia Dodd."

"Dat little lawyah niggah?! Sheeeyit."

"Quit worrying, Milly. Who's gonna be at Lois's in all this snow?"

"De abomabul snowman, das who! Go on then, Lewis. I'll send someone to back you soon as they come clear. Be careful!"

I left Adelle a fat tip. Anyone waiting tables at sixty-plus has earned one. Lucia, I noticed, also left a sizable tip. She insisted on paying her half of the tab. I didn't argue.

# Shepherd of the Wolves

"I got a lead!" I announced to Lucia.

"Well. Move over Charlie Chan," she replied. I couldn't tell how she meant that.

We stopped twice on the way out to Saddle Mountain Lodge to chain cars out of ditches. The snow kept coming, quiet but heavy. It was going to be a blessed day for area body shops.

As we drove, I gave Lucia some background on Lois Ross. She asked me what Ivy Joe had told me about her the day he died. Nothing, I answered, he just said the name. I told her of Pierce's vague suspicion that the truck might have been pushed through the guardrail. I emphasized, however, there wasn't a shred of hard proof to support the suspicion; it was only an experienced lawman's hunch. There was no real evidence upon which we could rule out a simple accident.

"Sheriff Cody," Lucia Dodd said, staring out the steamed glass in her door at the passing snow-blanketed woods, "would you agree it is a fair statement to say that my grandfather was a licensed, practicing automobile driver in these mountains for at least fifty years?"

"Yes."

"And do you know that in all that time, over half a century, he never had a single traffic accident?"

"Sure. It's in Pierce's report. The motor-vehicle division has no record of Mr. Joe even receiving so much as a parking ticket."

"Then doesn't it seem odd to you that he should die carelessly, in broad daylight, driving off a dry clear road he'd traveled all his life?"

"Miss Dodd, that is something that nags at me and my chief deputy, too, but, A., it's possible, and B., it brings us to the grand question: Why would anybody have wanted to kill Ivy Joe Culpepper?"

Lucia looked at me with her huge dark brown eyes. She sniffed derisively. "Since when does a 'nigger' need a legitimate reason to get himself killed in this country? Thousands in this nation have died just because they were black."

"Aw, horse shit," I responded, maybe a little too emphatically. "Spare me the ethnic self-pity. I went to high school here when the schools integrated. There was not one incident in this whole county, not so much as a name calling. The black kids just showed up one year and kept to themselves. The whites mostly ignored them. Orderly, nonviolent integration just happened, here and in most of the rest of America. Nowhere in the records of this county is there anything to substantiate a racially motivated murder," up to now at least, I refrained from saying. "I don't buy the ethnically paranoid notion that somebody just motored merrily along County Twelve looking for a stray 'nigger' to shove off the road. 'What'd you do today Lem?' 'Oh, nothing much, hon, just the usual, got some gas, picked up some fence wire at the hardware store and, oh, yeah, I found a real live nigger so of course I bulldozed him off the decent white man's mountain he was smelling up.' That's tripe, Lucia. In fact, it's racist tripe. It suggests whites are murderers just because they're white."

"What about the Sloans?" she asked, fixing me again with those lovely soft eyes.

"Christ, I never said there were no racists in this county. Hell, some of them reside in deepest darkest East Hunter. I just said this isn't a racist county. There's a difference."

"I was a few years behind you, Sheriff Cody, but I went to school in this county also until I was fifteen years old. There may never have been any racial violence during integration here but we were certainly not welcomed with open arms. The hate, the condescension—it was all there. When I told my lily-white guidance counselor at Hunter County High School that I wanted to pursue a pre-college curriculum, she peered at me over her glasses and smirked. She smirked! 'Come now, Lucia,' she told me. 'Let's do be serious, dear.'"

"You know that cafe where we just ate?" I replied. "Food was damn good, huh? Well it's owned and operated by, and is the sole support for, an elderly widow named Lady Maude Harris. Back in the late fifties, only a year after she became a young widow with three kids to feed and no insurance, and in a time when the courthouse had three restrooms: men, women and 'colored,' Lady Maude, who is as white as all that snow, incidentally, showed up in front of the courthouse one Saturday and started passing out menus for her recently opened restaurant. The curious thing, people began to note, was that she was giving them to, oh-my-God, niggers, too! When she was asked by then mayor Albert Burns why she was handing out expensive menus to, 'you know, them,' she answered, 'Why not, Mayor? Niggers got to eat, too!' Mayor Burns pointed out to Lady Maude that such a gesture might motivate the, uh, 'decent' folks in town to eat elsewhere, something that could be the kiss of death to a struggling new small business on the square like Lady Maude's Cafe. 'Albert,' Lady Maude replied. 'Read the papers! Watch TV! Times are changing. Colored folks has been done wrong and it's time to fix it. I'm just doing my part. Now get out of my way!' All this is in the archives of the *Hunter Press*, by the way; the editor is a friend of mine, sort of. Anyway, it was a few days before an old black woman ambled into Lady Maude's one morning and, holy-shit-Lem, that nigger wasn't applying for a job in the kitchen—she was here to eat! Lady Maude served her personally like she was the Queen of England. Several of her regulars walked out and both her waitresses quit. She ran the place single-handed for several desperate weeks when it looked like she would fold. The bank, naturally, wasn't the least interested in extending her capital loan till things settled down, and Lady Maude damn near went under. But you know what happened in the end? People—black people and white people—just got hungry for good food and apparently asked themselves why race should keep them from a fine Southern meal. Finding no satisfactory answer for this question, they just said to hell with all this racial bullshit, I'm hungry. And slowly, one by one, they drifted back to the cafe. Today people drive all the way up here from Roanoke to eat supper."

Lucia Dodd stared at me briefly as I stopped talking, then turned her face away to look again out the window. Good thing. I was going to wreck the truck if I didn't pay more attention to the road and less to that beautiful face.

"And now, as Paul Harvey says, for the 'rest of the story.'" I looked to see if she was listening and found her watching me from the sides of those luscious eyes. "A year prior to all this, Lady Maude's husband, and the father of her three children not coincidentally—a farmer named Joshua Harris—went to Christiansburg one day to pick up a plow disc that had come in at the rail depot. On the way back, he saw two men standing by their car with the hood up, and he stopped to offer them a ride. The men shot Josh Harris in the face, took his clothes, money and truck and ran, leaving him naked and bleeding to death on the side of the road. Virginia State Troopers caught them near the North Carolina line, killing one in a shootout. Two days earlier, they had killed a teller while holding up a bank in Pennsylvania. Lady Maude sat through the trial of the remaining suspect who admitted that Josh Harris offered to give them what they wanted, that they'd just killed him for fun. The suspect raised a fist in a black leather glove to the courtroom. 'When the revolution come,' the transcript says he told the prosecutor, 'the Brothers is gonna rise up and kill all you whitebread motherfuckers!' "

We rode silently over the deepening snow.

We passed the gatehouse at the turnoff to Saddle Mountain Lodge. I noticed that Lois had posted no sentry today and there were no tracks spoiling the fresh snow in the long drive to the lodge. Those were good signs. The snow was hurting business.

"Now listen," I told Lucia Dodd. "You stay in the truck up here till I get back."

"Not on your life. I intend to meet this Ross woman head on and find out once and for all what, if any, connection she may have had with my grandfather."

"Wrong. You stay in the truck, period. You'll be about as welcome up here as a rabid badger. With you present, she isn't going to tell me shit about Joe's death. I promise you I'll tell you everything I learn but you stay in the truck. *Comprende?*"

Lucia pursed one corner of her mouth, drew a deep breath and let it out slowly. She nodded.

We proceeded up the drive to Saddle Mountain Lodge. Though there were some vehicles in the woods by the rental cottages, there were none in the lodge parking lot. Another good sign. I parked out of view to the side and left the truck running with Lucia inside. I then crunched through the snow to the front of the lodge, thinking whatever Lois Ross had to show me, it better be good.

I clumped across the broad porch and shoved open one of the heavy front doors. Instantly, a fist the size of a hamhock seized me by the front of my bomber jacket and yanked me inside like a rag doll.

# 13

~

## Oops

Complacency is the deadliest enemy of a lawman. Even the most professional cop falls victim to it sometime; I had to pick today. No sentry, no cars out front, no tracks, a snowy, quiet, broad daylight; who needed backup to call on a burned-out old floozy?

Another deadly enemy of the lawman is a gorilla like the one who helped me through Lois's front door, slamming it behind me. He was huge but, worse, he knew what he was doing. He took me off guard in the darkness, fast, and had jerked my gun from its holster while I was on my way to the dirty walnut floor of Saddle Mountain Lodge. I got had in a New York minute.

I got to my feet slowly, my eyes adjusting to the relative darkness in the barroom. The guy who took me was about Pierce's size and wore custom-cut hair and a suit with no tie. He looked like a studio wrestler coming home from church. He was pretty proud of himself, but most of his smirk was hidden behind his massive mustache. He impudently twirled my SigSauer nine millimeter around his finger—that was a good sign because it meant he was a fool with guns, which probably meant he was a beater, not a shooter. That was not exactly comforting news, given that fists his size could kill you as dead as bullets when correctly applied. I hoped that, if the pistol went off, it was pointed at him when it did.

# Shepherd of the Wolves

The other signs were not so thrilling. There were two other night creatures with him, also out-of-towners I'd never seen. There was Lois's black bartender behind the bar polishing glasses like he was all alone. Several of Lois's working girls were seated randomly about the bar and the booths bordering the dance hall, some smoking and grinning as though they were having a good time, others staring morosely at the floor. And standing nearby in jeans, a shiny blue Western blouse, cowboy boots and enough war paint to decorate a tribe of Sioux—looking just real pleased with herself—was Lois Ross.

"Well," I said, "I guess you're all wondering why I called you here today."

"Yeah, that's good, smartass," Lois snapped. "We'll see how cute you are when I'm done with you today. I warned you about fucking with me, Cody. I owe you, and today you get paid, big time."

I looked at her. "You enjoy yourself, Lois. You better have the time of your life, 'cause when you're 'done' with me, dead or alive, Pierce Arroe and my deputies will plow you and this whole place in lime. Depend on it."

Lois cackled like the Wicked Witch of the West in *The Wizard of Oz.* "Sheeeyit, Cody, they can be handled just like you! Remember the good Councilman Arnie Dreyfuss of Roanoke you smarted off to the other day, Sheriff? Well, motherfucker, he remembers you!" She cackled again and lighted herself a cigarette. I noticed her hands were trembling. Rage? Fear? Excitement?

Lois blew rancid blue smoke at me. "Cody, I'd like you to meet three of Councilman Dreyfuss's associates here. That's Jack there, with *your* gun!" A couple of Lois's tramps giggled and sucked at their stinkweeds. "And over here is Chick, and that's Larry. They're here to fix your little red wagon."

"I'm just so pleased to meet you fat faggots."

The smug smiles evaporated from the faces of Lois's contract help. "Hey, motherfucker!" Jack growled, striding quickly toward me. "You talk pretty damn cute for a son of bitch who's gonna spend the rest of his life in a fuckin' wheelchair!" He raised a mammoth fist and the other two moved toward me.

"Not yet, goddamn it!" Lois screeched. "Not till I tell you! Not till I tell you!" She walked up to me, quivering with rage and hate. "When I'm done with you, mother-*fucker!* When I'm done with you, you gonna need a nurse-maid just to take a shit!"

Lois's goons stood near and postured tough. Some of the girls tittered and looked on like wide-eyed gawkers at a bloody car wreck. One girl, sitting in a booth across the dance floor, got up and walked to the stairs leading up to the rooms off the circular balcony. "I don't want no part of this shit," she said nervously. "Me, neither," said another and followed. Still another stood quietly, then went up the stairs.

Lois shot them a furious glance and then turned back to me, now breathing rapidly. She aimed her lipstick-stained cigarette at my face. "I been waitin' a long time for this day, Cody. I figured Arnie Dreyfuss would know somebody who could tighten your smart ass up, and he did, and he was just thrilled to do it. Now you gonna find out what it costs to fuck with Lois Ross!"

"Like Ivy Joe Culpepper found out, Lois? Did you hire these cocksuckers to hit Joe, too, or did you kill him yourself?"

Lois's ugly face twisted like a prune. "I ain't got *shit* to say to you about that, Cody!"

I could see big Jack peeling off his suit coat and laying my gun on the bar. Chick and Larry were spreading their feet in position.

Soon.

I was going down hard; that was clear. The only options open involved how much damage I could do before they got me. My heart was thumping. I knew bone breakers when I saw them. Jack now stood slightly to my left front beside Lois, who was directly before me. Chick was at my left rear and Larry was on my right. These guys did this kind of thing for a living. I'd have to move first and fast to have a prayer.

I looked Lois hard in the face with my best wolf-eyed stare. Come on Clint, I said to myself, don't fail me now. To Lois I said, "Listen, you mule-faced old whore, you tell your baboons to do their thing and do it good but do it *now!*

Otherwise, I'm going to your phone and call my people, and we *will* settle accounts."

Lois's hate-fueled rage was building fast. "Tough guy, huh? By God, we'll *see* how tough you are!"

"Say, Lois, you heard from your lover boy lately? I mean the one I pitched through your bedroom window a few years ago. You remember."

Lois blew out. Her face shriveled like burning plastic. "You bastard!" She hissed, trembling. "Always the motherfucking *smartass!*" Suddenly, she stabbed at my eye with the cigarette. I wasn't expecting that move and was a nanosecond late jerking my head back. The cigarette sizzled into the sweat of my cheek. That's it, folks. Showtime.

I openhanded Lois in the side of her head and she flew into Jack, who was caught off guard. I kicked Larry, on my right, hard in the stomach. He grunted and staggered back, gripping his gut. I set my feet, spread and stiffened the fingers of my right hand and put all my weight behind a thrust at Jack's fury-widened eyes. He saw it just a hair too late, and though he jerked his head, my ring and little fingers harpooned him solid in his right eye. He roared like a stuck bear, clutched his face, careened backward and fell over a chair, crashing to the floor and scattering other furniture. Lois lay on the floor holding her head and howling like a brat. There were startled squeals from a few of Lois's girls.

I had not forgotten the third stooge, Chick, but all this had gone down in little over a second and I couldn't get them all at once. Chick hit me with his fist in the back of my head. I stumbled forward, tripped over the prone and squawling Lois and fell to the floor. Now Chick and Larry were all over me. I fought to gain my feet and almost did, but from somewhere came someone's pointy-toed cowboy boot which torpedoed me in the ribs. I couldn't move. I couldn't get a breath. I was hauled to my feet and held at each arm. When I opened my eyes, Jack was staggering toward me like a cyclops, blood flowing from one closed eye, and, friends and neighbors, he was not a happy camper. He drew back to give my dentist a vacation in Bermuda. I threw up both feet and kicked him hard in the chest. He backpedaled and fell over the very same chair and revisited the floor. I suspect he shared a learning curve with Lanny Sloan. My weight threw the other two goons off balance; one dropped me and I pulled the other to the floor with me. Assorted blows rained on me. They snatched me back up and pinned my arms behind me.

"Hold him!" Jack screamed. "Hold that son of a bitch!" My wrists rose up around my shoulder blades. Jack made another run on me. I pitched up to kick again, but he was ready this time; he stayed out of range until my feet fell, then he nailed me dead under the sternum. That's all folks. There was nothing left in me. A jolting blow hit me in the side of my face and I could no longer see clearly.

Now things began to get rude. They dragged me out into the dance hall and threw me on my back on a pool table. I got some of my vision back in time to see them rush up, each with a pool cue gripped by the small end. Here it comes, I thought, wishing I at least had enough strength to resist.

"Git him!" Lois yowled. "Git that motherfucker!"

One-eyed Jack stepped up and loomed over me, bleeding from his eye and consumed with rage. "Now you son of a bitch! The goddamn party is over for you!" He whipped the cue up high over his head and then the whole place sounded as if a bomb had gone off in it.

There were piercing screams and startled cries of "Holy *shit!*" Splinters of wood and pieces of brass and glass rained down all over the room. Suddenly, it got quiet as a tomb in the Saddle Mountain Lodge.

For there, standing by the bar, holding my smoking shotgun was Lucia Dodd, by God! I was never so glad to see anybody in my whole life.

I climbed down off the pool table with some difficulty. I would have laughed with joy if I could have. Everyone in the joint was frozen, gawking at Lucia Dodd in horror. The penultimate redneck nightmare, a 'nigger' woman with a shotgun.

What was left of the decimated old wagon-wheel chandelier, which was hung from the dance-hall ceiling, now swung, creaking overhead, casting moving shadows about the room.

# Shepherd of the Wolves

Finally Lois, who now stood leaning weakly on her old-fashioned jukebox, her hair rumpled and her shirttail hanging out, cried, "Who in the hell is *that?!*" Poor Lois. Things just weren't working out the way she'd envisioned them.

I walked painfully toward Lucia, staying out of the line of fire. "That's my new deputy, Herman," I croaked. "He dresses kind of funny but he's hell with a shotgun."

*"Whaat?!"* Lois was shorting out on all circuits. Her sense of humor was somewhat diminished at this point. Instinctively, she must have been sensing that a time of reckoning was drawing very near.

I could straighten up by the time I reached Lucia. I grinned at her gorgeous face and said, "What took you so long, Toots? Give me that thing." She handed me the shotgun. I racked another round into it and handed it back to her. "If any of these fucks moves, Herman, you blow 'em in half. That includes the witch by the jukebox."

I got my gun from the bar and holstered it. The bartender was cautiously getting up from the floor.

I went back to Lucia and took the shotgun. "Go out to the truck and look under the seat, Herman. There's a box of heavy plastic cable ties there. Bring it in here, please." She walked briskly out the door.

I surveyed the stunned assemblage. Lois looked like she'd just swallowed an outhouse leech.

*"Hey,* you maggots!" I yelled. "Guess who's coming to dinner!"

Larry and Chick now prudently let their pool cues slide from their hands and rattle to the floor. They glanced at Jack for desperately needed leadership. For his part, One-Eyed Jack was looking like the only guy in the chainsaw fight who just ran out of gas. He still held his cue elevated over his head in the adios-motherfucker position. I walked to a point just outside his reach and sighted the masterblaster on his remaining functional eye. "Use it or lose it, Jack," I said. He dropped the cue like it had suddenly burned him. He was a little slow on the uptake, but he wasn't entirely retarded. I faked to hit him with the shotgun stock. On reflex, he threw up both arms to deflect it, and I kicked him stoutly and upward in his crotch. He collapsed in a fetal heap, stoically, understanding there were now dues to pay. A low hollow groan seeped out of him.

I turned to Chick and Larry, whose eyes suddenly got real big. "Now just a minute, Sh—Sheriff!" Chick said, backing up.

"Face down on the floor, now," I said. They both did carrier landings.

Overhead from the balcony, I heard a door open and I threw up the shotgun. One of the three whores who had gone upstairs blanched and screamed. "Get down here," I said, "now!" Slowly they came down the stairs.

"The rest of you debutantes hit the floor," I ordered, "on your front sides for a change." None of them moved—they peered nervously at each other. I seized one by her hair and sent her sprawling onto the floor. "That was an order, not an invitation, damn it! *Move!*" They all got awkwardly to the floor and lay facedown. "Yeah!" I said. "What happened to all the smirks and grins, ladies? You nuns were sure happy enough when I was getting my career altered."

Lucia returned with the box of cable wraps. I exchanged the shotgun for them and began tying hairy wrists together behind backs.

Then, in the distance, I heard several sirens growing nearer. I glanced at Lucia Dodd, but I doubted she had called on my radio, since she had elected to take a more direct role. I looked at the three girls descending the stairs, and one of them looked back at me and then down at her toes. It was her, bless her heart! She must've called my office when the trouble started. I would remember that.

Lois was watching me. She was real worried and that was very appropriate.

Sirens screamed up out front and car doors thumped. The front doors exploded open and Pierce Arroe stormed in, covering the room with his shotgun. Haskel, Billy, Otis and a young Virginia State Trooper I knew named Boyce Calder followed like the marines coming ashore.

"Jesus, Lewis," Pierce said, peering curiously at Lucia Dodd. "Are you okay?"

"Oh, yeah, I'm just peachy keen. Thanks for the company. These three assholes were about to qualify me for handicapped tags when Herman here killed the chandelier. Otis?"

"Yeah, Lew?"

"Ya'll take these three guys outside. Be gentle now, hear?"

"Why sure, Lew, we treat these fine gentmuns with velvet gloves, don't chu know." Whereupon Otis and Haskel heaved Jack to his feet and propelled him into the front doors so hard they blew back and Jack went headfirst down the split-log steps into the snow. Caught up in the festive atmosphere, Trooper Calder and Billy dragged Chick and Larry to the porch and heaved them yowling onto Jack, who was really having a bad day.

Otis and Haskel returned. I collared Otis. "Run these girls off with instructions that they no longer work here or anywhere else in Hunter County, but go soft on the three by the stairs; one of them dropped the dime on me, I believe."

When the girls and the bartender were herded out, I gave Lois a menacing look to maintain her apprehension. She backed gingerly across the room toward the kitchen. To Lucia Dodd, I whispered, "Listen, everything you are about to see is an act. Just watch and don't interfere." She looked at me solemnly. Damn, she was a lady of few words.

I gave Lois the wolf eyes. "Pierce," I said grimly, "be a nice guy. Take Miss Dodd outside . . . and close the doors behind you."

"What?" Lois croaked. "Now wait just a minute!"

"Shut up!" I shouted. Lois jumped. "Beat it, Pierce. Take her with you." I nodded at Lucia.

Pierce took his cue from our code, "nice guy," and fell into the role.

"But, Sheriff!" he said, melodramatically, "you can't—"

"The hell I can't!"

"Can't *what?*" Lois shrilled.

I walked at Lois. "You made another real big mistake today, woman. This is the second time you hired somebody to put me to sleep."

"Goddamn it, I want my lawyer!"

"Sheriff!" Pierce called with Oscar-winning alarm.

"Get out! Both of you! This cutthroat bitch is *mine!*" I grabbed Lois by the hair and dragged her stumbling across the floor toward the kitchen.

"Stop him!" Lois shrieked. "I got my rights! I want to—aaaah!"

I shoved her into the kitchen. She turned a high-heeled cowboy boot and fell against a stainless-steel rack of pots and pans. They clattered down and she fell among them howling like a scalded cat. I dragged her out by the foot, roaring and trying to look as deranged as I could.

One of the steel sinks was full of dirty dishwater. I grabbed Lois up, stuffed her head under the soapy gray water and held it. She kicked like a beetle on its back. I yelled and beat the sink with a large serving spoon. When I pulled her out, she choked and screamed like grim death.

I bellowed in her ear, "You murdered Ivy Joe Culpepper!" Then I stuffed her head back in the water. Her feet thrashed the air and her arms flailed about, knocking cookware onto the floor. I jerked her out of the water, her wet hair slinging back a stream of suds. "Murderer!" I yelled.

"No! Jesus! God! I swear I didn't kill him! I swear to God I—"

Splash.

Thrash.

Gurgle.

"Haak! Cuhg! Ah-huhg! Oh God, no!" Lois screamed. "I didn't kill him, I swear! Please—"

"You lying bitch! He was seen out here! He said your name when he died!"

I suddenly saw a gift from heaven, one of those genuine horror-movie meat cleavers! I snatched it up. "You killed Ivy Joe Culpepper! Now it's your turn!" Alfred Hitchcock would have been proud of me.

"Aaaaaaaaaaaaah!" Lois was getting hoarse.

Right on cue, Pierce ran in between us. "No, Sheriff, wait! Maybe I can get her to tell us about Ivy Joe!"

"She won't talk!" I yelled and lunged at Lois with the cleaver. Pierce convincingly struggled to restrain me. "She won't talk!"

"Yes I will! Yes I will!"

"She won't talk!" I swished at the air with the cleaver.

"Yes I will! I swear to God I will!"

Pierce heaved me back and held up his hand like he was warding off Dracula with a cross.

"Lady, you listen to me!" Pierce whispered urgently to Lois. "I don't know how much longer I can hold him off! If you know anything about Ivy Joe Culpepper, you better make words fast."

"I didn't . . . I didn't kill him." Lois gasped, fighting for breath.

Pierce took Lois by the neck with a giant hand and pulled her close to his face. "Don't you give me no bullshit, woman, or, so help me God, I'll just walk right out of here and leave you to the sheriff!" He released her and she sat down hard on the wet floor.

"I swear to you . . . I didn't kill him." Lois glanced at me with fear.

Pierce said, "I'm warning you, Lois, he was seen out here. We got witnesses."

"Yes! He was here! I admit that."

"You better admit a lot more than that, and fast. What the hell was he doing out here? Was he dealing for you?"

Lois looked at Pierce with shock. She glanced at me as though amazed and released a nervous laugh. "Ivy Joe Culpepper dealin' for me? Are you nuts? That ol' nigger never broke a law in his whole damn life!"

"We found some of your pills in his truck!" I said.

Lois's eyes widened and she licked her lips. Mascara streaks trailed down her cheeks. "Now wait a minute! I don't got no idea what you found but it wadn't nothin' of mine!"

"Three hundred controlled uppers! You want to bet we can't turn this place and find some just like them?"

"It's a frame! They're trying to frame me!"

"They?" Pierce demanded. "Who?"

"Lanny Sloan! The Sloan brothers!"

Ah-ha. Velly interlisting, Charlie Chan would have said.

"Bullshit! Why would the Sloans want to frame you?"

"We done some . . . business together. It . . . ah, didn't work out and they were pissed at me."

"Out of the way, Pierce!" I said, gripping the cleaver. "She's stalling us with bullshit!"

"You ain't gonna kill me with that thing!" Lois said, regaining some of her brass. She was beginning to suspect a play.

I jumped forward suddenly, raised the cleaver high and drove it down hard into the wooden floor between her spread thighs. It hit with a jarring thunk about three inches from her professional inventory, and Lois turned white. I had finally gotten through to Lois Ross.

I leaned over and whispered hot in her ear, "Headline in tomorrow's *Roanoke Times:* 'Hunter County Tavern Operator Killed While Assaulting Sheriff with Meat Cleaver!'"

"You're fuckin' crazy!" Lois squeaked.

"'Lois Ross, a known local police character, enraged at the failure of an attempt upon the life of Hunter County Sheriff Lewis Cody by thugs in her hire, assaulted the sheriff with a meat cleaver yesterday afternoon!'"

"No!" Lois was losing it. "You're insane!"

I drew my pistol and placed the heavy black muzzle on the bridge of her nose. "'In the struggle, Sheriff Cody *shot and killed Ross!*'"

"Get him away from me!" Lois pleaded, trembling, looking cross-eyed down the tube of death on her nose. She turned her ear from my mouth. I jerked it back.

"'Ms. Ross was a prime suspect in the recent murder of longtime Hunter County resident Ivy Joe Culpepper.'"

"No!" Lois was weeping now. "No, please. I didn't kill him!" She sobbed. "I swear to—"

"'Funeral services for the late Ms. Ross are unannounced,'" I hissed in her ear.

"No!" Lois wept, exhausted, broken. "Please. I swear to God I didn't kill him. I don't know nothin' about no pills on him. It's Lanny Sloan trying to hang it on me. They been stealin' cars and alterin' the serial numbers. They stripped some of them in the woods off County Nine near Lover's Overlook. I was sellin' some of the stereos and shit for 'em, and I know a guy who can counterfeit car titles. We had a thing goin'! Lanny wanted to up his cut and I told him to go fuck himself. He told me he'd get even. He seen Joe out here once. Lanny *was* dealin' for me! He had plenty of pills. He musta put them pills on Joe. He said he was gonna kill Joe anyway! Somethin' about his girl, Peggy. That's all I know! I swear to God that's all I know! Lanny musta done it." Lois sobbed, shaking. Her nose ran. Her wet hair hung in her eyes. "I swear that's all I know! Don't kill me. Please . . . don't kill me." Lois was lost in tears.

I took Lois's face in my hand and made her look at me. "A few loose ends, Lois."

She wept, ruined.

"Listen to me!" I demanded. "Why was Joe out here and why did he say your name when he died?"

Lois was almost useless by now. "Let me up!" she cried. "Let me up. In my apartment. I'll show you . . . I'll show you why he said my name."

Pierce and I helped Lois to her feet. She staggered, sobbing, from the devastated, wrecked kitchen past the bar and across the dance floor to the hall leading to her private rooms.

Lucia Dodd stood by the bar with her arms crossed, staring at me in an odd way. I nodded at her to follow us.

Lois led us through her office and into her inner sanctum, a stale-smelling but surprisingly well-decorated apartment with the upright piano I'd seen from her office the day before. There was a dirty fireplace across the room with one of those gold-framed and lighted portraits of Jesus over it that looked new. Lois shakily sat down at the old piano.

"This is it," she said. "Nobody but me and him knew about it."

"What's 'it'?" I asked.

"The pianer," Lois said softly, stroking the keyboard with her hand. "Ivy Joe was teachin' me the pianer." Lois began to plunk out something on the keys that only in the roughest way resembled "Rock of Ages."

Slowly it began to sink into me.

"Raaacck of aaagess . . ." Lois howled, torturing the old piano.

There were several sheets of notebook paper on the top of the piano that bore the rudiments of musical notation and included instructions written in the shaky hand of an old person.

". . . cleft fer meee . . ."

One of the handwritten notations in the border of a sheet of simple music read, *"Miss Ross, practice this six times a day. When I come back next week, you should be able to play it without looking."*

I handed the sheet to Lucia Dodd. She read it and passed it back to me with a pained expression in her eyes. "It's his hand," she said.

Mercifully, Lois stopped playing. She slumped at the bench and seemed to be speaking to the piano. "He was teachin' me the pianer. I was really learnin' the pianer from him." Lois sniffed loudly. "Ivy Joe was bringin' me to Jesus. I told that ol' nigger . . . that old man, I told him I'd fix him up with whatever he wanted if he'd teach me the pianer. Hell, that old Mrs. Baxter from in town, that holy bitch, she woulda never come out here to teach me for no amount a' money. Old Joe didn't want no grass, dope, booze, girls, nothin'! He said he'd teach me free if I'd just listen to him talk about the Lord for ten minutes of every hour he taught me pianer. Hell, I thought he was crazy! I'd a' paid him a hunnert dollars a hour to teach me. But you know . . . that old man had a way about him. When he'd talk about God and Jesus, he made you want to listen to him!"

"I don't be*lieve* this!" Pierce muttered, but I waved him off.

Lois began to sob again—deep racking sobs. She stuck her elbows on the keys and the old piano sounded a discordant *chong*. She placed her face in her hands and wept. In a moment, she raised her tear-flooded, hideous face to me.

"Why would I a' killed Ivy Joe Culpepper, Sheriff Cody?" Lois wept. "That old man was the only decent thing that ever happened to me in my whole goddamn life . . ."

Lois began to bang the piano again. *Chong. Chang. Plong.*

"Raaack of aaages . . ."

I looked at Pierce, then at Lucia. The same horror I felt at witnessing the wretchedness of Lois Ross was reflected in their faces.

". . . cleft fer meeee . . ."

We fled the room.

# 14

## Reckonings

Pierce and Lucia Dodd and I walked down the steps fronting Saddle Mountain Lodge. It was beginning to get dark, snow fell silently and the air had a bitter taste. Lucia went to the truck at my instruction.

One-Eyed Jack and Chick and Larry lay widely separated, shivering in the snow by Pierce's cruiser. Otis and Haskel had three billfolds with driver's licenses and sundry items laid out on the hood.

I went to Trooper Calder and offered my hand. "Your momma still teaching school down in Polk County?" I asked.

"Yes, sir!" He beamed.

"Well, you tell her Sheriff Lewis Cody said hi, will you?"

"Yes, sir, she'll be pleased to hear it, Sheriff."

"Also I'll be dropping your supervisor a note, too. You did a good job and I'm grateful for the timely help."

"Shoot, Sheriff, I just wish we'd got here in time for the fun."

"You got here soon enough. We can take it from here. You can go on back on patrol."

Trooper Calder paused. He looked at me, then at Jack and chums, and back to me as the meaning sank in. "Ah, right. I'm outa here. See ya'll." He crunched off to his blue and gray state police car and glided away down the drive.

"Hey!" Chick demanded, a distinct note of panic

creeping into his voice. "What the hell are you guys fixing to do?"

Pierce, Otis, Haskel, Billy and I gathered around silently. Chick watched Pierce like he really was Frankenstein's monster.

"This ain't legal!" Larry wailed, his eyes widening. "This is police brutality!"

"We got our rights!" Chick yelled, his voice now cracking. "I want a law—lawyer!"

"Yeah!" Larry parroted, "You cain't do this! We'll sue you!"

Jack's pain-filled bear growl filled the cold air. "Aaaaaaaaah, *ssshut up, you assholes!*" Jack groaned with the exertion of his shout and toppled back on his bound wrists in the snow. "Aaaaah."

Chick and Larry eyed Pierce nervously. I squatted down by Jack, well out of earshot of everyone else. His right eye was blue, caked with oozing blood and swelled shut. His lips bled and he had a slight gash on his forehead. With some effort, he squinted up at me with his good eye—wet, cold and aching.

"Been one of those days, huh, Jack?" I said.

"Sometimes you dance," he replied. "Sometimes you trip on your dick."

"We got rights!" Larry squawled, as Pierce hauled him to his feet.

Jack roared, "I said shut the fuck up, Larry!" To me he quietly asked, "Sheriff, is there a deal in this somewhere?"

I was beginning to like ol' Jack.

I grinned. "You bribing me, Jack?"

"Oh, hell no, sir. I ain't got enough money to my name to offer a good bribe. Besides, that dipshit Arnie Dreyfuss said you cain't be bought. I'm just saying that if there's any way me and my boys can sort of, well, work this thing off, you know? I mean, if we could, we'd be real grateful and you'd never see us in your county ever again. Never. No, sir."

"How good are you at answering questions, Jack?"

"I'm a goddamn encyclopedia, Sheriff. World Book, Britannica, I'm the whole fucking Library of Congress. What do you want to know?"

"Hmmm. I wonder how truthful the answers might be."

# Shepherd of the Wolves

Jack sighed. "Let's face it, Sheriff. I'm talkin' for my ass now. Our asses. I ain't in no position to shit you."

I admired the way he included his buddies and cut through the crap. "Any of you done time, Jack?" I asked.

"No, sir."

"Wanted for anything, anywhere?"

"No si—no wait! Chick jumped bail on a DWI down in North Carolina. That's all. I swear."

"Anybody hurt on the DWI thing?"

"Chick!" Jack yelled. "Did you hurt anybody on that DWI thing in Winston-Salem?"

"What?" Chick responded, baffled. "Uh, no!"

"Goddamn it, you better not be shittin' me! It's important!"

"I ain't, Jack!" Chick cried. "Some fuckin' sheriff—aaah! Some officer of the law saw me weaving and pulled me over. I didn't hit nobody, honest!"

"Now for the biggy, Jack," I said. "Feel up to it?"

"Is a duck watertight?"

"Who paid for this job on me?"

"Ross did."

"What did Arnie Dreyfuss have to do with it?"

"Nothing. I mean, he called me with the Ross woman's name and said she had a good job for us. The woman made the deal and she paid us."

"How much?" I asked, curious to know what the going rate for crippling a sheriff was.

"Well, she offered us five hundred each. I told her she was crazier than a baboon on LSD, that we wadn't gonna take no cop for less than five thousand apiece!"

"Good for you, Jack. That's tellin' her."

"We settled on two thousand apiece!" Jack said proudly. "Half up front, half when we done the job."

"Six thousand lousy bucks to kill me?" I exclaimed, downright indignant.

"Oh, fuck no, Sheriff! Do I look like a hit man? The six grand was just to do you bad enough so you couldn't hold office no more. We was just gonna break your arms and legs and hands. That's all, I swear!"

"Oh, well, hell, Jack, and here I thought you were going to hurt me."

"Well, we wadn't gonna kill you!"

"Not for a measly six grand anyway, huh?"

"Look, Sheriff Cody, we knock a few heads for a buck now and then, but truth is, present company excepted of course, most of 'em deserve to get knocked. Some guy beats his wife and her brother pays us to clean his clock—that sort of thing. But killin' people is outa our league." Jack was indignant now. After all, he had his standards.

"Ya'll ever hit on a cop before?"

"Hell no. An' I ain't never going to again. I knew this was a bad idea and I shoulda known better. But the money was about ten times what we usually get for one job. Besides, Dreyfuss said you was a pussy. He was full a' shit, too. I guess I just let the money go to my head, Sheriff. I was a damn fool and I deserve whatever you give me, but my boys there, they just do what I tell 'em. This ain't their fault. Maybe you could at least cut a deal for them?"

I thought for a moment. Pierce and the others watched us, wondering no doubt what was going down. "You know we got makes on all of you, Jack?"

"Sure, Sheriff."

"You know that if you make me look bad for letting you slide on this, that me and two of my best people will track your asses down and you will look and feel like you got fed through a tree shredder?"

"I can take a hint. Yes, sir, Sheriff. I can be counseled."

"One more thing."

"Name it."

"Does Arnie Dreyfuss fall down much?"

"Huh?"

"I mean, you know, does he ever, say, fall down a flight of stairs, carpeted stairs, say, so he doesn't get hurt very bad, just scared shitless?"

"Aaaah. Well, ah, I don't know."

"What?"

"I mean, yeah! I bet he does! I bet he might accidentally dangle by his feet from the fifteenth-floor balcony of the Roanoke Hyatt Regency, say."

"But he wouldn't fall, would he?"

"Oh, hell no! Not a nice guy like Arnie!"

"Reckon that such an unfortunate accident might encourage the good councilman to be more selective in his private endeavors?"

"Sheriff, I ain't got no idea what that means but I guaran-fucking-tee you Arnie Dreyfuss will understand it within a week!"

"Did we have this conversation, Jack?"

"What conversation?"

"Jack. Do we have an understanding?"

"Sheriff, is fuckin' fun?"

I am such a bad boy.

"Otis!"

"Yo, Lew?"

"You and Billy take these guys to the dungeon. Have Milly print 'em and photograph 'em and run 'em on the computer. If they're clean except for a DWI in North Carolina on the ugly one there, turn 'em loose."

"Release 'em, Lew?"

"Yep. Cut those tie wraps off and handcuff them before they get gangrene or something."

"Ten-fo', Sheriff. Git inna car, dudes! Let's go!"

"Pierce, you and Haskel go see what else Lois knows about the Sloans and Ivy Joe, if anything. I don't think she'll hold out on us anymore. And find out who's counterfeiting car titles for her, too."

"Right, Lewis."

"And Pierce? Tell Lois I said she's used up her ninth life in Hunter County. Tell her she's got a hundred and twenty days to sell this place and clear out, but we better know where to find her if we need her for a witness against the Sloans."

"With pleasure, Lewis."

The warm interior of my truck felt good. Lucia Dodd's perfume felt even better. I was stiff and sore and it was difficult to even hook my seat belt.

"Aaargh!" I groaned.

"Are you all right?" Lucia asked.

"I'm feeling some pain, but I'm a damn sight better off than I'd be right now if you hadn't come in when you did. I owe you. Thanks. How did you know I was in trouble?"

"I'm not used to being ordered around. I guess I got a

little rankled at being condemned to wait out here. When I got to the door, I heard the sounds of a fight, so I went back for your shotgun."

"Where'd you learn to use one?"

"When I was little, Poppy Joe—that's what I always called him—Poppy Joe would wake me up at dawn. We'd take two shells for his old pump-action Winchester model-twelve and we'd go to the woods. He'd shoot two squirrels and we'd have them for breakfast."

We pulled out onto the highway toward Hunter. I noted that the state had come through with a grader but the falling snow was already covering the graded portions of the road. Fortunately, there was almost no one on the roads, except a few kids in dolled-up four-wheel-drive vehicles happy to have the chance to pull other motorists up grades and out of ditches.

I was startled to feel a touch on my cheek. I turned and was acutely aware of the closeness of Lucia Dodd. She lowered her hand but still looked at me with that incredibly smooth and evenly sculpted face.

"You're bleeding," she said, without evident emotion.

I wiped my cheek. "I don't doubt it. I took a few solid hits before you assassinated Lois's chandelier." I smiled. She didn't. Sigh.

We rode in silence under snow-weighted pines overhanging both sides of the road like a tunnel. It was getting dark. I switched on my headlights. Lucia Dodd stared out her window.

Finally, I said, "I wish you wouldn't be so gabby; I can't get a word in edgewise."

After a moment, still staring out the window, she answered. "I'm still astounded at how you do business."

"What do you mean?"

"What do you think? The Sloans commit a relatively minor assault on me and you shoot up thirty thousand dollars worth of their equipment, beat them up at gunpoint and put them on your 'shit list,' as you call it. Then three hired thugs try to kill you and you order them processed and released. You drown Lois Ross and intimidate a statement out of her without so much as a Miranda warning. It's amazing. In any civilized jurisdiction in this country, you not only couldn't make a charge stick, you'd fall liable for prosecution yourself!"

"Right," I replied. "So what should I have done? You said yourself no case could successfully be brought against the Sloans, not because they didn't commit the crime, obviously, but because the victim was the only witness for the prosecution. By my way of 'doing business,' they paid for their crime, pronto. No hassles about warrants. No arrests. No chasing the bastards down at taxpayer expense and lawman risk for ignoring summons or jumping bail. No plea bargains. No farcical tax-expensive trials benefiting no one but lawyers. No postponements and endless continuances. No appeals. No appeals of appeals. No reduced and/or suspended sentences. No tax-expensive jailtime. No probation for them to violate. I rest my case."

"What about those men who assaulted you? You ordered them released after they tried to kill you for money!"

"Ah, those guys are just a trio of muscleheads out to make a buck the only way they know. They aren't killers or I'd be dead. They aren't even serious criminals. If they turn up dirty, we'll hold them, but otherwise what does society gain by playing out the above-mentioned charade on them? Besides, they didn't exactly go unpunished."

"And the Ross woman? Suppose she had confessed to killing my grandfather? You couldn't have made that confession stand up in court and you know it."

"Sometimes, the best you have going for you in law enforcement is your instinct. I've known Lois pretty well for a long time, and while I don't put anything past anybody, I couldn't get real high on the notion of her murdering Mr. Joe. I was confident she knew some things about Joe she wasn't telling but that she didn't kill him or order him killed. If I'd advised her of Miranda, which, incidentally, she knows better than you do, and played the game by the rules, she'd have just spit in my eye, and we would never have gotten enough out of her to eliminate her as a suspect or even know what Joe had to do with her. Or crack a car-theft operation in the process. As for any of them bringing charges against me for my unorthodox ways, they're all way too dirty to win a shit-slinging contest against me in Hunter County and they know it."

Lucia Dodd drank all this in. "You don't think much of the legal system and due process, do you?" she asked.

"I think we had the best legal idea in the world until lawyers began fucking with it, since you ask. Now it's just a big casino where lawyers go to gamble other people's lives for fun and profit. You're an experienced attorney. Look me in the eye and tell me the system reliably dispenses justice, that it actually protects the law-abiding citizen better than it protects the criminal."

She looked out her window again without speaking.

"The bottom line is the existing legal system doesn't work. It's grown obese and clumsy and choked with esoteric concerns that have nothing to do with guilt or innocence, right or wrong or protection of the law-abiding from the criminal. Corrupt practices such as plea bargaining and contingency legal fees are commonplace—"

"Corrupt?!" Lucia exclaimed. "Without plea bargaining, the courts and dockets would be so overcrowded the—"

"Agreed! But that's a fault of the system's own obesity and obsession with esoteric legal theory at the expense of purpose. It's not a justification for cutting sleazy deals with criminals so they receive less punishment than they deserve and are released prematurely to prey again on the—"

"Without contingency legal fees, the poor man could not afford good counsel!" Lucia was getting hot.

"Oh, bullshit! This is Sheriff Lewis Cody you're talking to, not some dewy-eyed debutante who's been sitting on her tush in a law school classroom for two years. The 'poor man' can't afford good counsel anyway—hell, even the rich can't afford the system these days! No lawyer will touch a contingency case unless it's so weighted in the client's favor he can't lose. And in such a case, a competent attorney could win it for a reasonable fee instead of gouging the defenseless client for a third or more of what is entitled to him. It's crooked! It's common practice but that doesn't make it right!"

"Attorneys earn their fees! They deal with people's lives and fortunes!"

"So do *pilots,* for God's sake, but they don't hold up passengers for thirty-three-plus percent to get them down alive at the right location! Lawyers should be affordable instruments of an affordable, functional legal justice system like professional pilots are to the transportation system. Instead, they have contorted the American legal system to where its primary product is not justice but windfall profit for lawyers!" I roared.

"Who the hell appointed *you* judge and jury?" Lucia shouted, inches from my face.

I don't know what came over me. I seized her by the back of her head and kissed her hard, deep and long. She didn't exactly kiss back, but then she didn't fight, either. I finally released her to keep from wrecking the truck. She recoiled to her own side of the truck, wide-eyed with astonishment. I was a little astonished myself.

"Gaaaahd-*damn* that was good!" I heard myself say. I wiped lipstick on the cuff of my jacket. I could still taste her heat and slippery softness. The wolf howled inside.

Lucia Dodd whispered in a strained tone, "You are certifiably insane."

"Let me see if I got this straight," I replied. "A man has to be insane to kiss you?"

"You know what I—"

"Sheriff One!" came Milly's voice on the radio.

"Hold it," I said, picking up the microphone. "Sheriff One."

"Sheriff, we been advised by the fire department that they dispatchin' a couple of pumpers to a housefire on Bram's Ridge. Way they talk, Lewis, sound like it might be your place!"

# 15

## Fire and Brimstone

My first thought was that Gruesome was in the house. My second was my gas stove. The third was of the twisted face of Lanny Sloan saying, "Your time is coming, Cody! We'll get your ass, and soon!"

I plopped a magnetic blue light on the roof, chunked the truck into four-wheel and leaned on it.

When we turned off the highway onto narrow Bram's Ridge Road, we came upon a half-dozen volunteer firemen struggling to get one of the county's antique firetrucks out of the ditch. It was clear to me a heavy truck wrecker was going to be necessary and the nearest one was in Christiansburg. One of the volunteers ran to my window.

"Sheriff Cody!" he panted. "It's your place, Sheriff! Arnold's up there with the first truck, says your barn's on fire, too! We done sent for some more boys and equipment!"

"Thanks, Jerry!" I yelled. "Call up there and tell Arnold my dog's in the house and my horse is in the barn!"

"Sure thing, Sheriff!"

We followed the deep tracks of the first firetruck. I knew it was the Sloans now. Both the barn and the house were on fire and they were two hundred meters apart.

It took eight long minutes to get up to the house. As I turned over the cattleguard rails into my yard, my heart sank and I started feeling ill. My cruiser was a charred, smoking hulk, riddled with bullet holes. The housefire was mostly out but that was because there wasn't much house left to burn. A portion of the back porch and lower floor remained, but otherwise there were only blackened, steaming, smoking timbers.

Down the ridge, the barn blazed out of control. I knew what had happened; Fire Chief Arnold Webb had come on the house, barn and car all burning. Having only equipment, men and water for one fire at a time, he wisely chose to concentrate his meager resources on saving the house. I gunned the truck past the house and down the trail to the barn.

I stopped halfway.

The barn was completely engulfed in raging flames rising a hundred feet in the air. I hoped they had let Moose out before they fired the barn, but I knew, even as I thought it, that this was a gesture of compassion wholly alien to the Sloans. I drove closer. The heat was intense, melting the snow back fifty feet. Where the snow remained, I saw vehicle tracks and human footprints.

But no sign of a huge and beautiful horse.

I drove back up to the burned house. Lucia Dodd, characteristically, had said nothing.

Arnold Webb walked up as I got out. His yellow turnout coat had luminescent stripes that glowed white like neon from the floodlights on the truck. His face was smudged with soot and he looked furious. He slammed his helmet into the snow. "Goddamn it, Lewis!" he said. "I'm sorry as I can be. One a' my people let the other pumper get away from him turnin' off the highway and went right in the ditch! Wadn't much we could do with one pumper and four men. Jesus, Lewis, I'm sorry!"

I looked at what was left of my grandfather's house.

Arnold blew smoke-blackened mucous onto the snow.

"Lewis, I know you're wonderin' about Gruesome. I got to tell you we ain't found him yet. But they's a section of the lower floor and east wall that survived and my boys are still digging around in there. All we saved was some a' your furniture." He looked toward the inferno that used to be my barn. "I guess ol' Moose is gone, Lewis. I don't know what to say."

"It's all right, Arnold," I said. "The roads are treacherous." I had a flash on the last words of Ivy Joe Culpepper. "I know you did all you could."

I felt sadness more than fury then. Sadness for my animals. Sadness for me. Moose and Gruesome were all the family I had. The reality of it all was only slowly settling in now.

Arnold sighed with exhaustion. "Lewis, I got to tell you it looks like somebody done a job on you. Not only was both the house and barn fired but your police car was burned, too. Ain't no doubt it's arson."

"I know," I said.

Arnold looked at me with squinted eyes, then he looked at Lucia Dodd, who had walked around the hood of the truck to stand nearby.

I walked toward the smoking ruins of my home. I couldn't help thinking that being burned alive was the very worst way to go. Haunting images of Tess's plane crash flashed in my head. I only hoped smoke had gotten my animals before the flames.

"Chief!" shouted one of Arnold's volunteers. Arnold caught up with me. The fireman walked up with something in his hand. It was the charred neck of a liquor bottle. The ashes of a cloth were visible in the bottle neck.

"Molotov," Arnold said, examining the fragment with a flashlight. "That clinches it. Look, Lewis." He pointed up to my bedroom window on the portion of the east wall that still extended to the second floor. "That window was broke out when me and the boys got here. We could see flames comin' outa it. I figure whoever done it threw this Molotov through your bedroom window figurin', since your car was here, you was inside asleep, maybe. Most of the gasoline musta went into the hall . . ."

I wasn't listening. I couldn't avoid searching the wet black debris for a charred mass of flesh.

"Hey!" yelled another of Arnold's volunteers who was several feet from the west side of the house. "Lookit this!"

By the fireman in the tramped snow were dark glots of frozen blood among several human and dog footprints. The fireman held a piece of bloodstained denim fabric.

"He got one of them," I said, almost to myself. "He bit

and drew blood and tore this off somebody, which means he made it out of the house. Maybe he's somewhere around here alive." I tried to tell where Gruesome might have gone by the tracks, but the snow was so tramped up, melted in places and covered with ash that tracking wasn't possible.

Headlights swung through the gate. I looked to see Coleby Butler and his daughters running from Coleby's Jeep. Coleby wore a distressed expression as he drew near.

"Lewis! Thank God you're all right! One of Arnold's people called to tell me they thought it was your home burning." He grabbed me in a tight hug as Anne looked on, understanding. Coleby finally released me. "My word, Lewis. I'm so sorry about your house!"

"Where's Gruesome?" Elizabeth squeaked, staring with sick horror at the smoking ruins of my home.

"And your horse, Uncle Lewis?" Anne asked.

I was suddenly finding it hard to talk. "Moose . . . is gone, Anne," I said. "Gruesome may have survived. It looks like he got out of the house long enough to bite somebody. We were about to look around for him . . ." I was very tired.

Elizabeth was crying. She ran toward the woods calling, "Gruesome! Gruesome!"

Anne said, "I'll go with her." Coleby nodded.

I became aware of Lucia Dodd standing near. I met her eyes. The brown Mona Lisa.

"You would be Miss Lucia Dodd," Coleby said warmly. "I'm Coleby Butler; I'm an old friend. Lewis understated when he described you as an exceptionally beautiful woman." The silver-tongued Ashley Wilkes lived.

"How do you do, Dr. Butler," Lucia replied, extending her hand to him and glancing at me.

Coleby took her hand in both of his own. "Call me Coleby, please."

I noticed a couple of Arnold's volunteers peering at us curiously. I didn't care. The shock was wearing off and I was beginning to have some very unfriendly thoughts about the Sloan brothers.

Ever the mind reader, Coleby said, "I presume we can take this to be the handiwork of Lanny Sloan and his foul family."

"Certainly looks like it," I answered.

"That would seem to accent the suspicion that they had a hand in the death of Ms. Dodd's grandfather, would it not?"

I struggled to order my thoughts. I was so tired. "This makes them prime suspects, I would say, Coleby. I found out only an hour ago from Lois Ross that Lanny was definitely in the pill business. It could explain the stash we found in Ivy Joe's truck. Lois also said they were stripping cars near Lover's Overlook. Lanny admitted they were on Saddle Mountain that day, although he denies any involvement, of course. And his pickup truck had some recent front-end damage, but he claims he got it pushing a stalled truck, and that's going to be tough to refute."

"Still . . ." Coleby mused.

"Yeah," I said. "This torch job wasn't just arson, it was a hit. They thought I was home when they firebombed the house. I imagine they waited outside with rifles in case I escaped. There are bullet holes in the body of my car. It proves they're a lot more worried than I thought. They wouldn't go this far—take this kind of a risk—for simple get-even revenge. They're afraid I'm on to something very damaging. I just wish I knew exactly what."

Arnold Webb handed me a thermos cup of coffee. I was cold enough and sore enough to forget for the moment that I didn't drink coffee.

Arnold squinted at me again. "Lewis, me an' the boys will haul your stuff down to the firehouse and stow it in the back garage till you figure out what you're gonna do. Don't you worry." Arnold studied his boots. "An' I got to say, Lewis, I'm sorry we couldn't at least save your animals."

"No apologies, Arnold. We both know it was all over before you even got the call. Tell your men I thank them for doing what they could."

There was a high squeal that startled us all. Elizabeth. We looked toward the sound to see Anne waving from the woodline. I knew they'd found Gruesome. From the tone of Elizabeth's cry, I suspected he was dead.

He wasn't, but he was close. He'd somehow crawled into a depression in the pine needles near a stump. He lay unconscious but breathing in a bubbly, struggling way. Blood covered his side and he had one front leg drawn up close to him.

Coleby pushed by, pulling a stethoscope from his coat pocket, and knelt by Gruesome's shaking body. He pressed the stethoscope to several places on Gruesome's side and breast. "He's got a heartbeat, Lewis, but there is some congestion in his respiratory system. I can't tell about his injuries yet. He's alive but he's hurt seriously."

I guess it all just caught up with me. I remembered the day I found him—a quivering maimed puppy lying on a bridge roadway after some creep tried to throw his litter off the bridge from a moving car. I sank to my knees, put my hand on his bloody muzzle and began to weep. Elizabeth cried uncontrollably, held by her older sister. I felt a hand on my shoulder.

Coleby said, "Lewis, let the girls and me take him to Hap Morgan's veterinary clinic. Hap and I will do all that can be done. I promise you."

I nodded and placed my hand on his at my shoulder and realized instantly the hand was too small and smooth to be his. I turned to see Lucia Dodd kneeling behind me. In her huge brown eyes, there was just a trace of . . . sorrow, pity, sympathy. I couldn't tell.

Coleby gingerly wrapped Gruesome in his expensive Abercrombie and Fitch coat and carried him to the Jeep, where Anne and Elizabeth were opening the tailgate and clearing a space.

I felt drained. Defeated.

I stood and wiped my eyes. It occurred to me I was sure crying a lot for a grown man lately. I wondered what that said about where my life was.

Lucia Dodd followed me back to the truck. Pierce Arroe had arrived and was flash-photographing my burned cruiser. Good ol' Pierce. He was already at work doing the equipment damage report to save me the trouble. Haskel and Billy stood nearby. Thank Christ for friends.

Arnold walked up. "Lewis, tomorrow morning we'll get ol' Jimmy up here with his backhoe and we'll bury your horse. Anyplace special you'd like?"

I stared at the smoking barn, now nearly burned out. Poor

Moose. Another creature in my care I'd failed to protect adequately. "In the far pasture, Arnold. Between those three pines and the woodline. Thank you. Have Jimmy send me a bill."

"Fuck the bill. You know Jimmy ain't gonna let you pay him, 'specially after what you done for his sister's kid."

I went to Pierce by his cruiser. In the glow from the truck lights I could see his jaw muscles tensing and releasing. "The Sloan boys, I guess," he said. His eyes were ice crystals.

"Looks like it. Arnold's boys found the remains of a Molotov cocktail in the house. I think they believed I was home. I think they were trying to hit me, Pierce, not just burn me out. I'm onto something serious about them; I just don't know what."

"When do we go for 'em?" Pierce asked casually, but I hadn't missed that look in his eyes as he stared past me toward the ruins of the barn.

"When the evidence is tight, Pierce. Let's let Arnold do his fire marshall's investigation and submit a report. We'll continue to work on it from the angle of Joe's death. In the meantime, let's get a couple of our informants in the right saloons. When the Sloans drink, they get loose at the mouth. When we can make it stick, we'll take 'em hard. Not before."

Pierce spat in the snow. "You watch your ass, Lewis. They'll try again when they find out they blew it this time."

"Noted."

"You gonna stay at Dr. Butler's? You know you're welcome to move in with us."

"Thanks, Pierce. Coleby has already made arrangements and Brenda has enough to do with your houseful without a long-term guest. I'll put up at Mountain Harbor until I can get things sorted out."

"What about insurance, Lewis? You gonna be able to rebuild?"

"I guess. I was insured, but no money will replace that beautiful horse. God, I hate those bastards!" I surprised myself with the outburst. "Arnold saved some of my grandfather's things. I don't know. I'll think about it later."

"Sure."

# Shepherd of the Wolves

I watched Coleby's Jeep disappear down the road, falling snowflakes glinting in the headlights. I knew Gruesome was in good hands, that there was nothing I could do for him. Coleby and Hap Morgan, the vet, would let me know when there was anything to tell.

Lucia Dodd stood near, looking at me. I couldn't have put my finger on exactly what it was, but there was a different manner about her.

"I'll drive you to Mr. Joe's place on my way to Mountain Harbor," I told her.

She followed me to the truck without reply.

We drove in silence down the ridge road, past the effort to retrieve Arnold's other firetruck from the ditch, and out onto the snow-muffled highway to Hunter.

I realized I was glassy-eyed. I felt sore, tired and emotionally wasted. At that moment, I thought that if Gruesome died it would be the last straw required to break the back of my strength, that I'd just fold then and say fuck it. I put it out of my mind. Such thinking was dangerous, particularly for men who carry guns. Besides, there were more immediate considerations, which I could actually do something about, that merited my attention.

I was suddenly aware that Lucia Dodd had spoken to me.

"I'm sorry," I said, "I'm . . ."

"It's all right, Sheriff. I just asked you what you were going to do about supper. You need to eat."

We turned onto Eldridge Street in East Hunter and rolled slowly toward Mr. Joe's little home. I hadn't thought of eating. I didn't feel hungry. I supposed I could get Polly to whip up something for me when I got to Mountain Harbor. I stopped the truck before Joe's house.

"I'm not hungry" was all I could manage to say.

"Nonetheless," she replied sternly, "you need to eat properly. Come with me."

I looked at her. She met my eyes briefly, then, to my astonishment, she reached over, switched off the ignition and got out, taking my keys with her. She strode briskly for the house and went inside, leaving the door slightly ajar.

I sat dumbfounded for a time. Then I turned off my headlights and I entered the house of Ivy Joe Culpepper.

# 16

<hr/>

## Brimstone and Fire

**A** man's home can tell you a lot about the man. Old Joe's
house smelled of wood smoke, though it was heated by a
large brown enamel kerosene stove on a steel plate at one
end of the living room, which ran the length of the front of
the house. Off this largest room, to the rear, were a kitchen
at the left and a bedroom at the right. The place was clean
enough to do surgery in. A long, thick, worn, hooked rug
covered most of the living room's walnut floor. The right
wall behind the kerosene stove was a wall-to-wall, floor-to-
ceiling bookcase filled to capacity, and more books were
stacked in piles before the lower shelves. Against the rear
wall, between the doors to the kitchen and bedroom, was a
polished upright piano with a patina that would have given
an antique dealer an orgasm. On it, and to both sides of it,
were stacked hymnals and droves of sheet music. The
room's only other furniture items were a huge, faded,
overstuffed sofa from the thirties with a plump matching
chair near the stone fireplace that dominated the left wall, a
couple of freestanding shaded lamps and a small walnut
table by the chair on which sat a large and weathered old
Bible. Covering every square foot of wall space remaining
in the room—over and lining the sides of the fireplace,
around the doors and windows, flush up to the edges of the
ceiling, walls, windows, doors, piano and bookcase—were
hundreds of framed photographs. Some were recent and in

color, but many were black and white and a few were turned
brown with age. Some were large; some were small. Many
were of posed graduating classes. Others were of homecoming parades, packed school buses, football or basketball
games or staged plays. Still others were of individuals in cap
and gown or in sports attire or smiling from playground
equipment or hugging a shy and mildly embarrassed old
Negro janitor. Some were taken in snow, some in balmy
weather, but all, all of them, were of the children of Hunter
County, hundreds and hundreds of children enshrined in
the heart and the home of Ivy Joe Culpepper.

Unfortunately, a man's home didn't necessarily tell you
so much about his granddaughter. Lucia Dodd let her coat
slide from her shoulders and come to rest on the sofa, all in
one graceful fluid move.

Lucia must have taken in my walking-dead look. She
unzipped my bomber jacket and tugged it off me like she
were undressing a child. I was more tired than I thought.

"Make us a fire," Lucia said, pointing to a stack of cut
wood in the corner. "I'll make us a drink."

Us?

She went into the kitchen. I stacked kindling, boosted it
with newspaper and lit it. I sat down on the embracing old
sofa, pulled off my boots and felt the growing, popping
flames melt my tired eyes.

Lucia returned with two steaming mugs of something
dark, which I drank without question. It was pungent, hot
and heavy but immensely satisfying.

"Jesus. What is this shi—uh, stuff?"

"It's hot cider, cinnamon and rum," she answered.
"Drink it. It's good for you." She sat down in the chair,
kicked off her own boots, drew one foot beneath her and
drank of her own concoction. All the while those hypnotic
huge brown eyes never left me.

"It has always amazed me," I told her, suddenly aware of
how fast the drink was charging through my empty stomach
to my brain, "how you girls can sit on your landing gear like
that. Excuse me. 'Girls' is supposed to be a slur these days,
isn't it? I forgot. You 'women,' then. Or should I say 'you
African-American, wholly liberated and independent female individuals'? Will that keep me out of trouble?"

"I'm not particularly sensitive to labels, Sheriff Cody. I conduct myself according to my own personal definition of feminism, which I find differs radically from what is popularly passed off under that term. I have, in fact, been accused by both feminist and black political extremists as being loyal to neither cause. I'd appreciate it if you could find a gentle synonym for 'nigger,' or 'bitch,'" she said concisely, "but beyond that, you can call me whatever you wish as long as it isn't demeaning. Is that too much to ask?"

"What a relief," I said, suddenly wondering how I got on this tack. "Actually, the word 'girl' is one of the dearest in my vocabulary, occupying a special place of affection, and is in no way disrespectful, trust me."

Her eyes narrowed ever so slightly and a touch of a smile tugged at the corners of her mouth. "Of you, I might have guessed that" was all she said.

I pulled my eyes from her and drew another long sip of the hot liquid, letting it slide down my throat, burning all the way. My eyelids weighed 192 pounds. Each. I was utterly devoid of energy. My breathing slowed. I sank into the cushions of the sofa. With enormous effort, I rolled my head to look at my watch. Almost seven P.M. I'd rest my eyes a little, then call my office.

A moment later, I looked again at my watch, then shook my head and looked again. It was eleven-twenty P.M.! I became aware that I was reclining on the old sofa, covered by Lucia Dodd's down coat. My boots stood together near the hearth, where coals now barely glowed orange.

"Jesus Christ!" I said, standing. The room was dim, lighted only by a small lamp in a corner. The door to the late Ivy Joe Culpepper's bedroom was closed and no light shone beneath it. I blinked and looked about for a telephone.

Lucia Dodd's soft voice came from behind the bedroom door. She sounded sleepy. "Your office knows you're here," she called. I could hear her moving around.

"Are you sure?" I asked, wondering if I had marked out on the radio when we arrived, remembering I couldn't have because Lucia had turned off the ignition, and thus the radio, and had taken my keys before I could have called in.

The bedroom door opened. Lucia Dodd stood in the

# Shepherd of the Wolves

doorway in a satin-like lavender dressing robe and matching slippers with a slight heel. Her shining black hair was released from that severe bun and was now combed back from her face in light, feathery waves. She stood with most of her weight on one leg, with her hip cocked. The bedroom light was now on and it shone through her gown, silhouetting her bust, slender waist and long lovely legs spaced about a hand's width apart.

Oh, Lordy.

Oblivious, thankfully, of all the bells and lights going off in me, Lucia said, "I called your Sergeant Stanford about seven and told her where you could be reached. I told her you were sleeping and you should not be disturbed if it wasn't important."

"Oh, great," I said wryly. "Effectively, you told her we were sleeping together and don't bug us. I bet she loved that. Did you call Lady Maude's Cafe and issue a press release?"

"Oh, Sheriff Cody. Are you concerned that your constituency will . . . cut your dick off . . . if they think you're . . . sleeping with a 'nigger'?"

My gaze snapped from the coals back to her as she parodied the Sloan brothers' vicious words on the occasion of their stripping her. I was relieved to see no acrimony in her expression—only a peculiarly mischievous twinkle.

I decided to let her question go unanswered. "Did Milly leave any messages?" I asked.

"No," Lucia said, looking directly into my eyes. "She just asked if you were all right and suggested she should come by to see if you needed anything. I told her that would not be necessary, that you were in good hands and not to worry. I don't think she likes me very much."

"You didn't give her a lot of reason to in your brief encounter. Besides, she cares very strongly for me in a motherly way and she's suspicious that you mean me harm."

"So I gathered. She told me in no uncertain terms that you risked your newly elected career a few years ago by promoting her from jailhouse cook to desk sergeant. She said to me, 'Anybody what even want to mess up Sheriff Cody's hair will have to *kill* my black ass first. You hear, girl?' "

I smiled. "Yeah, well, nobody will ever accuse Milly of failing to say what's on her mind, and she protects those she loves with vigor."

"I was impressed. I know enough about the climate in these mountains to appreciate how bold a move it was for you to replace a white man with seniority with a . . . 'nigger' female maid."

"It wasn't all that bold. The guy I blew away was a thief and an incompetent, a crony of former Sheriff Oscar Wheeler. He wasn't missed. Besides, Milly never gave me a single occasion to regret promoting her. She worked hard and earned the respect of the whole department."

Lucia considered this for a moment. "Would you liven up the fire?" she asked. "I'll get your dinner."

I watched her walk into the kitchen; when she turned on the light, that same silhouetting effect burned into me again.

I stoked the fire and went into the bedroom to the adjoining bath to wash my face. A big freestanding, claw-foot, white porcelain tub filled the little bathroom. A curved rod held a shower curtain, and a pipe wound up the wall from beneath the tub to an elevated shower head. The sink had white porcelain faucet handles. The icy water reminded me of the weather. I pulled aside a small curtain at the window and looked out at the night. Snowflakes continued to float down. In the darkness, I could not tell how deep it was.

In the bedroom, a lathed cherry four-poster bed, covered with a colorful thick quilt, stood between two cherry nightstands. On the wall were several more framed photographs, which I paused to examine. One old black-and-white was of Mr. Joe, about sixty years removed, with a smiling young black woman at his side. Joe wore baggy, cuffed trousers held up by suspenders and the woman wore a twenties vintage flowered dress and feathered hat. There were shots of a younger, sad-faced woman—Lucia's mother?

Beneath were numerous gold-framed photos: a beautiful black girl-child propped on Joe's knee; the child standing by Joe with cane pole, fish and grin; still another of the girl, now about sixteen, with hair in ringlets; a later shot of the girl in cap and gown; a yet later one of a very serious young woman standing by a door bearing a brass plate which read: H. LUCIA DODD, ATTORNEY AT LAW.

I heard her footsteps and smelled her perfume. Perfume? I turned to look at her. "Old Mr. Joe was devoted to you."

"My mother was his only child and I was his only grandchild. My grandfather had a lot of love and only the two of us to bestow it upon." She stood nearer. "My grandmother died in 1942. My mother died in 1978. Scrubbing other people's floors . . ." she added with a bitter note. "Your dinner is hot."

The kitchen had a thirty-year-old electric range standing on a cast-iron slab where I was sure once stood a wood-fired stove. On a faded white wooden dinette table were several steaming dishes.

"The neighbors have been generous with food," Lucia said. "I'm glad to have someone to help me eat it."

I scooped broccoli, potatoes and roast beef onto a cracked china plate and sat down. Lucia set another mug of the rum-spiked cider by my plate and left the kitchen. I ate like a starving wolverine.

When I finished, I reloaded the old chipped china plate and ate again. I washed the dish and took the rest of my cider back to the living room. Lucia Dodd sat on one end of the couch, staring at the dancing flames and holding her drink. Shadows flickered about the room.

She looked up at me when I sat at the opposite end of the old carpet-cloth sofa. My breath caught briefly as it dawned on me she had freshened her hair and lipstick. I couldn't help pondering why she would do that under the circumstances. Mere vanity didn't seem to account for it adequately. Either I was engaging in male fantasy or the possibilities were stunning.

Lucia sipped at her drink. "I called your friend Dr. Butler about nine o'clock to tell him you wouldn't be out there tonight. He's a very gracious man. He said your dog is stable at Dr. Morgan's veterinary clinic. He said the dog has some broken ribs and other minor injuries but that he will recover. Dr. Butler asked about you." She met my eyes. "I asked him about you."

I looked back into those massive soft brown eyes.

"He told me about your daughter," Lucia said. "I'm sorry."

"Coleby talks too much," I groused.

"Don't be angry with him. He seemed to want me to appreciate you as much as he does."

"Coleby is a fine, gentle, loving man. He's the best friend a man could have. He's a damn sight better husband than his wife deserves, I can tell you."

"Also your deputy, the big fellow, came by to check on you. You're lucky to have such caring friends."

"Pierce is good people, with a worthy, loving wife."

"He said to mention to you that people are in place in case the Sloan brothers get 'talky.' He also said to remind you of the funeral of Cassie Shelor tomorrow at one P.M. Who was she?"

"A local kid," I answered, thinking how inadequate that summary sounded. "She had a heart problem. We found her dead the day after Mr. Joe died. People are dropping like flies these days . . ."

Lucia rose and warmed herself near the fire. The glow shone through the lavender gown again, making subtle but unmistakable statements about her shape. The perfumed scent of her was warm and musky and sweet. My blood mobilized for maneuvers. What was happening here?

Lucia seemed entranced by the fire. "I started calling him 'Poppy Joe' when I was a baby. He loved it and I never called him anything else." The firelight gave her skin a polished copper appearance. "Sheriff Cody, what do you really think happened to him?" Her gaze rose slowly from the fire to my face.

I thought for a moment. "I'm not sure yet. It appears that the only person with any motive to harm Mr. Joe was Lanny Sloan et al., but so far any case against him is too weak to get an arrest warrant, let alone convict him. We'll know more tomorrow. I'm going to try to talk privately with Lanny's daughter Peggy. There's something she knows that hasn't been told yet, except perhaps to Mr. Joe himself. Something that went on between Ivy Joe and Peggy Sloan that we need to know more about."

"You don't mean anything physical, surely. He would never—"

"Hell, no. He was too good a man, too smart, not to mention too old, for that. But there was something else and I have a feeling it'll shed a lot of light. Trouble is, getting past Lanny Sloan to Peggy will be tough. Whatever she knows, he won't want her talking to me. Or you. Damn. If Cassie Shelor was alive I could work it through her—she was about the same age. I'll figure something out."

"Yes," Lucia said, "I believe you will."

I looked up at her and was struck. Her face was jeweled with a generous broad smile of soft red lips, perfect white teeth and skin that glowed gold in the firelight. It was the first time I'd ever seen her smile. Her eyes shone. She was a woman you don't forget.

"Good God, you are beautiful when you smile," I told her impulsively.

Lucia sipped her hot drink, watching me from the corners of her eyes. "Are you charming me, Sheriff Cody?"

"I sure hope so," I replied. She smiled again.

I stood and walked on my sock feet to join her by the fire. She held her drink with both hands.

"Would it be presumptuous of me to ask you to call me Lewis, *Ms.* Dodd?" I asked, locked on her eyes.

I noticed her own eyes flick from mine to my lips and back. "No . . . Lewis. I suppose we've progressed to a first-name stage of propriety."

"I sure hope so," I said again.

She smiled again. Her eyes were framed in long curving lashes.

I set my drink on the stone mantel, put my hands on the mantel at either side of her head and leaned to kiss her, slowly, to give her time to think and react as she might be moved to. She didn't budge, except to tilt her face to mate mine when our lips came together.

I tell you, it is hard to find words to describe how good an early kiss with a lovely woman is. It wasn't a tonsil washer, you understand, just a firm, gentle, tasting kiss. Her lips were soft and wet and hot and she smelled wonderful. When I pushed, gently, she pushed back. Her lipstick was slippery.

She made me hard enough to chip concrete.

I could hear her draw a deep breath and hold it, then her breath came out warm and moist. My nostrils flared as I sucked in the smell and heat of her.

Shortly, it became difficult for both of us to breathe gracefully through our overloaded noses. We sounded like runaway respirators, so we parted by mutual agreement and came up for air.

Lucia's breasts rose and fell with her breathing.

"Ooh. Ah." She breathed hoarsely. "Let me see if I understand what's happening here." She heaved for breath. "Am I being seduced . . . Lewis?"

"God, I hope so," I answered. I kissed her lightly on each cheek as her eyes darted rapidly about my face. I took her drink from her shaking hands and placed it by mine on the stone. I put my hands on her waist—her slender, silky waist—and gripped her firmly.

She leaned into me. Her breasts, pressed against my chest, felt marvelous. Coming against me compressed her gown, forcing out of it a rising, intoxicating wave of warm air scented with her perfume and her heat and that musky smell unique to an aroused woman. I put my face against her neck and breathed in slowly, savoring it. She emitted a little moaning sound and moved her head against me.

I lifted my face to hers and kissed her again, slowly again, gently again.

She parted from me, struggling to get her breath. "What makes you think . . ." She kissed *me* now and parted again. ". . . I'd want to . . ." She kissed me again with a bit more fervor. ". . . Make love to you . . ." Another kiss, *serious* this time. ". . . White boy!"

I smiled wryly at her, then seized her hair with my hand and held her ear to my mouth and ran my lips lightly over the ear buried in soft black tresses, saying, "What makes *you* think . . ." I sucked gently at the lobe and whispered slowly. ". . . I'm offering you a *choice*, Ms. Dodd?"

Lucia surprised me with a short happy laugh, the first time I'd ever heard the woman laugh. She slid her arms around my neck and pulled me to her. I nibbled at her ear with somewhat more gusto and she moaned, arched against my knee and kissed me hard, wet and probing. Simultaneously—a feat I thought—she took my hand from her waist and slid it inside the front of her gown to her breast where the nipple was a half-inch wide and long, and as stiff as porcelain.

We parted our lips and, with no small difficulty, I said, "'Atta girl, play hard to get."

Lucia laughed again with delight and buried her face against my chest. She giggled again, like laughing was some new and magical experience, like it had been a long, long time since she had last laughed.

I swept her up from the floor in my arms like Rhett goddamn Butler and she clung to my neck. On the way to Ivy Joe Culpepper's little bedroom, I told her, "There won't be any finesse, Lucia. It's been so long. I need you so bad."

"I know," she whispered. "I understand. It's been a long time for me, too."

Her breath was warm and moist against my neck.

# 17

## Integration

I laid Lucia Dodd, literally and figuratively, on the quilted old cherry bed, starving for her, craving her, needing her too much to give a damn about anything else. The only light in the room was a dim presence of firelight from the living room. She untied the dressing gown and let it fall away from her. Beneath it she wore a shimmery, lavender, thin-stringed camisole and those loose panties with no elastic in the legs. I shrugged off my clothes and she slipped the panties from her ankles. When I came to the bed, she slid her thighs apart and I lay between them. The contact with her was electrifying. I could feel her breath rapid upon my face.

"Acch . . . God, that's sweet," I said as I slid into that sweet, hot, oily crevice and God it was. She burned all the way in. She released a short cry, not quite of pain, then I felt her lips at my ear.

"Yes! Oh," she whispered, "it's . . . been . . . so . . . long!"

She drew her knees up and gripped me with her calves and I went deeper into her and held her there, frozen in ecstasy. If I moved a millimeter, I'd explode and she knew it. We held tightly, not moving but struggling for breaths. In a moment, I don't know how long, the first wave of urgency slowly receded. I probed her slowly and she rotated her hips in response—a slow, rhythmic, undulation done while looking me full in the eyes, a carnal intimacy that almost put me over. We moved and countermoved, sought and found, until I felt the last great wave coming with force from way offshore. Lucia clung to me and whispered in cadence with our ever more frantic hunching: "Do it! Yes! Do it to me! Do it to me! Do it to me! Oh!"

I obliged her. The hot wave swept up from within me and I poured into her with a tight cry, clutching her to me desperately, as if I could absorb her through my skin. It had been a very long time and I seemed to gush on forever. I was releasing about a thousand years of compressed loneliness, and in the same act, I was purging the ghosts of Tess and Elaine and even Cassie Shelor.

After a time, I raised myself up and looked at her. Her eyes were wide and she wore a sort of pleased smile. I had never seen a face more beautiful than hers at that moment.

She gripped me with her arms and thighs. "Don't leave, Lewis. Not yet, please."

"I won't. Here, straighten your legs a moment."

She did, and staying inside her, I held her tightly at her waist and rolled onto my back. There she lay on me, her head on my chest. I whipped the heavy quilt over us.

And like that we slept.

In an hour or so, I awoke to a soft donging noise. It took me several seconds to identify it as the grandfather clock in Ivy Joe Culpepper's bedroom. Lucia stirred on top of me. The warm perfumed smell of her wafted up from beneath the quilt. My system sounded general quarters and my blood rushed for battle stations.

Lucia felt me growing. She looked at me with amusement, kissed me and slid off me. She walked with sway and grace into the bathroom, wearing only the silken top to her sleepwear. The door closed and the water ran and I stared at the ceiling and wondered if all this was happening or was I just going to wake up to my alarm clock in my bed on Bram's Ridge, as usual. Thinking of her sounds and smooth warmth caused me to tent-pole the quilt, which felt nice.

The light clicked out in the bath, the door opened and I could hear her hurry to the bed. She slid under the quilt and clung close to me, her thigh between mine. "Cold," she said.

The longer I held her the finer she felt. I put my hand

under her nightie and indulged in some deliberate fondling. She drew a little breath and her thick nipples grew stiff. I circled them with my fingers and then pulled gently at them. She made a long, low humming noise you could call a purr if you could have called her a cat.

I submerged beneath the quilt and positioned between her thighs and slid the nightie up above her breasts. Obligingly, she drew it over her head and tossed it. Her squirming nude body beneath me was a quantum joy to my senses. I kissed her ample brown breasts and tongued her nipples. She pushed a shoulder forward and held my head to her breast.

The sounds of an aroused woman are in their own right the most erotic sounds on earth.

She threw the quilt back. We weren't cold anymore.

I slid farther down and stroked her smooth belly with my face and felt it rising and sinking ever more rapidly.

I took her knees and spread her and ran my hands along the fine soft flesh of her inner thighs. I held her legs apart and lowered my face into the furry folds where her lush and tender thighs came together. Lucia flinched and stiffened, then slowly relaxed and worked herself against me. My nose and tongue slid easily between the soft, slippery, parted lips, and Lucia entwined her fingers in my hair. I foraged gently until I found the small swollen lump near the top and I teased it with my tongue. Lucia stiffened again and lifted herself against me. I sucked at her until her breathing began to come in gasps and moans. I slid two fingers into her and fluttered them in her hot, slippery depth. She grew frantic, closed her thighs about my ears, clutched me to her and hunched spasmodically, crying out again and again.

And then she was still.

I stayed motionless so as not to disturb her afterglow. I was in no hurry, if the truth be known. When she had savored the last rays of it, she gradually relaxed her grip upon me, stroking my hair in silence.

In time, I moved alongside her and propped my head on my hand. She found my other hand and held it in her own. We said nothing. I watched the slight glow dancing about the ceiling of Ivy Joe Culpepper's living room, caused by the waning flames in the hearth. I felt her push me onto my back. She placed a leg over me and lay her head in the hair on my chest.

The only sound was the soft swing of the pendulum in the old clock, until she spoke. "Where have you been?" she whispered.

"Pardon me?" I asked.

Gently she repeated, almost crying, "Where have you been? Where have you been for so *long?*"

When I knew she was asleep, I gently disengaged from her, slid out from beneath the quilt and walked carefully in the darkness into the living room. The fire was now only ruby coals, and as I was nude I was cold. I groped into the kitchen and dialed my nightwatch duty sergeant and asked him how everything was going.

"Sheriff, it's quiet all over the county. Almost nobody on the roads, thankfully. State called. Says they're hurtin' for snow-removal equipment, what with the size of the storm and all. Says it'll be late tomorrow—uh, today—before they can clear the Roanoke Highway. I got the county boys out with a couple a salt trucks, but it ain't doin' much good."

"What's the forecast, Gary?"

"Winter storm warnin's out until fourteen hundred local, Sheriff. Looks like we gonna be blessed with a little more snow."

"Okay. You know where to reach me, right?"

He repeated the phone number.

"That's right," I said.

"Okay, Sheriff. That's out at Dr. Butler's right?"

"Ah, no, another, ah, friend of mine."

Gary paused, waiting for me to elaborate. I didn't.

"Ah, right. Say, Sheriff, Pete Floyd called from the newspaper. Wants you to call him."

"Did he say what for?"

"Naw, I asked him, but he just said it was important and call him first thing in the morning."

"Okay, Gary. Thanks. Good night."

"'Night, Sheriff."

I supposed Pete was calling for more details about Ivy Joe or Cassie Shelor. It could wait till morning.

On my way back to the bedroom, I paused long enough to stoke up the fire and pile on several logs. The fire built and the heat felt good.

When I slipped back into the bed, Lucia held my head, kissed me, then clung tightly to me as though she were a scared little girl. I could not see her face, but for a moment I thought she was crying.

"Are you okay?" I asked her.

"I'm frightened," she whispered, holding tight to me. "I'm assailed by a million disturbing feelings all of a sudden. I . . . you may not believe . . . I can count the number of men I've made love to in my life on one hand, or at least I could a few hours ago. I mean it may sound silly but I'm one of these women for whom sex and . . . well . . . love, sort of go together. Now I'm in bed with . . . you, and I'm having all these scary feelings and, my God, they feel like . . . love! One moment I'm scared to death you're out there in the living room, dressing to slip quietly out of the house and not come back to me, and the next moment I'm asking myself how I could be so foolish as to fall for a *white* guy, a cop for God's sake! It's disturbing, Lewis. I'm not used to being out of control of my feelings and it frightens me."

I held her and stroked her soft hair. "Yeah, I can appreciate how you feel. It would be foolish for me to fall for a white guy, too."

She laughed and punched me. "Oh, hush. You know what I mean. It isn't a matter of race exactly . . ."

"I hope not."

"It's, well, let me say it this way. If forty-eight hours ago, people had told me I'd be naked in bed with the white sheriff of Hunter County, let alone having all these awful love feelings, I'd have thought them insulting or insane. I have never before even considered a . . . an intimate relationship with a white man. You are . . . were the personification of all I've despised since childhood. You're an enforcer for the traditional Southern white establishment. Yet . . . all of a sudden, with you, none of that has the meaning for me that it had two days ago. That's very unsettling, Lewis. I'm not prepared."

"Beg to correct you, madam. I'm an enforcer for the legal system which, as far as I'm concerned, at least, doesn't have any color."

"I'm sorry. I didn't mean that in a racist way but I guess it came out sounding like it."

"I think I know what you're saying. We're all prejudiced to some extent; it's a byproduct of human insecurity. But a person doesn't become a bigot until their prejudice has grown to affect their judgment and common sense. I think you and I are both prejudiced but neither of us is bigoted yet."

We lay quietly for a while. Then she spoke low, as though to herself. "I've had some . . . difficulty . . . with my personal life the last two years or so, Lewis. It's . . . left me very vulnerable in ways."

I waited in silence for her to expand on this, but apparently the subject was closed for now. So be it. I wasn't too crazy about my own personal life these last years either.

More comfortable silence passed.

"You know, since we're having true confessions here, I've been struck by you ever since you walked through my office door. Beauty and sensuality are different things for different men, but you're both for me."

Lucia kissed me on the neck and then bit me gently. "It's the Mandingo syndrome, right? The white master secretly lusting for the seductive slave girl?"

I found that amusing. I'd thought of Lucia Dodd as many things, but a slave wasn't one of them. "You almost sound like that scenario turns you on," I said.

"Doesn't it turn you on? Admit it. The power of literally owning a woman to do with her whatever you please?"

"Like the power of knowing that as a beautiful seductive woman you can command the man in spite of himself, because he's helpless in his lust for you?"

Lucia laughed through her nose and snuggled close. "Something like that, I guess."

"Well, lust for you though I do, it's your abundance of grace that holds me. I admire that quality above all others in a woman." I cupped one of her breasts in my hand. "Even these."

"Animal," she said, blowing in my ear. I started to get hard again, and Lucia felt it against her thigh. I'd been celibate for so long I couldn't seem to get enough of her.

"Ooh," she said, taking me in her hand. "What have we here?"

"What's it look like?" I answered. "A frog?"

She laughed that rich, throaty, musical laugh. "If I kiss it will it turn into a prince?"

"On my solemn oath as an officer of the law, I swear it will, yes."

Lucia laughed happily again as she slid beneath the quilt and kissed and licked at me till I twanged like a jew's-harp. Exquisite.

"No prince!" she said with suspicion.

"Well, hell, what do you expect? You have to work at it. This is—ah-hanh!" She engulfed me in her mouth. Her tongue was devastating. "This . . . this is the twentieth century. Princes don't come easy. Ah. No pun intended."

Lucia laughed while bathing me with her lips, and there is no sensation on earth like that.

We went on for more than an hour. As I lay with her afterward, I knew a peace; yeah, I spelled it right; a peace, a tranquillity I hadn't known in years—no—for as long as I could remember.

"Mmmm," Lucia murmured, her thigh and arm draped warmly over me. "Dear God. I haven't been in love since . . . I had forgotten how wonderful it is . . . I hope I'm not scaring you with the *L*-word, Lewis."

"Love is always scary. But I know I don't want you to feel any differently."

"I love easily. It's always been my weakness and has cost me more than one broken heart. But it's a no-strings sort of love, Lewis. I can't help feeling it, but I know it doesn't give me any right to expect anything from you and I don't."

"I understand. I don't yet know how I feel except that I'm very drawn to you. Things have sort of happened in a hurry with us the last few hours. My head is still spinning."

We lay entwined in each other, alternating between periods of silent mutual understanding and talk of our lives up to this night.

# Shepherd of the Wolves

Lucia's mother left Hunter and moved to Washington when Lucia was fifteen. All over the nation, rural blacks had been gravitating toward the big cities. The hope was for a better life, but in the case of Lucia's mother, like millions of others, it amounted only to an urbanization of poverty and struggle.

Lucia's father was a Hunter County tenant farmer who earned the dubious distinction of being the last official casualty of the Korean War, dying two years after it ended from liver complications resulting from a gunshot wound. "I never knew him," Lucia said. "I was too young to even remember what he looked like. But Momma loved him so much she never even removed her wedding ring, let alone remarried.

"The year we left Hunter, Poppy Joe said to me, 'Child, there are two things that can raise you where I know you want to go. One is money and the other is your grades. You ain't got no money but you gets good grades. You better keep them, child. They's your ticket to the future. They's the secret. Don't you forget that, baby girl.'"

Lucia didn't forget. She entered law school at American University ten years after the assassination of Martin Luther King, Jr. Law was where the power was, law was where the money was: all the intelligent, politically active young blacks knew that. Law!

Lucia proved to be not only academically accomplished but also a shrewd semantic tactician in the courtroom as well. Ultimately, she drew the attention of two partners in Washington's most prestigious black law firm. In time, partnership for Lucia herself came as well.

Lucia seemed to jam up when her historical account arrived at the last few years. I debated whether trying to draw her out would be prying. At one point, I gave her an opening to tell me about the 'difficult personal life' she had referred to, but she only said softly, "I knew a guy . . . it didn't work out."

With no preamble, she suddenly said, "I've got a little midnight snack for you," whereupon she rose to her knees, straddled my face and clutched me with her thighs.

Conversation wanes at a time like this.

I smelled a spicy aroma in the chill air of Ivy Joe Culpepper's bedroom. What woke me was a single ring on the kitchen telephone. I could hear Lucia taking the call, but I could not make out what she was saying. In a moment, she hung up. Shortly afterward, she quietly opened the bedroom door.

"Oh, good, you're awake. You're office just called." She entered carrying a steaming cup. Hot spiced tea. I could smell it. Her smile was a work of art; those brilliant white teeth shone against her brown skin. "Good morning!"

"Yes. The best I can remember in a very long time, now that you mention it," I said. Lucia handed me the cup and bent to kiss me.

"What time is it?" I asked.

"Eight-oh-five. Milly Stanford said not to wake you and not to give you coffee because you hate it. She was only calling to tell you she talked to Dr. Morgan and—Gruesome, is that his name?—is up and eating with some difficulty."

"That's a relief. That poor old dog has sure paid some dues. We need to get going swifto. We have a lot to do today, and I have to attend Cassie Shelor's funeral this afternoon at one."

Lucia untied her dressing gown and let it slide down her body to the floor. In the light of day, her flawless brown skin, pointed breasts and rounded hips were overpowering. A thin trickle of pubic hair extended up from her mons to her navel. She was amazingly sexy. "Damn, you look nice . . ."

She took my hand. "Get up, Sleepy. Let's take a shower."

I leaped out of bed and followed her into the bathroom. "Oh, well, what the hell. Since you insist."

We closed the door, turned on the hot water and kissed and touched each other all over as the steam clouded the little white tile bathroom. Ultimately, I sat down on the closed commode and leaned back against the tank, cold against my shoulders. Lucia sat, straddling me, facing me. I kissed her breasts as the tip of my cock kissed her cervix. In the steam and heat we slid wetly against each other, frantically arching, thrusting, until semen, sweat and vaginal oils glistened our thighs. We held each other in the shower until the hot water faded, clutching each other until the water was too cold to bear. Then we toweled each other dry.

"Poppy Joe's razor is in the cabinet if you want to shave," Lucia said. "I'll make us some fast breakfast."

As I shaved with Ivy Joe's ancient ivory-handled straight razor, I studied the stranger who stared at me from the mirror, his face masked in white cream. The stranger seemed dazed at the dizzying pace of recent events in his hitherto sleepy mountain county and his lonely life. The deaths of Ivy Joe Culpepper and Cassie Shelor, the torching of his house, an assault by hired goons, the violent encounter with the Sloans, the threats, the rumors, Lois Ross and . . . and the sudden extraordinary intimacy, the wet heat, the draining sexuality and the emotional narcotic of one Lucia Dodd.

My God.

After Tess died and Elaine left me, I came to regard love as a devastating mental disease of the young that—once contracted, suffered and recovered from—left its victim with some degree of immunity from catching it again. Who, after all, would voluntarily resubmit themselves to such misery?

Now, much as one senses the vague pre-fever uneasiness at the onset of flu, I was having these murky, nebulous feelings of warmth about Lucia Dodd. They were troubling. I knew it wasn't just having slept with her, having shared such intense physical intimacy with her; I'd taken a few other women to bed in the years since Elaine, and I wasn't stricken with these unsettling longings of the heart then. I had the uncomfortable sensation that I'd be having these feelings about Lucia even had we not just fucked each other blind. I had begun having the feelings, in fact, from the time she had walked into my office, when we were hardly likely to become lovers. That's what really worried me.

Falling in love with Lucia Dodd was clearly a losing proposition for us both. Even if race could be discounted as a practical consideration, just as our hearts discounted it as a romantic one, even if Lucia Dodd as a lover, let alone wife, of mine might not redefine my electability for sheriff in Hunter County, even if I as a lover, let alone husband, of hers might not redefine her career position with Washington's premier black law firm . . . no, even if all this could be discounted, there were still the radical differences in our ages, our incomes, our educations, our aspirations, our backgrounds—hell, even our geography. I was no spring chicken; I knew that one sweet-violent night of lust does not a solid marriage make. No, sir. I was no dummy.

Damn. Then why was I indulging myself in little white picket fence fantasies about her? Why was I allowing her to make me feel so happy? What the *hell* was the matter with me? Maybe if I took a couple of aspirin it would go away.

Not to worry, I told myself, washing my smooth face. Even if you were schoolboy enough to fall for her, which of course you're not, *she's* not dumb enough to fall in love with you. She did not work that long and that hard—achieve that much, suffer that painfully—to trash it all on some silly love affair with a poor white country cop. Not lately. There were too many black Mercedes-driving quiche-eaters in Washington—six-digit guys with advanced degrees and proud pedigrees who would be infinitely more suitable for Lucia Dodd, and she would not be so childishly heartstruck as to overlook this. I was confident that, even as I now spoke to the nut in the mirror, Lucia was standing in the kitchen under the cold light of day realizing full well how stupidly hopeless the idea of any ongoing relationship between *us* was. Any minute now, she would compose herself, stride confident before me and say words to this effect: "Lewis, we were lonely and hungry last night. We had a lovely time together and I'll always remember you but . . . let's not lose sight of reality here. Let's not spoil what we've shared with any foolish notions of love. I have my life and you have yours, and we both know they can never be merged." She would say something like that.

I walked naked into Ivy Joe Culpepper's little bedroom to find Lucia Dodd standing in the doorway in her robe. She wore a look of stern concern. Bless her heart, I thought, she's trying to find a way to let me down easy.

"Lewis," she began. Here it comes, I thought. I tossed the towel on the bed. She glanced briefly down at my plumbing and snatched her gaze away, struggling to compose her speech. "Lewis, I've been thinking."

I said nothing. She walked toward me, looking anywhere but at me, clenching her fists by her sides. I could see tears forming in the corners of her beautiful soft brown eyes.

"Lewis I, I . . ." She turned away from me, beginning to cry. "Oh, God, look at me. I'm crying like a baby!"

"Lucia . . ." I began, groping for some way to make this easier for her. It hurt me to see her so troubled.

"Nanh!" She cried out sudden and loud, startling me. She spun about, the dressing gown spinning out from her body, and she launched herself at me, crying. She seized me about my neck desperately and sank her forehead against my chest. Stunned, I held her to me.

"Oh, Lewis, I'm sorry—"

"It's okay, darlin'," I said, kissing her hair. "It's okay. I understand."

"I'm sorry. I love you! I love you so very much. I know I do. I don't want to, Lewis. I'm so afraid but I know I love you. Oh, God. What am I going to do? Please hold me! I love you, Lewis! I love you!"

"Yep," I said, holding her tightly and bending to kiss her. "We're in *big* trouble now."

# 18

## Thickening Plots

Over breakfast, Lucia and I planned to meet late in the afternoon. I had office work to catch up on and there was Cassie Shelor's funeral at one. Lucia had to start writing thank-you notes for the meadow of flowers and condolence cards Mr. Joe's funeral had drawn.

On the way in to the dungeon, I was pleased to see the snow had yielded to a blazing sun in a cloudless sky. It was still quite cold, and while the plowed and sun-heated pavement was clear and dry, a foot of snow stood unmelted everywhere but in the roads proper.

At the dungeon, I was treated to wide-eyed, raised-brow glances from the office staff and a blatant smirk from Sergeant Milly Stanford. "You lookin' kinda tuckered out there, white boy," she observed, enjoying herself immensely.

"Shut up," I growled, walking into my office where a fire blazed in the old stone hearth. Milly cackled softly. Okay, so the whole office was teeing off on the story of where and presumably with whom the boss slept last night. Well, screw 'em. I'd plead the fifth. Let 'em guess forever.

Milly wasn't guessing. She waddled in with a cocky swagger and leaned on the mantel to warm her hands. "Mmm, mmm, mmm," she said, casually, "I think that little lawyah niggah done wore your white ass out."

"Oh, well, don't hold back, Milly," I said with exasperation, "don't mince words, just speak your mind! Jesus. What do you know?"

Milly went tee-hee, shaking all over. "Sheeeyit. I'm a woman, ain't I? I done talked to that little gal twice on the phone. Once she tell me I don't got to come by an' check on you, that you is in 'good hands.' I'll bet!" Milly howled like that was the richest thing she'd ever heard. I glanced at the open office door, fervently hoping the staff was busy.

"So wha—"

"Then! Then I done call this mornin' and that girl sound all mellow, tired-out and happy, an' ain't but *one thing* make a woman all them things at once!"

"Aw, bullshit, Milly. Will you keep your voice down?"

Milly fairly bayed. She was having a field day. She waddled over to the closet and withdrew a neatly pressed uniform with my insignia on it and laid it across a chair. "Put this on before you go to that funeral," she said, walking toward the door. "Dat uniform you wearin' look like, oh, well, les' just say it look . . . kinda fucked up." Milly wiped her eyes, laughing.

"Close the damn door!" I called. She did, but I could still hear her howling.

Nobody but Lucia Dodd and I could know what went on in that little house.

I was startled by my office door opening so swiftly it whammed into the wall. Cindy Poff stalked in looking as beautiful as always but with fire in her eye. She marched up to my desk and slammed down a serving tray, spilling some of the hot chocolate from its mug. She spun on her heel and stormed out, slamming my office door behind her. Well, I considered grimly, clearly somebody *thinks* they know what went on.

There were messages on my desk to call Hap Morgan the vet, Pete Floyd the editor, my State Farm insurance agent and Dr. Coleby Butler.

I called the clinic for Coleby first. He sounded fatigued, wasted. Like I'd seen and heard so many battle-weary grunts look and sound, picking them up after all-night firefights with the NVA. I knew that if I could see Coleby through the phone, he'd have that thousand-yard stare.

"Good morning, Lewis," Coleby said, obviously emotionally drained. "I hope you got the word on Gruesome. It looks like he's going to be fine."

"Yes, Coleby, thank you. I did get the word, and I hope it goes without saying I'm very grateful to you and Elizabeth and Anne for being there and for taking care of him so well. I wasn't up to it. I have a message here to call Hap, but I wanted to ring you first. I gather Lu—ah, Ms. Dodd advised you I wouldn't be spending last night at Mountain Harbor. She was kind enough to insist on fixing me some supper when I took her home, and I was so exhausted I fell asleep right there on the couch."

"Yes, Lewis, she told me. We had a long and charming talk on the phone last night. I'm very impressed with her, Lewis. She seems to be one of those rare mergings of the physical and maturity curves we talked about. She is quite lovely and very engaging."

"Yeah," I stammered. "Ah. She's . . . very unusual. I, well, I like her . . . a lot." Jesus, I hoped I didn't sound as stupid as I felt I did.

"Lewis," Coleby said, pausing to sigh as though reluctant to convey bad news, "there may be a problem. It may be nothing, but I want you to know about it. Can we have lunch today at Mountain Harbor? I'll have Polly fix us some splendid Reubens. It won't take long. I know you need to attend the Shelor funeral at one."

"Of course, Coleby. Are you all right? You sound awful, my friend."

"I've been better, Lewis. Things are getting . . . worse with Sarah. She—well, let's talk about it over lunch. Sarah's gone shopping in Roanoke with Elizabeth all day. Anne and I went riding this morning, but she has a luncheon date with a VMI cadet this afternoon. Is eleven-thirty all right with you?"

"Eleven-thirty. I'll be there, Coleby. I'll see you then."

There may be a problem with what? I wondered, hanging up the phone. Or with whom? He meant with Sarah, obviously. He'd said as much. Damn that woman.

I called Hap Morgan at his veterinary clinic. He told me Gruesome was up and about and cranky as hell. He said I could take him home in two days if his prognosis held. I passed on mentioning that I didn't have a home to take him to anymore. "You oughtta feed that animal something besides beer and table scraps, Lewis—he's a dog, not a garbage disposal!" Hap admonished me. I told him thanks and I'd be by later to visit.

I picked up the phone to call Pete Floyd but then set it back in its cradle. Pete would want to know why I wasn't going to the morning meetings of The Gentry lately and what was happening with the Ivy Joe Culpepper investigation. I didn't feel like answering questions about either right now.

I called my insurance agent, who said he'd been out this morning to inspect what was left of my house, where he'd met Pierce Arroe and Arnold Webb, the fire chief. He said I was in what he called "good shape." Easy for him to say. We set a meeting for later in the week.

I spent another hour on routine administrative matters, phone calls, the payroll, and arranging with Vaughn Chevrolet to obtain and outfit another police interceptor package unmarked patrol car to replace the one torched by the Sloans. I remembered Moose again, and acid thoughts about the Sloans gurgled in my belly. I hoped a solid case against them fell into place soon. I looked forward to going after them, perhaps a little more than I should have.

At ten-thirty, Pierce and Arnold Webb stamped in with a handful of Polaroid photographs and a bag full of sundry charred flotsam. Pierce seemed pleased about something.

"Well, Lewis," Arnold began, warming himself by the fire, "if they was ever any doubt, they ain't no more. It was arson for certain. The device was a common Molotov cocktail made from a Jack Daniel's whiskey bottle with a shop rag stuffed in the neck. I ain't sure of the agent, but they ain't no reason to believe it wadn't plain old gasoline. As you know, your old granddaddy's house, your home, was all old and very dry wood. Even the interior walls was pine paneling, they wadn't no drywall when that old house was built. It didn't take much to make it burn like an old Christmas tree."

This grim assessment only seemed to amuse Pierce.

"They didn't bomb your barn, near as I can tell," Arnold continued. "Probably just tossed a match in on all that dry straw and . . . whoof."

Whoof. A pretty succinct statement when voiced by a fire investigator. What the hell was Pierce grinning about? I was damned if I could tell what was so funny about all this.

"Lewis," Arnold went on, "we had ol' Jimmy bring his backhoe up on the ridge and doze into the ruins of the barn. You know, to bury your horse and all." Now Arnold was grinning, too! What the hell? "We found your tractor; 'course it's ruint. But, ah, Lewis, we didn't find no horse!"

I sat up suddenly. Pierce smugly tossed a Polaroid picture on my desk that brought tears to my eyes. It showed a grinning Pierce Arroe standing in the snow by the blackened foundation of my barn next to a somewhat sooty but obviously quite healthy Belgian draft mare.

"She's alive, Lewis!" Pierce exclaimed. "Moose is alive! She got out of there somehow. We found her down near that same stand of pines you told us to bury her in. She was a little jittery but she's okay. Arnold's having his boys truck her out to Dr. Butler's stable till you can rebuild."

I dabbed at my eyes. "What a miracle" was all I could manage. It struck me that what I wanted to do most right then was to call Lucia Dodd with the good news.

Pierce said, "Yeah! I don't know how she did it but—"

"Shit," Arnold grunted. "I know how she done it. That's over a ton of horse there. When that fire got hot enough, she got busy makin' her own door outa that barn. I'm just glad I wasn't in her way!"

"Lewis," Pierce said, "I talked to all your neighbors on Bram's Ridge to find out if anybody saw anything. Turns out Paul Waters was on his tractor towing straw up to Clement Machevski's place on the ridge when he almost got torpedoed between the headlights by a speeding pickup truck about the same time Arnold got the call on your place. Paul knows it was Lanny and Danny Sloan because they broke his nose about five years ago when he caught them poaching on his land. He remembers them real well and he got a good look at them in the front seat of the truck. Said they was a third person in there with them, but he didn't recognize him. Probably Lanny's punk kid. Anyway, they were hauling ass, which is why they nearly hit Paul's tractor. Don't leave much room for doubt in my mind."

Pierce stood up with a look on his face like the residents of Tokyo must've seen when Godzilla came to town.

"Now, Lewis," Pierce continued, "How about me and some of the boys goin' up there and snatchin' them white-trash maggots right off their mountain, *now?* I got enough outa Lois yesterday to indict them for grand theft auto and intent to distribute controlled substances. Lois *will* testify."

I thought about this for a moment while Cindy Poff came in with coffee and chocolate. She pointedly served Arnold and Pierce and left me to pour my own. On her way out, she paused just long enough to fire me a look that would cause cancer in lab rats. I sighed.

"Pierce, let's hold off on the Sloans a while longer. I know you're anxious to take them and so am I. But when we go for them, chances are they're going to go hard. It'll be dangerous; somebody could get shot. If we're going to do that, I want it to be for more than petty dealing and car theft. It's still a stretch case in court to prove they torched my place and we can't yet indict them for Ivy Joe's death."

"The Sloans killed Ivy Joe Culpepper?!" Arnold exclaimed.

"You keep this under your hat, Arnold," I said. "You hear me?"

"Sure, Sheriff."

"We don't know what happened to Ivy Joe yet, but I've got a burning hunch Lanny's daughter, Peggy, knows something that might knit all this together. I'm trying to figure out now how to interview her without tipping off Lanny, who would beat her brains out for talking to me."

"Aw, come on, Lewis," Pierce said, "maybe if we tumble them, they'll confess. Lanny's probably too tough a nut to crack, but that piss-ant brother of his would give up his mother for a buck."

"No. Not now. The Sloans aren't going anywhere; they're grafted to these hills. They'll be there when we're ready. Let me talk to Peggy Sloan somehow and then we'll rethink it."

Pierce sighed. "You're the boss, Lewis," he said, but I knew he wasn't happy.

As Arnold and a disgruntled Pierce left my office, I

reflected that it was a damn good thing Pierce was on my side of the law.

And how about Moose!

I drove the truck out to Mountain Harbor and pulled around back. Polly had a worried look on her face when she let me in.

"Dr. Butler will be down in a minute, Sheriff Cody," Polly said. "Would you like some good hot herb tea?"

"Sounds good," I answered, following her into the long brick-floored kitchen. "Polly, what the hell is going on out here?"

Polly sighed, pouring my tea. "I don't know, Sheriff Cody. Ms. Butler, she just cain't seem to give poor Dr. Butler no peace. I swear he done everything a mortal man could do to make that woman happy, but don't nothin' seem to do no good. Ms. Butler, she don't say much around me, but that poor little Elizabeth come cryin' to me sometime. Ms. Butler, she want a divorce and she want to take Elizabeth and move away, but Lord knows how that girl love her daddy, Sheriff Cody. She'd just die if that was to happen. So would Dr. Butler. You know that."

"Yeah." I did.

"Now . . ." Polly sniffed. "Dr. Butler, he having me make him margaritas at ten in the mornin' . . ." Her huge shoulders shook as she cried.

I put an arm around her. "I'm sorry, Polly, I didn't mean to upset you."

"Aw, that's okay, Sheriff Cody. This is surely one upset house these days."

I took my tea into the den. Coleby came down the winding staircase. In the bright sunlight shining through the den windows, he looked pale and haggard. Though he evinced no signs of the slightest inebriation, there was a slight smell of alcohol about him.

"Lewis!" he said greeting me. His mouth smiled slightly but not his eyes. "Thank you for coming out. Polly, we'll have lunch in my study."

In the library, Coleby told me Sarah was growing impatient and was becoming increasingly vitriolic. "She profanes me, Lewis, she profanes me before my daughters. She accuses me of impotence in front of them, although she's rebuked every physical advance I've made long before she could know if I was impotent."

Coleby allowed himself a grim chuckle. "I'm not impotent," he mumbled.

I didn't know what to say to comfort him. Coleby slowly drew a hand down the length of his face. As the hand passed, the face revealed a renewed strength. He smiled again, having apparently put his agony behind him for a while. "But, Lewis, that isn't why I asked you to join me. I . . . know how lonely you've been since Elaine left and I know you—I can see you becoming drawn to Lucia Dodd. She's a beautiful woman, to be sure, but . . . there's a problem that you need to know about, I think."

This was a startling tack. I sat quietly. I knew Coleby would make himself quite clear soon enough.

Coleby looked at me carefully. "Lewis, her name is uncommon and it rang a bell. I couldn't place it for the longest time and then I remembered. I made some calls to colleagues in Washington and confirmed what I am about to tell you.

"Please hear me out, Lewis, for I mean Ms. Dodd no disrespect, but I think you should know something about her. Three years ago, she defended a black surgeon who practiced at George Washington University Hospital. She defended him on a malpractice case. The malpractice was pretty blatant. It seems the surgeon had been under the influence of alcohol when he accidentally severed a nerve, inducing permanent partial paralysis of the patient's left arm. The patient was a professional basketball player. Even more unfortunate, Ms. Dodd apparently fell in love with the doctor over the many months the case was litigated. He had been a medic, a corpsman in the navy in Vietnam. Like so many veterans of that terrible war, he carried psychological damage from it. A failed previous marriage and"— Coleby paused to look me in the eye—"the death of a child, combined to drive the physician to drink. In any case, Ms. Dodd fell in love with him. They lost the suit and a huge judgment was awarded, some seven hundred thousand dollars of which was not covered by insurance. The doctor did not have the remainder and attempted suicide by overdose but was discovered by Ms. Dodd and was saved. In keeping with the theme of desperation in this sad story, she cosigned loans with him to cover the balance of the damage award. Shortly thereafter, the emotionally destroyed surgeon took his life. Now Ms. Dodd is the subject of collection lawsuits that seek to take her home, offered as collateral, of course, and her other assets. She may have to declare bankruptcy, which, aside from wrecking her financially, will probably jeopardize her position with her firm. She's in serious trouble, Lewis."

Coleby gave me time to soak in all this before continuing. "I have, of course, questioned that I have any business bringing this up. It smacks of gossipy meddling, but my chief concern is . . . well, this lovely young woman is almost certainly under immense strain, Lewis, which has every indicator of becoming worse. I wanted you to be aware so you can be better prepared to deal with the inevitable effects of the situation as they bear on you. My ultimate concern is that I'd hate to see you become enmeshed in another terribly unhappy situation. I think you're . . . closer to a breaking point than you let on. I know you pretty well and I see in your eyes that look of . . . quiet misery. I've seen it before in the faces of men and women who became suicides. I know how empty your life has been, and it leaves you vulnerable. Just be careful as you grow to know her, Lewis. Don't let her grief become yours."

I stared back at Coleby for a moment, then I carried my tea to the window. Down the draw and across the creek, I could see a horse trailer being towed up to Coleby's stable. I watched as two men led Moose from it into the long barn. She looked well from this distance.

I turned back to Coleby, who had risen and was watching me through pained eyes—eyes that had felt entirely too much pain these last years. I set the tea down, walked to him and we embraced each other as only two battle-weary soldiers can appreciate.

I drove back to the dungeon on mercifully dry and clear roads, considering the foot of snow that bordered them. I changed into my dress uniform, borrowed a marked cruiser and drove to the Weeks's Funeral Home for the last farewell to Cassie Shelor. On the way, I suffered a headful of roiling, flashing emotions about Lucia Dodd and even poor Cassie Shelor. I felt empty inside and vaguely afraid without really knowing why. I found myself overwhelmed by an urge to weep, but even as I tried, the tears would not come, yet the urge would not go away. What disturbed me deeply was I knew I had been having this problem more often lately. Was I closer to a breaking point than even I knew?

Lawrence Weeks was quietly and efficiently plying his difficult trade. I saw him ushering a hunched-over Helen Shelor to a waiting limousine. Cassie still looked very nice, considering she was dead. I was disturbed to find myself growing hard at the vision of her squirming naked in the mud by Bram's Creek. This is insane, I thought, and I moved away from the casket for the last time. Adios, Cassie, my love. You were an original, darlin'. In my odd way, I will surely miss you.

Coleby had said he wasn't up to attending the funeral, and he wasn't at the church ceremony. Outside in the cemetery, however, as I stood well to the rear of the dozens of weeping schoolgirls and other mourners, I was surprised to see a lone, well-dressed figure standing a hundred yards away on a rise near the trees. Dr. Coleby Butler. Poor, big-hearted, loving Coleby Butler. The shepherd of Hunter County.

A shadow engulfed me and I turned to see Pierce towering over me. "Lewis, call Milly ASAP. She says it's important."

I walked to the Episcopal Church office and called the dungeon. Milly told me, "Lewis, some female called here a few minutes ago. Say she got to see you right away. Wouldn't give her name but, Lewis, I swear I think it's that same little Sloan girl who called the night the Dodd woman got into trouble out there. She left a number."

Milly gave me the number and I dialed it immediately. I pushed the office door closed. The phone answered halfway through the first ring. It was indeed fifteen-year-old Peggy Sloan, whose terror was obvious in her trembling voice.

"Sheriff Cody! Oh, thank God!" Peggy Sloan began sobbing out of control.

"Peggy, Peggy, honey, try to calm down a little for me. I can tell you're upset and I'm going to help you. Just tell me where you are, darlin', tell me where you are."

"I, I'm at Slayer's General Store, you know out the Trace Mountain Road? I ran away! I ran away! Daddy's tryin' to find me! Him and Uncle Danny are looking everywhere for me. Sheriff Cody, they're gonna kill me! You got to help me! They're gonna kill me!" Peggy Sloan was on the verge of hysteria.

"Peggy," I said calmly, "listen to me, honey. I'm not going to let anyone hurt you, I promise you. I'll come get you right away. You stay there. Abe Slayer will take care of you till I get there."

"Hurry, Sheriff Cody! Please hurry! I cain't take it no more, I'm so scared! I know! They know I know! They're gonna kill me, Sheriff Cody! Daddy's done said so! Please hurry!"

"I'm on the way, Peggy. Try to relax. What is it you know, honey?"

"Everything!" Peggy Sloan screamed into the phone. I held it back from my ear in pain. "I know it all! What Daddy done! What they done to your house! What they done to Ivy Joe Culpepper!"

I could hear the phone clatter at the end of its cord and I could hear Peggy Sloan weeping in wretched horror.

# 19

## Dark Secrets

"**P**eggy!" I called into the phone, but the handset only swung on its cord and rapped against something. I could hear Peggy Sloan sobbing. "Oh God! They're gonna kill me! They're gonna kill me!"

I heard the phone being picked up and old Abe Slayer's voice sounded, "Hello? Hello?"

"Abe?" I replied. "Abe, this is Sheriff Lewis Cody."

"Sheriff Cody? That you? Say, Sheriff, this little girl of Lanny Sloan's come a runnin' in here a-cryin' and all. Keeps a-sayin' somebody's gonna kill her. And she looks like somebody already tried; she been whupped up on."

"Listen, Abe, I'm en route to your store right now. Can you hide her in the back till I get there? I think the Sloans may be looking to do her serious harm."

"Why sure, Sheriff. Sure thing!"

"Listen, Abe, if the Sloans show up, tell 'em she's not there, but if they use force to search your place or take her, don't get yourself hurt. I'll deal with them when I catch up with them."

"Shit, Sheriff Cody, I been runnin' my store since before you was born and ain't nobody never took nothin' out of here I didn't want 'em to take."

"Don't get in some Hollywood gunfight, Abe. I'll be right out there."

"Take your time, Sheriff. This little gal is safe as the goddamn Queen of England."

I called Lucia at Ivy Joe Culpepper's little cottage.

"Hi!" she said with charming enthusiasm.

"We may have a break in Mr. Joe's case," I told her. "I'll pick you up in about five minutes and I'll be in a hurry. Be ready."

"I'm ready, Lewis."

Under blue lights and siren, I hit the road and radioed Milly at the dungeon. "Milly, I'm leaving the cemetery. Do we have anybody closer to Abe Slayer's store than me?"

Milly paused, waiting for any of the monitoring patrol units in such a position to respond. No one did.

"Disregard," I said, and hung up the mike.

Lucia was standing out front when I came down Eldridge Street. She wore boots, jeans and a red sweater under her down ski coat. She got into the car and we took off.

We screeched through town, quickly but carefully edging past cars that were pulling into the snow to the right of the road to let us pass, and zipped out the road to Trace Mountain. It took us nearly ten minutes to get there. I switched off the lights and siren while still a mile away. There were no vehicles in the lot before the store but I'd had that tune sung to me before. I slipped up onto the porch of the old clapboard store and peeked around the edge of one window. Old Abe sat before his kerosene stove, watching a soap opera on TV. Across his lap was a scoped deer rifle. I waved to Lucia to join me and went inside.

"Well, hey, Sheriff!" The bearded Abe Slayer groaned, getting up from his chair. I had a tense moment as he swung the rifle muzzle past my middle. He placed the weapon under the worn wooden countertop covered with bulk candy jars. He went in the back and returned with Peggy Sloan, and I began to understand her hysteria.

Fifteen-year-old Peggy Sloan looked like she'd made Mike Tyson real mad. Her hair hung in her eyes. Her upper lip was blue and puffed, one eye was swollen and she had a red abrasion on her right cheek. I remembered noting, the night the Sloans stripped Lucia Dodd, that Lanny Sloan was left-handed. Peggy wore jeans, a T-shirt and a frayed light jacket. On her feet were only wet socks. She looked utterly terrified, trembling visibly and crying. She bore the defeated, frightened look of a chronically abused dog.

"Look at this girl, Sheriff," Abe said. "Anybody treat a kid this way ought to—"

Lucia Dodd came through the front door and Abe looked like E.T. had just waddled in.

"She's with me," I said. "Come on, Peggy, darlin', nobody will hurt you now, I promise. Let's go to town and you can tell me everything. I'll take care of you."

Peggy moaned. "They're gonna kill me. They're gonna kill me." She cowered by the doorway, not moving.

Something told me not to go near her just yet. She seemed close to the edge of her control.

"Peggy, I promise to keep you safe. I won't let them hurt you."

Peggy gasped for breath; she was very near a breakdown.

I felt Lucia's hand on my arm and looked at her as she stepped slowly around the end of Abe's candy counter. She held out her arms to Peggy Sloan.

"Come to me, child," Lucia said.

Peggy wailed and rushed into Lucia's arms. She buried her face in Lucia's bosom and wept uncontrollably. "Oh God, I'm so scared! Oh God, don't let them kill me. Oh God . . ."

"Lewis." Lucia looked at me, holding Peggy and rocking side to side. "She doesn't have any shoes. Her feet are bleeding."

On my way out of Abe's Stone Age store, he handed me a new pair of heavy woolen boot socks. "Don't sell no shoes." He grunted. I knew better than to offer him payment.

We drove to the dungeon, Lucia in the back seat with Peggy, who remained cradled in Lucia's arms, struggling to get her breath. When we arrived, we led Peggy into my office.

"Milly," I called, "get us something hot to drink. Send somebody to Lady Maude's for a cheeseburger and some fries and send somebody else to Ed Ramsey's store for a pair of size-six shoes and a size-medium winter coat for a girl. Tell Ed to bill me."

"Yes, sir!" Milly said, scribbling furiously on a notepad.

"Say, Lewis, Pete Floyd with the paper, he been trying to get you."

"I don't have time to talk to him now, Milly. Get a recorder and come on in here. Tell Cindy I don't want to be disturbed for anything but the food and clothes."

Peggy Sloan stared vacantly at the fire in my office and said nothing while we waited for the food. When it arrived, she attacked it like a rescued POW.

"Easy, sweetheart," Lucia told her. "Chew it up slowly or you'll get a stomachache."

The clothes were brought in. The shoes were the pink ankle-high ski type that were the teenage rage at the moment. Peggy looked at them on her feet and then looked up at me. Only the faintest hint of a smile tugged at the edges of her swollen lips.

I nodded at Milly who switched on the tape recorder.

"Peggy," I said, "do you feel a little better now?" She nodded slowly, chewing her hamburger, the wariness still in her eyes. "Let's talk a little bit, can we?" She nodded again. "Peggy, this is a tape recorder so we won't forget anything you tell us, okay?" Again, she nodded slowly.

I voiced the time, date and place and the names of the persons present for the tape. "Interview with Peggy Sloan," I said. "Peggy, how are you, now?"

Peggy looked at the recorder, then at me. "Okay. I . . . I'm okay."

"Peggy, do you feel like telling us what has happened to you and answering some questions?" She nodded. "I need you to speak out loud for the tape, honey," I told her.

"Yes. Yes, I do."

"Okay, darlin', you're doing real good. I want you to relax now. You're safe, nobody is going to hurt you. You just take your time and tell us why you called me today."

Peggy looked slowly at Milly and Lucia and then back to me. Her expression became grim again. She looked at the floor.

"I . . . I'm so afraid. Daddy and Uncle Danny, they're . . . Daddy said they was gonna kill me. They killed Ivy Joe. They—"

Lucia leaned forward in her chair as if to ask something, but I waved her off.

# Shepherd of the Wolves

"Gonna kill me."

Peggy was beginning to cry again. She stopped talking.

"Peggy," I said, "why do you think your father and uncle want to kill you?"

" 'Cause I know," she replied, looking at me, the fear creeping back into her eyes. " 'Cause I know they killed Ivy Joe and they think I'm gonna tell. Daddy said if I ever talked to anybody about . . . about . . . he said he'd kill me! Uncle Danny, he just do whatever Daddy say." She looked from Milly to Lucia. Lucia looked at me.

"How do you know they killed Ivy Joe, Peggy?" I asked.

" 'Cause . . . he knowed. Ivy Joe knowed." Peggy stared at the floor. "They was afraid he'd tell. They said they was gonna kill him." Peggy began to weep again. "He . . . they . . . they killed that nice old man because I told him!" She looked up at me again in abject misery. "He knowed!" she cried. "Poor old Ivy Joe died because I told him! They killed him on account of *me!*" Peggy wept in despair. There was agony in Lucia's face as well.

"Because you told him what, Peggy?" I asked gently. "What was it you told him, sweetheart?"

Peggy struggled to breathe against her weeping. Milly handed her a box of tissues. She blew her nose and dabbed at her eyes. She breathed deep and looked at me, but her gaze fell immediately to the floor.

"He . . . Ivy Joe . . . he was so nice. He was so kind. He come up on me in the band room one day. He—"

"When was that?" I asked.

"Aw. About a month ago, I reckon. I was crying and he ast me, 'Why is you crying, Peggy?' He . . . Ivy Joe knowed everybody's names. He was always so nice, like he really cared about you, you know?"

I nodded. Peggy resumed staring at the old hook rug.

"Well. I couldn't take it no more! I couldn't take it no more, so I told Ivy Joe! I told him everything! Everything!"

I waited. Peggy wept and shook her head slowly. Lucia leaned forward and propped her chin on her hand, a tight wrinkle of concern on her brow. Milly glanced at me, then at Peggy, who still shook her head, sobbing.

Gently, I coaxed her. "What did you tell Mr. Joe, Peggy?

What did you tell him that made your father want to kill him?"

Peggy sniffed. Tears ran down her nose and dripped to the floor. She continued to slowly shake her head and weep. Then she mumbled something I could not understand. I looked quickly at Milly and Lucia, who both shrugged to indicate they hadn't understood her either.

"Peggy, darlin', I know this is hard for you. You take your time. There's no hurry. But can you please speak up, hon? We're having a hard time understanding you."

Peggy's crying became more pronounced. She struggled to speak between sobs, staring between her knees at the floor. She mumbled again, rocking her head slowly, fighting her sobs. Again Milly and Lucia shook their heads at me.

I sighed. "Peggy, we—"

"He *done* it to me!" Peggy suddenly shrieked at the floor, startling all three of us. "He done it to *me!*" she screamed hysterically. She pitched back on the old leather sofa and covered her face with her hands. "He done it to *me! Me!*" She lost all control and cried, drowned in her misery.

Lucia sat up. Milly stood. I leaned forward. All of us were in shock.

"Peggy. Who did what, honey?"

"Daddy!" she wailed. "Daddy done it to me! He done it to *me!* Over and over and over . . ." She sobbed.

Lucia looked at me with amazement. Milly dabbed at her own eyes.

"Peggy," I said softly, "honey, I know how hard this is for you, but I need you to help me here. Are you telling us your father, Lanny Sloan, has had sexual intercourse with you?"

"Yes! Yes! Oh, God. He done it to me, he done it to me . . ." She wept wretchedly.

"When, Peggy?"

"Last night! Last night, but he's been doing it to me for over a year! I cain't take it no more!" Peggy sobbed. "I cain't take it no more, Sheriff Cody! It ain't right! I cain't take it no more!"

"You don't have to take it anymore, Peggy. It's over, I promise you. He'll never touch you again." I paused to think. "Peggy, honey, we need to ask you some more difficult questions. I know it's distressing for you."

# Shepherd of the Wolves

Peggy shook her head violently, her face still in her hands. I looked at Lucia. She walked to the couch, sat by Peggy and gently took her hands in her own.

"Peggy," Lucia said softly, "sweetheart, we have to ask you some unpleasant questions now and you must try real hard to answer them truthfully. We know this is hard, but it's important. Can you help us?"

Peggy nodded and sniffed.

"Peggy, are you telling us that Lanny Sloan placed his penis in your vagina, is that what you're saying? Be very sure."

"Yes!" Peggy stammered, struggling to maintain what thin composure she had. "Yes. Yes, he did. He . . . you know, he got . . . hard and all . . . and he put it in me and he done it to me."

"And did he do anything else to you of a sexual nature, Peggy?" Lucia continued.

Peggy looked into Lucia's soft eyes. "Well, he . . . he . . . put it in my mouth, you know? He held my head and put it in my mouth and he made me . . . you know . . ."

Lucia asked, "Are you saying Lanny Sloan placed his penis in your mouth, Peggy? Is that what you mean?"

Peggy stared at Lucia, wondering no doubt why she was belaboring the painfully obvious. I knew why. The lawyer in Lucia intended to leave no room for confusion on the tape.

"Yes," Peggy answered.

"And did he do anything else to you of a sexual nature, Peggy?"

"Well, he touched me all over a lot and he, like . . . put his finger in me sometimes, you know?"

"Are you saying that Lanny Sloan fondled your breasts and vagina?"

"Yes."

"And are you saying Lanny Sloan placed his finger inside your vagina?"

"Yes."

Lucia looked at me.

"Peggy," I said. "When did Lanny Sloan first have sexual intercourse with you?"

Peggy sighed and sniffed and lay back on the couch, looking up at the ceiling. "It's been over a year, Sheriff

Cody. I think, yeah, it was sometime, I don't remember exactly when, summer before last summer."

"How many times, Peggy?"

Peggy sat forward, placed her elbows on her knees and cradled her face in her hands. "I don't remember, Sheriff. I . . . a lot of times." She began to cry again. "A lot of times."

"Would you say more or less than ten times, Peggy?"

Peggy's crying increased. "Oh, more! A lot more than ten!"

"Peggy, I'm sorry to push this, but it's important that we be specific, that we tell it like it is. Would you say he had sexual intercourse with you more or less than fifty times?"

"I don't know! It was a lot of times but maybe not fifty. It was only once for a couple of months at first. He come in my bedroom one night when he was real drunk. Later, it was whenever they was nobody around but him and me, and lately it's been a couple of times a month. He done it to me last night. I said no, please, but he always hits me if I say no."

"And did you tell Ivy Joe Culpepper all this that day, you said about a month ago, when he found you crying in the band room at the high school?"

"Yeah." Peggy sighed. "But I didn't actually say . . . you know . . . I just said he done it to me. I didn't tell Ivy Joe the, you know, the details and all. Ivy Joe promised me he wouldn't tell nobody but he told me I should go to you and tell. But I was afraid to."

"I understand. And how did Lanny Sloan learn that Ivy Joe Culpepper knew that he had sex with you?"

Peggy continued to eke out words between sobs. "It was, I don't know, a week ago. He, Daddy, he done it to me again, but this time I couldn't take it no more. I fought him and he beat me up again. I yelled at him that I couldn't take it no more and I was gonna tell! He slapped me around again and choked me and he wanted to know who I told! I told him nobody but he kept hitting me! He just kept hitting me! He hurt me! I told Daddy I only told old Ivy Joe but Ivy Joe swore he wouldn't tell! He just told me to call the sheriff! He promised he wouldn't tell! But Daddy screamed at me about tellin' and he chased me and hit me some more! He said, 'You just made a dead man outa that old nigger! I'll kill him! I'll kill him!' Oh, God, Sheriff Cody!" Peggy wept. "They killed that poor old nice man on account of me!" Peggy collapsed on Lucia, weeping out of control. Lucia held her and rocked her.

"No, sweetheart," Lucia said softly, "it wasn't your fault. None of this was your fault. You couldn't help it. None of this was your fault, Peggy. You only did what you had to do. It was not your fault."

"I never wanted for them to hurt Ivy Joe!" Peggy wailed. "He was such a nice old man!"

"It wasn't your fault, Peggy," Lucia repeated gently, rocking her. "It was not your fault, sweetie."

There was a knock at my door. Milly opened and Cindy leaned in. "Sheriff, can I talk to you, please?"

This was a bad time, but I knew Cindy would not have disturbed us unless it was important. I joined her in the outer office. She leaned close to my ear, which was distracting, but what she had to say got my attention off her perfume and cleavage.

"Sheriff, somebody who sounded like a grown white male just called here demanding to know if we had Peggy Sloan here. I said, 'Who's calling?' and he yelled, 'Is she there? You ain't got no goddamn right to talk to her!' and he hung up."

"Lanny Sloan?" I asked.

"Could have been, Lew—Sheriff, I can't be sure. I've never heard him talk in person."

"Thanks, Cindy, you did good."

Back in my office, I continued to question a somewhat more composed Peggy Sloan.

"Peggy, like Ms. Dodd has told you, none of this is your fault, and you should not feel that it is. It is not your fault Mr. Joe was killed. You could not help it. You are one of the victims in this. You didn't cause any of it. We're going to protect and help you, but we need to ask you just a few more questions. Do you feel up to it?"

Peggy was still miserable, but she nodded. "Yes."

"Who else knew about the sex between you and Lanny?"

"Nobody! Nobody! Daddy said he'd kill me if I told anybody else, and he told Uncle Danny and my brother that Ivy Joe tried to rape me!"

"Peggy, there are two matters we're dealing with here. One is the statutory rape of you and the other is the death of Ivy Joe Culpepper. We've talked enough about the rape for now. What knowledge do you have that Lanny Sloan or anyone else killed Ivy Joe Culpepper?"

Peggy drew a deep breath. "They . . . the day Ivy Joe was killed, Daddy and Uncle Danny left the house in Daddy's truck with their guns. I heard them say they was gonna find Ivy Joe Culpepper and kill him. Daddy *said* it was for Ivy Joe trying to rape me but it was because Daddy knew I told Ivy Joe about him doing it to me!"

"I understand."

"Then, when I heard Ivy Joe was dead, I knew they done it. That was it. I couldn't take it no more. I was thinkin' about tellin' you when Daddy come at me last night. I said no, but he made me again! I cain't take no more, Sheriff Cody!"

"Easy, Peggy, you don't have to take any more. You've done the right thing. Did you hear Lanny or Danny talking about killing Mr. Joe anytime after you heard he was dead?"

Peggy thought for a moment. "I never heard them say they done it, but I heard them joke about him being dead and all. Plus I seen the front of Daddy's truck was bashed in like he'd hit something. He told my brother it was a bear, but him and Uncle Danny laughed. They done it, Sheriff Cody. I know my daddy and I know he done it."

"What do you know about the fire at my home?"

"The day after this . . . lady . . . come out to the house and you came that night and shot your gun, they was all crazy. They got drunk and took some gasoline and their guns and they said they was gonna get you for good. When they came back a couple hours later, they was bragging and joking about burning your house down, and Uncle Danny was done bit by your dog and he was bleeding."

That was enough to obtain warrants for murder, statutory rape and arson. Pierce was going to get his wish. We were going for the Sloans.

"Peggy," I said, "you have done good, sweetheart. I know it's been tough, but you've been tough, too, and we're proud of you. You've been through some terrible times, but they're over. You're going to be all right. I'm going to take care of you and we're going to put your father and uncle where they can never harm you again. Now I need you to do one more important thing for me. I need you to go with me to the courthouse to see Judge Lemon, okay?"

Peggy nodded sadly. I got the impression there was something else on her mind.

"Peggy, before we go, is there anything else you want to tell us, darlin'?"

"Yeah," Peggy Sloan said, choking up again, gasping to hold back tears. "Yeah, there is." She began to sob again. "I'm . . . I'm pregnant!"

The child wept.

# 20

---

## Trouble in River City

Milly and I went to the outer office, leaving Lucia to console Peggy Sloan.

"What a sorry, rotten, asshole motha*fuck*ah!" Milly hissed with her characteristic charming subtlety.

"Yeah," I said, "but we're about to fix that. I'm taking the tape and Peggy up to Judge Lemon's chambers to obtain warrants for Lanny Sloan for murder, incest, statutory rape and arson, and for Danny for murder and arson. Find Pierce, tell him to drop whatever he's doing and bring all the toys because we're going for the Sloans. Call in Otis, Thomas and Collen off patrol, call Art, Billy, Haskel and Elgin in from home. Get hold of Trooper Boyce Calder, too; I want all the manpower we can muster. Tell everybody to meet me here in an hour."

Over Milly's shoulder, I could see Cindy already picking up the phone.

Lucia and I drove Peggy to the Hunter County courthouse and were quickly ushered into the chambers of Judge Holden Lemon, a tall emaciated old man who always looked like he'd been dead for a week. When introduced, he eyed Lucia sharply, then extended his knobby, varicose-veined hand. "I'm pleased to meet you, young lady," he told her. "I'm familiar with your senior partner, Ernest Pelham—as fine a jurist as ever stood the bar."

"Thank you, sir," Lucia replied. "I'll relay your courtesy to Mr. Pelham."

Judge Lemon turned to the mortified Peggy Sloan. "And who have we here, Lewis?" He smiled at Peggy. Judge Lemon's expression was genuine but bore an unfortunate similarity to a buzzard eyeing fresh roadkill. Peggy gulped, wide-eyed, and she stepped closer to me.

"Judge, this is Miss Peggy Sloan, aged fifteen, the daughter of one Lanny Sloan, of whom I know you are familiar." I held up the tape. "I'm afraid we have some unpleasant matters to discuss with you, sir."

Judge Lemon's eyes narrowed as the tape played. Peggy stared at the floor. When the tape ended, no one said anything. The tocking of an old brass wall clock was the only sound in the office for many seconds. The judge rotated his long frame in the high-backed leather chair.

"Young lady," he addressed Peggy. "Did you at any time encourage Lanny Sloan to have sexual intercourse with you? Did you entice him in any way at any time?"

Peggy Sloan gaped at Judge Lemon. She looked at me and then at Lucia and then back at the old judge. "Sir," she said, "do you *know* my daddy?"

Judge Lemon said, "Answer me, please."

"No! God, no! He hurt me! I hated it!"

"Did you fight him or resist on each occasion?"

Again Peggy looked at me like she thought Judge Lemon had the IQ of a fern plant. To him she said, "Sir, you fight my daddy and he'll *kill* you!"

"Miss Sloan," said Judge Lemon, "I will ask you one additional question. Have you ever had sexual intercourse with anyone other than Lanny Sloan?"

"No! No!" Peggy looked at me with distress. "Sheriff!"

"At no time before, during the time in question or since?"

Peggy began to cry again. I knew what Judge Lemon was doing. He was ascertaining that Peggy's pregnancy could be attributable to no one else but her father, Lanny Sloan. I just wished there was a gentler way.

"Sir!" Peggy said in heartbreaking despair. "Look at me. Do I look like a homecoming queen to you? Nobody ever touched me before Daddy and nobody has after neither."

Peggy collapsed in tears and added, "An' ain't nobody never gonna, neither!" She cried.

Lucia had tears in her eyes. She rose to comfort Peggy but froze as Judge Lemon lifted a withered hand into the air without taking his eyes from Peggy.

"Look at me, young lady," Judge Lemon commanded, but in a gentle tone. Peggy regained her composure and looked up at the judge.

"My dear young woman, I do not fail to appreciate the suffering you've been through as a result of these events. However, I am called upon to make decisions here that may result in the imprisonment of at least two men. Possibly, those decisions may ultimately manifest in capital punishment. Execution. I am empowered to instruct the good sheriff here to capture, with force if necessary, these dangerous men, an endeavor which entails deadly risk to my officers of the law. I must know the complete truth to make these decisions correctly, and to know that truth I am compelled to ask you these hurtful questions. It is neither my intent nor my desire to cause you further pain and distress, and for that unavoidable side effect I offer you my profound, heartfelt apology."

Judge Lemon's eloquence may have been a little beyond Peggy, but maybe not. Her crying ceased and she seemed to relax.

The judge rotated in his chair to face me. "Sheriff Cody, you will forthwith bring before me Messrs. Lanny and Danny Sloan. My staff will prepare the appropriate warrants within twenty minutes."

"Yes, sir," I replied. "I'm going to the jail to brief my men, Judge. I'll be back in half an hour for the warrants."

With Peggy in tow, Lucia and I hurried down the granite-floored hall of the courthouse, our footsteps echoing among portraits of Hunter County venerables. My head was whirring with planning details of the Sloan apprehension when it occurred to me I had forgotten the poor victim.

"Peggy, we're going back to the jail. Sergeant Stanford will arrange for State Child Services to pick you up. You'll stay with them until a court decides what's best for you." I stopped in the hall, turned to Peggy and grasped her by the shoulders. I looked into her puffy, tear-reddened eyes.

# Shepherd of the Wolves

"Peggy, you listen to me, darlin'." She met my gaze. "Honey, things have been rough for you and there are going to be more unpleasant times and ugly questions for you as all this moves through the court system, but I promise you I won't let Lanny or anyone else hurt you again. You'll be safe at State Child Services and you'll have my phone number. If you're afraid, if you're frightened, if you need to talk, you call me anytime. My office always knows where I am. I'll be there for you. You're going to be all right, Peggy. The worst of this nightmare is over. Better times are coming. I'll take care of you. Understand?"

For the first time I'd ever seen, Peggy Sloan smiled. Then she threw her arms around my neck and clutched me. "Thank you! Thank you, Sheriff Cody."

Lucia shone that beautiful smile of hers on the scene.

My Tess would have been seventeen this year.

As the three of us trotted down the steps of the courthouse, Peggy held my hand tightly. On the far side of the small park that constituted the town square, I saw Trooper Boyce Calder in his blue and gray cruiser headed for the jail. I waved but he didn't see me.

My mind was racing, planning the arrest of the Sloans. They would go hard, and preparation was crucial to minimize the considerable possibility of violence and reduce as much as possible the risk to my people. I reviewed the geography of the Sloan farm in my head and considered different approaches to arrive undetected and cover all the exits while maintaining cover. We would have to—

I wasn't conscious of being in the street outside the courthouse until I heard the straining howl of carburetors sucking wind and tires screeching under hard acceleration. I glanced to my left instinctively and saw a large black car closing on us fast. I'd never seen the car before, but I sure knew the men in it. The Sloans had come to town.

There was no time. I shoved Peggy ahead of me and she sprawled to the pavement out of the path of the car. I planted my feet, spun and pushed Lucia backward. The car was now on me and there was nowhere to go but up. I jumped and landed on the hood, slid up against the windshield and cascaded off the right side of the car. I came down on my holstered gun and my hip felt seared. The car lurched to a stop as I fought to clear the pain in my hip enough to draw my weapon. There was a painful explosion, my ears rang and pavement chips sprayed into my face. I struggled to see beneath the car to where Peggy lay on the other side. At the same time I rolled, knowing a second shot would come any second.

Looking underneath the car, I saw boots on the ground on the other side and I saw Peggy Sloan snatched up from the ground, screaming. I rolled away and looked up at the passenger-side window of the car in time to see the evil eye of Lanny Sloan squinting down the ribbed sight of a Colt Python at me. My hip was numb and would not respond to command. I rolled again as Lanny's gun went off. The slug hit the pavement where I'd been, stinging the side of my head with pavement fragments. The Sig was now in my hand, but as I brought it up to bear, Danny Sloan rose up in the back seat of the car. Over my gunsight, I could see a hysterical Peggy Sloan held up as cover. The engine roared and an acrid cloud of blue rubber smoke emitted from the tires in front of me. Lanny leaned out for a departing shot, but his aim from the careening car was off and the bullet hit a parked car behind me.

Then I saw a vision I will always remember. It was the triumphant leer of Danny Sloan, who peeked from behind the frail, tortured body of Peggy, her face distorted with horror, screaming, her desperate hand extended toward me from behind the rear window of the fleeing car as though reaching out to me. I will always know that vision.

As I struggled to my feet, it was as though loud and confusing sound had just been introduced to a previously silent movie. Women were screaming, men were shouting, people were pointing and running. Tires squealed and carburetors howled as the black car lurched to the left around the square then hard back to the right onto the Roanoke Highway. There was no chance of a safe shot at them with Peggy in the car and citizens everywhere. I cried out in frustration and holstered my gun. I turned to see Lucia getting up from the ground, her face ashen. From my right, there came the high yelp of a siren. I looked to see Boyce Calder's state police cruiser squealing around the town square at me, blue light bar flashing. He slid to a halt by me and threw open the passenger door. Limping, I scrambled to the cruiser and dove in. The tires were singing before I had the door shut.

Boyce bore hard around the square, trying to steer and talk on the radio at the same time.

"Gimme that!" I yelled over the roaring engine and wailing siren. "I'll talk, you drive. Don't lose 'em!" He pitched me the microphone without taking his eyes from the road. We whipped left, then right onto the Roanoke Highway. Boyce floored it and the big Chevrolet lunged down the highway after the Sloan car. The black sedan was a quarter mile off and going away. It swerved left to overtake a car in its own lane and forced an oncoming car to dodge onto the snowy sidewalk to avoid a head-on collision. Boyce's cruiser built speed fast.

I stabbed at buttons on the radio console, selecting the frequency the state police shared with my department.

"Sheriff One, emergency traffic!"

In a second that seemed an eternity, Milly answered. "All units, hold your traffic. Go ahead, Sheriff One."

"Milly, I'm with Trooper Calder. We're in pursuit north on the Roanoke Highway from the town square of a black older-model Ford sedan with Virginia tags unknown. Shots have been fired. The subjects in the car are the Sloan brothers and the oldest Sloan son. They have abducted Peggy Sloan from my custody. Call Roanoke County and have 'em roadblock the county line. Advise State and tell 'em we need a helicopter. And get Rescue and one of our people up to the square. Several shots were fired by the suspects and someone may have been hurt. You got all this, Milly?"

"Ten-fo', Sheriff, I got it." In the background of Milly's transmission, I could hear feet thumping, doors slamming and sirens lighting up as my men raced to join the chase.

"Repeating, they are armed, shots have been fired, they have a hostage. Let's everybody keep our heads here, people. No wrecks, nobody hurt."

"Ten-fo', Sheriff."

"We're now north on Main, passing Jackson Street," I said, holding the mike close to my mouth to be heard over the siren.

"Ten-fo'. All units, the pursuit is now north on Main, passing Jackson. All units, use extreme caution. Suspects are armed. Shots have been fired."

The cruiser bounded over a dip like a Boston whaler on a high sea. Boyce was pursuing like a trained pro—fast but not foolish.

Virginia cops can ram a fleeing vehicle under certain defined circumstances, but, satisfying as it sounds, it is only rarely feasible, and this was not one of those times. The strategy in almost all police vehicle pursuits is not to catch the fleeing vehicle, per se, but to stay with it and not crash. In nearly every case, the excited and untrained driver of the fleeing car, unused to the stress of the event, will wreck his vehicle shortly. Boyce was skillfully following this strategy, staying close enough to keep them well in view but not so close as to push the fleeing driver to higher speeds or risk a collision. But Lanny Sloan's twenty-three-year-old kid had hot-rodded these roads for years—I knew my people had written him many citations—and the Sloan car, probably stolen, had a big engine, and I could see antisway bars had been installed beneath it. Boyce was hard put to keep the black car in sight.

I yanked a seat belt around me and cinched it tight, watching the black car lean severely, speedily negotiating the mountain turns. The road was dry except that, in the banked turns, runoff from the snow bordering the road flowed in slick streaks from the high shoulder to the lower. Mercifully, with the weather, there was little traffic on the highway. What there was moved smartly to the shoulder as Boyce's screaming, flashing cruiser bore toward them.

I reached and pressed a yellow button beneath the steering post and the electric clasp that secured Boyce's twelve-gauge police shotgun between the seats sprang open. I pointed the barrel out my window, racked a round into the chamber and safetyed it. I opened the glove box and stuffed three handfuls of shells for the gun into my coat pockets. I put another in the storage tube to replace the one now locked and loaded.

The chase had now cleared the town and had picked up to speeds over ninety, swift for two-lane mountain roads. The Sloan kid was hitting blind turns and rises way too fast to react to anything he found on the other side. I hoped he wouldn't encounter a stopped school bus or some farmer on a tractor.

My people were on the radio, professionally, not cluttering the channel but reporting into the chase. I heard Pierce order one disappointed deputy to fall out and check the situation on the square.

"They're headed straight for Roanoke County," I said on the radio. "We're crossing the Saddle Creek Bridge now."

Boyce closed on the big black Ford as the turns were becoming tighter and it was harder to keep the chased car in view. I could not see either Danny or Peggy Sloan in the back seat, but I did see Lanny get onto his knees facing rearward in the front seat and extend his gun hand out the right side window.

"Watch it!" I called to Boyce over the shriek of the siren. "He's going to shoot at us." We both lowered our heads to near dash level and Boyce weaved the car as much as control would permit to make us harder to hit. I saw Lanny's big magnum Python jump twice. I hoped he didn't hit the radiator or a tire, not to mention one of us, either of which could remove us from the chase or even the living. The third time the gun bucked there was a loud *crack!* The interior of the car was filled with flying glass particles. I flinched and the car swerved, but Boyce recovered it. I felt a cold wind suddenly whistling in the car and I became aware of an object in my lap. I looked down to find the rearview mirror lying there among crystals of glass. I examined myself for injury but found none.

"Are you all right?" I shouted over the wind and siren, which were even louder with the hole in the windshield.

"I don't feel nothin'!" Boyce bellowed, intent on the road. "I guess I'm okay!" The cruiser dove for the inside line on a right turn.

We entered a series of sharp banked turns and Lanny seated himself in the black car, apparently to reload. I ached to shoot back at him, but with Peggy in the car it was out of the question. Sure enough, as we drew closer to them, Danny Sloan held Peggy up to view in the back window to discourage just such a thought. I could not hear her, of course, but I did not need to hear the child to know she was screaming in terror, her mouth open wide, her eyes bulging from being held by her hair, thrashing her head from side to side. My blood boiled. I nearly cried out with the anguish.

This would not last long, I knew. The speeds were too great. Lanny's kid couldn't keep this pace up indefinitely. It was only a matter of a short time before the great unbreakable law, the law of averages, finally caught up with him. I hoped Peggy would not be injured when they wrecked. Briefly, I considered breaking off the chase to reduce the risk of a wreck injury to Peggy, but it did not take Columbo to figure out the Sloans didn't abduct Peggy from the law at gunpoint in broad daylight to take her to a church social. I knew they'd kill her if they escaped. Poor Peggy was between a rock and a hard place, and her best hope, her only hope, was me.

We both swept out of a right-hand slider. The black car drifted into the left lane, forcing an oncoming car to yank to its right and career into the snowy trees.

"Sheriff One," I hollered into the radio, "we're coming up on the intersection with six-twelve. Pierce, have somebody check the motorist who was just run off the west side of the road about a half mile this side of the school."

"Ten-four, Sheriff One! Sheriff Eight, do it."

"Sheriff Eight; ten-four!"

"Sheriff One; we're now—stand by!"

It was finally happening. The Ford bounded over a rise where the road hooked sharply to the right. Lanny's boy was late braking and was too hot going in; the back of the car swayed outboard as the rear wheels contacted a strip of icy runoff. He drifted left and steered into the skid, but when the rear wheels hit dry pavement the car straightened with a vengeance and he could not remove the steering correction fast enough. The black car snapped into a counterclockwise rotating slide and went off the road backward, colliding with an elevated embankment. It bounced back into the road, spinning fast to the right now, and it decelerated quickly, sliding sideways. It lurched to a stop crossways in the road, the driver's side to us, the trunk lid swinging up over a crumpled rear end. Boyce went down hard on his brakes. It all happened so fast there was no time to get off a radio call.

# Shepherd of the Wolves

As Boyce's cruiser slid up to the left side of the Sloan car, Danny Sloan made the last mistake of his life. He opened the left rear door, put his feet on the road, aimed an automatic handgun through the open door and fired directly at us. At least one round hit the windshield frame. With a guttural bellow of rage, Trooper Boyce Calder simply lifted his foot from the brake pedal. Lanny's kid in the driver's seat threw up his hands and opened his mouth to scream. At the last horrible second, it clearly registered in the eyes of Danny Sloan that his race was run. Four thousand pounds of wailing police car slammed into the Sloan vehicle, blasting it twenty feet sideways and crushing the legs off Danny Sloan.

On collision, I decelerated painfully against the seat-belt straps. In the same nanosecond, Danny's upper body snapped forward through the door window of the Ford, rebounded off the hood of Boyce's cruiser and whipped back into the rear seat of the Sloan car. The gun he held flew away.

I could not see Peggy or Lanny, who were evidently thrown to the floor in the impact with the embankment and the resulting spinout. I kicked open my door and bailed out with the shotgun. Boyce dived out his side. In the rush, neither of us turned off the siren which continued its deafening injured-dog shriek. I looked at the Sloan vehicle in time to see the bulk of Lanny Sloan disappear from view on the far side. Then his heavy bearded face popped up in the window, his gun extended toward us and three shots boomed in rapid succession. I hugged the side of the cruiser and held fire because I still hadn't located Peggy. Boyce must've had the same thought because he wasn't shooting either. Lanny ducked from view.

The siren howled maniacally. We could barely hear the kid in the driver's seat screaming, "I give up! I give up! Don't shoot me!" He was bleeding from the face.

Then, at last, I saw Peggy Sloan appear from behind the black car, scrambling to my right on her hands and knees, tears streaming down her face. She fell into the snow-filled ditch on the right side of the road. Now that it was open season on Lanny, I could not locate him. I couldn't see what Boyce was doing.

Shots exploded from the other side of the cruiser. I raised high enough to see Boyce and Lanny exchange several fast shots at each other, Boyce behind his open door and Lanny firing over the hood of the Ford. Lanny's boy covered his ears in the driver's seat, screaming. Boyce grunted and went down, holding his middle with his free hand. Lanny stood on his toes to elevate high enough to fire down on Boyce in the road. I threw the shotgun up to aim, but before I could shoot, Lanny saw me and dropped behind the front of the car. I flattened against the road hoping to fire beneath the Sloan car and cut a foot off Lanny, but the muffler and exhaust pipe had been loosened by the crash and blocked any shot. My chief concern now was to keep him away from Peggy and Boyce. Any second now, half the cops in Virginia would be arriving in force and we *would* take Lanny Sloan.

"Boyce!" I yelled, but I heard no reply.

I tore my eyes from where I last saw Lanny and looked to the ditch. Peggy was there on her knees, utterly consumed with hysteria, wailing in terror. She saw me. To my consummate horror, she stood, sobbing, extended both arms to me like a little girl entreating her daddy to pick her up, and she began to walk toward me.

"Peggy, *no!*" I screamed. The siren shrieked. *"No!* Get down! Get down! Stay—"

A shot boomed from somewhere behind the black car. A red spray emitted from the left side of Peggy Sloan's head and sparkled like rubies in the sunlight. Strands of her hair followed the exit of the bullet. Her eyes rolled back and she collapsed in the roadway like a rag doll.

I have no clear recollection of what happened next. I do remember charging around the rear of the black Ford to find Lanny lifting his weapon at me. Pierce would later say that he and Otis Clark arrived to find me drenched in the blood of Lanny Sloan, methodically pounding his mutilated corpse with the blood-slick barrel and breech assembly of Boyce Calder's shotgun. The state police investigation would reflect that I pumped seven loads of buckshot into him, beat him with the empty shotgun until the stock broke and then continued to beat him with the steel portion until Pierce and Otis arrived to pull me away. I do not remember. I am glad I don't.

# Shepherd of the Wolves

Lanny Sloan was very, very dead.

I wrenched myself loose from the restraining grips of Pierce and Otis and I collapsed weeping on the tortured, abused remains of poor Peggy Sloan, in her new coat and pink shoes crusted with snow. Another innocent child I had promised, and failed miserably, to protect. I was unaware when he did it but I would later learn that Pierce disarmed me briefly for fear that I might try to harm myself. This was how Lucia found me when she and Milly arrived on the scene.

"It's all right, Lewis!" Lucia whispered to me, holding me as I sobbed over the lifeless little girl on the bloody side of the Roanoke Highway. "It's all right!"

But it wasn't.

# 21

## Untidy Ends

The road was choked with state and county police vehicles and ambulances. The state police helicopter landed nearby with the Roanoke district commander aboard. Officers were everywhere, photographing, measuring, bagging evidence, taking statements.

The Sloan boy was a handcuffed nervous wreck, locked in the back of a state police cruiser. Danny Sloan's body lay in the back of the black Ford, the legs dangling askew by muscle and cloth from the crushed door. A blood-soaked sheet covered what was left of Lanny behind the Ford and still another somber stained sheet covered the savaged body of Peggy Sloan in the ditch.

Boyce Calder had taken a bullet through the edge of his waist, which bled profusely, but nothing vital was hit. He insisted on walking to the helicopter.

Pierce was directing my people in aiding the state police investigation. Several groups of citizen gawkers and a small herd of cows looked on from the snowy pastures bordering the road.

I sat in the front seat of Pierce's cruiser, Lucia at my side with her hand on my shoulder. I was lost in a vision, the hideous vision of Peggy Sloan's horror-stricken face. "Why have you let them do this to me?" she wailed from the vision. "Why have you let them hurt me?" The animal revenge of my assault on Lanny Sloan was little solace. Too late. Too late. Too late for poor Peggy Sloan.

Pierce walked up, his immense shadow shading me from the bright autumn sun.

"How you feel, Lewis?" Concern was obvious in his face.

I sighed. "I'm okay, Pierce. I'm . . . okay." I looked up at him. My mouth opened and closed and opened again. "I . . . she just . . . she just stood up, Pierce. She just stood up in the middle of it all and started walking toward me!"

"Lewis, it's all right," Pierce said. "You couldn't—"

"The Whelen unit was still on yelp. I yelled at her to get down . . ."

"It wasn't your fault, Lewis. It—"

"She just kept walking. I yelled . . . I yelled. . . . The bastard killed his own child, Pierce! He just blew her away!"

"I know, Lewis, I know." Pierce lay his huge hand on my arm. "You couldn't have helped it, Lewis. You did all you could. Thank God, you killed the miserable son of a bitch," he hissed, his breath becoming foggy puffs in the cold air.

"She just kept . . . walking!"

"Lewis, Lanny's boy is pretty shook up, but I think he's tellin' all he knows. He says he just did what Lanny said, that he was terrified of Lanny and just did what he was told. He says he wasn't with them the day they went to hit Ivy Joe, but he confirms what Peggy said about them saying they was gonna kill Joe for messin' with her and that they went to do it that day in Lanny's truck. He also overheard Lanny and Danny joking about Joe's death afterward. And he swears he didn't know nothin' about . . . about Lanny and Peggy. I think he's on the level."

I drew a deep breath and let it out slowly. It was time for me to get back to doing my job. I stood. "Yeah, you're probably right, Pierce. I think the boy is almost as much a victim as Peggy was. Goddamn Lanny, that evil bastard."

"Yeah, well," Pierce said with notable satisfaction, "thanks to you, it's gonna take three funerals to bury all his pieces." He gave me a grim smile.

I thought for a moment and looked around. "Where do we stand here, Pierce?"

"Well, State's handling the investigation, of course. We're assisting where we can. I got the road detours set up and men handling the traffic. I had Otis taking pictures and Thomas videotaping the statements you and Boyce and the kid gave. It's pretty open and shut, Lewis. The state boys are busting ass to get it wrapped up and the road cleared by sundown. Milly says wasn't nobody hurt up on the square when the shooting went down. They's a couple of motorists with damaged cars, but looks like nobody but Boyce got hurt. The Sloan brothers are sucking eggs in hell, of course, but that's tough shit."

"Thank Christ no citizens got hurt," I observed.

"Look, Lewis, Milly left here as soon as she knew you were with, uh, as soon as she knew you were all right. She's back at the jail taking care of everything there. I got it all under control here. You've given your statement to State. Why don't you let Thomas drive ya'll back to town? Get some food and rest, Lewis. I'll call you if there's anything you'd want to know, you know that." Pierce surveyed the macabre scene, fogs of his breath floating past his squinting eyes. "It's terrible about Peggy Sloan, Lewis, but at least you got the killers of Ivy Joe Culpepper. Got 'em hard and final."

Lucia and I walked silently past idling, flashing police vehicles and ambulances and wreckers, the latter two waiting patiently like jackals and buzzards for State to release the bodies and wrecked cars.

"You're limping!" Lucia suddenly exclaimed, frowning like she'd caught me in a deceit.

"I'm okay," I said, wincing at the pain in my right hip. "When I fell off the Sloan car at the square I landed on my gun. It's just bruised."

"Hmph!" Lucia sniffed. "You are going directly to that clinic of Dr. Butler's and have him check you over!" Her tone left little room for negotiation.

"I'm okay. I—"

"Nonsense, Lewis, you have to do it for workman's comp reasons if nothing else, and you know it."

She had me there. You can't argue with a lawyer.

"Lewis!" came a male voice I recognized. Pete Floyd, the newspaperman, had finally caught up with me. I turned to see him hustling as fast as his bulk would allow, hastily deploying his cameras and tape recorder. He gave Lucia a strange look as he hurried up to us. "Lewis, I need to get a statement from—Jesus! Are you all right? You look like shi—uh, you look awful!" To emphasize his point, he snapped several quick shots of me.

"I look exactly like I feel, Pete." I really didn't want to deal with Pete right now. I just wanted to go someplace without gunshots and sirens and blood, and drink until I washed away the vision of ruby crystals sparkling in the autumn sunlight. Then I wanted to sleep for about two weeks. But Pete had a legitimate role in this sordid affair, and I owed him and his readership at least a brief statement. I stopped and waited for Pete to organize his tape recorder.

"Pete, we're still investigating, but right now we know this much: Lanny Sloan's fifteen-year-old daughter, Peggy, came forth today offering testimony to the perpetration of . . . a number of crimes, by Lanny and Danny Sloan. The Sloan brothers, together with the oldest Sloan son—I forget his name, you can get it from Pierce Arroe—abducted Peggy at gunpoint on the square about an hour ago. A pursuit ensued, by Trooper Boyce Calder and myself, which ended when the Sloan car crashed here, killing Danny Sloan. Several shots were fired. Peggy Sloan was slain by a shot fired by Lanny Sloan. Another shot fired by him struck Trooper Calder, who has been medevaced in satisfactory condition. I engaged Mr. Sloan and shot him fatally. That's about it."

"Ah, Lew—uh, Sheriff Cody, what crimes were the Sloan brothers implicated in by Miss Sloan's testimony that motivated them to abduct and murder her?"

"At this point, Pete, it appears the Sloan brothers had a hand in the death of Ivy Joe Culpepper. We further suspect they were part of an organized car-theft ring operating out of Roanoke County. We have additional indications of drug trafficking as well." I had no illusions that the incest of Peggy Sloan would remain secret, or even that it should; I just couldn't talk about it right now. I didn't trust my composure to hold up.

"Sheriff Cody, why did the Sloans kill Ivy Joe Culpepper?"

"We believe they learned that Miss Sloan confided in him

with regard to the crimes, and they may have sought to prevent him from revealing what he knew."

Pete chewed on this for a moment, glancing at Lucia Dodd. He thrust his microphone at her as though he intended to ask her a question, but he pulled it back, apparently changing his mind. He pushed the microphone at me again.

"Sheriff Cody, when did you first—"

"Excuse me, Mr. Floyd!" Lucia interrupted firmly. She must have read his name from the press pass Pete wore like a red badge of courage at every newsworthy event he attended. Pete gawked at Lucia. "Sir, Sheriff Cody has sustained some injury in the course of these events and he is en route to Dr. Butler's clinic for examination." With that, she seized me by the arm and towed me away, leaving Pete gaping and holding his microphone in the air for no one in particular. He recovered and chased after us.

"Sher—Lewis! I'm gonna need something in-depth on this! I'm gonna—"

"Pete," I called over my shoulder as Lucia dragged me toward Thomas Bonner's cruiser, "I'll meet you at your office at ten in the morning." Pete's *Hunter Press* was a weekly that didn't come out for another three days. Tomorrow would be soon enough.

"Okay! Okay, Lewis, ten o'clock! I got something I need to talk to you about!"

"I'll be there," I reassured him as Thomas drove us away. That was odd. Pete usually wanted information. He never gave any away.

I radioed Milly to call Coleby and make sure he would be at the clinic. In a couple of minutes, she called back to say he was aware of the situation and was waiting for me.

By the time we reached the clinic, my right thigh and hip hurt so bad I needed both Thomas and Lucia to help me hobble inside.

"Lewis!" Coleby exclaimed, hurrying across his small lobby to meet us, pushing a wheelchair.

"I'm fine," I grumped. "I don't need a—"

"He is not fine!" Lucia insisted, forcibly rotating me to sit in the chair. "He's been run down by a car, he's been in a car accident and he's been in a gunfight!"

Coleby wheeled me swiftly down a hall to one of his examining rooms. At the door, he turned to Thomas and Lucia and asked them to wait in the lobby. Lucia was about to protest, but I interrupted.

"Ah, Ms. Dodd, this could take a while. Suppose I have Thomas drop you at Mr. Joe's house and I'll meet you there when Coleby releases me?"

"Excellent idea," Coleby said, smiling at Lucia.

Lucia looked skeptically at both of us. "Very well, Dr. Butler. I have things to do and I could make us some supper." She reached out and touched my cheek, looking into my eyes. She seemed to suddenly become aware that her affection was showing and she recovered herself. "Well. Deputy Bonner, if I may trouble you for a ride."

Before they left, I arranged for Thomas to have my new cruiser brought to the clinic from the square outside Judge Lemon's office, where we'd left it a couple of fateful hours and three violent deaths earlier.

Coleby went over me minutely, his healing hands moving my limbs, probing for signs of internal injury. He shined lights in my eyes, listened to my heart and took my blood pressure. He had me exercise my right leg, which hurt like hell but worked okay. He decided an X-ray wasn't needed. As I got dressed, he sat in his office in an adjoining room, writing me a prescription for pain. I limped into his office and sat down.

Coleby slid the prescription across his desk to me and leaned back in his crimson leather chair. "In the morning, Lewis, that acetabulum joint and the peripheral musculature are going to be very stiff and probably painful. I want you to stay in bed at least a day."

"Fat chance."

Coleby sighed. "Why not, Lewis? You've solved the mystery of the demise of Ivy Joe Culpepper and accounted for his killers in a manner which rather effectively limits recidivism. All at no small risk to yourself. I'd say you've earned a rest, my friend."

"I haven't earned shit, Coleby," I said softly. "I got Peggy Sloan killed."

"Oh, Lewis, no, you—"

"I told her I'd take care of her, Coleby, just like I told my

Tess I'd take care of her. 'I'll protect you,' I told her. I did a real slam-bang job of that. I let her down, too, Coleby. Just like I failed Tess. I—"

"Lewis, you couldn't have—"

"I grossly underestimated the savagery of Lanny Sloan," I mumbled. "I should have been prepared, but I never knew they were there until they were all over us. And now another child is dead."

Coleby put his hands together, placed his fingertips against his lips and studied me. "Lewis, the Sloan family has been the scourge of these hills for decades, everyone knows that, yet I am certain no one in the county would have foreseen his slaying his own daughter. You think you're the shepherd of Hunter County, Lewis, but you can only control events just so far. Some inevitably happen on their own, no matter what anyone does."

I rubbed my face. "Did Milly tell you why Lanny was desperate enough to kill Peggy?"

"Yes, she did. What a brute that man was. What an irredeemable brute."

"Lanny must have known that even if I could not convict him of the murder of Ivy Joe, the incest would be enough to send him to prison. He probably also knew that even penitentiary inmates take a very dim view of child molesters, a view that is often fatal to the molester."

"He was a desperate, treacherous man, Lewis, and one not without a certain hideous cunning."

I closed my eyes and leaned back in Coleby's plush parlor chair. I winced at the pain in my hip. "So many deaths, Coleby. Ivy Joe, Cassie Shelor, Peggy, the Sloan brothers. This was such a peaceful and quiet community, and now it's fucking Dodge City."

"You mustn't blame yourself, Lewis. There was no way you could have foreseen, let alone prevented, Ivy Joe's murder. Certainly you could have done nothing about Cassie Shelor's heart attack. The poor Sloan girl was an innocent casualty of an utterly inevitable battle between a duly appointed guardian of civilized society and a sociopathic outlaw. You did what your duty and survival demanded, Lewis. You did what you get paid to do. Miss Sloan was but one of a sad legion of pathetic innocents in our world who are in the wrong place at the wrong time. You did not invent these factors, Lewis, you merely coped with them as you had to. You were very nearly a victim of them yourself."

I stared out Coleby's office window at the darkening evening sky.

"Get some food and rest," Coleby continued. "Rest content in the satisfaction that you resolved the death of Ivy Joe Culpepper and rid the world of an evil and dangerous man."

"I'm not so sure," I said.

"What?" Coleby replied, his eyes narrowing.

"I guess I ought to feel relieved to put the question of Ivy Joe's death to rest, Coleby, but I don't."

Coleby sat forward intently. "Why not, Lewis? You had it from other sources, your deputy Otis Clark and Lois Ross among them, that Lanny Sloan threatened to kill Ivy Joe. Peggy Sloan's revelation was the clincher, wasn't it? Milly told me on the phone that Pierce informed her this was borne out by the confession of the older Sloan boy, correct?"

I rubbed my eyes. "I don't know. All I really have for certain is intent and opportunity. I can't prove they actually killed him. All the witnesses are dead. I'm having Pierce see if he can match up the damage to Lanny's truck to Joe's pickup, but that's a long shot at best."

"But, Lewis, while clearly a confession is not forthcoming, you have overwhelming circumstantial evidence to support a motive, a means and an opportunity for the Sloan brothers, including testimony by intimate members of their own family. Isn't that enough to put it to rest?"

I studied Coleby as though the answer might be in his eyes. "Maybe. But there is a loose end. The story is untidy in my mind."

"What do you mean, Lewis?"

"Ah, maybe I'm just tired, Coleby, maybe I'm making too much out of a small thing, but the night Joe died he said what sounded like the word 'shot.' We both know he wasn't shot. Why did he say that? And why did he seem to name Lois?"

Coleby pondered these questions, his hand at his lip. "Lewis," he said, "consider this. The Sloans were raised on guns. Isn't it likely, even certain, they would have carried weapons with them on their mission to kill Ivy Joe? Maybe they took or threatened to take shots at him, missing him, then after running him off the road and injuring him sufficiently to kill him, they elected to accept the windfall of letting it look like an accidental death. Thus Joe might have mentioned gunshots."

"It's possible," I admitted. Even likely.

"As to Lois Ross, you told me he was trying to bring her to Christ. He was a kind, giving, religious man who would indeed do such a thing. Isn't it possible he simply had her, his most recent salvation project, on his mind facing death and her name just spilled forth in the confusion and trauma of the moment? He was extremely aged, Lewis. And he was doubtlessly in severe shock. I think it may be a mistake to attempt to attach too much logic to his words uttered under those circumstances. It is highly unlikely for anyone, let alone a man over ninety years old, to be rational at such a moment."

I thought about that and had to admit it made sense. "Yeah, Coleby, you're probably right. I just hate it when these things don't tidy up neatly but, then, they almost never do. I guess I just have to accept that.

"Thanks for your input, Coleby, my good friend, but enough of this. Tell me. How goes it with you? Things any better at home?"

The interest in Coleby's patrician face faded quickly to sadness—a fatigued, weary sadness. His lips smiled slightly and he looked away out his window. "It goes poorly, Lewis. Sarah is becoming increasingly restless and she becomes more neurotic with every passing hour. She wants out of the marriage, which I could abide at this point, but she still wants to wreck me in the process. Her property settlement proposal will ruin me financially when a reasonable settlement would leave her quite comfortable. She wants it all, even Mountain Harbor, which she has no desire to live in or even to sell; she simply wishes to expunge me from my home, evidently for sheer spite.

"Worse, she continues to demand exclusive custody of Anne and Elizabeth. Anne has not gotten along with Sarah for years now and she is old enough to resist domination by

Sarah, which is why, I suspect, Sarah is attempting to take all my assets and holdings, in a crazy attempt to control Anne by controlling her means of support.

"But Elizabeth is only ten, Lewis. Like any child that age, she wants to have both her parents, but she is undeniably a daddy's girl. It would break her heart to be deprived of me. And it would certainly kill me."

"How the hell could Sarah be awarded exclusive custody, Coleby?" I asked. "The courts won't go for that."

"My attorney tells me she is attempting to make a case for my being a bad influence on Elizabeth."

"What? On what grounds?"

"Sarah claims I don't love Elizabeth, that I am negligent of her. She cites my frequent absences of the past several months as 'callous disregard for Elizabeth.' You know why I've been away so much Lewis. The acrimony is so intense and painful at home; Sarah is so vitriolic and bitter. It was easier on everyone to simply evade going home than to try to maintain civility and peace there in the face of her continuous emotional offensive. But I've tried hard to make Elizabeth know how much she means to me. We've done many things. I bought her a new horse. She knows—"

"Of course she knows, Coleby. I can see it in that child's eyes every time she's in your presence. She's crazy about you."

"To complicate things, Elizabeth is exceptionally mature for her age. Of late, she has become acutely aware of Sarah's machinations against me. She resents it and says so. In her paranoia, Sarah sees her objections as some plan hatched by me to alienate Elizabeth from *her* and this only intensifies her determination to remove Elizabeth from any trace of influence by me. The harder she tries to denigrate me, the more resistance she encounters from Elizabeth, and so on. A vicious cycle is in place by Sarah's own doing that is driving a wedge between her and Elizabeth."

I could readily see all this occurring but I also knew it would be very difficult, if not impossible, to illustrate to the satisfaction of a court, and I told Coleby. "The custody laws in this country are for the most part woefully obsolete and biased along pro-mother lines," I added.

"So my attorney confirms," Coleby acknowledged. "He

tells me there is a virtual certainty Sarah will win controlling custody of Elizabeth, and there is a possibility she may be able to bar me from visitation. I could not, I would not, live under that, Lewis."

"It won't come to that—"

"I will *never* abandon Elizabeth to be raised and irrevocably influenced by so self-centered and mean-hearted a person as Sarah has proven to be. Never." Coleby's words were soft-spoken but they quivered with force.

I was alarmed by his uncharacteristic vehemence. "It won't come to that," I assured him. "Surely the courts aren't so totally out of touch with reality."

Cradling his head in his hands, Coleby said, "I wish I was confident of that, Lewis. I wish my attorney were as well." He looked up at me. "I'm frightened, Lewis. It's all becoming too much. It's getting out of control."

"All divorces are hell, Coleby. They seem worse when you're in them than they eventually prove to be. Have courage, my friend. In time, this misery will pass."

It was dark out now and snowing again.

In the pale glow of his desk lamp, Dr. Coleby Butler looked older than Ivy Joe Culpepper.

## 22

## Hurt, Heat and Harmony

The warmth from the little house on Eldridge Street bore the odors of wood smoke, the tantalizing smells of hot foods and the fragrance of Lucia Dodd.

I limped painfully to the fireplace, threw my leather jacket in a corner and put my handcuffs and pistol on the mantel. I turned to face Lucia, who still stood by the closed front door. Her hair flowed past her ears in shimmering, feathery black waves. She wore an American University sweatshirt over snug jeans and sock feet and she did look good.

"Honey, I'm home," I said. "I had an unusual day at the office."

Lucia walked to me with a scolding expression. "Don't you dare joke to me, Lewis Cody," she said, putting her arms around my neck and laying her head upon my chest. "You were almost killed about seven times today." She clutched me tightly.

I hugged back. She felt better than good, she felt . . . healing. "So were you. I'm sorry, I was so preoccupied with my own concerns today. Were you hurt?" I buried my face in her clean soft hair and felt her shake her head.

"No. I have a scuff on my right hand and a sore bottom from being shoved to the pavement by a certain cop."

"Sounds like police brutality to me. Want to file a complaint?"

"I guess I'll let him get away with it this time, since it was preferable to being run over by a carload of murderers. My God, Lewis, I was so scared. I just froze."

She pushed back gently and held me at arm's length. Her lovely huge brown eyes studied me carefully, then fixed on my own eyes.

"It was a terrible, violent experience, Lewis. Tell me the truth. Are you all right?"

"My hip is killing me. Coleby says I'll have a lot of stiffness and soreness tomorrow, but otherwise I'm fine."

"I mean emotionally, Lewis. I know you're a war veteran and an experienced police officer, but you went through a lot today. You killed a man and you . . . endured the murder of Peggy Sloan. He can rot in hell with my blessing. But Lewis, are you okay inside?"

I pulled her back against my body and she clung to me.

"I guess I'm all right, Lucia. It'll take some time to be sure. I'm at peace with killing Lanny Sloan. My only regret is that I didn't get him before he got Peggy or shot Boyce. I can get very distressed if I think about the tragedy of Peggy Sloan, so I'm being careful not to think about it."

"You'll think about it, Lewis. Coleby Butler told me about your daughter. You'll think about Peggy Sloan a lot, no matter what I say, so just get it out of your system. But don't let me catch you blaming yourself for the death of either child. Coleby says you think you are the shepherd of Hunter County; you think you can protect everybody from everything and then you castigate yourself when you can't. That's not being fair to yourself."

"I underestimated Lanny Sloan," I told Lucia. "It never occurred to me he'd try to hit me in my own town in broad daylight, let alone that he'd actually kill his own child. I should have seen that coming somehow."

Lucia towed me toward the bedroom. "Go take a shower. I asked your deputy to go to the fire station where they've stored your things from the house and bring all your seasonal clothing here. There's some underwear and jeans and socks and other things in those cardboard boxes by the bookcase. You've two clean uniforms in Poppy Joe's closet."

228

I smiled, ruefully. "Thanks. That ought to remove any and all doubt that the sheriff is playing house with the woman from D.C."

Lucia smiled. "You mean your men will think you're sleeping with a 'nigger'?"

I saw mischief in her face, not any bitterness.

"Actually, racism disappears in men somewhere about the waistline," I said. When it comes to racism, none of my people can hold a candle to the town's Christian little old ladies who go to church every Sunday morning and Wednesday night and wax righteous about God's universal love. They'll scream for my ass when they hear about us, but they'll get over it."

Lucia smiled slightly. "I thought you said this wasn't a racist county," she teased.

"It isn't, as a county," I answered, unbuttoning my shirt, "but it has its share of people who let their prejudice cloud their judgment, just like D.C. or Zimbabwe or the Vatican. It's a human thing, not a geographical one. Some of those Christian hypocrites screaming for my ass for spending the night alone in the same house with you will be black, in fact."

"You don't seem too worried. Aren't you concerned about the next election? It's late this month, isn't it?"

"No. First of all, no one is running against me, so the voters don't have a whole lot of choice, do they? Second, there's a limit to the price I'm willing to pay in freedom and privacy to get elected. Besides," I reflected grimly, "I just slew the local maggot king. I could probably get elected governor in this county right now."

Turning on the water in the shower, I realized why I was sniffing at Lucia. I was afraid of being alone with my thoughts. I was looking for anything to protect me from the ghost of Peggy Sloan. In the steamy shower, the ghost caught up with me. I saw that horror-stricken face and those outstretched, pleading arms and that ruby mist in the cold autumn air. I sank to a fetal heap in the floor of the tub and wept. I seemed to be doing a lot of that lately. What was wrong with me?

We dined by candlelight at Ivy Joe Culpepper's white wooden kitchen table. I had found some loose khaki pants and a favorite old denim shirt to wear. I ate fiercely, to my surprise, as I hadn't thought I was hungry. Lucia dined with her customary flawless grace.

"I'm going back to Washington in the morning," she said, out of the blue. For reasons I wasn't clear on, this news disturbed me.

"So soon?" was all I could think of in the way of reply.

"I have buried my grandfather. I, you, have closed the question of his death. I have a number of . . . other matters . . . in Washington to take care of, not to mention my case load."

I recalled Coleby's tale of Lucia's troubles with the ill-fated surgeon and the crushing debt she was strapped with. I wondered if she'd ever tell me about it.

I groped awkwardly for something to say. I thought of something. "You're aware that I still can't conclusively prove the Sloans killed Mr. Joe?"

Lucia looked at me intently for a moment. "Under the law, as you know, Lewis, you need not prove a case absolutely, only 'beyond a reasonable doubt.' I had the nauseating misfortune to learn firsthand and graphically what the Sloan brothers were like. That they had the means to have murdered Poppy Joe is unquestionable. I was also privy to testimony from Lois Ross and from Peggy Sloan, corroborated by her brother and, indirectly, by your Deputy Clark and his source, which conclusively established their motive, and they even admitted their opportunity. Clearly, the case will always remain circumstantial, but in the court of my mind the Sloans are guilty beyond a reasonable doubt. I'm content with that. You should be, too." We studied each other.

"You make a very tight case," I said.

Lucia leaned forward and took my hand in hers and fixed me with those bottomless infinite eyes. "Conversely, Lewis, consider this clincher. You were at my grandfather's funeral; you knew him all your life. He was a phenomenally loved, harmless, gentle old man. Who else but the Sloans could possibly have had any motive to wish him ill will, let alone murder him?"

# Shepherd of the Wolves

I had, of course, already considered that. I reconsidered it. She was right. Having eliminated Lois, there was no one but the Sloans remotely likely to have had an unkind thought, let alone a deadly one, for Mr. Joe. I was beating a dead horse. I was physically and emotionally tired, and I was dwelling foolishly, obsessively on my doubts. What doubts? There were no doubts. The Sloans clearly had the motive—the only conceivable motive—and the means and the opportunity to kill Mr. Joe. Not another soul on earth did. It was time to let it rest.

I squeezed Lucia's hand. "You're right," I said. "I'm just tired and—"

"Darling, you are exhausted. You have the war-weary eyes of Abe Lincoln. Go stoke the fire and sit down in the living room while I put the dishes away."

"I'll help—"

"No. I'll be quicker if you're not in my way. Go. Go sit down." She kissed me on my cheek and pushed me toward the door.

I was too wasted to argue. I hobbled into the living room and chunked some wood on the fire. As the flames grew and radiated, their heat bathed me. I sat down on the old couch to rest my eyes.

"You promised," she reminded me. Her skin was dried and cracked and drawn tightly against her skull like a starved Holocaust victim. She held her hideous face near mine, the desiccated lips drawn severely back from gumless teeth, the eyes only a dim blue glow coming from deep within dark cavernous sockets. Her tone was rebuking but gentle, almost pouting, like that of a little girl denied a cookie. "You promised," she repeated. The sparse brittle hair dropped in clumps from her scalp as she tilted her head to peer more intently into my eyes. "You promised you wouldn't let them hurt me," she said. "You said you'd take care of me!" She began to cry. Red tears of blood flowed from the black sockets and trickled down her yellowed skin and into her mouth. The bloody tears stained her teeth and dripped from her chin. She held out her withered arms and came to me. I recoiled. I wanted to flee but I couldn't move. I trembled and twitched as she lay her rancid head on my chest and the blood ran onto me. She wept now. "You promised!" she said, sobbing. "You prom—"

The room was dark and I was breathing hard and my heart was pounding. There was a face before me dimly visible in the orange glow from the fireplace. But the face was not repulsively decayed; it was vital, fresh and beautiful, the face of Lucia Dodd. I lay on the couch. Lucia knelt beside it on the hooked rug and she lay across my chest. A blanket was wrapped over us both.

"Ssssh," she was whispering. "It's all right, Lewis, it's all right. I'm here. I'm with you. It's all right."

I drew a deep breath and let it out slowly. I put my arms around her and held her tightly. Finally, I said, "Sorry. I was paying a little dues for getting Peggy Sloan killed, I think."

"Hush," Lucia whispered. "You hush. You don't owe any dues. Try to sleep, Lewis. Try to rest."

In time, the fire began to wane, and I led Lucia Dodd to the old cherry four-poster. There, entwined in each other, we slept deeply.

No ghosts dared intrude.

I awoke as dawn began to dilute the darkness in Ivy Joe Culpepper's little bedroom. Lucia stirred, her head on my chest, her leg over mine. I kissed her and she snuggled close and tugged the quilt about us tightly against the cold morning air.

She sighed. "What are we going to do?" she asked at last.

It was a simple question, but there were no simple answers to it. In the excitement of new love and the heat of passion, it had been easy to postpone consideration of some very graphic problems. Now, in the growing light of day, the day Lucia would return to Washington, the questions could no longer be put off. We were of different races, which clearly didn't interfere with us personally but which, as a factor in our careers, had to be weighed. Our careers. They were 280 miles apart in statute mileage and about three galaxies apart in social and financial content. By one slightly-less-than-romantic way of looking at it, we had to have been idiots to have become so drawn to each other. But who thinks love?

"I don't know," I said brilliantly.

Several seconds ticked by before Lucia spoke again.

"Do you love me, Lewis? Do you feel anything for me?" Her question did not accuse; it simply asked.

"Yes, of course, I feel something for you, Lucia. I know I'm very drawn to you; I know I'm pulled to you by forces other than sexual, but isn't it too early to know if what we feel is love?"

"Not for me," she replied softly. "I know. I love you."

I held her tightly to me. "Have you considered the difficulties a love between us might entail?" I asked.

"Are you kidding? That's all I've thought about for the last two days, when I wasn't being assaulted, run down and shot at by maniacs. I can't count how many times I've called myself a dummy for falling for a white rural police officer! My God, I still don't believe it. Any second now I'm going to wake up lying next to a gorgeous black hunk who's a, a, an engineer for the federal government or something unweird like that."

"Or a chicken rancher or anything but, oh my God, sheriff of the Bastion of White Ignorance!"

Lucia laughed lightly. "Okay, okay. So I'm given to overstatement on occasion. It's a handicap of my profession. But seriously, Lewis, soon we must get up, put our clothes back on and go about our lives. What are we going to do? Where do we go from here?"

The old grandfather clock began its stately donging while I pondered her questions.

"I'm far from an expert on this sort of thing. How did I get stuck with having to answer 'the big question'?"

"Because I'm a skilled, college-trained semantic tactician and I tricked you into it. So answer it."

"Oh. Well that clears that up." I thought for a moment. "Maybe I'm overlooking something, but, at least in theory, it doesn't seem too complicated. We continue to meet the demands of our lives as best we can, we try to make as much time to see each other as we can, given the phenomenal diversity of our lifestyles, and we see where the relationship goes. If our . . . feeling endures, we'll find some way to overcome our problems. If it doesn't . . . hopefully we part friends, a little richer for having known each other. Sound reasonable?"

Lucia propped up on one arm and looked down at me, smiling. "Wow. And I thought I was a semantic tactician. Yes, Lewis, that sounds as reasonable as any affair of the heart could be." She smiled again and kissed me and then said brightly, "Thank you!"

"You're welcome—for what?"

"For not trampling the fragile flower of hope under the callous heel of practicality. I know things are never simple and real problems lie between us and happiness together, but I'm so glad you let hope flower. I needed that."

"Yeah. Well, as it happens, I could do with a little hope myself these days."

We lay quietly for a while, the only sounds a distant rooster crowing and the majestic tocking of the ancient clock.

"You know, Lewis, I think I could live down here again except for one huge problem. I grew up here and I've always loved these mountains even when I hated what I thought this community was. And I'm not in love with Washington. The colossal problem, of course, is even if I were to find a position down here I could be happy with, it couldn't possibly pay a fraction of what my Washington practice pays and I . . . I have . . . a lot of bills to pay."

She let the last sentence trail off. I waited for her to elaborate on it, but it became apparent she wasn't going to. I decided to let Coleby's story of her financial woes slide for now.

"Tell you what," I said, "it'll take a few weeks for me to get caught up with all the events of this week. By then, I'll need a vacation, big time. Maybe we could take a couple of weeks off together."

Lucia brightened visibly. "Oh, do you mean it, Lewis? I'd love that! Maybe we could take a cruise! But can't we see each other sooner?"

"I certainly hope so. Let's see what our schedules leave us and we'll work at it."

# Shepherd of the Wolves

She hugged me tightly. "I love you, Lewis."

Over an orgasmic breakfast of biscuits with gravy, bacon, eggs and, yes, by God, grits, we firmed up some details. Lucia offered me the use of Mr. Joe's cottage to live in until I could rebuild, and I accepted. It was closer to the dungeon than Mountain Harbor and it would spare me the awkward tension in the Butler household.

I called Stout's Texaco, which had recovered Lucia's car from Trace Creek, and Jim Stout confirmed the car was ready. "Carpet's are still kinda damp, Sheriff, but otherwise it's good as new."

I called Milly at the dungeon to see if I was needed for anything.

"Pete Floyd keep calling, Lewis, done left about ninety messages. Say he got to talk to you. I figgered I best not tell him where you be . . ." Milly let that trail off snidely.

"Nice thinking, Sherlock. Call him and tell him his office at ten, please."

"Sho' thing, Lewis. Say, Lewis, they's one mo' thing."

I didn't like her tone now.

"We . . . ah, we got a call last night from the Sloan boy, you know the young'un, he about seventeen?"

"Yeah. What's wrong, Milly?"

"Well, Lewis, his momma, Lanny's wife, killed herself sometime last night. Relatives what gathered over there 'cause of all the goings on went to wake her this mornin' and found her dead. The deputies out there now say look like she OD'd on some a' them pills Lanny sold. Say she left a note sayin' she didn't want to live without her baby girl."

There was a long pause.

"Lewis?"

"Yeah . . . Milly. Thanks. I'll . . . I'll check in later, uh, before I go to Pete's." I hung up.

"Goddamn it!" I exclaimed in frustration.

Lucia ran in from the kitchen. "Lewis, what is it?"

I told her. "Lucia, what the hell is going on?" I asked. "I've had more unusual deaths in my county in the last four days than I've had in the previous four years! Jesus, I want to remember to check on that younger Sloan boy and make sure he's all right before he's the *next* body I have to plant around here. *Damn* it!"

"Lewis," Lucia said softly, "Dr. Butler is right. You can't protect everyone all the time."

"So many deaths, Lucia. So much grief."

Lucia lay her head on my chest. "Ssssh. Hush. You can't do it, Lewis. You can't be the shepherd of Hunter County."

# 23

## Who'd a' Thunk It?

Lucia's Lincoln Towncar looked none the worse for wear at Stout's Texaco, but it smelled damp inside from having been rolled into Trace Creek by the Sloans. Sleep tight, you miserable bastards.

I moved her bags from my cruiser to her trunk, no small feat on a right leg that felt like one huge stubbed toe.

Eventually, a pregnant moment evolved as each of us searched for an appropriate gesture of parting. I noticed Stout and his mechanic and the kid who drives his wrecker peering at us from the counter room of the station.

"Come on," I said, "follow me in your car. I kiss better when I don't have an audience."

I led Lucia out the Roanoke Highway. I had a difficult moment passing the scene of the carnage of the preceding day. I successfully avoided looking at the ditch where poor Peggy Sloan met the terrible end of a cursed life. I could not help noticing a dark smear in the pavement where even fire hoses could not wash away all the black blood of Lanny Sloan.

I made a mental note to follow up on the survivors of the Sloan family to assure the younger Sloan boy was in good hands with relatives. I grimly reflected that these mountain clansmen could and did bear grudges for decades; this seventeen-year-old kid I was so concerned about might well have it in mind to kill me some day.

The older Sloan boy was legally an adult and would be in the hands of the court system for a long time. Him, I didn't have to worry about.

About fifteen minutes away, there was a private place near the county line, a small overlook with a weathered green picnic table concealed from the highway by a stand of pines. We both parked and stood taking in the white-carpeted Shenandoah Valley. Wisps of steam rose over tiny towns in the distance. Our breath formed clouds of vapor in the cold autumn air. Lucia pulled her suede coat about her and leaned back against me. I stood behind her, holding her, and we gazed out on the valley in silence for several minutes, each of us reluctant to part.

"My God," she said at last, "I lived up here for fifteen years and somehow I never saw the beauty of this land."

"Yeah," I answered, "you grow up here and you tend to take this natural majesty for granted. Living in Washington, D.C., will cure you of that real fast, though."

More silence passed.

"I'm scared, Lewis. I have a fear that I'm never going to see you again and I'm even afraid of wanting, needing to see you again. For a brief while this morning, I tried to write off my feeling for you as just the temporary sexual reaction of a lonely woman to an attractive man. I'm afraid of loving you. Yet . . . I do love you. I know it. And it scares me to death."

I squeezed her to me. "Why are you afraid?" I asked her.

"I . . ." She seemed to struggle for the words. "I . . . my . . . life is very . . . complicated right now, Lewis. I guess I'm afraid of anything that will make it more complex. I'm pulled between that fear and my need for you. That alone makes things more complex."

I mulled quietly on the tale of the tragic doctor. "Anything I can do to help?" I asked, looking away at the white valley.

A long silence endured. I glanced down at her face and thought I saw a lip trembling.

"No," she said at last. "No, Lewis, thank you. These are old problems. I'll tell you about them some better time."

She turned to face me and seized me desperately. "Oh! Hold me please, Lewis! Hold me!"

I did.

I watched Lucia's car go out of sight toward Roanoke. The taste of her was still vivid on my lips, her tears still wet on my cheek, her soft heat still on my hands.

I had the vague, depressed feeling you get when you come out from a good movie and confront dull reality. I felt painfully alone and anxious without knowing precisely why. How deep was this woman into me? What would happen to us now? A year from now, would we treasure these last few days or would we be desperately attempting to forget them?

"Sheriff One," Milly's voice came over my radio. I limped to my car.

"Sheriff One. Go ahead, Milly."

"Lewis, Pete Floyd is on the phone. Says you supposed to meet him at his office."

Damn, I thought, looking at my watch. ten-twenty A.M.

"Thanks, Milly. Tell Pete I apologize, I've been tied up, but I'll be there in fifteen minutes."

"Ten-fo'."

On the way back to Hunter, I chided myself for letting my preoccupation with Lucia interfere with my duties. I had flat out forgotten my meeting with Pete, even though I knew he'd been after me for two days.

The offices of the *Hunter Press* were in a painfully plain building enclosed in one side of the town square. The door squeaked when it opened and your immediate impression was always the pungent odor of printer's ink. The interior was a fire marshal's nightmare, a seemingly chaotic jumble of oily printing machinery, stacked supplies and tear sheets tacked up everywhere. *The Washington Post* was in no danger of a hostile takeover by the *Hunter Press*.

Pete's private office was enclosed in glass so old it was visibly wavy. Through that glass, I could see Pete at his desk, wearing the frayed blue button-up sweater he always wore from late September to April and smoking a cigar that would make Taipei smog smell sweet. On the wall over his desk was a sign: TO HELL WITH HOW THEY DO IT IN NEW YORK! I could also see James Chilton, the county school board chairman, and a stranger in a blue suit who could only be an accountant or worse, a lawyer. I presumed Pete was busy and would talk with me when he finished his business with the other men, but he waved me in right away.

The stranger was introduced as Simon Kingman of the Roanoke law firm of Markham, Kingman and Waters. My alert system went to DEFCON-1.

"Sorry I'm late, gentlemen," I said, shaking hands.

Pete Floyd had a distinctly odd look on his face, as did James Chilton. The lawyer, Kingman, was impassive. What the hell was brewing here?

Pete leaned back in a creaking office chair, drew on his magnum death weed and exhaled a noxious cloud. "Lewis," he began, "has, uh, where is the Dodd woman right now?"

Hard right rudder, all ahead full. Sound general quarters. What was this all about?

"She's on her way back to Washington, as far as I know. Why?"

Pete looked at Chilton, then back at me. He sighed.

I was getting tense. "Will somebody get busy telling me what the hell is going on here?"

Pete looked at his desk. James Chilton looked at the floor. Finally, Pete spoke.

"Lewis," Pete said with an uncomfortable smile, "you've often accused me of printing anything without regard to consequence. A . . . situation . . . has developed which I hope may give you reason to reconsider that view."

Jesus, I wish he'd get to the point, I thought.

He continued. "Some . . . uh . . . information . . . has come to light which could be the biggest story in this county in fifty years, but I've decided to sit on it at least until it is shared with you and you decide where you want to go with it." Pete looked at the ceiling, searching for words. "Where to begin . . ." he mumbled. After what seemed like a year's pause, he said, "Lewis, on the day Ivy Joe Culpepper died, I routinely submitted his obituary to the *Roanoke Times,* as well as other papers, knowing there were people all over the state who would want to know of his passing. Simon"— Pete nodded at the lawyer—"you want to pick it up from there?"

Simon Kingman cleared his throat and adjusted his

glasses. "Of course. Sheriff Cody, like many large law firms, we detail a clerk to read the obituaries every day. As a result, it came to our attention that Mr. Culpepper had passed away. As we have long represented Mr. Culpepper's interests—"

Mr. Culpepper's interests?!

"And we wrote and are charged with implementing his will, we were naturally concerned."

"Ivy Joe Culpepper left a will?" I asked slowly.

"It gets better, Lewis," Pete said.

Simon Kingman continued. "In his will, Mr. Culpepper provided a rather generous college scholarship fund for worthy but indigent Hunter County High School students, and ample funding for a new library for the school as well."

*"What?"* What planet was I waking up on?

"Fasten your seat belt," Pete said with relish.

"Consequently," Kingman continued, "I immediately contacted Mr. Chilton, here, as the appropriate representative of the school system. Mr. Chilton, perhaps you should take it from this point."

James Chilton straightened in his chair. "Well, Lewis, you can imagine my shock and surprise—"

"You bet your ass I can," I said tersely.

"But that soon gave way to elation and, as a favor to Pete, I wanted him to know. So—"

Pete could contain his excitement no longer. "So! James called me. Immediately, I put two and two together and I knew that if Ivy Joe had any estate, especially one large enough to build libraries, that fact could, how do I say, significantly alter the picture where the circumstances of his death were concerned. I told James to sit on the revelation for a while till you were informed. He agreed. I got James to give me Simon's name and number and I called him for more detail. And if you think all this has been hard to absorb up to now, just wait. Simon?"

Kingman explained. "Mr. Floyd did, as he indicated, call me, and from him I learned the details of Mr. Culpepper's . . . shall we say . . . peculiar . . . passing. At that point, my partners at the firm and I decided you should be made aware of certain . . . facts."

"What facts?"

Pete fairly shouted, "Like Ivy Joe Culpepper left an estate of *two-point-seven million dollars,* that's what!"

"Ivy Joe Culpepper was a *janitor!*" I exclaimed, exasperated. "He didn't make a tenth of that in his whole damn career!"

"Actually, Sheriff Cody," Simon Kingman said, "Mr. Culpepper, while doubtless a man of simple tastes, was nonetheless a well-read man and a man not without a certain innate vision. He had the foresight to invest initially small sums in oil stocks in the late teens when many people still thought the horse would prevail. Later, he read about something called Univac; he decided computers might catch on and he invested there as well."

"Two-point-seven *million* dollars?" I choked.

Simon Kingman frowned. "Sheriff Cody, I realize this is a bit of a surprise—"

"Yeah! About like that bright flash was to the residents of Hiroshima!"

"Sheriff Cody, the secret to Mr. Culpepper's relatively impressive holdings is *he never spent any of it.* He just kept turning his gains over and over in renewed wise investments for nearly *seventy years* while he subsisted on his janitor's pay. He was very insistent that no one, absolutely no one, know about his estate. We formed an investment company under an alias, and we handled all the transactions. No one but Markham, Kingman and Waters were to know of it. We handled the taxes—everything. Mr. Culpepper was concerned to the point of *obsession* that, if it became known about his wealth, his relationships with everyone he knew would be adversely affected."

I was beginning to catch up now. "How much of the two point seven goes into the scholarship and library funds?" I asked.

Kingman shuffled through numerous documents. "According to the provisions, Sheriff Cody, the scholarship fund comprises seven hundred thousand dollars, part of which is to be invested to sustain the fund."

"And the library?"

"An endowment of one million dollars is provided for construction and equipping of the library, any surplus to supplement the scholarship fund."

# Shepherd of the Wolves

I looked at Pete, who was about to bust, then at Kingman. My heart began to pound as some very unsettling implications settled in like acute heartburn.

"Okay," I said, "you want to tell me where the other cool million goes?"

"I thought you'd never ask!" Pete exclaimed.

"The balance of Mr. Culpepper's estate goes to his sole heir, Hannah."

"Hannah? Who the hell is Hannah?"

Kingman coughed and adjusted his glasses. "Ah . . . that would be Ms. Hannah Lucia Dodd. Hannah stands to inherit slightly more than nine hundred thousand . . . uh . . . dollars."

I stood and walked to Pete's office window and stared out at the sight of the abduction of the late Peggy Sloan, my heart thumping. My God, I thought, what has come over this county? What happened to the tranquil, simple peace that made living here so unique?

"Mr. Kingman," I said after some thought, "as I understand this, no one was to know of Ivy Joe's wealth, is that correct?"

"Absolutely. He was adamant about that."

"So there is no way Lu . . . Miss Dodd could have known that she stood to inherit a medium fortune. Is that correct?"

"Oh, yes. Unless, of course, Mr. Culpepper himself elected to inform her."

I nodded, continuing to stare out the window, deep in thought.

Kingman coughed again. "Uh, Sheriff Cody, there is one recent development which may bear on your position in this matter."

I turned to face the lawyer as he went on.

"Early this month, we were instructed by Mr. Culpepper to draft for his review a revised will, a revision negatively impacting Ms. Dodd."

"He was going to disinherit her?"

"Not exactly. His instructions were to draft it in such a way that she would inherit his relatively meager property holdings, the house and contents. His, ah, let's see, his 1953 Studebaker pickup truck was to go to the mechanical shop class at Hunter County High School."

"Never mind the truck. Where did the million dollars go?"

"Yes. Well. Ms. Hannah Lucia Dodd was, by the revised will, to receive a bequest of one hundred thousand dollars, the remaining nine hundred thousand was to revert to the United Negro College Fund, for Virginia residents."

"But the revised version was never . . . completed, right? The will that prevails is the one leaving Ms. Dodd the full million. Am I right?"

Kingman pursed his lips. "That is correct, Sheriff Cody. Mr. Culpepper was to have signed, and thus validated, the revised will on the day he died. He, ah, well he never made it to our offices. The revision is, thus, effectively worthless. The original will remains in force."

"Did he ever discuss the proposed revision affecting Ms. Dodd with her?"

"To be certain, Sheriff Cody, we at Markham, Kingman and Waters told no one. Whether Mr. Culpepper himself told Ms. Dodd, or anyone else, is subject to speculation."

"Don't you see it, Lewis?" Pete Floyd asked. "It's unfolding like some Agatha Christie novel! Ivy Joe dies under mysterious circumstances while on his way to sign a nine-hundred-thousand-dollar reduction in the sole heir's inheritance! The motiveless murder now has a motive!"

"Yeah, Pete," I said, "I see it."

My mind was racing. Thank God that Pete didn't know Lucia was in debt better than seven hundred grand, because of the suicidal doctor, and that the wolves were at her door. Her part of Mr. Joe's original estate would have saved her home and bailed her out clean with a neat sum to spare. But if Joe cut her to a hundred grand, it would still leave her better than six hundred thousand in dutch, would cost her her home, would bankrupt her and would seriously threaten her career. Further, she wouldn't see a dime of Joe's estate in either case unless Joe died, and prior to the Saddle Mountain incident, he was possibly years away from dying.

There was no question that all this made the case of Ivy Joe Culpepper more than a little untidy, to say the least. It hung a flashing neon suspect label on Lucia if Joe's death turned out to be murder. But Joe loved Lucia; why would he cut her off? And she loved him. Even in the face of ruin, could she have killed him? And how? Her car was undamaged. And why did Joe name Lois, if he did? And what about him saying he was shot? And where did that bag of uppers come from? Damn!

Suddenly I had a thought that struck me like a broadhead deer arrow. It made my throat dry.

"Lewis?" Pete must've said for the third time.

"Ah. Well," I said brilliantly. "Anything else I need to know?"

No one said anything.

"Okay. Thank you all for your consideration and cooperation. Special thanks to you, Pete, for putting it all together and containing it. It will take me a few days to hammer down some loose ends. I'll advise you all then so you'll know how to proceed."

Pete stood. "Lewis, I want to know everything exclusively on this."

"All I have right now is a lot of questions, Pete. When I get some answers, I'll share them with you first. One more thing. Mr. Kingman, have you contacted Miss Dodd yet, with regard to Joe's will?"

"No. In view of the circumstances, we decided to suspend contacting Ms. Dodd until after discussing the matter with a competent authority."

"Very well. Gentlemen, may I prevail on you to hold all this strictly in confidence for another three days?"

"Sure, Lewis," James Chilton agreed.

Kingman spoke. "My firm will hold the matter in suspension until you advise us, say, not later than close of business this Monday?"

"Fine. Thank you. Pete?"

Pete sighed and shook his head slowly. "Lewis, I go to press on Monday, you know that. Can I know something by Sunday night?"

"Let's say I get with you Sunday night and let you have whatever I know at that time."

"Fair enough."

"Thanks, Pete. I owe you."

I hobbled through the outer jail office, ignoring greetings from Millie and the staff, and slammed my office door as a signal I did not want to be disturbed. My "broadhead deer arrow" thought already had me very disturbed. I went quickly to the huge old walnut desk where, as usual, Millie had organized the mess I always left into a semblance of order. To the right, there was a stack of small sheets of paper I'd jotted odd bits of information on. I sorted through them and froze on the one I sought. I flopped into my chair and leaned back, staring at the ceiling.

Damn.

I had considered in Pete's office that Lucia Dodd's car was undamaged and thus she couldn't have shoved Joe off Saddle Mountain, the revelation of her inheritance notwithstanding. I remembered writing down Lucia's tag number that first morning she stormed into my office. It was then that a terrible thought struck me. Now I had confirmed it.

I hadn't picked up on it the day I wrote it down, distracted as I was by my initial encounter with Lucia, but today I thought I remembered the tag began with an *R*. Now I stared at the scrap of paper on which the tag was scribbled and there it was: RCT241.

In Virginia, all nonpersonalized license tags beginning with *R* are registered only to rental cars.

I told myself that there could be a dozen good reasons why Lucia could have been in a rental car. Maybe she flew into Roanoke and rented something to drive up here. Maybe she leased her car and the leasing company carried rental tags on it. What I couldn't think of a dozen good reasons for was why Lucia didn't say the car was rented the night the Sloans rolled it into Trace Creek. Inconclusive, Pierce would say, but curious.

I contemplated where to go from here. I dreaded where it might lead me. Then I walked into the outer office to the DMV computer terminal and ran a listing on the tag. It came back listed to Rudenhour Lincoln Mercury Leasing and Rental Division in Roanoke. Back in my office, I got the number from information and called them, asking for their rental division.

"Rudenhour Rental. This is Judy, how can I help you?"

"Hi. I'm calling to ask you about a rental of yours—the tag is RCT241—a Towncar?"

"Yes, sir?"

"I'd like to know who rented it and when, please."

"Well, sir, we don't—"

"Sorry. I should have mentioned I'm Sheriff Lewis Cody of Hunter County. This is in connection with an official investigation. You can dial my office back if you need to confirm."

"Oh. Ah, no, that won't be necessary, Sheriff. One moment." I could hear her pecking at a keyboard. "Yes, here it is. It was rented last Monday morning to a, ah, Hannah L. Dodd of the law firm of—"

"I have that, thank you. Can you tell me why the car was rented?"

"Well, sir, the computer only says it was a referral from the service department."

"Thank you. Can you transfer me to Service, please?"

After a pause, a country good ol' boy came on the line. "Service Department, Wilson."

"Mr. Wilson, this is Sheriff Lewis Cody of Hunter County. I need—"

"Holy shit! Is this about that asshole brother-in-law of mine? I tole Darlene not to loan that shithead her car! Did he—"

"Hold it, Wilson, I just need to ask you a question about one of your customers."

"Ah, Jesus, I'm glad to hear that! What can I do for ya?"

"Monday, a Hannah Dodd rented a car from your rental division referred by the service department. Did she leave a car to be worked on?"

"Hmmm. Dodd, Dodd, Dodd. Hol' on while I git the work order up on the screen. Hmmm. Oh yeah, here it is. Yeah! I remember this woman, good-lookin' colored lady. Left us a Mark VII, said she needed it in a hurry and, just between you and me, Sheriff, she even slipped me a hundred to get it in the first thing. Yeah. We got it all fixed and ready to go now!"

"What was wrong with it?" I asked, terribly afraid I already knew.

"Oh. I thought you already knowed, Sheriff. It was in the body shop. She brung it in with the front end all tore up."

# 24

## Muddy Water

Before I hung up with Rudenhour Lincoln Mercury in Roanoke, I asked Wilson if they'd photographed the damage to Lucia's car before repairing it. He said they had not as Ms. Dodd had indicated she would be paying cash for the repairs and would not be submitting a claim to her insurer. I also asked him not to mention our contact to Ms. Dodd when she arrived to claim her car, as I suspected she would be doing soon, and to ask the rental-office girl to keep quiet, too; he assured me he'd take care of it.

Now, slumped in my cracked leather office chair, staring at the old tintype of my great-granddaddy on his bellicose-looking mule, I felt sick. I was physically and emotionally tired, I was hungry, my right leg was killing me, I was cold and I was lonely for Lucia in spite of everything. Worse, I had a suspicious death case dogging me that was beginning to stink more and more like a murder committed by the first woman in years to evoke love in me. Oh, hot damn, life is grand.

What was I going to do now? I wondered. I never questioned that I had to pursue it to the end or I'd never be able to look at Lucia again without wondering if she jammed a kind-hearted old man off Saddle Mountain to his death. The thing I wondered about right now was how to proceed. According to Wilson at the car dealership, the parts removed from Lucia's car were already on their way to a scrap-metal yard in Pennsylvania. Even if by some miracle I was able to find the scrap-metal truck and distinguish which of thousands of junk parts on it were from Lucia's car, the evidenciary chain of custody had already been broken in a dozen places. I'd never make a case for murder from it, something a lawyer like Lucia would be quick to appreciate. Without specific forensic evidence, like paint transfers, to connect the damage with Joe's truck, she could easily claim she damaged the car some other way at some other time.

I felt immense distress as the romantic in me warred with the cop in me. I saw Lucia's lovely, soft brown eyes and the tender, vulnerable soul beyond them. I couldn't accept that a woman of Lucia's passion and warmth and love was capable of coldly bulldozing her beloved old granddaddy off a mountain for money. You moron, the cop in me replied, you're thinking with your dick instead of your brain. Anybody is capable of anything under enough pressure. How do you know she even loved Joe at all? Because she told you so? By her own admission, she had not been to see him for years; was that the behavior of a doting granddaughter? Even if she did love him, people have murdered loved ones for a hell of a lot less than nine-tenths of a cool million, setting aside the intense heat she must be under because of her debt problems.

I reflected on a case several years ago when I was a D.C. cop. A nine-month-old baby had apparently been kidnapped from her understandably distraught mother. For days, the DCPD scoured the city for the "tall thin black man" the mother saw in the laundromat just prior to leaving the baby for a moment to go out to her car. There were countless replays of television interviews with the weeping mother pleading to the abductor: "Please! Please bring my little baby back to me! I love her so much!" Sob, sob, sob. Ultimately, she confessed that she suffocated the baby because it wouldn't stop crying, and she led homicide investigators to the west bank of the Anacostia, where the little body floated facedown in a pool of garbage.

Lucia wouldn't necessarily have to be as black-hearted as the smother-mother to have waxed Ivy Joe. The stress she could have experienced in the episode with her suicidal lover, and the resulting crushing debt, could drive a lot of people to a moment of murderous desperation. It only takes a moment.

A knock at my door intruded on my morose contemplations.

"Come in."

Pierce lumbered in and we discussed some peripheral issues connected with the Sloan shooting. The state police had some minor questions. Lanny Sloan's oldest kid, who had done the driving during the chase, had given investigators the rest of the story introduced by Lois Ross about the car-theft ring operating out of Roanoke County. Arrests were being planned there. Boyce Calder would recover nicely. I made a mental note to call him at the hospital in Roanoke later in the day. I asked Pierce about the younger Sloan kid, and he told me the boy was with relatives.

Pierce also revealed the autopsies performed on the Sloan brothers in Roanoke showed PCP and cocaine in their blood. I wasn't surprised.

"And they found a high lead content in Lanny's blood . . ." Pierce quipped with poorly suppressed amusement. "And a car bumper in Danny's blood!" Pierce was enjoying himself.

What was left of the Sloan clan had mercifully set separate dates for the funerals of the Sloan brothers and Peggy and her mother. I felt compelled to attend the funeral for Peggy but wondered if it was wise. I wouldn't exactly be a stellar guest welcomed by the family and it would probably wreck me emotionally.

I debated whether to let Pierce in on the revelation of Ivy Joe Culpepper's astounding estate and its effect on the question of his death and the suspicion now heavy on Lucia. In the end, I decided to keep it quiet for now. It was just easier than trying to answer all the questions Pierce would have.

I did need to talk about it with someone, though, and I knew who it should be. When Pierce returned to his office, I called Coleby at the clinic.

"Lewis!" Coleby answered. "How do you feel?"

"Physically I'm fine Coleby. How about you?"

"How is your leg, Lewis?"

## Shepherd of the Wolves

"Just like you said it would be, stiff and sore, but I'm getting around okay."

"Are you running any fever? Feeling any nausea? Having any vision problems?"

"No, no, Doctor, I'm fine. What about you? You sound tired, my friend."

There was a pause and a sigh on the other end of the line. "I'm exhausted, Lewis," Coleby replied softly. "The situation at home grows more atrocious by the hour. Anne went back to school in Fairfax County last night, but the strain is taking an enormous toll on the rest of us. What are you doing this afternoon, Lewis? I need to talk desperately."

"Funny you should say that, Coleby, I was just calling you for the same reason. I can get away in a couple of hours. You?"

"I'd say we both need and deserve a break, Lewis. Suppose we take the horses up on the ridge?"

"Great idea. I'll see you at your place about two. Is that okay?"

"Wonderful. I'll have Arthur saddle our horses. Thank you, Lewis."

Hap Morgan's veterinary clinic was a far cry from those urban pet palaces that charge seventy-five bucks to trim the nails of Lhasa Apsos named Reginald of Clyde. Hap did more dairy cattle and horses than dogs, and what dogs he did had names like Sooner, Old Red . . . and Gruesome.

Hap's receptionist led me down a cluttered hallway to his office, where Hap sat reading a copy of *The American Horseman* and Gruesome lay on an old horse blanket by the fireplace.

Gruesome went into a whimper frenzy on sighting me and struggled painfully to get to his feet. I sat on the floor by the hearth and lifted him gingerly so his head lay on my thigh, and I rubbed his ears. He whined and lapped at my hands. I fought tears.

Hap Morgan tossed the magazine on his desk. "That animal is a fighter," he said. "If he wasn't, I'd a' been tempted to put him down. Like some people, some animals just give up when seriously injured, others fight to live. His fight was the only reason I was able to save him. He's a good ol' mutt."

"Yeah, Hap," I agreed, "he's a fine friend." I looked up at Hap. "How hurt is he?"

"He's got two broken ribs and some internal bruising from whatever hit him. Some cuts to his jowls. His diaphragm was so swollen the night it happened he could hardly breathe. You cain't imagine how hard it is to intubate on a snout like his. He'll be okay. Incidentally, Lewis, I drove out to Coleby's this morning at his request and checked ol' Moose over. Near as I can tell, she's just fine."

"I owe you more than your bill, Hap, thanks."

"Not on your life, Lewis. Maybe you forgot, but I ain't forgot that night you caught my boy driving drunk. He'd a' never done it except his fiancée had just broken it off with him and he was ruined by it. But the FBI woulda rejected his application if you'd booked him, and you knew it, so you brought him home to me. Now my boy is a happily married special agent in Sarasota. Your money ain't never gonna be no good in this clinic."

Hap wanted to keep Gruesome two more days. I thanked him again and drove my old truck to Vaughn Chevrolet to pick up the new unmarked cruiser Milly had told me was now ready. Vaughn's people said they'd store my truck till I had someplace to put it.

There's nothing like a new car to make an American male feel better, but even this sweet-smelling new police-package Chevy couldn't dilute my glum mood. There was what you might call a niggling little detail on my mind that was becoming increasingly more difficult to ignore, as much as part of me wanted to ignore it.

Professionalism and legal prudence now dictated that I wash my hands of the case of Ivy Joe Culpepper and hand it off to the state police, forthwith. Why? Because, the investigator sleeping with the prime murder suspect is another of your little no-no's in the law-enforcement business. It could have poisoned a successful case against Lucia and it could possibly have destroyed my career. The only smart legal thing to do, now that a motive for Lucia to have done Joe had surfaced, was to give everything I knew to the VSP and let them handle it from there. What was jabbing me in the conscience was that the very reason I should turn it over to the state police was also the reason I hadn't already done so. I was . . . intimate . . . involved with . . . I cared for . . . Jesus, I had trouble saying it! I loved her! I was in love with the damned prime suspect!

I thought. The case against Lucia was still strictly circumstantial. A lot of questions remained unanswered. Suppose she didn't do it? Would she be able to forgive me for complicating her life with a murder investigation without so much as asking her about it first? Didn't I owe it both professionally to the law and personally to Lucia to at least see if there was any substance to the suspicions before putting more wolves at her door? Jeez, I hate it when the shitstorms blow. Maybe the ride and a long talk with the always calm and analytical Coleby would help me arrive at a decision.

Speaking of storms, Milly's voice came over the radio as I approached Mountain Harbor, advising all my units that the National Weather Service had just issued a new winter storm warning for the night. The forecast was for twelve to fourteen inches of new accumulation by tomorrow afternoon. My roads wouldn't be dry much longer. Wonderful.

I turned off the road between the two stone gateposts. On one was a large bronze plaque reading MOUNTAIN HARBOR. Coleby's paved driveway was lined with tall trunk pines that formed a tunnel as the drive wound its way up the white pastured mountainside to the huge old home at the crest.

I was startled to see, running down the pine tunnel toward me, Elizabeth Butler wearing soaked house shoes, jeans and a light sweater. She was sobbing and breathing rapid puffs of vapor from a nearly one-mile run from the house. I had flashes of a nude Lucia on the road to the Sloan farm. I stopped quickly and got out.

"Elizabeth! What are you—"

"Uncle Lewis! Oh, Uncle Lewis!" Elizabeth cried, sobbing miserably as she ran to me.

"Girl, what the hell are you doing? What's wrong?"

As she drew near, I could see an ugly welt by her left eye.

"Oh, Uncle Lewis!" Elizabeth wailed, crashing into me. She wept out of control. I held her for a moment, then swept her up and carried her to the car. I got in and turned up the heat.

"Uncle Lewis!" Elizabeth cried. "Mother hit me! She said she was going to take me away from Daddy, away from Mountain Harbor! I said I didn't want to leave my daddy and this is where I live and I wouldn't go and she hit me!" Crying overcame her. I held her while she wept and then examined her swollen cheek. She'd taken a stiff shot but there was no permanent damage. I dropped the car in gear and moved up the driveway toward the house.

"I'm sorry, darlin'" was all I could think of to say to her.

"I don't want to leave Mountain Harbor, Uncle Lewis! I don't want to leave my daddy!"

"I know, sweetheart, I know. Where's your dad now?"

"I don't know. He and Mother had a big fight and Daddy rode off on his horse. I hate it when they fight, Uncle Lewis, I hate it!"

A broad, lone figure wrapped in a long coat and scarf came into view waddling down the driveway toward us. Polly had Elizabeth's snow boots in one hand and her coat in the other.

"My Lord, child," Polly said to Elizabeth as we drew up. "You'll catch a cold, sure! Running out of the house with no clothes on! Hi, Sheriff, glad you come along when you did. Things are getting out of hand. Mrs. Butler, she's drinking again and she started in on Dr. Butler again. He's done the only thing he can do when she gets like this; he left. Rode off on his horse toward the captain's grave. My Lord, Sheriff, Mrs. Butler hit this child! Just hauled off and hit this child in her face! My Lord, little girl, you face is all swole up."

"Polly," I said, "how about you take Elizabeth up to your quarters till things calm down? I need to go find Coleby. Take Elizabeth to your apartment. If Sarah comes for Elizabeth before I get back, don't let her in. I don't want her trying to drive under the influence with Elizabeth in her car. If Sarah gets violent, call my office. I'll have a portable radio with me, and I'll get back down here and get her under control. Do *not* turn Elizabeth over to her till I get back."

"Okay. Yes, Sheriff. I understand."

I drove them both to the rear of the giant house and watched Polly lead Elizabeth up the stairs to her apartment over the six-car garage. I crunched across the packed snow

# Shepherd of the Wolves

on the veranda and knocked at the curtained French doors. A long moment passed before the door opened to Sarah Butler.

It's sad how hate can make a beautiful woman ugly. Sarah was, as always, impeccably dressed and her hair and make-up were flawless. But wrinkles appeared at the corners of her eyes and the sides of her nose from the contempt she viewed me with. She stared at me for a few seconds, then shoved the door shut in my face. I kicked it hard at the base just before it latched and it crashed open against the wall.

"Damn you!" Sarah said, snarling. "Get out! Get out of this house this instant! How dare you force your way into my house? Get out!"

I walked into the huge high-ceilinged den, gazing about at an overturned lamp, a book sprawled open on the carpet and a cocktail glass laying by the broad fireplace. Sarah was furious but composed, though she swayed slightly and the room had an odor of alcohol.

"Get out of my house, Lewis. You leave this instant or I will bring a legal action against you that will leave you penniless! It shouldn't take much to do that."

"In a minute, Sarah," I answered. "Let's us have a little fireside chat first."

"I have nothing to say to you. Get out!"

"Where's Coleby?"

"I don't know and I don't care! He rode away on his horse, the perfect metaphor of the pathetic anachronism he is. On the dawn of the twenty-first century, he still gallops about like some antebellum plantation squire. He could have been somebody! He could have been an exceptional surgeon or a noted research scientist instead of some house-calling country GP. He could have *been* somebody!"

"He *is* somebody, Sarah. He's what he wants to be, which is the ultimate success. Further, he's something you wouldn't understand; he's the shepherd of Hunter County."

Sarah barked a mean laugh. "Oh, please! That's what he calls you: 'the shepherd of Hunter County.' Spare me the cheap platitudes, Lewis. Romance is not your strong suit, believe me. You're as nauseatingly sentimental as Coleby. Get out of my house this instant!"

I walked slowly toward Sarah. "In a minute," I said. "First, a couple of not-so-sentimental words for your delicate ear."

"Go to hell!" Sarah spat, and she spun on her heel to walk away.

I seized a fistful of her hair and yanked her back.

"Damn you, Lewis!" She screeched and she flailed at my face with both hands. I pulled down and back on her hair until she gritted her teeth from the pain. I dangled my handcuffs before her enraged face. Her eyes bulged.

I put my mouth to her ear. "See these handcuffs, Sarah?" I whispered, shaking the cuffs before her eyes. "If you ever, *ever* hit that little girl again, I will get a warrant for your arrest for child abuse from Judge Lemon and I will put these very handcuffs about your wrists like a common criminal and I will *personally lock you in a cell!*" I threw her away from me.

Sarah rubbed her neck, seething with rage. "I'll sue you, you bastard! I'll sue you and this county and I will break you both. So help me God, I will!"

"Yeah. Well you can sue the Pope for paternity, too, but collecting will be about as likely. You got no evidence and no witnesses, so take your best shot. Just don't you forget what I told you, woman."

Sarah glared at me, considering my remarks.

"No," she then said. "No, Lewis, I have a better idea. I have a much better idea. I'll make Coleby suffer, you bastard, and you know I can do it. I've lived with that man for eighteen years; I know his every tender, sensitive weakness. I know how to make him cry, and for you, Lewis, just for you, I will make him miserable. I promise you that. For you, I will make him hurt every way I know. And I know."

My fist clenched and my arm snapped back but I caught it. I strode quickly into the kitchen, knowing that if I stayed another instant I'd crack and beat her to death. I could feel the rage bubbling in me that presages murder.

I yanked open the double door of the refrigerator, tucked four bottles of cold Norwegian beer into my bomber-jacket pockets and took a fifth back into the den with me.

Sarah stood tall and confident, fully aware she had scored a hit on me.

## Shepherd of the Wolves

I twisted the top from the beer, sailed the cap into the fireplace and drew hard on the icy brew till my eyes watered. I held the bottle up to Sarah in a toast.

"What goes around, comes around," I said to her, and I walked out toward the stable.

I heard the door slam hard behind me.

# 25

## Grave Concerns

Crossing the wooden bridge over the creek that ran between the house and Coleby's sumptuous stable, I gulped more biting beer. So much misery these days. So many tears. So many hurt people.

Coleby's elderly stable hand, Arthur, glanced with curiosity at the beer bottles sticking out of my coat pockets as I strode down the broad, dirt-floored, center aisle of the stable. He was feeding an apple to my monster horse, which he'd managed to get a saddle on. Moose stood taller at the withers than Arthur did at the head. She looked like the massive steeds of the Conan legends.

"Afternoon, Sheriff Cody. I had to rig an extension on the cinch, but I finally got a saddle on this elephant of yours." He stuck another apple under Moose's nose. "She's a fine animal."

"That she is, Arthur, thank you. Any idea where Dr. Butler is?"

Moose stirred, snorted like a 747 reversing thrust and nuzzled at me as I came near. I looked her over; as Hap Morgan had said, she looked none the worse for her narrow escape from the burning barn.

Arthur sighed. "These is troubled days at Mountain Harbor, Sheriff Cody. I reckon Dr. Butler be up at the captain's grave. He like to go there and think sometimes.

# Shepherd of the Wolves

You don't have to bring no beer with you, though. Dr. Butler already took a fifth of Jack up with him."

I had to stand on a stool to get a foot in the stirrup. Mounting Moose was like climbing onto a propane storage tank. As she shifted her footing, anxious to go, Arthur stood clear of her sixteen-inch-wide, white maned hooves. I clucked at her and ducked my head as she clopped out of the stable. I aimed her and gave her her head and she slid into a wavy lope, glad to be free of the confining stable, blowing huge puffs of breath in the cold clear air. Chunks of snow flew as her hooves rose. Cody the Barbarian rides again.

The Mountain Harbor estate lay mostly on a wooded plateau that cleaved sharply on its western side to a panoramic view of the Shenandoah Valley. Captain Hiram Braithwaite's grave was set among a stand of withered, wind-twisted pines. The captain lay beneath an elaborate marble sarcophagus enclosed in the same sort of wrought-iron spear fencing that surrounded my dungeon downtown. After ten minutes of riding at Moose's casual but extremely long-gaited canter, I arrived at the grave to find Coleby nowhere in sight.

I reined in Moose, her sides bellowing as she stepped nervously about, anxious to get under way again. I examined the tracks in the snow outside the grave enclosure. Evidently, Coleby had dismounted and walked in to stand by the sarcophagus for a time. Now the horse's tracks disappeared north into the trees along the edge of the plateau.

I felt a shot of alarm as I recalled that in that direction on a rocky outcropping was a hawkbill overlook where Coleby and I often went in the summer to play chess and watch the sun set. What alarmed me was that anything that went off that overlook dropped about two hundred and fifty feet onto a jagged rockfall. I gigged Moose, and she jumped, dug her heels in and loped away, obliterating the tracks of Coleby's mount.

The beautiful Arabian stallion stood at drop rein in a small clearing at the foot of the rocky path that rose to the overlook. It started at Moose's approach and jumped back several feet but settled down there. I tied Moose to a tree, a big tree, and I scrambled on foot up the narrow path, slipping on the snow-blanketed rocks.

He was standing on the precipice in a full-length leather riding coat and the high polished black boots he wore when playing polo in Washington. He stared out toward the valley miles away, his hands thrust into his coat pockets.

I froze, trying to assess exactly what was happening here. "Coleby!" I yelled.

After a moment, almost absently and without turning away from the valley below, he answered, "Hello, Lewis."

"Hey, listen, Coleby," I said, "if you're going to jump, you mind if I keep the horse? He'd be a jolly good addition to my polo stable."

Now Coleby rotated his head to look over his shoulder at me. A weak smile offset the misery in his face. He even laughed lightly. "Oh, I think I'll ride him a little longer, Lewis." To my relief, he walked toward me over the snowy rocks.

"Well, hell," I said. "And here I thought I had me a new horse."

He came to me and we embraced like Russian brothers. There was a faint scent of fine Tennessee whiskey to him, but he exhibited no signs of inebriation. We returned to the clearing where the horses stood, and I broke dry twigs from the bottoms of pines while Coleby gathered firewood in his two-thousand-dollar coat. I used the pioneer method of firestarting, taught me by my grandfather the woodsman; I hosed the kindling down with Coleby's whiskey and threw a match at it from four feet away. In three minutes, a cozy blaze was cracking and popping. We sat near it on a fallen tree trunk. The pine boughs had sheltered the clearing from any significant snow accumulation. I opened new beers for Coleby and me and stowed the remaining two in a pocket of snow in the rocks.

We stared at the fire, letting the heat warm us and soothe our eyes. Wood smoke hung in the still air.

Coleby sipped his beer and said, "Sarah says only the working class drinks beer." He smiled and drank again.

"To the working class," I toasted, and drew a healthy glug. "Coleby, was there a time when she was a sweet and loving woman or was she born a ballcutting shrew?"

Coleby smiled wanly again. "Now that you ask, Lewis, it

does seem difficult to recall her as ever being loving. Certainly she has not been for many, many years." He rubbed his eyes. "She had grace and poise when I met her in Baltimore after Vietnam. My mother was a lady of a vanishing genre of grace and poise, and I mistook Sarah's possession of those traits to mean she had my mother's heart and character as well. A woefully flawed presumption, it develops."

"She was drinking when I got to Mountain Harbor," I said.

"Aren't we all," Coleby observed.

"You know what I mean."

"Yes. Yes, I do. There's no denying she's at least border-line alcoholic. I've tried to discuss it with her for a couple of years, Lewis, but I'm afraid any productive discussion between us died out long ago."

"She socked the hell out of Elizabeth. I found her—Elizabeth—running down the drive toward the highway."

Coleby rotated his blond head to look at me. "Was she hurt?"

"A swollen cheek and a bruise. She wasn't permanently marked, but next time could be different. When alcoholic parents go to whacking on the kids . . ."

"Don't I know," Coleby mused. "I've treated scores over the years." He stood and held his gentle, healing hands to the fire. I stood and tossed more sticks on it. A galaxy of sparks rose.

"What am I going to do, my friend?" Coleby asked, his voice colored with pain. "What do I do with this awful, hurtful situation? Where do I go with it? How do I seek a resolution? I'm out of ideas. I'm out of options."

"I think all you can do is sue Sarah for divorce and custody of Elizabeth. Anne will be a legal adult next month and she can remain with you at her will. Sue Sarah and let the chips fall where they may."

"That's the problem, Lewis. Where do the chips fall? My attorneys tell me the probability is I'd lose a custody suit."

"To an alcoholic child abuser?" I asked, exasperated.

"Proving she's alcoholic is highly improbable in this case. She's always refused to seek treatment. As for child abuse, the mental kind is next to impossible to prove in a court, and one slap in the face isn't going to qualify her for physical child abuse. The custody laws in this country stem from an era when women were chauvinistically assumed to be better parents. Time and research have since debunked that myth, but it has not adequately translated into the law yet, so my attorneys tell me. Courts automatically award custody to mothers except in the most extraordinary provable instances of unfit motherhood, and sometimes not even then. It's wrong, but it's the law in America." Coleby pronounced the word *law* with subtle sarcasm.

I squinted, my eyes burning from a drift of the smoke.

"I tangled with Sarah at the house just now. I told her if she ever hit Elizabeth again I'd lock her up for assault. She said she'd get even with me by hurting you. She said she's lived with you for eighteen years and she knows how to make you cry."

Coleby sighed. "That she does."

"I'm sorry."

"Don't be. I'm just about cried out these days. There is little left, even to her cruel imagination, in the way of innovative new ways to hurt me. What worries me most, Lewis, is it's all getting out of control. Until now, the acrimony, while vicious, has been civilized, confined to rhetoric and legal action. But the pressure on us all has escalated to where the situation is hemorrhaging at the seams. The signs are all there. She drinks more and more, and she throws books and cocktail glasses at me. And now you tell me she's struck Elizabeth. I fear I can't contain it much longer, Lewis. I can't evict Sarah—Mountain Harbor is legally her home, too. I can't vacate myself because that would leave Elizabeth to cope with Sarah alone. Aside from that, Mountain Harbor is my home as well! There's a frightening momentum to events which grows by the minute. I fear something terrible is going to happen soon and I'm powerless to prevent it."

A silence ensued, punctuated only by the snapping of the fire. Coleby was transfixed. He seemed to have said all he knew to say. I rose and refueled the fire.

"Coleby, I think Lucia Dodd murdered Ivy Joe Culpepper."

## Shepherd of the Wolves

Coleby slowly raised his head, his eyes fixed on mine. He stood. "Lewis, no!"

"Yeah. How about that? First girl I've met since Elaine who makes me feel love, who seems to feel love for me, who puts some promise of meaning and happiness in my life and, bingo, she turns out to have iced her saintly old granddad. Is that poetic or what?"

"Lewis, what are you saying? The Sloan brothers killed Ivy Joe Culpepper! What earthly motive could Lucia Dodd possibly have had to murder her grandfather?"

I pointed to the fallen tree trunk from which Coleby had just risen. "Better have a seat, my friend. I've got some real bizarre news for you." I laid it all out for Coleby. I reminded him that, in spite of all the circumstantial evidence against the Sloans in Mr. Joe's death, there had remained a shred of doubt in my mind. We never did account for the bag of pills in Joe's truck or for the odd words he uttered at his death. The Sloans never admitted to killing Joe and I couldn't yet connect the damage on Lanny's truck to Joe's old truck. Coleby was as astonished as everyone else at the revelation of Joe's secret estate, and, of course, he already knew of Lucia's financial woes due to the episode of the suicidal doctor in Washington. Then I told Coleby of the last-minute change Joe had ordered in his will, which all but excluded Lucia, and I detailed my discovery of Lucia having covered up damage to her car, which was known to have occurred about the time of Ivy Joe Culpepper's death. When I finished the whole sordid tale, I pulled my gaze from the fire and looked at Coleby.

He sat on the log with his elbows on his knees and his face in his hands. In a moment, he raised his eyes to mine and I saw there were tears gleaming in the corners. I suddenly felt very selfish at having dumped my sadness on top of Coleby's own.

"Coleby, I'm sorry. This is a bad time to be unloading all this on—"

He raised his hand and shook his head, silencing me. He stood again, lifted his head and held himself with the confident posture of an aristocrat, of a man of strength and character fully up to the task at hand.

"Nonsense, Lewis." He put his hand on my shoulder and

smiled. "Misery loves company. Now, correct me if I'm wrong, but, from what you've related to me here, it appears your case against Lucia Dodd is also only circumstantial."

"That's true, Coleby, but it's also pretty goddamn substantial; she clearly had method, opportunity and a compelling motive."

Coleby studied the fire. "Hmmm. Can Lucia account for the time frame of Ivy Joe's death?"

"I doubt it, all things considered, but I don't know. I haven't talked to her since this morning, when she left for Washington, before all this new information came to the surface."

"What are you going to do?"

"I don't know, Coleby. I don't know what to do. No. That's bullshit. I know exactly what I should do. I should dump it all on the state police, ASAP, and let them run with it."

Coleby's eyes narrowed as he looked into mine. "But you aren't going to do that, are you?"

"Goddamn it, I don't know! I can't believe she did it, Coleby. I swear to God I just can't believe it. I haven't known her very long, but I have known her intensely and intimately, and I just can't convince even the suspicious policeman in me that she did it, evidence be damned. There must be some explanation for it all!"

Coleby spoke softly. "You love her, don't you, Lewis?"

"Hell, I don't know! I don't know what love is anymore. But I know this. I know she hurts and I don't want her to. I know she's miserable in her life but I make her happy and that makes me feel good. I know I damn sure don't want to sic a murder investigation on her if there's any chance she didn't do it because it could be the straw that breaks her and/or drives her from me. And I know this. I know when I look into her eyes I don't see a murderess." I looked at Coleby, who was watching me intently. "Christ. I guess that means I love her."

"So are you going to inform the state police, Lewis?"

I stared at the dancing flames for nearly a minute. At some point in that time, a decision took hold in me.

"No. Not now. Not before I talk to her. I'll fly up there

tomorrow night and confront her. If she can't account for the evidence against her, then I turn everything over to the state police and let them move on her. For better or for worse, that's what I'm doing."

Coleby looked visibly relieved. "I think that's wise, Lewis. I'm sure she couldn't have killed her grandfather. I'm sure she will somehow convince you of that truth."

We kicked out the fire and mounted our horses. We rode slowly in silence past Captain Braithwaite's grave in the orange glow of a setting sun.

Three hundred years ago, the men who walked this land were Powatan Indians and they believed in spirits. I liked to think I was a more enlightened man in a more enlightened time, yet I was also a tired, sore, hungry, sad, hurt, worried . . . haunted man. Somehow the beauty of the cold sunset, the dignified symbol of death in the captain's snowy tomb and my own exhaustion combined to overwhelm my defenses, and I was invaded by the Ghosts of Innocence Lost.

The souls of my Tess and of Peggy Sloan came into me on a chill wind, and I was swept by a pervasive sorrow, a soaking remorse. Moose sensed something and she stopped. I slid down from her, staggered a few steps toward the disappearing sun and sank to my knees in the snow. The sobs welled up from deep within me in slow heaving waves of wretched sorrow. I was permeated with an abiding remorse for the senseless, violent loss of two young and innocent girls in my charge—two who had asked of the world only to laugh and love and who were instead consumed by the rotten luck in life or the sheer evil in men, two I had been given to protect yet, somehow, had let go to wholly unwarranted deaths way, way . . . way before their time.

My sobs carried on the cold wind.

Coleby sat quietly on his horse until my sorrow was purged once again. I heard his boots in the snow and the rustle of his leather coat behind me. I felt his hand rest upon my shoulder. When I regained my control, I rose and together we stood in the evening wind whistling up from the Shenandoah, watching the sun melt into the distant Appalachians.

"Tess," I said. "Peggy Sloan. Even Elizabeth."

Coleby thought for a moment. "I know," he said. "I understand."

"Well," I said emphatically, starting back to my horse. "Now that I've had my sob session I—"

"Don't chastise yourself, Lewis," Coleby said sternly, still staring at the fading western glow. His voice tightened with his own heavy grief. "Lately, I've been thinking a lot of a proverb from the Japanese classic, *RAN*. 'Man is born crying,'" Coleby spoke, "'and when he has cried enough, he dies.'"

The sun was gone.

# 26

## Resolve Dissolved

**T**he disturbingly young airline captain I saw through the open cockpit door on boarding the 737 must have gotten his takeoff clearance at the same time he was cleared on the runway. As soon as he nosewheeled her into alignment, he shot the throttles to the rock-and-roll position, and I was sucked back in the seat. Roanoke fell away below.

It was snowing again. I'd worn all my tribal talismans, my sheephide bomber jacket with a favorite old white Irish turtleneck sweater, faded but clean blue jeans and my worn but polished brown boots. I also wore a rain-stained old fedora Coleby had given me years before because, as he had said, "This hat is you, Lewis; it's a hat worthy of a modern-day shepherd." I looked like Indiana Jones or Freddy Krueger, depending on your movie orientation.

No pilot ever sleeps on airplanes unless he's exhausted. He doesn't sleep when he's doing the flying, of course, and he sure as hell doesn't sleep when someone else is flying the machine because he knows all the things that can go wrong. The fact that they rarely do go wrong is precious little comfort. Such paranoia makes for good pilots but lousy passengers. When the plane leveled off I was grateful for the distraction of a sweet-smelling stewardess brushing by my shoulder. I know, they're "flight attendants," but when you've got a stewardess fetish, "flight attendant" just isn't adequate. Maybe it's their uniform or the service theme, who knows? Who gives a damn? Whatever it is, it feels good. That's all we Cro-Magnon throwbacks require, thank you.

Fortunately, on this Saturday afternoon, most people were fleeing Washington, not flying to it, so the window seat next to me was empty, which took some of the cramp out of being six-foot-two in a flying sardine can.

Idly, I perused a copy of the *Roanoke Times* left in the seat pocket and was particularly drawn to a minor blurb on page two of the city section: *"Councilman Dreyfuss Assaulted,"* the header read. *"Roanoke City Councilman Arnold C. Dreyfuss, 41, was seized by a trio of unidentified men yesterday and was suspended upside down from the fifteenth-floor balcony of the Roanoke Park Hotel, sources close to the councilman reported. Councilman Dreyfuss was unable to describe his assailants to police nor could he provide any motive for the attack. Dreyfuss was uninjured but was admitted to Lewis Gale Hospital overnight for treatment of acute anxiety, hospital sources confirmed."* Hmmm. My, my, what was this world coming to?

When Coleby and I rode back down to Mountain Harbor from Captain Braithwaite's grave the previous evening, we found that Sarah had gone on a rampage and left for parts unknown. Her Mercedes was gone from the garage.

I helped Coleby, Elizabeth and Polly pick up books, lamps, overturned furniture and broken ceramics. A large ornately-framed wedding photograph of Coleby and Sarah was impaled on the staircase banister post; glass shards dotted the carpet. Everyone went about cleaning up the disgraceful spectacle in silence.

Elizabeth's cheek was now blue, but she seemed emotionally adjusted, as much as any child could be as a player in a crashing family. At one point, she saw Coleby standing quietly by the hearth, the misery heavy on his face. She went to him and threw her arms about his waist. He clutched her to him, and she said with remarkable calm, "I love you, Daddy. I'll *never* leave you." Coleby's face quivered with his futile attempt to hold back tears.

I ached for him. He was running out of strength. He was

breaking down, day by day, right before my eyes, and there was nothing I could do to stop it.

Later, after Polly had fed us and we'd put Elizabeth to bed, Coleby walked me out in the darkness to my cruiser in a light but steadily falling snow. I cranked the big engine to let it warm and used a windshield squeegee from the equipment box in the trunk to clean the snow from the windows, defroster intake and lights. I closed the trunk and turned to find Coleby staring at me oddly. He stepped near and seized me in a desperate embrace. I held him until he released me. He stepped back and said, "Go to her, Lewis. I'm sure she will convince you she didn't kill her grandfather. Give her that chance."

"I will, Coleby. I hope to God you're right."

I opened the car door and looked once again at Coleby. The light from the house fell on his face; his agony was vivid.

"Lewis," he whispered, and he extended his hand toward me, his palm raised and his fingers spread. His hand trembled. It was as though he was trying to transmit something to me through his hand. I didn't know how to react. "You are the shepherd," he said, and he turned and walked away.

At the gate to Mountain Harbor, I stopped for headlights approaching on the snowy highway. Abruptly, the lights swerved toward me. Sarah Butler's crimson Mercedes rocketed between the stone pillars and slid to a stop alongside my cruiser. Sarah was clearly drunk and the alcohol accentuated the hate with which she now glared at me.

She tossed her hair and floored the Mercedes. Its engine howled and the car spun away, throwing a cascade of snow behind it. I hoped to Christ she just went to bed when she got to the house. Coleby was too near the edge for any more misery tonight.

I went into town to the dungeon, checked my messages and left some orders with the nightwatch sergeant.

There was a note on my desk from Pierce outlining a trap he and the men were setting for the Roanoke car thieves who had worked with the Sloan brothers. Pierce also wrote that the bartender at Saddle Mountain Lodge had called to report that Lois Ross had disappeared, taking none of her belongings with her. That was strange. Now what the hell had happened to Lois?

By the time I parked the cruiser in front of Ivy Joe Culpepper's little cottage on Eldridge Street in East Hunter, the snow was a couple of inches deep on roads that had been clear at noon. I gazed with amazement at the little house, the tiny, ridiculously modest home of a secret millionaire. I wondered briefly if I had just dreamed the events of this day, but I knew I could not have been so lucky.

Inside, I lit the kerosene stove and took a hot shower. By the time I was dried and dressed in a VPI sweatsuit, the house was cozy. There was a faint fragrance of perfume in the air that evoked erotic images of the sweet, brown, writhing body of Lucia Dodd.

I built a fire and lay on the overstuffed sofa and contemplated Lucia. Should I call her or just show up unannounced? Should I give her any warning? How would surprise affect the likelihood of forthrightness?

I walked into the little bedroom and sat on the ancient cherry four-poster where I had made such intense love to a woman whose mother was probably conceived and born in the same bed two generations ago. I picked up the phone and put it down again. What was I going to say, "Hi, sweetheart. Gee, suppose I drop by tomorrow and we have a romantic little tête-à-tête about you murdering grandpa, the millionaire janitor"?

In the end, I decided to call her but give her no warning of the true reason for my visit. I didn't want to just barge in unannounced; that would only provoke suspicion on her part and offered no tactical advantage. Yet to give her any hint whatever of why I was coming would precipitate a discussion on the phone which I wanted to avoid. I wanted to be face to face with her when I broached the issue, so I could see her eyes, read her body language, observe her unrehearsed reaction.

I picked up the phone.

Now, at twenty-seven thousand feet over the Blue Ridge Mountains, I still felt a little guilty at my deception. Lucia had sounded so thrilled to hear from me. When I suggested

# Shepherd of the Wolves

I fly up the next night, she was so excited she reminded me of a time when I told Tess I was taking her to Richmond to the circus. Lucia had all but jumped up and down. "Oh, Lewis, I'm so happy!" she had said, "We've only been apart a single day, but already I miss you so I ache! I won't ask you what made you decide to come so soon, I don't care! I just want to be in your arms. Hurry, my love!"

Never mind, I told myself, booting aside my guilt, staring out the airliner window at the snow-blanketed Blue Ridge. This isn't a social call; it's business. As soon as I get there, I'm going to level with her and we're going to have it out. If she can't come up with some goddamned miraculous explanations and some diamond alibis, then I will surely have her charged with the murder of Ivy Joe Culpepper. Depend on it.

The moment I walked into the concourse at Washington National Airport and took one look at Lucia Dodd, my resolve dissolved. She stood leaning against the back wall, dressed in a powder-blue leather skirt and jacket over a silky white blouse and matching blue heels. Sensuality is different things to different men, but my definition now stood against the concourse wall, five feet four, skin of soft brown and lips of red framing perfect white teeth.

I was four feet from her when she pushed off the wall and strode to me with a purpose. She hit me with a thump, threw her arms around my neck and kissed me like the Fourth of July. When in Rome, I figured. I grasped her tightly about her waist and straightened. Her feet dangled a foot above the floor; she curled one shapely leg at the knee. She was exotically perfumed, slippery wet and frantically probing. I became uncomfortably hard in spite of the people gawking at us. It was a moment to remember, trust me.

When I set her down, Lucia laughed nervously and glanced with embarrassment at the people watching us, some with smiles, a few with ill-concealed disgust. "Sorry," she whispered breathlessly, "I guess I got a little carried away."

"Excuse me," I choked out, turning away from her, "I'm going to reboard the plane so I can get that welcome again."

"Come here!" She giggled, pulling on my arm. "We'll do it again later, I promise. Come on! I'm so glad you're here!" She took my arm and towed me through the flow of people trafficking the concourse. Walking briskly along, hand in hand, I looked to find her watching me with those hypnotizing lovely brown eyes, eyes which seemed to me to be full of adoration.

This was going to be a lot harder than I expected.

On the plane, I wondered what, if anything, Lucia would say when we got to her car to account for the difference between it and the rental car she drove to Hunter. Then she said, "We're taking a taxi, Lewis. I hope you don't mind. Washington drivers, excluding me of course, lose their minds in snow. Did you check a bag?"

"No," I replied, indicating the leather duffel slung over my shoulder, "just this; I can only stay the night."

"Ssssh," Lucia said, a sudden solemnity appearing on her face, "I don't want to think about that right now."

We walked silently for a while through the phenomenally diverse throng in the airport. "Jeez," I said to Lucia, "I'm sure glad you're here to be my guide; otherwise, I'd be lost in the Land of the Quiche Eaters."

Lucia smiled. "Lost, my foot. You were a cop in this town—a pretty good one, I hear from one of my lawyer friends who once had a go at you on the stand."

"Yeah, but I never really felt at home here."

"Odd," she remarked softly, "I never have either." Suddenly her demeanor brightened. "Tonight will be a true test of our relationship, Lewis," she said.

I looked at her curiously. I had had the same thought—on the plane I spent a lot of time pondering tonight. If she killed Mr. Joe, the relationship between us was impossible and must end. I could not forgive her even if she did not ultimately dim the lights at some penitentiary or spend the rest of her life in a cell. If she didn't kill him, she probably couldn't forgive *me* for accusing her, for using our personal relationship to probe a professional matter, for slipping invited through the defenses of her battered heart to stab her with new grief and trouble. Tonight would indeed be a test of Lucia Dodd and me, but how could she know that?

"Beg your pardon?" I said.

# Shepherd of the Wolves

"Tomorrow we will know what we're made of. Know why?"

What was she leading up to here? "No, but I'm dying to find out."

"Because!" she answered, her devastating model's smile lighting her face again. "Tonight I'm taking you to the indisputably best Mexican restaurant in North America! If you're man enough to eat the food and make love to me with jalapeño breath, we'll last forever!"

I laughed with no small relief.

"Are you hungry?" she asked.

"Starved," I replied. "And I could use some food, too."

Her laughter was sweet, sexy music.

The place was in the Adams Morgan section of northwest Washington. It was an old-world, hardwood, dignified establishment that thrived on word-of-mouth advertising among the locals. The service, by dark-skinned Mexican waitresses exotically dressed in peasant skirts and off-shoulder blouses, was swift and efficient. The rooms rang to the traditional Mexican music of a strolling mariachi band, which looked as though it just rode in out of the dust with Gregorio Cortez. The food was all Lucia had suggested it would be. We ate until our eyes watered.

I didn't see anything to be gained by spoiling such a fine meal with talk of murder. I would wait until we got to Lucia's home, away from the public eye, in a quiet, controlled surrounding. There and then, we would discuss massive debts and secret inheritances. We would talk of concealed repairs to a damaged car and of death on a mountain.

As soon as we got home.

We departed from the restaurant into the cold oil-scented air of the nation's capitol. We walked quietly, arm in arm, across the Taft Bridge in gently falling snow. We crossed Connecticut Avenue and soon came to a high-rise condominium building called Everett House. There, a uniformed, elderly black security guard held open the shiny brass door and said, "Good evening, Ms. Dodd." He peered suspiciously at me.

As we crossed the plush carpeted lobby, past a bank of

gleaming brass mailboxes, Lucia whispered to me, "Henry doesn't approve of you."

"Who?"

"Henry, the doorman. I can see from his expression he disapproves of my choice of . . . companion."

"Me? Why? Because I'm white?"

"Precisely."

"Wait a minute," I said as the elevator doors closed on us, "I thought all the bigots in the world were back in the ol' bastion of white ignorance."

Lucia suppressed a rueful grin. "No, Henry isn't a real bigot. He's too nice an old gentleman to hate you without knowing you. In fact, it's really me he disapproves of, not you. He thinks I've sold out to the white establishment. 'Bitch think she too good fo' the brothers!'" Lucia mimicked.

"He told you that?"

"Of course not. I happen to be vice-president of the condominium association which signs Henry's check. He'd have a seizure if he thought I knew he said that. Celia Rodriguez, the daytime desk clerk, is a world-class gossip who feeds off Everett House like an intestinal parasite. When she isn't busy telling me everything she knows about everybody, including Henry, she is, I'm sure, telling everybody everything she knows about me. Suitably embellished, of course."

"Of course."

We walked along the deep carpeted hall of the sixteenth and, according to the elevator numbering, top floor. I pondered for the millionth time how I was going to open the kettle of worms I'd come to explore. I dreaded it. She was so happy. She felt so good to me. I'd forgotten how good it was to be loved by a woman of quality. By a murderess?

I suddenly had an alarming shot of professional paranoia. Suppose Lucia knew a lot more than I thought she did? If she did in fact kill her harmless, doting old grandfather, then it was not at all beyond consideration that she could kill me, too, if she saw me as one of her problems instead of one of her solutions.

Lucia chose that moment to grip my arm and lean her

head against my shoulder as we neared the door to her apartment. "I'm glad you're here, Lewis," she said, almost with sadness, I thought.

It was an elegant but not showy corner apartment, the outer two walls of which were floor-to-ceiling smoked glass shrouded in expensive drapes on electric runners. The dining area was a bay with a hundred-and-eighty-degree wraparound view. In the distance, past a sea of buildings and treetops, the upper third of the Washington Monument glowed under thin blowing snow. The apartment was comfortable, a place where an established attorney could entertain important clients or just kick back and relax. It was fine carpet, indirect lighting, oak paneling and smoked glass. It was original paintings, Ansel Adams photographs and objets d'art of apparent African origin. I mentally compared it to my grandfather's late farmhouse on Bram's Ridge, out of view of any other residence, with its walnut floors, threadbare rugs and furniture from the thirties.

In the corner of the outer wall where the living room area began, there was a gleaming ebony Yamaha electric piano on which lay several sheets of music. I didn't know why that surprised me—what adored granddaughter of Ivy Joe Culpepper's would not have been taught the piano?

Lucia opened a polished wooden console containing a bank of black-faced electronics components. She touched a button and an easy flowing Branford Marsalis jazz piece filled the apartment as if Marsalis and his musicians were in the room.

I felt awkward, almost ashamed, staring out at the sparkling city lights. I was a guest in Lucia's home and in her heart, perhaps even in her bed, yet . . . this is bullshit, I told myself angrily. Get your head out of your ass, get your badge out of your heart and do what you came to do. Pronto.

I shucked out of my jacket and laid it across the back of the large, modern, white-leather sofa facing the draped living-room windows. When I turned to locate Lucia, I saw her bending to place a different CD in the console player. Her blue leather skirt was now stretched tightly across her bottom and had pulled up in the rear to reveal a tantalizing soft brown inner thigh above the top of a stocking, the sort of stocking with an elasticized lace band at the top to keep it up.

Lucia stood up, tall in her blue heels. She shrugged slowly out of her leather suit jacket and let it slide down one arm to the floor. As she walked toward me, the CD cut in and the Righteous Brothers began the slow, low lead-in to their classic "Unchained Melody."

The light in this end of the long room was low. It was a combination of dim glow from the dining-room chandelier and the blue-ice radiance of city lights shining through a section of the smoked-glass wall where the drapes were drawn back. Wavy hues of blue rippled in reflection from the shifting satiny sheen of her blouse as she walked.

She stopped an arm's length away and stood staring into my eyes as though asking me if I wanted her to come closer. I did. I put out my left hand and she took it in her right. I drew her to me, put my other hand on the soft leather at the small of her back and we swayed together in dance. The emotional intensity of the great song swelled, and Lucia put both arms about my neck and lay her head upon my chest. I grew hard against her belly, acutely aware of her breasts, her thighs sliding against me as we moved. Her perfume and her heat scorched. I could feel her breathing faster. Then she lifted her lovely face to me and her lips parted with heavy breathing. We kissed slowly at first, just light brushing touches. Soon our hearts pounded, our tongues explored and we sucked at each other's souls.

We parted to get our breath and rocked slowly against each other to the flowing, surging music, her face pressed in the bulky knit of my Irish sweater. I realized then she was inhaling the smell of me through the thick wool. I gripped her waist tightly to me, and in concert to our dance she began to subtly push against me, her lower belly against my upper leg, as we danced, an ancient, instinctive, erotic hunching.

We rolled about the rug, leaving articles of clothing in our wake. When we arrived at that meld of mind and body where salmon jump waterfalls, stallions kick down fences and wolves howl, we mated with sound and fury. It was primal lust, awkward, ungraceful, human and satisfying far beyond the capacity of mere words to convey.

There is no substitute for woman. Everything else is second best.

We soaked together in a steaming shower, bathing each other, sometimes just holding each other under the hissing hot stream of water. It was at some point there in the steam that I knew I loved Lucia Dodd. It was then I became certain that it was her, not merely fucking her, that I loved.

My God, I thought. What will I do now?

In her bedroom, illuminated only by the blue glow of city lights, I stood nude, watching the snow fall, the heat from the ceiling ventilator drying my hair.

Coleby, I called silently out over the city, Coleby my troubled friend, tell me, what do I do now? I could not hear his answer.

Lucia emerged from the bathroom wrapped in a towel and carrying an ornate crimson jar of pearlescent cream. I turned away from the window and met her at the bed. She smiled impishly and handed me the jar. She let the towel fall and she lay facedown on the bed, her head upon her hands, and she watched me over her coppery shoulder.

But for her face and hair, I rubbed that cream slowly and gently into every square centimeter of her splendid body. When I did her breasts, her nipples twanged against my fingers. I creamed her legs and feet and toes one by one.

She parted her legs and I slid my slippery hands high along the tender insides of her thighs, where isolated strands of curly dark pubic hair crept down from the thick growth above. A small clear trickle of oil ran from her and disappeared into the soft cleft below.

We did not fuck this time, we made love. We looked into each other's eyes and held hands and thrust slowly, exquisitely for a very long time before melting and fusing together and falling into deep blessed sleep.

I awoke in the darkness and looked at the digital clock in Lucia's VCR: *04:10*. I reached to touch her, to hold her, only to discover she was not there. I retrieved a pair of dark blue sweatpants from my bag, tugged them on and tied the drawstring. I padded barefoot through the dark apartment to the living room.

"Lucia?" I called.

"I'm here, Lewis," I heard her say, and in the dim blue light from outside I could see her silhouetted, standing in the extruded bay of the dining room, her arms crossed, looking out at the night. She wore my sweater, which extended nearly to her knees. As I drew near to her, she turned and ice blue light reflected from tears running down her face.

"Lucia, what's wrong?" I asked, and I held her to me. She began to cry softly.

"Oh, Lewis. I love you." She wept.

"I love you. Why are you crying?"

She pushed back from me and covered her eyes with her hand. She took in a deep breath and released it slowly.

"We have to talk, Lewis," Lucia said, walking away in the darkness toward the living room. "There . . . there are some things I have to tell you, things I'm afraid to tell you. I'm in a lot of trouble, Lewis. I've done a terrible, terrible thing."

# 27

## Black Truths

My heart sank. Apparently, I would not have to accuse Lucia of murdering Ivy Joe Culpepper. It seemed she was now about to confess. I felt no satisfaction, no relief, only a terrible sadness. I almost willed her to say no more, but it was time at last for the truth to rule.

She sat on the white leather couch, tucked her feet beneath her and tugged my sweater about her thighs. I slipped my sheephide jacket about my shoulders and settled into a black leather recliner near the window. In the darkness, I was aware of my heart beating more heavily than normal.

"Do I need to read you your rights?" I asked, in a joking effort to relieve the tension, only to suddenly realize the remark might be more appropriate than either of us thought.

The faux pas was not lost on Lucia. "I'm a trial lawyer," she said, fighting tears, looking at me through pained eyes, "I know Miranda and I waive my right to counsel, but for the record, Lewis, I'm not talking to the sheriff of Hunter County now; I'm talking to my lover."

I said nothing. I decided we both understood that if she confessed murder to her lover, the sheriff of Hunter County would still have her arrested.

"First of all," Lucia began, wiping her eyes and sniffing, "I have never lied to you, Lewis. Everything I've ever told you was true. Unfortunately, though, I omitted some salient details, some of which you should have known then, all of which you should know now." She began to cry softly again in spite of her efforts not to. "Oh God, Lewis. I was, I still am so afraid it will drive you from me." She wept.

I was dying. The woman I loved was about to inflict me with the duty of destroying her. I wanted to go to her, take her in my arms, dry her tears and tell her she need tell me nothing. But I didn't. I sat silently, waiting patiently for her to deliver herself into handcuffs. And I hated myself bitterly for it.

Lucia suddenly yanked herself under control. She stared past me at the distant floodlighted point of the Washington Monument.

"Lewis, about three years ago I was in love, like I'm in love with you now, deeply, desperately, out of control. It was a huge mistake then, but I made it anyway. He was a client, a black physician named Rayfield Hollander. I called him Rafe. Rafe had been a navy corpsman with the marines in Vietnam, some place in the central highlands called Dak To. There was a battle one night—a "firefight," he called it—and Rafe crawled into the woods, the jungle, looking for wounded marines he could hear crying out in the darkness. He was caught, captured by the North Vietnamese and taken to some encampment in Laos where he was brutalized over several days for information. They left him poorly guarded at one point, thinking he was unconscious, and he escaped. In the process, he came upon a single NVA soldier returning unarmed—from using the bathroom, Rafe thought. He was only a boy, Rafe said, no more than fourteen. He saw Rafe and opened his mouth to yell, but Rafe seized him and covered his mouth. Rafe never wanted to hurt him, but the boy panicked and struggled. Ultimately, Rafe choked him to death and escaped. He walked barefoot for three days before hearing helicopters. He ran into a clearing to wave and get their attention. The helicopters were American, of course, but they were also gunships. I guess the pilots only saw a running, barefoot, dark-skinned man in dirty green clothing, far from where any Americans were thought to be. They took him for the enemy and strafed him even as he waved at them. Smaller helicopters came and landed to search his body, and it was only then that they realized he was American and he was still alive. He did eight months in Bethesda Naval Hospital, recovering. But he was never the same, he often told me."

Somewhere in the dark snowy city, I could hear the faint whine of sirens.

"Later, Rafe graduated from Meharry Medical College in Nashville and specialized in surgery. He was good at it and he made something of a name for himself among the community of black professional athletes, mostly football and basketball players. He used to laugh about how a patient once told him he was 'the only nigger with a knife who could give a man back his career instead of ending it.'

"Rafe was married and they had a son, but Rafe suffered a lot of psychological aftereffects from the Vietnam experience. He wasn't easy to live with, I'm sure, and eventually his wife left him and took the boy. When the child was six, he was killed by a drunk driver on his way home from the swimming pool one summer."

Oh God, I thought.

"Rafe started drinking too much. About a year before I met him, he drank until three in the morning and then attempted a ligament procedure on a patient's elbow at ten the same morning. He . . . slipped, he made a tiny wrong move and somehow he severed the ulnar nerve. What started out to be a relatively simple operation resulted in the paralysis of the patient's left and dominant hand. The patient was a star forward for the Washington Bullets so his career was effectively ruined.

"The plaintiff sued Rafe for thirty million dollars, ten million compensatory and twenty million punitive—absurd figures, of course, but not unheard of in cases where million-dollar-a-year athletes are injured. The anesthesiologist testified to smelling alcohol on Rafe's breath while scrubbing for the operation."

"And you represented him," I said.

"Yes," she whispered. "Somehow we fell in love. One late-night deposition here, one strategy dinner there—aaaaah. There was no excuse. It just happened. He was so beautiful a man, Lewis. He had such heart and he hurt so much and I thought I could save him and make him happy again. Oh, what a love-wrecked fool I was . . ."

In the dim blue glow through the curtains, I caught the gleam of a tear on her cheek.

"I poured my heart and soul into his defense, and in the end it devastated us both. The best I could do was get the judgment against him down to three-point-six million dollars. Rafe's insurance covered only part of it. He liquidated his assets, but even that left almost eight hundred thousand dollars outstanding.

"By now, Rafe was an emotional basket case. I called him one night when I knew he was home and he didn't answer. I had a key to his home in Silver Spring, and when I got there I found him on the bathroom floor from an overdose of something. He'd just taken it and they got him to a hospital in time to save him. He recovered."

"All this must have taken a toll on you," I observed.

She shivered. "It was the worst time of my life, Lewis. It was horrible. Hoping Rafe would regain his will to live if he were free of the crippling debts, I helped him arrange loans for the balance of the judgment against him. I cosigned actually, putting up everything for collateral. My stocks, my shares, even this apartment.

"Then . . ." Lucia covered her eyes with a hand. "Then last year he reached a point where his hurt and his shame were so great"—Lucia fought back sobs now—"and his defenses were so weak then. He could bear it no longer and he sat in his car in his closed garage with the engine running. This time . . . I couldn't . . . I couldn't save him." Lucia wept. "This time I couldn't save him."

I left her crying and went into the bathroom, where I ran hot water into a towel and squeezed it out. I took the damp towel back into the living room and handed it to Lucia. I ached to hold her and comfort her, but something held me back. She held her face in the hot towel for a moment and regained her control.

"Aside from what losing Rafe did to me emotionally, Lewis, it also wrecked me financially. Without Rafe's income to contribute, I have inevitably fallen way behind on the loan payments—so far behind that the creditors have filed recovery actions. I'm on the verge of bankruptcy. Bankruptcy would result in the loss of my home and virtually every asset I own, but worse, Lewis, it would mean the end of my career! The senior partners were less than thrilled when I became the lover of a key client while in charge of his case, even less inspired when I lost it. That alone severely strained my position with an established firm which prides itself on its long-standing reputation for traditional, unquestionably ethical practices. A bankruptcy for someone in my position raises serious question of one's ability to conduct one's affairs competently. The firm could hardly then entrust me with the affairs of important clients; my partnership would become a liability, one they could not and would not tolerate. They'd force me out, and with a legacy like that I'd be lucky to get pro bono work at some Anacostia storefront legal clinic." Lucia drew a deep quivering breath and held it.

She killed him, I thought. She's building a case in her lawyer's way, laying down all this groundwork so that her one-man jury might understand the stress and desperation that drove her to push an old man off a mountain to preserve and deliver his fortune to her salvation. I will listen, my Lucia, my love. I will listen. I owe you that.

Lucia went to her kitchen and brewed some tea for us in silence. The rich liquid felt good going down in these dark hours of a cold morning.

"There's more," she continued, sipping her own tea. "You're going to swear it's impossible, but it can be verified. My grandfather was not exactly the pauper Hunter County thought he was. Lewis, Poppy Joe was worth over two million dollars."

She looked at me carefully. I wondered if I should feign surprise, to prevent her from suspecting I knew any of this, but I wasn't up to the effort. I just looked back at her through steam rising from my tea.

"I didn't know that until I graduated from law school," Lucia went on. "I had a partial scholarship and I waited tables on the side, but there still wasn't enough money to pay for a law degree. Somehow, Poppy Joe always seemed to make up the difference, I assumed through struggle and sacrifice.

"When I took up my practice, I set about repaying Poppy Joe for his contribution. He refused to let me repay him, saying my success and my love were all the repayment he needed. I considered him semi-indigent, so I devised to submit a regular monthly check directly to his bank account, since he kept sending my earlier checks back. At some point, I accidentally forgot to sign a check and it came back to me under the letterhead of a Roanoke law firm. I couldn't understand how this occurred, and when I made inquiries of the firm, I was bluntly told they were not at liberty to discuss my grandfather's affairs.

"Wondering what kind of trouble he was in and how I could help, I confronted Poppy Joe with this; he swore me to secrecy and finally explained it all. He started out investing small sums through a trusted white friend way back in the teens, Lewis! He had enough insight, and he was aware enough, to suspect where oil was going as an investment. Later, he had the same timely foresight with the computer industry. All the while, he labored and lived off his paltry pay as a janitor for the Hunter County School Board. He just kept reseeding his investment earnings over and over for seventy years! He leaves an estate worth almost three million dollars!"

Lucia waited for me to react.

"Why didn't you tell me this in the beginning, Lucia?" I asked her. "You knew it was germane to any investigation of Mr. Joe's death. Why did you withhold it?"

"Yes, I knew! Of course, I knew. I wanted to tell you, but I couldn't. I—" She groped in agony for the words. "Look, Lewis . . . I haven't told it all yet. It gets worse, I'm afraid."

Yes, I thought. I know it does.

"When Poppy Joe told me about his estate, I was thrown into shock! Why did he let us struggle so hard for so long? Why did my mother have to work until her dying day? Why did I have to wait tables in white restaurants and then study until three in the morning to make it through law school? Why did he waste himself for over half a century, mopping school floors, when he could have lived well with pride? Where was he when he could have made a contribution to the fight for racial equality? Why did he play Stepin Fetchit for decades when he could have been an example for struggling young blacks?"

"He wasn't a Stepin Fetchit," I interrupted. "He was his own man in great dignity. He did what he did because he damn well wanted to, and he lived the life of a man of character."

Lucia rose and walked to the window with her cup. She looked out at the falling snow for a while. She sighed and spoke. "I know that now, Lewis. At least, I understand it better, but in those days I was young and naive and full of social revolutionary zeal and black pride, and I did not understand it at all. I was outraged and incensed. He tried to explain that he feared the corruptive effects of wealth, that he was afraid that we would never achieve our personal potential as long as we had money to fall back on. He was concerned that people known to be wealthy are treated differently, that friendships, loves and acquaintances lose their innocence and purity when large sums of money are associated. We had what we needed, he argued; our struggle made us strong. But at the time I threw all that back in his face as hypocrisy. I challenged him to make what I saw as his due contribution to the black cause, but he refused.

"The event estranged us. For years afterward, I avoided him. You stung me bad that day in your office when we met, Lewis. You charged that if I loved him so much, why had I never come to visit him? That hurt because you were right. I guess I was punishing him for not being the grandfather and black American I so righteously decided he should have been.

"In recent years, with maturity and experience, I had begun to question my position with Poppy Joe, but by then I was absorbed in the Rafe Hollander affair. I was trapped then. Although Poppy Joe never knew of my involvement with Rafe or of my financial straits, I felt that to attempt to repair Poppy Joe and me now would be seen as financially motivated, as going to him strictly for a bailout. Inside, I guess I feared that might actually be part of my motive. I couldn't go to him as long as I was in distress for money, Lewis! Then I would be the hypocrite! Poppy Joe would be proven right about wealth affecting love and relationships."

Lucia took my cup, leaving a warm sweet scent behind her as she walked to the kitchen. She refilled the cups and returned to the white leather couch. She sighed tiredly and continued.

"About two weeks ago, Poppy Joe called me, Lewis, the first time we'd conversed in years. I was stunned. He told me he had originally structured his will to provide an even one million dollars for me. What he called to tell me was that, in view of my success, as he put it, he felt that the money would be better placed in the United Negro College Fund and was that all right with me? What a hellish question that was, Lewis! I needed that money so very badly! Yet what was I going to say? After ten years of snubbing him for my perception of his failure to support the black community, was I now to thwart that very effort on my own personal behalf? Did that not prove beyond any further question the wisdom of Poppy Joe hiding his wealth? Would not that make me the ultimate hypocrite? It was the second toughest decision of my life to tell him no, of course I didn't mind, that I was pleased to see him make that contribution to our people. He said he would instruct his lawyers to implement that change in his will immediately. After that, we talked, Lewis, for the first time in nearly a decade we talked to each other! I promised to come and see him soon, and he seemed overjoyed at that. When we hung up, I wept with misery and shame. Who was I to have judged him? Who appointed me God?" Tears trickled from the lovely brown eyes of Lucia Dodd.

"The toughest decision of my life came a few days later when I decided to throttle my pride, stain my image in Poppy Joe's eyes, accept responsibility for my own hypocrisy, and go to him, hat in hand. I would explain my dilemma and ask him to bail me out. Then I would beg him to forgive me for letting money, not just love, be what finally brought me back to him. The prodigal daughter would go home in shame."

What went wrong? I wondered. How did good intention turn to murder? I waited for her to tell me. I felt very old.

Lucia continued. "I—last Monday I set out for Hunter in my car to see Poppy Joe. I didn't tell him I was coming; I just went. Somewhere down between Roanoke and Hunter, my cellular phone rang, but the connection was too weak to understand, so I stopped at a pay phone to call my office in Washington. My secretary told me there was a message to call a woman in Hunter, a longtime friend of Poppy Joe's, and she had said it was an emergency. 'Oh, no!' I thought, 'Please, God, let nothing have happened to Poppy Joe! Not now!' But he was dead. Worse, it looked like his death was murder. There were rumors of Lois Ross and of threats by the Sloan brothers and—"

Lucia stood and began to pace nervously. What was happening here? I thought rapidly. Was Lucia saying Mr. Joe was dead before she ever saw him for the first time in a decade?

"I—I was grief-stricken, Lewis! I was beside myself! He couldn't be dead! Murdered! Not on the very day I was going to him to reconcile us after so long. Don't tell me that, after ten years apart, I was to be only two hours too late! I ran back to my car and drove recklessly, way too fast, almost as if by speeding to Hunter fast enough I could outrace time and see Poppy Joe before he died! I was crying and talking to myself and to Poppy Joe, begging him not to be dead, praying there was some mistake! Then I lost control of my car in a turn, ran off the road and hit a fallen tree. It was expensive damage, but I wasn't hurt and the car was still drivable. When I calmed down a little from fear and guilt and grief, I backed onto the road and continued toward Hunter at a sane speed."

Lucia's breathing had quickened and her face was twisted by her pain.

"Then, at some point as I drove, I began to consider my situation from a lawyer's point of view. If I showed up in Hunter in a front-end-damaged car when the rumor was that Poppy Joe had been forced off the road, if the circumstances of Poppy Joe's estate came out, especially if it were to be contrasted with my financial situation and Poppy Joe's intent to reduce my inheritance, well—I—well you can see it, can't you Lewis? It would make *me* appear to be the prime suspect!"

Yeah. I could see it.

"It would become still one more disaster for me to contend with at a time when I couldn't stand another,

Lewis. Emotionally, I couldn't bear to even be accused of harming my own grandfather for money! The scandal would swamp my already storm-ridden career boat. Worse, it would inevitably distract, perhaps even eliminate any meaningful investigation into what really happened to Poppy Joe! I couldn't allow that to happen, Lewis! Can't you appreciate that?" Her eyes pleaded.

I said nothing. It was not a time for me to talk. Lucia looked hurt by my silence.

"So I turned around and headed back to Roanoke, where I dropped the car at a Lincoln Mercury dealer, rented another and drove on to Hunter. I spent that evening in East Hunter gathering information from the black community about what was known of Poppy Joe's death. On Tuesday morning, I went to see you. You know the rest."

I stared at her intently. She met my gaze, then looked at her lap and began to cry softly. My God. If she was acting, it was Oscar quality, but then again, if she was acting, she was doing so with her life at stake. I sighed and ran my fingers up my forehead and through my hair. I thought carefully, turning it all over slowly in my mind.

"Lucia, did you report that accident to the police?"

Her brow wrinkled in confusion. "No. No, I didn't. It involved only me. There was no injury or property damage other than my own car, which was drivable, so I—"

"It didn't occur to you that your insurance carrier would demand a police accident report?"

"Not at that moment, Lewis, no. I was still in shock from learning of Poppy Joe's death and I was frightened by the accident. Later, when I got to the Lincoln Mercury dealer, I thought about that, but by then it was too late."

"Why did you tell the service writer at the Lincoln Mercury dealer you'd pay cash for the repairs instead of making an insurance claim?"

"Well, because I—" Lucia's eyes suddenly widened. She drew in a deep breath. "Lewis, how do you know about—"

"Answer my question, Lucia."

"How—"

"Answer me, goddamn it!"

"I—because—by the time I got to Roanoke, I was not only aware I had inadvertently become a suspect, I was scared to death of it! It was in my interest to keep my accident off the record as much as possible! Lewis, tell me how—"

"Where did the accident happen?" I hammered at her.

"Lewis . . ."

"Talk to me, Lucia! Where did you run off the road?"

"I—I'm not sure, Lewis! Somewhere between Roanoke and Hunter. I didn't—"

"Come on! That's over fifty miles. Can't you be more specific?"

"Oh, God, Lewis! You don't think I killed Poppy Joe, do you? Is that why you're here? Is that why you came?" Tears welled up in her eyes again.

"You just made the case against yourself, didn't you? Did anybody see you make that call to your office or the subsequent call to the neighbor in Hunter?"

"Lewis!" Lucia cried, her voice breaking. "Lewis, please tell me this isn't why you came here tonight! How much of this did you already know?"

"Who saw you make the *calls?*" I demanded.

"No one! No one I know of! I called from a public phone near a closed and abandoned gas station. But, Lewis, the long-distance phone records will—"

"Will verify the time and location of the calls, Lucia. But what the phone records won't indicate is whether your car was already wrecked when you made them!"

"What are you saying, Lewis?" Lucia pleaded, crying miserably.

"I'm saying that if your car wasn't wrecked when you made those calls, your story floats. If it was wrecked before you made the calls, then you could have already shoved Mr. Joe off Saddle Mountain to his death and have been fleeing when your cellular phone rang and you stopped to make those calls! That's what I'm saying!"

"My story floats? Oh, Lewis, no! You think I killed him!" Lucia stood and backed away toward the dining room as though I were metamorphosing into an python right before her. "Is that why you're here, Lewis?" she asked, her voice quavering. "Is that what I am to you, Lewis? A *suspect?* Tell me, *Sheriff* Cody! Do you always use this interrogation technique to—"

"Lucia, listen to me—"

"Do you always *fuck* confessions out of your female suspects?" she flared. "Or just the gullible *nigger* tramps!"

I leaped out of the chair and stabbed an accusing finger at her. "Don't run that shit at me, Lucia! You know damn well—"

"Or . . ." Lucia wept anew now. She dropped to her knees on the deep carpet, her clasped hands sliding between her thighs. "Or . . . do you just break their hearts instead? Oh God, Lewis, I can't believe you think I could have killed Poppy Joe. I thought you came here . . ." She sobbed in slow wretched heaves. "I thought you loved me."

I spun away in anger, partly in disgust with myself, partly in intensely agitating confusion. Was she telling the truth or was she just a world-class actress acting for her life? I stalked away, unable to bear her misery, the agony that I had thrust upon her in her most vulnerable time. I slammed the door to her dark bedroom behind me, but I could still hear her crying. Suffering.

I went to the bedroom window and stared out at the snowy city dawn. Confusion assailed me. God knew I wanted to believe she was innocent, but there had to be proof or it was all a sham. Proof of her innocence would now swing around times, the times of those calls versus the time of Ivy Joe's death, both of which were fairly verifiable. I hoped with all my heart that there would not be enough time for Lucia to have made it from Saddle Mountain to the site where the long-distance records would show the calls were made. I wished there were some way to verify that the damage to her car had been done by a tree and not the rear end of a '53 Studebaker pickup truck. Lucia's personal Lincoln, a heavy luxury car, was plenty big and powerful enough to have pushed Mr. Joe's . . . a heavy luxury car . . . the damage . . . her car . . . car . . . Lois Ross!

My heart stopped.

Lahz Roz! Roz Rahz! Oh, dear God, *no! No!*

At first I could not generate enough breath to scream, then all I could manage was a hoarse hollow cry, a cry of horror.

I knew.

## Shepherd of the Wolves

I reeled backward in the dark, fell over Lucia's vanity bench and crashed hard to the floor.

"Lewis!" I heard Lucia call, on the run. She rushed into the room. "Lewis! Lewis, what's wrong? What is it?" She slid to the floor by me on her knees. "Lewis, darling, what's wrong? What's—"

I seized her. I clutched her to me. I began to do some serious sobbing of my own. Lucia held my head to her breast.

"What is it, Lewis? You're frightening me!" she whispered. "Tell me, my love, tell me what's wrong. *What's wrong?*"


It was almost twenty minutes before I could talk, and when I did, it was on the phone to Milly at the dungeon in Hunter.

"Mornin', Sheriff!" Milly said brightly. "Where you at? You still up in—"

"Listen to me, Milly," I said, exhausted.

"Lewis, you okay?" Milly asked with sudden concern.

"Is Pierce in yet?"

"Yeah, Lewis, he in his office. Are you—"

"Put me through to him, Milly."

The tone of Pierce's basso voice sounded as though Milly had alerted him that something was wrong. "Hey, Lewis. Everything okay? Lewis?"

"No . . . no, Pierce, everything's not okay. Listen to me carefully."

"Sure, Lewis, how can I help?"

"Get hold of Judge Lemon, ASAP. Wake him up if you have to."

"Okay, sure. What—"

"Tell him this, Pierce. Tell him I want immediate court orders to exhume the bodies of Ivy Joe Culpepper and Cassie Shelor."

# 28

## Lois Ross

Snow quieted the world. The land was white and the sky was gray at a little past noon. The season's second snowstorm, another heavy one falling even now, hard on the heels of the first, had deeply carpeted the road from Hunter to Mountain Harbor. Fog and the still falling snow had visibility at less than a quarter of a mile.

I felt isolated, alone on the planet. The battered old silver Ford truck floated over the snowy road, the only sounds being the muted engine, the slap of the windshield wipers and my own labored breathing.

I turned the truck between the dignified stone portals at the entrance to Mountain Harbor, thinking of my encounter with Sarah there two evenings before, seeing again her look of scathing hatred. When the driveway became steep, the rear wheels spun. I got out and locked the hubs; by the time I got back in, the heavy snowfall had peppered my Stetson and the fleeced collar of my bomber jacket. I tugged the coat over my holstered gun to keep it dry.

The truck clanked as I engaged the front axle, and then it moved easily up the rising tree-lined drive.

I stopped when the mansion barely came into view through the misty fog. I cut the engine and studied what I saw, which wasn't much. I decided to close the remaining three hundred meters on foot.

# Shepherd of the Wolves

"County, Sheriff One," I said into my radio. "Milly, I'm out with my portable at Mountain Harbor."

Static hissed and then: "Ten-fo', Sheriff One. Twelve twenty-six."

"Sheriff One." Pierce's distinctive grumble came from the radio as I slipped it into my jacket pocket. I turned up the collar of the coat, and my boots crunched in the snow.

"Sheriff One," Pierce repeated. "Lewis, you sure about this? I can be there in twenty minutes."

I held the radio to my face. "Negative, Pierce. Thank you, but this is something I have to do alone. I'll advise if I need assistance. If you haven't heard from me in two hours you can come looking for me."

There was a long silence as I plodded toward the Butler home. I knew Pierce wasn't happy with how I had insisted on handling this. Finally I heard the frequency open; I could hear Pierce draw in a deep breath and let it out. "Ten-four, Sheriff. Two hours."

High on the plateau of the Mountain Harbor estate, a stiff cold wind now carried the snowflakes horizontally. I stopped and examined the front of the stately old house, but there were no signs of life.

I zipped the bomber jacket tight at the collar against the bitter wind and I walked around the house to the rear. Sarah's Mercedes and Coleby's Jeep were the only cars in the six-stall garage. There were some tracks on the veranda slowly disappearing under falling snowflakes.

I froze.

One of the French doors stood open on a dark den, and snow lay on the carpet several feet into the room. I hadn't expected this. That door had been standing open in a raging snowstorm for some time.

At the doorway, I saw there were no lights on inside, in spite of the dark gray day. Heat from within warmed my face.

"Hello!" I called. "Anybody home?"

Nothing.

"Hello!" I bellowed, louder.

I heard only the tocking of the antique grandfather clock in the foyer beyond the spacious, sunken den. I drew my nine-millimeter and entered. I didn't know why I felt I needed to be armed, but something was very wrong; I could sense it.

"Anybody home?" I yelled.

Silence, but for the slow tocking of the old clock.

I found nothing in a slow, cautious search of the lower floor—nothing in the big stone-floored kitchen, in the exquisitely furnished living room, in Coleby's library or in the other downstairs rooms.

In the foyer beneath the heavy crystal chandelier, I peered up the winding staircase before ascending it.

The huge master bedroom, which had been exclusively Coleby's since Sarah moved permanently to one of the guest rooms years ago, was vacant, the bed unmade.

The guest room I used was immaculate.

I found the door to Sarah's study ajar; I eased it back with my foot and tensed. My breathing quickened.

Sarah Butler lay still on the floor, staring at the ceiling, staring with the same kind of clouded, dead eyes that Ivy Joe Culpepper and Cassie Shelor had gazed at me with. She was dressed only in a plush bathrobe that had, apparently in struggle, come untied and now lay open at the breast. Her hair was wrapped in a damp towel and one thigh extended through the front of the robe, crooked beneath the other leg.

I knelt by her, felt beneath her jaw and confirmed that she was dead. She was still warm. I drew the robe back from her nude body but saw no blood, no wounds or bruises—no marks at all.

I covered Sarah's body with the robe and studied her face. Even in death, her brow was knotted with contempt and there was a mean set to her mouth. The eyes were dead but they still beamed hate up at me. I closed them.

What goes around, comes around, I had recently said to Sarah.

I hurried now, almost in a panic.

Anne's room was spotless. I approached Elizabeth's room with a dread very close to horror. I pushed Elizabeth's door open like one lifts a rock under which one expects to find a spider; I pushed it hard and yanked my hand back.

Only when I found the room clean and unoccupied, the

canopied bed neatly made, only then did I realize how hard I was breathing.

I rushed through the rest of the upper floor, but at the top of the stairs, I remembered I had not checked the bath off Coleby's bedroom.

But it, too, was vacant.

I thought for a moment and then it came to me. I holstered the pistol, charged down the curved staircase and ran to the stable across the creek. As I'd suspected, Coleby's favorite Arabian was missing from its stall. Hurriedly, I swung open the heavy gate to Moose's stall and towed her into the broad stable aisle.

Arthur was nowhere to be found, which worried me, but I found the saddle he'd fashioned for Moose. In two minutes, I bent low over her neck as she loped out of the stable into the heavy blowing snow.

At the captain's grave there were faint disappearing indentations in the snow which had been the tracks of a man and a horse. I gigged Moose; she snorted and galloped away toward the hawksbill overlook.

Through the pines, near the clearing at the base of the rocky path to the overlook, I could see the stallion standing alone.

I rode into the clearing in the tall pines and halted Moose.

There at the fallen log, near the ashes of the fire we'd built two days ago, Dr. Coleby Butler lay leaning against the log watching me. His eyes were tired but they were alive.

"Hello, Lewis," he said, smiling sadly. "I've been expecting you."

Coleby's doctor's bag, the old-fashioned top-opening black leather type, lay on the pine needles beside him, open. Coleby wore riding boots and the same knee-length leather riding coat he'd worn when we were here last. His hair was windblown and his face showed exhaustion, but, oddly, it seemed at peace for the first time in years.

I slid down from Moose.

"Lewis," Coleby sighed. "I'm glad you're here. I am about to give myself a lethal injection and—"

"The hell you are!" I said, and I started for him.

Coleby quickly reached beneath his coat and withdrew an

old army-issue Colt .45 automatic pistol which he cocked and held to his head.

"Stop, Lewis," he ordered. I did. "Please, Lewis, don't make my children have to endure a closed casket funeral for me. Don't carry the memory of my exploded head with all the other horrors you bear, my friend. Please."

"Coleby, listen to me. It doesn't have to end this way. You can plead insanity, you weren't yourself, you've been under so much pressure! You—"

"No, Lewis. It can be no other way. No." Coleby sighed again. He waved the gun at the ashes. "Build us a fire, Lewis. I'm so cold. I'm glad you're here now." He uncocked the gun, but he laid it close in his lap. "Build us a fire, my friend, for we've much to talk about."

The pines sheltered the grove from the worst of the snow. I found enough dry kindling and wood to get a good fire going. I sat across from him, eyeing the gun still near in his hand in his lap. The horses watched the fire crackle.

The wind howled above the pines.

"You were sleeping with Cassie Shelor," I said softly.

Coleby laid his hand atop the pistol. A trace of a smile showed beneath his exhausted eyes.

"How did you know?" he asked, weary, breathing slowly and deeply.

"Cassie had a passion for older men. I found that out vividly almost a year ago. Her mother told me at her funeral that, about six months ago, Cassie stopped dating and told her mother she was tired of boys. Helen Shelor said Cassie continued to go out regularly, sometimes overnight, but always claimed to be alone. She said Cassie was very happy for a long time, but she grew depressed just before her death. Cassie was a daddy's girl and she was desperately lonely. You . . . you were lonely, too. It didn't register then, but the last time you and I played chess, the day Cassie died, you told me, 'there is nothing on earth more lovely than a beautiful girl in her late teens, nature is her kindest to them then . . .' I thought you were referring exclusively to Anne, but you were talking about Cassie also, weren't you?"

Coleby lay his head back on the huge fallen tree trunk and gazed up at the sheltering pines.

"I don't know how it happened, Lewis. I didn't mean for

it to, I swear it. She . . . Cassie came to me nearly a year ago for a birth-control prescription. I gave it to her, but I also had a long talk with her about the risks inherent in an active sex life, especially at her age. I knew her father was dead, of course, and I felt she could benefit by my counseling. Lewis, I swear that was my only motive. I never intended—"

"I know, Coleby. I know you and I know what Cassie was like."

"Then, about six months ago, she started making repeated appointments to see me for this or that. I never found anything wrong with her, and at some point, it dawned on me that Cassie wasn't coming to me for medical reasons. On one occasion, she simply walked up to me and laid her head on my chest; it just seemed natural to hold her, to comfort her. That's all it was, I told myself. She just needed a little fathering."

"But that wasn't all, was it?"

"At first it was, Lewis, but then I found myself looking forward to her visits. Her sweet, adoring, feminine sensuality was such morphine to the agony of Sarah. Where Sarah scathed me, Cassie praised me; where Sarah ridiculed me, Cassie worshiped me; where Sarah was mean and cold, Cassie was so loving and warm . . . no . . . not warm . . . Cassie Shelor was hotter than the sun."

"She was pregnant when she died, wasn't she?"

Coleby looked at me. "My God, you're perceptive, Lewis. How did—"

"Just a good guess. An unused birth-control prescription, an empty tampon case . . . a reason to kill her."

"Oh, dear God! At first there was no sex, Lewis, I swear! I enjoyed . . . no . . . I *needed* her company so acutely. She was all that enabled me to cope with the ever-increasing pain and pressure from Sarah. I became concerned that my staff at the clinic might become suspicious of her frequent 'appointments' so I suggested we go to Roanoke one Sunday for dinner. She was overjoyed, so excited, so happy! Sarah didn't care where I was; I didn't even have to explain my absences. Cassie and I . . . we . . . she . . ." Coleby stammered for the words. "God, Lewis, she felt so good! She was like a narcotic!"

"And just as addictive."

"More! Once it started I couldn't get enough of her. She made no secret of wanting us to make love together. She made the most incredibly erotic overtures—"

"I know, Coleby."

"But I resisted at first. She was a patient! My God, she was almost an adolescent, a contemporary of my daughter! I resisted because somehow I could justify the morality of our involvement as long as it remained platonic yet . . ." Coleby stared into the blazing fire as it lashed in the howling wind. "Soon that facade collapsed. I hadn't had sex in *years,* Lewis, you know what Sarah was like. But Cassie. Sweet Jesus, she was a beauty, but it was much more than that, Lewis. She made me feel like a *man!* Like I had some *worth!* I'd forgotten what that was like. And she herself had such a *need!* She made me feel like I was cheating *her* by *not* making love to her! You can't *imagine* what she was like!"

"Yes, I can."

"Once we . . . once we . . . made love the first time, all my reservations dissolved and I could not get enough of her, Lewis! She was inexhaustible, yet always so grateful and appreciative. She made me feel like a *god!* Oh, Lewis, my friend. She was indeed a narcotic. And I was indeed addicted."

Coleby pulled his coat about him tightly, the gun still in his lap. I stoked the fire, and sparks rose into the wind.

"She became pregnant," I prompted.

"I was astounded and terrified, Lewis. We were heaven on earth for months, and then it all came crashing down in flames when she told me she was pregnant. She'd simply stopped taking her pills. She said she knew she could never have me but she could have my baby. She said she knew I would never have consented so she did not allow me that option. I was scared, Lewis! Terrified. I don't believe in abortion, you know that; besides, Cassie insisted on having the baby. She swore that she wanted nothing from me and no one need know it was ours, but that was impossible! You can't keep secrets like that in Hunter County!"

"I know."

"Worse though, Lewis, you know what the scandal would have done to me. Legally, it would have handed my head to

## Shepherd of the Wolves

Sarah on a silver platter and it would have destroyed my position in the county and in my profession. But far worse than even that, Lewis, Cassie was a peer of my daughters'; Anne and Elizabeth would never have understood! They could never have forgiven me, and I could not bear that!"

I sighed. "So you killed her."

Coleby cried out in agony. "Yes! Yes . . . I killed her. I . . . I couldn't see any other solution. I . . . I knew no other way! I knew about Cassie's heart murmur, of course, and . . . oh, God the trust I've betrayed, my friend. I was the coroner. I would do the autopsy myself."

Coleby's voice became strained, taut.

"We met at a spot on Lover's Overlook, well . . . you know that, I suppose."

I nodded.

"She'd been complaining of nausea from the pregnancy, so I told her I would give her an injection to relieve it. I gave her three hundred milligrams of Demerol and I sat with her while she grew sleepy." Coleby began to weep. "She held my hand, Lewis," Coleby cried. "She held my hand and talked about how happy she would be with the baby. Oh dear God, Lewis, I have done so wrong. I have done so wrong!" Coleby shook with deep sorrowful sobs.

"But that isn't all of it, is it, Coleby?"

"No!" he cried.

"Ivy Joe Culpepper's dying words to me had nothing to do with Lois Ross, did they, Coleby? It wasn't Lois Ross he was telling me, was it?"

"No. Oh God, no . . ."

"He was saying *Rolls-Royce!* He was telling me what he saw in his mirror moments before he was bulldozed to his death. Only I was hearing what I wanted to hear, not what he was saying. He wasn't saying Lois Ross, he was saying *Rolls-Royce!* Your Rolls-Royce, Coleby. You sent it to Washington to repair front-end damage, not the top actuator!"

"Yes! Yes. Oh my God, Lewis, I have done so wrong. I have done so wrong."

More gently now, I asked, "What happened, my friend? The confession is not yet complete, Coleby, you are not free to die. What happened to Ivy Joe Culpepper?"

Coleby was abject misery. His gaze broke my heart.

"Cassie died gently, Lewis. She just faded away painlessly in her mother's car, dreaming of our baby . . . Aaaaah!" Coleby screamed suddenly, startling me. "I killed my own child, Lewis! I killed my own child by killing its mother!"

"Ivy Joe Culpepper, Coleby! What happened to Mr. Joe?"

"He was there! Ivy Joe Culpepper was there! When I got out of Cassie's car to walk back to the Rolls, he was there, down on the roadway, looking up at me from that old red truck. He saw me clearly and my car. I think he must've just recognized the car in a strange place and had stopped to see if he could help. I froze when I saw him. He seemed to perceive that something was going on that he did not want to know about, for he looked right at me for several seconds and then he drove away casually.

"I panicked, Lewis! There was a witness! He couldn't have known what I had done, but later, when Cassie's body was found, he'd know! He'd remember. He would have the character to report my presence at that time and place to you. I'd become a suspect and obviously someone else would do the autopsy. The Demerol and her pregnancy would be discovered and it would all be known! I couldn't let that happen! It would ruin me and rob me of my daughters! I couldn't—"

"So you killed Mr. Joe, too," I said with profound sadness.

"I didn't intend to, Lewis! At first, I only meant to chase him down and try to explain some plausible reason for my presence that would satisfy his curiosity, but as I sped after him, I realized there *was* no explanation! He had seen me where Cassie would be found dead. There would be no way I could contain the situation if that information became known.

"By the time I caught up with Joe on County Route Twelve, I hoped to get him to stop so I could give him a lethal injection, and try to explain it off as a heart attack as well. Oh my God, Lewis, I was so desperate! So afraid! But Joe wouldn't stop! He was no fool; he knew something was wrong. I blew my horn and pointed to the shoulder, but he wouldn't stop!"

# Shepherd of the Wolves

Coleby was heaving now, sitting against the log, the gun still at his hand.

"He wouldn't stop. 'Stop!' I yelled, but he wouldn't. Then I thought, I'll just hit him enough to make him stop and give him the injection and say he had a heart attack due to the accident. At least then there'd be nothing to connect me with Cassie Shelor. By now I'd lost ground on Joe's old truck, so I floored the heavy Rolls to catch up with him. But as I closed on him, for some reason I'll never know, he slowed suddenly. I hit him before I could even get a foot on my brakes. He lost control of the truck. It crashed through the guardrail and disappeared down the mountainside! I was hysterical by now, Lewis. But I was in so deep there was no turning back. I got my bag and ran down to the wreck. Joe was alive! That frail, gentle old man was still alive, trapped in the wreckage. He was severely injured, but I couldn't risk that he'd remain alive long enough to talk to anyone. So I prepared another injection of Demerol, but I discovered there wasn't much of the drug left in the vial. I wasn't sure the amount was adequate, but I gave him all there was."

"That's why he said he was shot, or at least he said the word 'shot,'" I remarked.

"Before I fled, I went back to my car and took some prescription amphetamines from samples given me by pharmaceutical salesmen over the years and poured them into a bag which I secreted in the glove box of Joe's truck. I was hoping in some perverse, insane way that it would cast suspicion upon him which might divert any investigation you might do. Then the dripping gasoline ignited and I ran. I ran from my own horror."

"Then you went back to Cassie's car and swept your fingerprints and tracks."

"I was not only a monster, Lewis, I was a fool to think you'd never figure it all out eventually. Yes. I had worn surgical gloves from the time I entered Cassie's car so fingerprints could not be left. All I needed to do was sweep the dirt with a pine bough as I backed away, erasing my own tracks and those of my car. My car. I drove the Rolls to Roanoke where I hired a driver to take it on to Washington to be repaired. I called Arthur to come pick me up in my Jeep and I told everyone I sent the car to have the top actuator repaired."

The wind blew, and the fire flared. I fueled it anew before finally asking the one question of many that I feared most.

"Coleby, I found Sarah. Anne's in school at Madeira. Where's Elizabeth?"

Coleby studied me. "Oh, Lewis. You don't think I could have hurt her, do you? Is that what I seem like now, even to you?"

"You killed three people that I know of, Coleby," I said evenly. "Four if you count the baby. Where are Elizabeth and Polly and Arthur?"

Coleby sighed sadly. "It's a fair suspicion under the circumstances, I suppose. They're quite safe in Roanoke, Lewis. I knew what I had to do today, and school is out because of the snow. So I sent Polly and Arthur to take Elizabeth to Roanoke for a movie and some shopping. Arthur checked in by phone when the snowstorm reports went bad—I told him to take three rooms at the Hyatt and drive in tomorrow. Oh, Lewis! I wanted so badly to speak one last time to Elizabeth, but I knew I would break down if I tried!"

Coleby sobbed. I pondered trying to rush him before he could get the gun from his lap.

"This whole terrible thing just went awry," Coleby continued, "out of control like a derailed train! Once Cassie became pregnant I had to kill her or lose my daughters and my family estate and . . . my profession, my whole existence. Once Joe saw me at the scene of a murder I had to kill him, too, in order to keep the terrible secret. Then, when the false hope of the whole black affair dying with the Sloan brothers faded as you investigated deeper, I knew you'd figure it all out sooner or later. I knew it would all come out and then, of course, Sarah had to go too or she would control my estate, and Elizabeth would be left to her exclusive care. And that could not happen."

Coleby seemed lost in the fire. I slowly gathered my feet beneath me.

"Sarah had to go . . . it was awful, Lewis. She struggled. I finally got the needle into her. Before the drug took effect, she tried to get to the phone in her study. We fought and she died hating me to her last breath. And the terrible irony is . . . I'd come at last to deserve her hatred. Desperate for love and warmth, I'd become a, a, a serial murderer! A despicable animal worthy of Sarah's hatred! I had ended my career as a professional healer by becoming a killer. There is only one thing for me to do now, Lewis, you know that."

Coleby took a syringe and a large vial from his bag. He inserted the needle into the rubber cap of the vial and drew the syringe full of the clear liquid.

I charged right through the fire and dove on him. My first objective was the gun, which I threw away from us. We wrestled on the pine needles for control of the syringe, which I finally took from him, the needle still inserted in the vial.

"Lewis . . ." Coleby said, heaving for breath, his eyes gentle.

I got to my feet. "Get up!"

"Listen to me, Lewis. You know you will not condemn me to live out my life in prison or some mental institution, enduring the shame of my daughters, prolonging their shame and suffering. You will not do that to them, Lewis, and you will not do that to me. This is the only way, Lewis. It is the only path for me to take."

I trembled and struggled to breathe. He was right, and I knew it. An insanity defense would never cut it. He'd killed three innocent people, at least two with clear presence of mind and intent. He had not been insane; he had been lonely, frightened, desperate beyond reason, but not legally insane, not unable to distinguish between right and wrong. They might eventually execute him after years of misery, shame and expense for all involved. More likely, and worse for Coleby than death, they would institutionalize him, they would incarcerate a proud, sensitive aristocrat with criminal dregs or with the truly insane, there to rot away or actually go insane, an endless source of suffering for himself and his daughters. I fingered the drug vial and syringe and I wished I were far away, removed from this awful scene.

Coleby sensed my quandary, my struggle between duty

and the love of a friend. He pressed, looking me hard in the eyes. "Give me the syringe, Lewis. You know there is no other way."

"Coleby, how do I explain to Anne and Elizabeth that I let their father, my best friend in this fucked-up, sorry world, that I just let him kill himself?"

"You don't, Lewis. You don't explain anything to anyone. You found me dead. You had no role in the event. This dosage is fast, Lewis, fast and painless. It's the same thing I . . . used on . . . Cassie. I'll feel immense peace and relaxation, I'll grow sleepy and then I'll rest. While I'm asleep, my respiratory function will arrest, and a minute or so later my heart will stop. You found me dead, Lewis. You need explain nothing."

I shivered uncontrollably in spite of the roaring fire and the exertion of the struggle with Coleby. "I can't, Coleby. I can't let you die, too. So many deaths. So much hurt. Not you, too, Coleby. You're my friend. I love you, goddamn it."

"I know that, Lewis, and I love you. But it is because of the love we share, not in spite of it, that you must let me die. You know what the system will do to me, Lewis, and you know I could not endure that. Moreover, you know me. You know that I cannot live with what I have done, that I can never reconcile it with my conscience. More important, you know what having an institutionalized murderer for a father would do to Anne and Elizabeth, and you know they deserve better. You know you would hate yourself the rest of your life for binding us all over to that. Give me rest. Give me peace. Give my daughters a future free of what I have become, Lewis. Give me the syringe. Please, Lewis, must I beg?"

I sat down hard, my tears running cool into the corners of my mouth. I gazed into the fire, wishing I were dead, wishing I were free of the terrible decision before me. Who appointed *me* God? I thought. I'm eminently unqualified.

I looked through the dancing flames at Coleby. He looked back at me, knowing, even before I knew, what I would decide. He held forth both his wrists. I stood, withdrew my handcuffs and walked around the fire to him. I looked down at him and he never took his eyes from mine.

The handcuffs slid from my fingers and clinked to the

pine needles at my boots. I knelt before Dr. Coleby Butler and gave him the syringe still impaled in the vial. I slumped against the fallen tree trunk. Wasted. Surrendered. No longer swimming, just swept with the current.

Coleby injected the clean death into his arm and set the syringe on the ground by the vial and my handcuffs. I was gripped by a sadness far beyond weeping. I made no sound, though tears streamed down my cheeks. Coleby reached out to me and I took the hand of my closest friend to see him to his final breath.

Coleby smiled at me with clear gratitude. "Thank you, Lewis. I know you hurt, my dear friend, but in time you will come to know this was the right thing to do."

"Coleby," I whispered, my agony cracking me wide open, "Coleby."

He squeezed my hand. "Don't make yourself crazy trying to explain all this, Lewis. Sometimes there just are no reasons."

"Coleby, my good friend." I wept. "I love you. I will miss you so."

He engaged my eyes with his own. "Listen, Lewis, there is little time now, and there is one thing left we must talk about.

I looked into his oddly peaceful gaze.

"Lewis, I've one more grand favor to ask of you and one last great gift to give you. You were never the same after Tess died, my gentle, loving friend. I, better than anyone, know how you loved that child and how her death destroyed you. I know how empty it has left you all these years. Listen to me, Lewis. You must now raise my daughters. You must take Anne and Elizabeth as your own to raise and love and protect. They will need you desperately, you know that. This terrible thing I have done will hurt them deeply for a long time, and they will need you to guide them to adjustment and beyond. Anne is seventeen and a young woman, but she is also a daddy's girl, and a girl's need for her father doesn't end with adolescence. Elizabeth is only ten, still a baby, my baby. She will need you most. Sarah has no family, save her aged mother who never took any interest in the children. My family is all gone. It must be you, Lewis. For your sake and for theirs. Take care of my children for me, Lewis, and let them put the meaning and purpose and love back into your own life. Please, Lewis, time is short, please tell me you will be the father they deserve."

"Coleby," I struggled to speak, "I love Anne and Elizabeth as my own, you know that—"

"And so do they love you, Lewis. That is why—"

"But I'm not worthy of such a trust, Coleby. I've failed so—"

"But you are, Lewis! You are! Tess's death, even the breakup of your marriage, was not your fault! Peggy Sloan was not your failing, my friend. You are the shepherd, Lewis, but no shepherd can protect the whole flock from all evil and misfortune all the time. Not even you. Raise my daughters, Lewis! They need you now, and you need them. And me, Lewis. If I have any right remaining to ask any relief, I need to know you will be there to protect them and guide them and love them. Please, Lewis! The drug is taking effect. Please!"

I could see it in his face. "You already know my answer, don't you, Coleby? You always know before me."

"I know you are the shepherd, Lewis," Coleby said, his speech beginning to slur. "The shepherd of Hunter County. I know you will not refuse me. More importantly, I know you will not fail my daughters. And in their way they will in turn be your salvation."

Coleby's eyelids lowered slightly; his breathing slowed.

"Soon, Lewis," he said. "Soon."

"Coleby, I swear to you, on the love I hold for you, that Anne and Elizabeth will never know a moment's need. They will never fear, I swear to you, my friend."

Coleby reached forth a hand and touched my face like Ivy Joe Culpepper had only a week before. "I know, Lewis. I know. You are the shepherd . . ."

Coleby lay his head on my thigh and clutched my hand to his mouth. His breathing grew even slower. There was peace in his face.

"Goodbye." I wept. "Goodbye, my great friend."

But he was gone.

# Epilogue

Four saddled horses stand idly grazing on the lush summer grass. Moose shakes her massive head and looks at us.

We stand by the captain's grave, Elizabeth and I. She clutches my hand as we gaze out upon the tranquil beauty of the hazy green Shenandoah Valley far below. Small birds sing nearby, and in the distance a red-tailed hawk floats on the warm current flowing up from the valley.

Elizabeth smiled once last week. It was fleeting but notable, as it was her first smile in almost eight months. It was a treasure of a sight. She is healing.

Coleby left a will written two years prior to his death. In it he provided that, in the event of the simultaneous passing of he and Sarah, I was to be named trustee of his entire estate until Elizabeth's twenty-fifth birthday at which time the estate would pass equally to Anne and Elizabeth. He left generous bequests to me, to Polly and to Arthur, and he provided that Polly and Arthur could live out their lives at Mountain Harbor.

Sarah left no will. She was buried in Baltimore in her family plot. Thirteen people attended the funeral.

Coleby willed that Luciano Pavarotti's recording of "Panis Angelicus" be played at his funeral. The magnificent Italian tenor's voice rang down the mountain in the cold November air, that terrible month of so many funerals. Coleby asked that I spill his ashes on a rare westerly wind so that they might settle down the west face of the Blue Ridge. I scattered them from a rented Cessna 172 on the twelfth of December, and they blew toward the valley from above Mountain Harbor.

No one acted from any forethought, but it just made sense that I move into Mountain Harbor. Polly keeps the house and feeds us, and Arthur and I keep up the estate.

I remain Sheriff of Hunter County, re-elected unopposed in late November.

There has been the predictable bevy of legal problems, of course. Anytime an estate of several million dollars is involved, in today's litigious society, they are inevitable. I initiated a fair dispensation from the estate to Helen Shelor, but she refused it, saying we had all suffered in ways no money could relieve. Relatives of Sarah's, obscure and otherwise, have sued the estate for larger shares than Coleby's generous will provided them, but the chief counsel for the estate seems to have it all under control.

I turn and look toward the captain's sarcophagus where stands Anne, lovely and graceful, shaded by the gnarled old pines. She sees me looking and she smiles at me warmly. She is well bred and strong, a survivor. She, too, is recovering. Anne has decided to study pre-law at UVA in the fall.

I think Anne's career decision was affected largely by the chief counsel for the estate, a lawyer somewhat new to Hunter County, even to the Virginia Bar, but an attorney with extensive experience and skill. And heart.

If you counted the horses, you've noted there is still one person unaccounted for. You've surely guessed it was ridden up here by none other than the chief counsel for the estate, one Hannah Lucia Dodd, newly with the small but respected Hunter law firm of Whitney, Whitney and Dodd. God, how lawyers love those name trains.

This lovely brown beauty walks to me now with love in her eyes. I bend to kiss her as a warm breeze bathes our faces. There is a fragrance of honeysuckle on the wind. The summer sun feels good.

I am occasionally moved to question my atheism.

# About the Author

William Slusher was born in Virginia, raised in Tennessee and now lives in Charles Town, West Virginia. He proudly lays claim to all three states. He is a veteran of Vietnam and two marriages, all three of which he lost. Mr. Slusher is completing a sequel to *Shepherd of the Wolves* when he is not riding his horse, Shiloh, or flying a medevac helicopter for the Fairfax County, Virginia, Police. Mr. Slusher would like to extend to you his heartfelt thanks for spending your hard-earned money on his book, and he sincerely hopes your life is a little better for having read it.

# DON'T MISS THESE EXCITING POCKET BOOKS MYSTERY AUTHORS!

## Nancy Pickard

Confession/78261-4/$20.00
Bum Steer/68042-0/$4.99
But I Wouldn't Want to Die There/72331-6/$5.50
Dead Crazy/73430-X/$5.50
Generous Death/73264-1/$5.50
I.O.U./68043-9/$4.99
Marriage is Murder/73428-8/$5.50
No Body/73429-6/$4.99
Say No to Murder/73431-8/$4.99

## Jeremiah Healy

Rescue/89877-9/$20.00
Act of God/79559-7/$5.50
Blunt Darts/73742-2/$5.50
Foursome/79557-0/$4.99
Right to Die/70810-4/$4.99
Shallow Graves/70812-0/$4.99
So Like Sleep/74328-7/$4.50
Staked Goat/74284-1/$4.50
Swan Dive/74329-5/$4.50
Yesterday's News/
69584-3/$5.50

POCKET
BOOKS